A great first book from an exciting new author! A vicious enemy, a family secret, a thirst for revenge, and a need for reconciliation all drive *The Hunted* from intriguing beginning to thrilling conclusion. The skillful prose and great story-telling make Mike Dellosso a writer to watch. I can't wait for his next book!

—KATHRYN MACKEL
AUTHOR OF *VANISHED*

With hints of Frank Peretti and Stephen King, *The Hunted* is a chilling debut. Author Mike Dellosso is certain to make his mark in Christian fiction.

—CRESTON MAPES
AUTHOR OF *NOBODY*

Mike Dellosso's pins-and-needles thriller hurtles the reader down a dark and twisted path. Flickers of faith light the way, and fateful decisions determine the outcome of a horrifying climax. I dare you to take this one home!

—JILL ELIZABETH NELSON
AUTHOR OF TO CATCH A THIEF SUSPENSE SERIES

From page one *The Hunted* grabbed me by the collar and wouldn't let go. It is full of intrigue, supernatural undertones, and true-to-life characters. I highly recommend this superb debut novel.

—C. J. DARLINGTON
COFOUNDER AND BOOK EDITOR, TITLETRAKK.COM

The Hunted places Mike Dellosso on the list of authors to keep your eye on.

—VENNESSA NG
AOTEAROA EDITORIAL SERVICE

Something's coming for you...and you might not be able to stop it. Read this someplace safe as you experience the incredibly descriptive world of *The Hunted* through the vivid writing and spine-tingling imagination of Mike Dellosso. And sleep with the lights on.

—AUSTIN BOYD
AUTHOR OF MARS HILL CLASSIFIED TRILOGY

Mike Dellosso delivers a spine-tingling tale of hidden secrets, buried hopes, and second chances. Interwoven through page-turning drama is the truth about vengeance and the triumph of God's mysterious ways. *The Hunted* is a story best read with all the lights on and an extra flashlight handy—just in case!

—AMY WALLACE
AUTHOR OF *RANSOMED DREAMS*

THE HUNTED

MIKE DELLOSSO

REALMS
A STRANG COMPANY

Most STRANG COMMUNICATIONS/CHARISMA HOUSE/SILOAM/FRONTLINE/
REALMS/EXCEL BOOKS products are available at special quantity discounts
for bulk purchase for sales promotions, premiums, fund-raising, and
educational needs. For details, write Strang Communications/Charisma
House/Siloam/FrontLine/Realms/Excel Books, 600 Rinehart Road, Lake
Mary, Florida 32746, or telephone (407) 333-0600.

THE HUNTED by Mike Dellosso
Published by Realms
A Strang Company
600 Rinehart Road
Lake Mary, Florida 32746
www.realmsfiction.com

Design Director: Bill Johnson
Cover Designer: studiogearbox.com

Visit the author's Web site at www.MikeDellosso.com.

Library of Congress Cataloging-in-Publication Data

Dellosso, Mike.
  The hunted / Mike Dellosso.
    p. cm.
  ISBN 978-1-59979-296-5
  1. Missing persons--Fiction. 2. Lions--Fiction. I. Title.
  PS3604.E446H86 2008
  813'.6--dc22
                                        2008004118

08 09 10 11 12 — 987654321
Printed in the United States of America

For Jen

I wouldn't have wanted to share this journey
with anyone else.

ACKNOWLEDGMENTS

THEY SAY WRITING is a solitary endeavor, and maybe the writing itself is...but the making of a book is anything but. No individual is capable of performing all the tasks that must be accomplished to take a story from a mere idea and watch it take on a life of its own on paper.

To those who partnered with me to make my dream a reality, I say thank you:

- My wife, Jen, for encouraging me when I was ready to throw in the pen and for believing in me when I didn't believe in myself; also for her exhortation: "Live like it's already happened!"

- My three lovely daughters, gifts from God, for giving me inspiration and the drive to press on even when I had no idea where I was going.

- My parents, for praying and encouraging and believing; I need them in my corner.

- My agent, Les Stobbe, for taking a chance on me and for his wisdom and guidance through the murky waters of the publishing world.

- Kathryn Mackel, a wonderful author whose writing inspired me before I ever met her, for seeing the potential in my three chapters and patiently answering all my newbie questions.

- The wonderful team at Realms, for catching the vision and seeing this thing through to the end.

- Lori Vanden Bosch, for her careful editor's eye and thoughtful suggestions for making this story the best it could be, and Deborah Moss, for making sure my manuscript's hair was combed and shirt tucked in before going out in public.

- The readers who offered suggestions, encouragement, and an editorial education: Eileen Key, Ed Scheuerman, and Kari Van Zante; their advice and comments made a huge difference.

- My home church, Calvary Bible Church, for the encouragement and constant question: "When's the new book coming out?" Here it is!

- Physical Therapy & Sports Injury Center, for giving me a quiet place to write.

- And to all those too numerous to mention by name, but they know who they are, who encouraged me, prayed for me, answered my questions, and encouraged me some more. Their words were not in vain.

Arise, black vengeance, from thy hollow cell!
    —WILLIAM SHAKESPEARE, *OTHELLO*, 3.3

Vengeance is mine; I will repay, saith the Lord.
    —ROMANS 12:19, KJV

PROLOGUE

Yates Woods, Franklin County, Pennsylvania
Six months earlier

THE DARKNESS WAS thick and stifling.

The large room was a musty, stone dungeon. Empty, save for a small pile of rotting boards.

Hands, raw and bloodied, scratched in the dirt floor, clawed at the brittle wood, groped for anything that felt...different.

There. A wooden box.

The hands caressed it, fingered the intricately carved grooves.

Laughter filled the dungeon, echoing off the cold stone.

A young man, slender and sinewy, tucked the box under one arm and hurried into the sunlight that filtered down the steps. He sat, placed the box on the dirt floor in front of him, rubbed his hands together, and studied the engraved lid. Smooth channels worked their way across the dark wood in a medley of zigzags and circles.

Open, a voice said. *Open.*

The man hesitated, rubbed his hands together again, and then lifted one hand to cover his eyes, resting the other on the lid.

Open.

He giggled, uncovered his eyes, and slowly lifted the lid with both hands. Inside was a tawny, twisted paw the size of a small dinner plate. Beside it lay a leather-bound book.

The man removed the paw from the box, sniffed it, probed it, and let the soft fur caress his cheek. He then replaced the paw and withdrew the book. It smelled of dust, dry leather, and mildewed paper. His eyes widened as he flipped through the crisp, discolored pages. Words jumped out at him like flashcards: *Africa...tribal...legend...shaman...devil... vengeance...death...vengeance...vengeance.*

1

Keep it, the voice whispered.

He smiled, his head bobbing up and down in a rhythmic nod. Yes. Yes. Yes.

Vengeance.

CHAPTER 1

Present day

CALEB SAUNDERS DASHED through the woods, dodging low-hanging branches, jumping fallen trees, snaking around saplings and undergrowth. He had decided to trek along the untouched forest floor rather than the well-worn path that wove through the trees all the way to Hunter's Creek.

The path the others were on.

His lungs burned in the chilly November air, but he pressed forward, faster and faster until the trees whizzed by in a brown blur. His eyes darted back and forth, scanning the uneven terrain, calculating, planning every step, every change of direction. Thickets pulled at his jeans and camouflage jacket like tiny claws, trying in vain to slow his progress. Leaves crunched as his feet found footing in the loose soil.

A spotted canopy of orange and red leaves provided the perfect shade cover, allowing only thin rods of light to poke through and slant toward the leaf-covered ground. There were so many hiding places, so many shrubs and fallen trees under which to find concealment, but Caleb knew where he was headed—he had been there a hundred times.

He ran faster, ignoring the slender branches that smacked at his chest and arms. He was the fastest kid in the fifth grade and knew these woods like his own backyard.

Caleb came to a descending slope, paused, quickly surveyed the best route—something he had become very skilled at doing—and then plunged down the hill. His arms flailed wildly, legs pounded the ground. In control, out of control, in control. He fought the pull of gravity and uneven terrain to maintain balance as the leafy ground below rose faster and faster to meet him.

In the small clearing stood his destination, a long-abandoned stone house that had been burned to a blackened shell long before Caleb was born, long before his parents were born. It was last occupied over eighty years ago by a hermit known only as Old Man Yates.

Rumor had it that Yates's ghost still haunted the site.

Caleb never paid much attention to ghost stories, though. He was getting too old for that. And besides, he'd used the hollowed-out Yates place as a hideout hundreds of times and never saw or heard any ghosts.

He approached the old stone structure and stood in the doorway, resting his hands on the moss-covered stone. The roof was gone and only the first-story walls remained, stained with the residue of ancient smoke and flames. Toward the back of the house there was only a partial remnant of the second-story floor, broken floorboards charred black and supported clumsily by what was left of the wall dividing the dining room from the living room.

In the distance, Caleb could hear the excited laughter of Jeremy and the others. *They make so much noise, I can hear them coming a mile away.* They would certainly find him if he used one of his usual hiding places— under the first-story staircase or around the back of the house behind the raspberry bush.

Caleb brushed a shock of sweaty hair from his face and searched the ruins for a place to hide, somewhere the others would never even think to look. Of course. The cellar. The boys had a standing dare between them to spend ten minutes in the old cellar. Caleb had been down there once, but he never left the security of the stairs and lasted only four minutes before his panicked nerves pushed him up and back toward the light of day. He had to admit, the place gave him the creeps.

Running his right hand along the rough, moss-and-vine-covered stone foundation wall and his left hand along the brittle wood railing, he slowly descended the chipped and cracked concrete stairs. There were no windows in the cellar, and any light filtering down from above was quickly swallowed by the thick darkness. A musty smell hung in the damp air mixed with the pungent odor of rotting meat.

When he reached the bottom of the steps, Caleb extended one leg in front of him and felt the dirt floor with his sneaker, searching for any obstacle that might trip him. Leaving his hand on the railing, he squatted next to the stairs, not daring to wander too far from the light. He remained crouched in the darkness for a few minutes, slowing his breathing and listening for the sound of his pursuers. Outside, in the world of light and fresh air, birds chirped, a squirrel chattered, and a flock of geese honked overhead, but there was no sound of Jeremy and the others. Maybe they were looking elsewhere, thinking the Yates house too obvious a hiding place.

Or maybe they're scared. Caleb grinned in the darkness. They'd be talking about this one for weeks.

All at once, the outside world fell silent. Dead silent. The cellar was airless, as if a great vacuum had been placed at the top of the stairs and sucked every last ounce of oxygen out of it. Caleb could hear nothing but the quiet wheeze of his own breathing and his pulse tapping out a steady rhythm in his ears.

He held his breath and listened. Something moved. Was that footsteps? He listened closer, straining his ears to focus on the muffled sound. It *was* footsteps, but not from outside, not even from upstairs. They were soft and barely audible, like someone walking barefoot or wearing slippers. But they were near.

He listened closer. A chill raced down his spine. The hair on the back of his neck bristled. His blood ran cold, and a clammy sweat dampened his forehead.

The footsteps were in the cellar with him! Yates's ghost!

His pulse pounded so loudly in his ears now that he could barely make out the faint steps inching closer. The footsteps fell too softly and unevenly; one was barely distinguishable from the other. Whatever it was in that cave of a cellar was not human.

Caleb shut his eyes and gripped the railing. The footsteps drew closer and stopped right behind him. He could now hear the thing breathing—long inhale; short, quick exhale—and feel its hot breath on the back of his neck. He wanted to run, scream, fight, anything, something, but fear paralyzed him, nailed him to his spot next to the stairs. He was frozen, eyelids pressed together so tight they hurt, the rough square edges of the railing digging into the soft skin of his palms while his body trembled uncontrollably.

Please God, please God, please God.

The thing behind him snorted, and its putrid breath filled Caleb's nose. He swallowed hard, holding back the bile that rose in his throat. An image of a hideous spirit, all tangled hair and rotted teeth and bulging eyes, screamed in his mind, tying his stomach in a knot.

Finally, after what seemed like hours but was actually only mere seconds, the footsteps retreated and then fell silent. Caleb slowly opened his eyes and turned toward the darkness. Something was there, a vague form, but huge, at least as large as a man. He made a quick move for the steps with every intention of bolting up them into the daylight and screaming for help.

But he was too slow.

The thing lunged out of the blackness, teeth and claws flashing death in the muted light.

At the edge of the woods, the trees met a field that had lain fallow throughout the year. A man's thin frame was silhouetted against the pale blue sky, breaking the monotony of tall, straight trunks of centuries-old oaks and walnuts.

The man twisted his face and took a long, deep breath, inhaling the aroma of the wild. "*Mmmm*, how's that suit ya?" he said in a low hiss.

He then changed his voice, high-pitched and feminine. "Don't fret, little Stevie; they won't be botherin' us anymore. Momma's gonna protect ya."

He pulled his hands out of his pockets and rubbed them together, shifted his eyes from side to side, and drew in another breath. "Yeah. Good. We make a good team, ain't?" His voice was back to the low hiss.

He ran a hand across his stubbled chin as his lips parted in a crooked smile. "I hear ya. I hear ya. You and me, Momma. You and me."

Exactly three hours later and ninety-five miles north, Joe Saunders had just slipped into a shallow sleep in front of the TV when his eyelids jerked open. He bolted upright on the sofa, forehead wet with sweat, hands trembling, heart banging behind his ribs like a tight drum. He dragged a cool hand across his brow and sucked in a deep breath.

Though he'd only been asleep seconds, he'd had a dream.

Still somewhere between sleep and full consciousness, he sat back against the sofa and closed his eyes. The images were still pasted to the inside of his lids, the vivid detail remarkable. Caleb, his brother's son, teetered on a rocky precipice. His arms flailed in wide circles. Fear distorted his face. Joe tried to reach for the boy's hand, but he couldn't. He was no more than five feet away, but it might as well have been a mile. He was out of reach.

Joe could hear the rush and crash, the thunderous roar of waves pummeling the rocks beneath them. He hollered Caleb's name. Panic gripped his chest like a vice. Sweat and tears stung his eyes.

Caleb's right foot slipped on some loose gravel, his arms shot skyward, and he tumbled backward off the cliff.

That's when Joe awoke.

He sat on the edge of the sofa and rested his elbows on his knees, head in his hands. Caleb loved the water, but to the best of Joe's knowledge he'd never acquired a heart for cliff diving. This was not a plunge for bragging rights. It was a tragedy.

What a dream. What a terrible, terrible dream.

He had to call Rosa and make sure Caleb was OK.

He picked up his cell phone.

It rang in his hand.

"Hello?"

"Joe." It was Rosa, crying. "Caleb's missing."

Joe held the phone to his ear, but only a few random things registered after that: the faint sound of rushing blood in his ear, the trickle of sweat that lodged itself on the corner of his nostril, the sweat on his palm making the phone slick. And Rosa's voice, weak and thready, fading in and out, "…woods…lost…Dinsmore…search party…pray…"

Pray. She wanted him to pray. But Joe had given up on prayer ten years ago.

"I'll be there as soon as I can," he said. And then she was gone.

CHAPTER 2

OFFICER ANDY WILT sat on the edge of an overstuffed chair across from Rosa. They were in her living room. "When was the last time you saw Caleb?" When he'd arrived, he shook Rosa's hand gently and asked her to please call him Andy. Rosa had noticed the pity that softened the strong angles of his face.

Before answering, she dabbed at her eyes with a white handkerchief. The one Caleb gave her last year for Mother's Day. He'd had the corner embroidered with her initials. "About twelve-thirty. He finished his lunch and said he was going to the woods to play with the Dinsmore boys. They do the same thing almost every Saturday."

At thirty-one, Rosa Saunders felt at least ten years older than she was. The dark brown hair she loved to run a brush through was already sprinkled with a few strands of wiry gray. Her hands, once soft and supple, were now dry and calloused, and she'd recently noticed the hint of subtle shadows under her eyes.

But what did she expect? She was a single mom, worked a full-time day shift at the paper mill and two evenings a week at Darlene's Diner. Not to mention attending Caleb's school functions, sporting events, and church activities. Ever since Rick died, she was doing the job of two parents.

"And what was he wearing?" Andy asked, dangling his pen between his index finger and thumb.

Rosa had to think about it. She pictured Caleb as he tore out the kitchen door, waving a quick good-bye. "Light blue, long-sleeve T-shirt, no logos or anything, just plain. Camouflage jacket, blue jeans, and sneakers. Black adidas."

Andy jotted the information down on his little notepad and paused as if deep in thought, tapping the pen against his dimpled chin. "Has Caleb ever had any problems with any of the other boys?"

Rosa shook her head. "No, of course not. Everybody loves Caleb. He is outgoing and friendly. He makes friends easily. The boys come over here all the time to play football in the backyard, play video games, watch movies on the TV."

"Has Caleb ever talked about running away?"

Rosa lowered her brow. The question had stung. "Why would you—"

Andy raised a hand in surrender, the pen laced between his thumb and first two fingers. "I'm sorry, ma'am. I know it seems awfully insensitive, but these are just routine questions I have to ask."

"I–I'm sorry," Rosa said, fixing her eyes on her hands. When had they become so worn? She hadn't noticed before. "He is all I have left. If anything happened to him..." Her voice trailed off.

"Ma'am, did he ever talk about running away or threaten to? I know sometimes when kids get upset about something, they say things they don't mean, but sometimes they act on it anyway. You know, to get attention."

She shook her head slowly. "No. Caleb never talked about anything like that. We have a good relationship. He is a good boy."

"Did—I'm sorry. Your husband, he died some time ago, didn't he?"

Rosa nodded. Memories of Rick threatened to flood her mind. Any other time she would have welcomed them. But not today. Not now. This was not the time. She had to be strong. "Yes. When Caleb was one. In a trucking accident."

Andy paused, then sighed. "I'm sorry. Did Caleb ever talk about his feelings about not having a father?"

Rosa shot a sideways glance at the tall, lean officer sitting across from her. She didn't know Andy personally, but word around town was that he was a fair and honest cop. He was young but tough on following protocol. She restrained the urge to brush off his question; he was just doing his job. He probably didn't like asking these questions any more than she liked answering them.

Andy dipped his chin and frowned. "I'm sorry, ma'am, I really am. I'm just looking for any kind of hidden resentment or anger Caleb may have. Anything that will help us with the search, narrow it down, give us some kind of clue. In a case like this, there's not a whole lot to go on."

Rosa forced a smile and twisted the handkerchief in her hand. "I know. He asks a lot of questions about Rick, and I answer them honestly. But he never seems resentful or angry over not having a dad. He is very mature for his age."

"I'm sure he is. He's been through a lot." Andy arched his thick eyebrows and looked at Rosa. "One more question?"

She nodded. "Sure."

"Did Caleb ever talk about meeting any other men or talking to anyone you didn't know?"

"Not that I know of. I teach him not to talk to strangers, to stay away from people he does not know. I'm sure if he met anyone or had any strange encounters with anyone he would have told me. We talk a lot."

Andy wrote something else in his notepad, clicked his pen, and slid it into the breast pocket of his shirt. "Thanks, Mrs. Saunders. Chief Gill is talking to the other boys at the Dinsmore house. I'll let you know what she finds out." He stood and hesitated. "Do you have a recent photo I can take along?"

"Yes, we just got his school pictures last week." She stood, went into the kitchen, and retrieved a five-by-seven photo of Caleb from the drawer of the hutch. His dark brown hair was neatly parted to the side, freckles dappled his nose and cheeks, and a wide smile stretched across his face. She clutched the picture in her hands as if it were really her dear son.

Lord, please let my Caleb be OK. Protect him.

Returning to the living room, Rosa swallowed the golf ball that had risen in her throat. "Here, take this one."

Andy took the photo and studied it. "Thank you." He looked at Rosa, and she found some solace in his warm eyes. "And I'm sure we'll find him. I know what you're worried about, and if it's any comfort, there hasn't been an abduction in Dark Hills in over three decades."

He turned to leave, then stopped and drew in a long breath, letting his eyes meet Rosa's again. "We *will* find him."

"I know." It was all she could say. If she opened her mouth once more, nothing but groans and sobs would shove their way out. After all she and Caleb had been through, she never thought God would lead her down this path. This was supposed to happen to other people, the poor distraught parents on television. The ones surrounded by reporters. The ones with hollow, bloodshot eyes, staring blankly into the camera. This was not the way it was supposed to work out. Not for her. Not for Caleb.

Why, Lord? Dear God, why? I can't bear this burden alone. I need Rick.

"OK, boys," Chief Maggie Gill said, pacing back and forth in front of the sofa where the four Dinsmore brothers sat—Jeremy, David, Michael, and Sean. "What were you doing in the woods with Caleb?"

At thirty-three, she was the youngest chief of police in the two-hundred-year history of Dark Hills, and the first woman. But Maggie knew how to handle herself—she came from a long line of Dark Hills police officers and had earned the respect of the small community.

Jeremy, the oldest at eleven, pushed some hair off his forehead and spoke first. "We were playing Man Hunter, and it was Caleb's turn to be the prey."

Maggie stopped and faced Jeremy. "I think I can figure it out, but explain to me what 'Man Hunter' is."

Jeremy shifted nervously on the worn sofa, shot a glance at his father, then back at Maggie. "It's where, like, one person hides in the woods and the others have to track 'em and find 'em. We play it all the time. Caleb usually hides in the same place, somewheres around the old Yates house. We were gonna go there first but went down to the creek instead. When he wasn't anywhere around there, we went to the Yates place, but he wasn't there either, so we just walked around until we got bored and then came home. We called his name, told him we were done and were going home. I guess we just thought he got tired of hiding and went home too."

"Sometimes that happens," Michael, the eight-year-old, said, shrugging his thin shoulders. "The hunted hides so good no one can find him. So we all just go home when we get tired."

Maggie removed her cap and sat on a well-worn, olive-colored chair situated across from the sofa in the cramped living room. She knew the rest of the story. The boys had returned home and two hours later phoned Rosa, asking to speak to Caleb. Only Caleb still wasn't home. Rosa called the police department, and Maggie set the wheels in motion, sending Andy out to speak with her. And she wound up here, talking to the Dinsmore boys.

When Maggie received the call from Rosa, a gnawing void had settled into her stomach. She knew what it meant for the kid. Best scenario, he was just lost, wandering around in the woods, wide-eyed and scared, like some puppy that had strayed too far from home. Worst scenario, she had a full-blown abduction on her hands—a thought she didn't want to entertain until she gathered more information.

Jerry Dinsmore, the boys' father, cleared his throat and said, "They were worried sick when they found out Caleb was missing." He leaned his thick shoulder against the doorframe, hands shoved in the pockets of his dirty jeans. Jerry was a foreman for Kingston Construction and had a reputation around town for being a hard-nosed, by-the-book man. Maggie knew to tread lightly in his presence, especially when questioning his boys.

"I'm sure we'll find him," Maggie said, trying her best to sound encouraging. "About how big of an area do you play this game in?" She looked at Jeremy for an answer.

Jeremy shrugged and threw his head back to clear his long bangs from his eyes. "I don't know. We play, like, from the alley to the cornfield to the creek and over to the dirt road that goes back to the Yates place."

Maggie quickly jotted the landmarks down, drawing a rough map on her notepad. It wasn't too large of an area, maybe three quarters of a mile to a mile square. Shouldn't take too much time for a search party to comb. She'd make a few phone calls and would have a group ready to go in a couple hours. "Jeremy, you're in Caleb's class, aren't you? And you're pretty good friends?"

"Yeah. He's prob'ly my best friend."

"Do you know if he has any enemies? Any other boys who don't like him? Maybe he got into some fights at school."

Jeremy shook his head. "No way. Caleb's one of the most pop'lar kids in school. He's friends with, like, everyone. Nobody messes with him."

"But does he mess with anyone else? You know, tease, bully. Anything someone might want to get back at him for?"

Jeremy shook his head again. "No way. Caleb's cool. Everyone likes him."

Maggie stood up, placed her cap firmly over her hair, and faced the boys once again. "One more question, guys, and I want the truth. No one's in trouble here. Did any of you ever see any strange men in or around the woods, talk to any strangers, or see Caleb talking to any strangers?"

The boys sat quietly, stealing furtive glances at one another.

Maggie looked at Jerry and raised her eyebrows. Better to let him use his fatherly persuasion than to step into the role of interrogator and intimidate the boys.

Jerry pushed away from the doorframe and stood at his full height of over six feet. "Boys," he said, his voice deep and gruff, "answer the chief."

Jeremy looked at his father, then at David, his younger brother by a mere eleven months, then at Maggie. "There was one guy," he said. "Stevie. He wanders 'round in the woods. Sometimes we see him at the Yates place just standing there lookin' all weird and stuff. Sometimes we hear him talking to himself and laughing. But we ain't never talked to him. He's a creep."

"He's a retard," David said. "Lives in the old trailer on the farm. Down by the pond."

Sean, the youngest at six, fidgeted in his place on the sofa and glanced at his father, then back at Maggie. "Sometimes we throw r–rocks at his house. He said if he ever c–c–caught us, he'd k–kill us all."

CHAPTER 3

SITTING NEXT TO his sister-in-law, Rosa, their shoulders touching, Joe Saunders wrung his hands nervously. Her living room felt smaller than it was, closing in on him. After she'd called, he'd emptied his drawers into two suitcases, blazed down Route 522, making the hour-and-a-half trip in just over an hour, and now listened intently as she filled him in on everything she knew thus far.

He'd been here before, ten years ago, sitting next to her, comforting her, listening, just...being.

And feeling guilty.

He should have done more with Caleb. Despite living almost a hundred miles away, he'd tried to visit often and tried to call even more often. But often wasn't enough. He should have been more involved, lived closer, called more...something. But his guilt had repeatedly gotten in the way. Every time he looked at Caleb he wanted to cry, wanted to beg for the boy's forgiveness. And now he teetered on the same ledge on which he stood a decade ago, a decision to make: step over and plummet even further into the bottomless gulf of guilt and shame, or step back and accept the responsibility that had been thrust upon him.

Ten years ago he'd chosen the former.

Tonight he would choose to stay, brush aside the urge to embrace the loathing, take responsibility, and find Caleb.

"When's the search party meeting?" Joe asked.

The sun had already dropped in the sky and had taken the temperature with it. Joe was an experienced outdoorsman and knew if Caleb were out there, injured or lost, he wouldn't last long. In a child, hypothermia would set in quickly. The meteorologist on the radio had said the temperature was to dip into the low forties overnight. Time would not be on their side.

"Chief Gill said they were meeting at seven o'clock in front of the old repair shop on McCormick."

Joe knew the spot exactly. He slipped his arm around Rosa's shoulders and gave her a gentle squeeze; she tensed under his grip. He could tell her nerves were well past the fraying point. Ever since Rick died, Caleb had been her world. She had told Joe before that Caleb was so much like his father it was almost like having Rick around. Caleb was lucky to have a mother like her. She was a strong woman, determined to make sure her son didn't miss out on anything a young boy should experience.

But now she looked weak and vulnerable. Her small frame was slumped on the sofa, her eyes swollen and red, her hair disheveled.

Just like she looked ten years ago.

If anything happened to Caleb, she'd die, Joe thought.

"We'll find him, Rosa," he said, putting on his best *staying positive* smile. "I won't let anything ha—"

"Joe, don't," Rosa interrupted. "Don't put this on yourself. If things...go bad, you don't need to carry around any more needless guilt."

Joe smiled and nodded. Just like her, always thinking of others before herself. And just like her to see right through him. He felt like the Visible Man model he had as a kid, transparent enough for Rosa to see past the outer façade and into the inner workings of his soul. It was the first time she'd ever mentioned his guilt. He'd known all along that she was well aware of the turmoil that boiled inside him like a cauldron of oil, but she never said anything. She let him have his privacy, no doubt waiting for him to make the first move toward discussing Rick's death. But he never did. Someday maybe, but not today.

He stood, slipped on his green field coat, and stuck his hands in the pockets. "We shouldn't think like that. We have to expect the best to happen. He probably just wandered too far and got lost, that's all." He knew the hesitancy in his voice betrayed his attempt to appear confident. There were parts of the woods that were thick and tangled with briars and octopus-like vines waiting to snatch little boys who wandered unawares into their wicked domain, and one could easily lose any sense of direction. But the entire rectangular wooded area could not be more than a mile by four miles. Easy to get lost, hard to stay lost. That is, if Caleb was even lost. Joe was well aware of the possibility that he'd stumbled upon a candy-constructed cottage, only to find the occupant a dirty old—

He drove the thought from his head.

Stay positive, Joe. Stay positive.

Inside his trailer home, Stevie Bauer lounged in a torn, brown vinyl recliner, his head relaxed against the back, legs extended, elbows resting on his hips, fingertips of each hand lightly touching. The flame of a single oil lamp threw odd-shaped shadows against the barren walls. He liked basking in the natural light of fire; something about the silent quality of the dancing tongue, the orange hue of the muted glow, soothed him and kept his ubiquitous fears at bay.

Stevie grinned and sighed deeply, fixing his eyes on the twitching shadows. "One down, Momma. One down. I'll make 'em all sorry for what they done. You watch. I'm gonna make you proud, real proud. Time for Stevie to stand up."

A strand of hair fell across his face. He pressed his palm against his brow and brushed it away, then pawed at the air as if batting at imaginary bees and let out a long hiss. Then, stroking a tawny severed paw in his lap, whispered, "No one will bother us again, Momma. I'll teach 'em. They'll learn. Stevie's in charge now."

Joe pulled his 1992 Ford pickup into the cracked and crumbling parking lot of the abandoned repair shop. McCormick Street dead-ended at the edge of the woods, and the garage was the last building before the asphalt ended. The shop was an old, square, brick structure with peeling gray paint and a faded red and white sign that read *Harrison's Garage*. The windows were clouded with dirt, four rusted gray oil drums were lined up alongside of the building, and a stack of used tires, bald from wear and dry-rotted from age, sat next to the wooden overhead door. A single sodium streetlight hummed above the lot, illuminating only the front of the abandoned building. It used to be Hank Harrison's garage before he died and the business folded. No one in the Harrison family bothered to take over the mom-and-pop outfit, and the building was left to decay.

Joe turned off the engine and got out of the truck. Rosa exited the passenger side and met him around the front of the vehicle. She'd told him she wanted to come along and stay at the repair shop while the search party looked for Caleb.

Rosa took Joe's arm and motioned toward the group of volunteers huddled by the garage. "Come. Maggie is over there. Let's see what she has planned."

Joe hesitated. Yes, Maggie. Somewhere between Rosa's house and the garage he'd forgotten he would be face-to-face with Maggie Gill again. His heart rate quickened.

"Are you OK with this?" Rosa asked.

Joe smiled, willing his heart to settle into an even rhythm. "Uh…sure. Of course. Let's go see what she has planned."

Maggie looked up and caught Joe's eye. She stepped out of the group to greet them. "Rosa," she said, giving Rosa a little hug. "I'm glad you came. Are you holding up OK?"

Rosa nodded. "I'm doing the best I can. Keeping hope. Thank you."

Maggie then turned and faced Joe.

"Maggie," he said, extending his arms toward her. "It's good to see you again."

She hugged him tightly and patted him on the back. "Hi, Joe. I'm glad you came. How are you doing?"

Joe let go of Maggie and stepped back. She still looked like a blonde Audrey Hepburn. The overhead lamplight glistened off her dirty-blonde hair and cast soft shadows across her face, highlighting her smooth features. There was sorrow in her eyes that seemed to mute the blue that was once as bright as the midday sky. Nevertheless, she was still just as beautiful as the last time he saw her.

"I'm ready to find Caleb." He dropped his eyes to the asphalt, then looked back up at Maggie. "It's been too many years, hasn't it?"

"Fifteen *is* too many," Maggie agreed, a half smile curling one corner of her mouth. Turning, she clapped her hands, calling the group together. There were about twenty gathered, more men than women, mostly dressed in camo or plaid flannel. Their grim faces and hushed whispers spoke of the seriousness of the situation.

While they huddled around her, Maggie handed out flashlights to those who hadn't brought one and gave instructions. "OK, people. Caleb is eleven years old, about five feet tall, dark brown hair, brown eyes, slender build. Here's a recent photo." She passed around Caleb's fifth grade school picture. "He's wearing a light blue, long-sleeve T-shirt, camouflage jacket, blue jeans, and black adidas. By our best guess, he's been missing for about five hours. We'll cover every square inch of these woods if we have to. Leave no leaf unturned. He could be anywhere. Officer Wilt will lead the search. Officer Warren and I have some other business to attend to. I apologize for the darkness. I know it'll make your job that much more difficult, but organizing something like this takes time, and we all knew the early sunset wasn't going to be on our side. Do your best." She clapped her hands together. "Get your gear and go to it. Let's find Caleb."

She turned to Joe and pulled him close. "The Dinsmore boys said Caleb liked to hide in the old Yates place. You remember where it is?"

"Sure," Joe said. "I used it as a hideout when I was a kid."

"I remember. Start there. I checked it out earlier, but you may find something I missed. A clue, anything."

Maggie spun around to leave, but Joe caught her by the arm. "Wait. Where are you going? What's this other business?"

"Jeremy Dinsmore said he and Caleb and the other boys used to throw rocks at Stevie Bauer's trailer. They've seen him wandering around in the woods and at the Yates house. It's probably nothing, but I want to check it out anyway to make sure."

"Who's Stevie Bauer?"

"A young man who lives on the backside of the Walker farm. He's odd but harmless. Apparently the boys liked to give him a hard time."

"Be careful, Mags," Joe said, giving her arm a gentle squeeze.

Maggie smiled and looked ten years younger. Audrey Hepburn in *Roman Holiday*. "It's been a long time since anyone's called me that. It really is good to see you again. We'll have to find some time to catch up when all this is over."

Joe returned her smile. "I'd like that."

Maggie placed a hand on Joe's arm. Her touch sent a wave of gooseflesh over his skin. "Don't worry. We'll find him. It hasn't been that long, and the woods aren't that big. The cards are stacked in our favor."

CHAPTER 4

C HIEF MAGGIE GILL stopped her patrol car in front of Stevie Bauer's broken-down trailer home. The metal box sat at the edge of the woods at the end of a long dirt lane that wound its way like a scar through Josiah Walker's farm. After Stevie's mother died, Josiah took the boy in and raised him. It was a strained relationship, though. At ten years old, Stevie was diagnosed with paranoid schizophrenia. Josiah did the best he could with the boy, but the two fought constantly. When Stevie turned twenty, Josiah bought him an old trailer and set it up on the other side of the farm, near the woods. It wasn't much of a home—all a poor, old farmer could afford—but Stevie liked having a place of his own, and it kept him close enough for Josiah to keep an eye on him.

The green and white trailer was rusting badly and supported clumsily on cinder blocks. The windows were frosted with grime—some were broken and patched with plywood—and the roof was partially covered with a blue tarp.

Maggie and Officer Gary Warren approached the storm door. Maggie knocked hard. The light that flickered through the window went out, and a bright overhead light popped on. Maggie could hear heavy footsteps inside; then the door swung open, scraping the linoleum floor in the kitchen.

Stevie stood motionless and silent behind the dirty, glass storm door. He wore a pair of torn blue jeans, a red University of Maryland sweatshirt, and a heavy flannel shirt, unbuttoned, sleeves rolled up to his elbows. His gaunt, angular face was partially hidden by shaggy, dark brown hair that fell across his forehead and covered one eye.

Maggie reached up and opened the door a few inches. "Stevie? It's Chief Maggie and Officer Warren. We'd like to talk to you."

A broad smile suddenly appeared on Stevie's face, exposing a mouth full of yellow teeth. "Oh, hi, Chief Maggie. C'mon in." He opened the door all the way and allowed Maggie and Gary to enter.

The interior of the trailer was what Maggie had expected—dirty and cluttered. The pungent odor of rotting food and sour milk hung in the air like a yellow haze. A card table and two metal folding chairs sat in the middle of the small kitchen, the once beige linoleum floor now faded and graying, spotted with stains and gashes. The trash bin overflowed with empty soup cans, TV dinners, cat food cans, and milk cartons. In the living room, a brown recliner and green vinyl sofa were situated next to each other, facing a decades-old TV with bent rabbit ears for antennae.

"Would you like a drink a'water?" Stevie asked Maggie, holding up a spotted glass.

"No thanks," Maggie said. "We won't be staying long."

Stevie shuffled into the living room, and Maggie followed. He sat on the recliner, leaned back, and extended his legs. Clasping his hands behind his head, he stared at the ceiling.

Gary remained in the kitchen. Maggie had told him on the way over to snoop through the cupboards and drawers while she distracted Stevie. "Find anything that may link Stevie to Caleb's disappearance," she'd told him.

"Fire away, Chief Maggie," Stevie said, then laughed and thrust both hands in the air over his head. "No, wait; don't shoot!"

Maggie chuckled politely and removed her cap. "How have things been going for you here? You like having your own place?"

"Sure do." Stevie smiled wide. "It's my bachelor pad, Chief Maggie. Maybe you should come over some time. We can hang together."

Maggie dipped the corners of her mouth. "Stevie, I'm a little old for you. And besides, I'm not very good at *hanging*. Too much cop in me. I'm a bore. Would you mind if I ask you a few questions?"

Stevie shrugged. "Shoot." Then made twin six-shooters with his index fingers and thumbs and aimed them at Maggie. "But be careful, I might shoot back. Bang! Bang!"

Maggie glanced toward the kitchen. She'd have to stall a little longer so Gary could finish searching. "You like going in the woods, Stevie?"

"Yup. It's peaceful there, y'know. No one to bother me. Not that there's anyone to bother me here in my humble adobe...I mean abode." He paused and furrowed his brow, his dark eyes darted about the room. "What is it? Adobe or abode? Where is that dictionary when I need it?"

Maggie took the opportunity to look around the room too. Scanning for any clues, any sign of Caleb. "Have you ever seen anyone else in the woods? Hunters, hikers, kids, anyone?"

Stevie shook his head emphatically. "Nope. The only person I ever seen is me. That's why I like it there. Just me, myself, and me."

"So you've never seen kids around here? No one's ever bothered you or snooped around your place?"

Stevie put a finger to his mouth and pretended to be deep in thought. "No, no, no. I never seen no one."

Maggie shifted her weight and shoved her hands in her coat pockets. She knew he was lying, but what was he trying to hide? "When's the last time you were in the woods?"

"Oh, not for several weeks now, months maybe, I don't know. I lose track of my time, y'know? I ain't been in the woods since the weather turned cold."

Gary suddenly appeared in the doorway between the kitchen and the living room. He gave Maggie a subtle shake of his head.

"OK, Stevie," Maggie said. "We'll let you enjoy your evening by yourself." She turned to leave, then stopped and spun back around. "Oh, one more thing. Have you ever been to the old Yates place in the woods?"

Stevie fidgeted and combed his hand through his hair. He cleared his throat, looked at the ceiling, and tapped the arm of the chair. "*Um*, yeah, sure. It's a pretty neat place. I been there once or twice. Why?"

Maggie smiled. "No reason. Just wondering. Have a good evening, Stevie."

Maggie and Gary left the trailer and closed the door behind them.

"Nothing," Gary said, securing his cap on his head. "No sign of anything but a slob."

"Did you notice all the cat food cans?"

Gary snorted and shook his head. "Why does Walker support that screwball? Talk about a ball and chain."

As they approached the cruiser and opened the doors, they heard a hideous shriek come from inside the trailer and Stevie yell, "That's right! Get out and stay out!"

Gary looked at Maggie and shook his head again. "What a freak. But I'd bet my left leg he didn't mess with the kid. Nuts like him are all the same. All talk."

Maggie returned the look and lifted her eyebrows. "He lied, didn't he? C'mon, let's get back and see how the search is going."

~

Thick darkness, like inky liquid, surrounded Caleb, oozing between his fingers, crawling up his back, putting his bones on ice. He tried to move, but the blackness had solidified, encasing him in a jellylike tomb. He tried to yell, holler, scream for help, but the ink swallowed any sound that escaped his mouth.

He was trapped in some dreamy netherworld between reality and the stuff of horror movies, buried alive, left for dead. He had no memory of anything, only a feeling, distant and vague, of *something* awful, evil, gruesome. *Something* wicked. Clawing, attacking, seething, putrid hate. He *must* be dreaming, but it was so…real, so vivid. More than a dream. A nightmare.

Then the panic set in. He writhed and pulled at his arms and legs, shook his head, arched his back, curled his fingers. But it was useless; he was pinned to a wall, stuck fast like a fly to flypaper.

Slowly, like the exposure of a Polaroid photo, the memory began to materialize. The sound of lungs sucking in air, the brush of fur against his legs, the smell of death. He had tried to scream, but no sound would squeeze past his taut vocal cords. He tried to move but…suddenly, the beast was before him, glowering like a demon from hell begging for his life.

He remembered the flash of fangs, the searing pain, the numbing fear. And those eyes, as monstrous and nightmarish as any he'd ever seen in any horror flick he'd ever watched without his mother's consent, the look of vile death in them. Then there was a dead zone, and the next thing he remembered was backing into a hole, losing himself in deep darkness, withdrawing from the claws and fangs that would tear him to shreds.

He was safe—for now. He would stay in this hole and never come out.

~

Joe's pickup rambled down the dirt lane that led to the Yates place. A thick cloud cover had moved in, making the darkness in the woods almost palpable, surrounding his truck like a shroud, pressing closer and deeper, looming just on the other side of the windshield. The light from the old Ford's headlamps barely cut through the blackness and illuminated only a small swath of road no more than fifteen feet in front of the vehicle. Beyond that was dense darkness, as if the world ended and just dropped into nothing.

Joe steered his truck off the road and stopped, pointing the headlamps at the deteriorating façade of the old Yates house. He turned off the engine, grabbed his flashlight, and jumped out of the cab hollering Caleb's name. His voice mingled with the distant calls of the other searchers and echoed into the darkness.

Entering the house, Joe swept the flashlight beam around the main room. It was empty with the exception of a few scattered leaves, some fallen branches, and a stack of old planks situated in one corner.

The old house had definitely seen better days, but its *better* days weren't better—it had a dark and shadowed past. The tale went that in the mid-1920s the townsfolk suspected Yates of witchcraft. Strange sounds— ghastly screams; low, gruntlike moans; and hollering of the most awful obscenities—had often been heard coming from deep in the woods late at night and into the early morning hours. When confronted by the sheriff and a local minister, Old Man Yates had produced a shotgun and threatened to blow them both to high heaven if they ever came calling on him again. Days later, a mob of angry and frightened townsfolk swarmed the Yates house and burned it almost to the ground.

Rumor had it that Old Man Yates was burned alive in the inferno, and now his ghost haunted the woods. When Joe was a kid, some of the older folk living in town had said that on quiet evenings they could still hear screams and moans coming from deep within the woods. At the time, Joe sat wide-eyed and gullible and hung on every syllable. Now he suspected what they had heard was nothing more than the sounds of a gaggle of hippy teens experiencing life on a much more psychedelic level.

Whether there was any truth to the horror stories or not, being inside the building brought back fond memories for Joe. He and Rick, his younger brother by two years, spent many summer afternoons playing soldiers and using the old house as their fort. His eyes moistened at the thought of Rick and his crooked smile. He could almost hear his high-pitched laughter bouncing off the stone walls. He missed him so much.

C'mon, Joe. Stay focused. He called Caleb's name again. *Keep your head in the game.*

Suddenly, Joe heard a rustling sound from somewhere in the house. He stopped and listened, shining the light from corner to corner and sweeping the floor from side to side. The rustling came again, faint, but definitely from the cellar. Joe's pulse jumped, and though it was nearly fifty degrees, a cold sweat wetted his brow.

As a kid, Joe had mustered up the courage only one time to enter the blackness that lurked under the old house. People said the cryptlike cellar was the center of the haunting, that the ghost of Old Man Yates resided there, waiting to pounce on any intruders who would dare trespass his domain. All those years ago, Joe had sensed there was something down there, something unseen and unnatural...a presence. And though he now supposed the incident was nothing more than the imagination of a boy star-struck with movie monsters, the very memory of his past experience in the cellar some twenty years prior made his skin pucker with goose bumps.

He stood at the top of the steps and pointed the flashlight into the cellar, scanning as much of the dirt floor and stone foundation as he could see. There was something dark splattered on the walls and floor at the bottom of the stairs. Paint? Oil?

"Caleb?" he called in a hushed voice. "Caleb? You down there, buddy?"

No answer. The only sounds that could be heard were the faint calls of the other searchers. They were moving farther away. East.

Joe took a deep breath and descended the cold stone stairs. The stink of the cavelike cellar hit him all at once, and it burned in his nostrils—rotted meat and mildew. He was fairly certain he would not find Caleb stretched out on a leather recliner, remote in one hand, Cherry Coke in the other, watching SpongeBob on a plasma TV.

As soon as his head cleared the first floor, Joe swept the beam of light across the cellar—nothing but more old planks stacked waist-high against the far wall. The ceiling beams were noticeably rotted, no doubt the work of an army of termites, and covered with cobwebs draped from one to another like garland. The floor was smooth. No footprints or disturbances in the packed dirt. He moved the light back to the bottom of the crumbling staircase. What *was* that on the walls?

Suddenly, it hit him with the force of a sledgehammer. "No." It was blood. Dark crimson blood spotted the wall and clotted on the dusty floor. He looked again and now noticed a trail of dried blood ascending the steps.

What happened here? Did Caleb wander into the cellar and startle a wild animal? Joe's heart banged and a chill climbed up his back. His mind raced then blanked out, raced then blanked, spinning him in circles. *Think! Think!* The only animals around these parts large enough to maul a human, even a child, were coyotes and black bears, and to his knowledge neither had ever been spotted in these woods. Unless Caleb had stumbled upon a rabid wild dog. They'd been known to stray into the area from time to time.

Joe turned to climb the stairs when, from somewhere above, he heard a growl. Before he even had time to look up, something solid and soccer-ball sized landed on his shoulder and dug its claws into his head and neck. He reached behind and grabbed a handful of bristled fur. As he squeezed it, the creature—whether a rabid squirrel, a spooked cat, or a snaggletoothed, steroid-enraged toy poodle, he couldn't immediately determine—howled in pain. Joe yanked the writhing animal from its perch, its claws tearing at his flesh like needles, and threw the beast across the room. He pointed the flashlight into the darkness, swept it across the cellar and back again. It was nothing more than a cat, huddled in the far corner, ears pressed against its head, eyes glowing yellow in the light.

"Stupid cat," Joe muttered, rubbing the back of his now tender neck.

He then ascended the steps and followed the blood trail to the front door, where it was lost in the leaves and grass of the clearing. Joe stepped outside and scanned the exterior walls and grounds. Weeds, waist-high, grew up along the charred rocks, connected by an intricate system of spider webs. He swept the light from side to side until the beam fell on the outhouse, a four-by-four structure patched together by rotting wood and rusted nails. It stood cock-eyed, leaning like a pillared trapezoid. Shingles peeled and curled on the caving roof. The door dangled precariously on one hinge.

Joe looked closer and noticed a puddle of black liquid glistening on the ground by the door. A muted tingle crept across his head and face. *No. No, no. Please, no. I don't know if I can bear it.*

He approached the old outhouse, reached for the wooden latch, swallowed past the swollen lump in his throat, and swung the door open.

His heart dropped out of his chest and landed in his stomach. But his stomach was in its own state of rebellion. Bile rose in his throat and a deep groan escaped his mouth.

NO!

There, on the floor, was Caleb's colorless form.

CHAPTER 5

STEVIE BAUER LAY prone on the floor of his trailer, arms stretched overhead, face pressed against the carpet. He was in a trancelike state, eyes rolled back, his breath quick and shallow. Occasionally his muscles would twitch involuntarily, sending his body into a violent spasm. It would last only a second or two, then subside, and he would relax again.

Voices, so many voices, chattered in his head. Some whispered, some shouted, some rambled on and on, but all of them vied for his attention—begging, urging, commanding, threatening. Images of people from his past, both young and old, swam in his mind, taunting him, laughing at him, their faces distorted and disfigured. Ghouls that lurked in the darkest corners of his brain.

But one voice and one image surfaced above the others—his mother. Momma. She was pleading with him, begging him to help her. Dark figures pounced on her, beat her, ripped at her clothes and skin, pulled her hair. They were from hell, the shadows. He was sure of it. Sent to torture and torment, maim and kill. And they were enjoying it. Their loud peals of laughter and howls of excitement sent ripples down Stevie's back. But it was Momma they were brutalizing, her body they were violating. Her face twisted with fear and pain, stretched into an elongated howl.

"Stevie," she cried, "help me. Stevie, help me!"

Her body was then engulfed in a cloak of darkness.

"Momma!" Stevie shouted from his trance. "I will, Momma. I'll get 'em all."

Then Momma's limp body appeared alone. The shadowy figures were gone; the taunting had stopped. There was silence. Her bruised and broken body lay in a heap, like a pile of soiled laundry someone had neglected. Stevie approached and knelt beside her lifeless frame. He bent over and looked at Momma's disfigured face; she had suffered such a beating, such a violent, merciless attack. And he had done nothing to help. Stupid! Stupid! Coward!

Suddenly, her eyes flipped open and fixed upon Stevie. "You still have a chance," Momma whispered, her voice strained and wheezy, her face a pasty white. "You can still help me." She reached up with a shaky hand, grabbed a fistful of his shirt, and pulled him within an inch of her face. Blood trickled out of the corner of her mouth, and a string of saliva stretched between her lips. "Stevie, help me!"

Stevie remained prone on the floor, his body twitching uncontrollably with muscle spasms, his breathing fast and heavy. "I will, Momma. I will. I *will* help you."

Then his body went limp and his breathing slowed. He eased his eyes open and rolled over to his back. His shirt was soaked with sweat; hair clung to his forehead. Every muscle in his body ached.

He stared at the ceiling for a long time before a soft purr in his ear brought him out of his trance. "Hey, Kitty, where you been?" he said, sitting up and taking the tan cat into his arms. "Silly me. I know where you been. You been a good kitty."

He stroked the cat's head and jaws and the purring increased. "Are you hungry? Can Stevie get you somethin' to eat? You gotta get your strength up; there's lots more work to be done."

───

Forty minutes northeast of Dark Hills (on a good day, driving comfortably over the posted speed limit), the ICU room of Southcentral Regional Medical Center was dark except for the muted light that filtered in from the hallway and the soft glow of the myriad of machines that surrounded the bed.

Caleb rested peacefully, his chest rising and falling in time with the rhythmic *swish-swoosh* of the ventilator. His left arm was heavily bandaged from shoulder to fingertips. Tubes snaked around his bed, entering his frail body at various sites. A bolt monitoring intracranial pressure was screwed tightly into his head. His legs were encapsulated with knee-high sequential pumps, keeping the blood from pooling. Machines blinked and beeped, ticked and whined as they kept close watch on Caleb's vitals—and kept him alive.

The scene was so surreal that Joe half-expected a bug-eyed, hunch-backed male nurse named Igor to enter the room and start fiddling with the instruments, turning dials, flipping switches, and checking pressure gauges—*Yes, Master, everything is going as planned, Master.* But Igor must have been on breakfast break or out checking his text messages.

Joe leaned forward in the gray upholstered chair next to Caleb's bed, his elbows resting on his knees, head in his hands. When he found his young nephew in the outhouse, Caleb barely had a pulse. Fortunately, Joe was able to put him in his truck and meet the helicopter from the hospital's shock trauma unit in the field behind the woods. Caleb was then airlifted to safety. Joe had watched as the chopper lifted off, stirring up a whirlwind of dust and debris, wondering if it would be the last time he would ever see Caleb alive.

Joe met the chopper at the hospital and remained there overnight, waiting for a report from the doctors. They had spent most of the night stabilizing Caleb, replenishing his blood supply, and repairing the damage to his left arm.

The first time Joe saw Caleb lying in the hospital bed, his small frail body looking more like a machine than a boy, he could not stop the flood of emotion and tears that poured out of him. He was angry—angry at himself for not being there to protect Caleb, angry at God for allowing this to happen, angry at the Dinsmore boys for not looking until they found him.

Joe had tried to pray, but it seemed so futile, like God had shut the doors to heaven and hung out a *Closed* sign. Old emotions he thought he had buried now surfaced, numbing his nerves and twisting his gut. He had sat in a room very much like this one ten years ago, except that time the *machine* in the bed next to him was his brother, clinging to life by the gadgets that supported him.

He thought of Rosa. She had lost her husband, her soul mate, and had found hope again, thanks to her strong faith in God and resolute belief in His goodness. Now she was faced with the reality that she may lose the only thing she had left in this world—her son, her Caleb. *Why, God? Why do this twice to the same family?* How much pain and heartache could one woman endure?

Joe sat back in the chair, closed his eyes, and was about to doze off when he heard a gentle knock. He opened his eyes and saw Maggie standing in the doorway, dressed in faded jeans and a black, fitted button-down shirt—her off-duty clothes.

"Hey, Mags," Joe said, forcing a smile. "C'mon in."

Maggie entered the room and approached Caleb's bed. She swallowed hard, trying not to let the lump in her throat rise any higher. It was always hard seeing someone like this, especially a child. Caleb looked so frail and small, so...lifeless.

She pulled the other chair over and sat down across from Joe, placing a hand on his. His hand was warm, and it made her smile. Memories of their past flooded her mind. She'd spent a lot of time holding that hand and used to think she would never let go. She'd spent her whole adolescence *hoping* she'd never let go. Funny how nothing had turned out the way she'd expected.

She met Joe's fatigue-clouded eyes and couldn't help but notice how he'd aged. His once rich brown hair had dulled some and appeared to be lightly powdered with moondust. The angles of his face had sharpened with time and, no doubt, the fatigue and stress of the past twelve hours. He looked sad and worn, like someone had reached right into his chest and ripped out his heart. She suppressed the urge to reach out and take him in her arms, stroke his hair, and promise him everything would be OK.

"So how's he doing?"

"Not good," Joe said, a frown replacing his smile. "He lost a lot of blood. His right lung collapsed. He suffered some head trauma, and the neurologist said his brain is swollen. They have him in an induced coma now, hoping the swelling will go down."

"And what about his arm?"

Joe sighed and shrugged. "Don't know. The orthopedic surgeon was just in and said they were able to reattach everything, but they won't know how much use he'll have with it until he wakes up and it heals. They had to do skin grafts on the whole arm. The doctor said it looked like the arm went through a farming combine." Joe looked at Caleb, and Maggie could see the glisten of tears in his eyes. "Something really tore him up. When I found him, his whole arm..." He paused and lifted a hand to his mouth. "I'm sorry."

Maggie squeezed Joe's hand. Tears burned behind her eyes, and her voice cracked. "It's OK, Joe. You don't have to tell me anymore." She knew the damage that was done. She'd spoken to one of the Dark Hills paramedics last night and was filled in on Caleb's condition when Joe found him. The boy's left forearm had been stripped of skin, exposing muscle, tendons, and blood vessels. His shoulder had been dislocated and almost completely severed.

Maggie removed a handkerchief from her pocket and dabbed at her eyes. "What are they saying about any lasting effects of the brain injury?"

"That's up in the air too. He's got youth on his side, but the neurologist said he had a pretty good-sized contusion on his brain and with all the blood he lost…it's kinda just wait and see."

"And how's Rosa doing?"

Joe sniffed. "Better than me. Her faith has always been strong. Even when Rick died, it never wavered. At least not that she let anyone see. She's down in the cafeteria now getting some breakfast."

"Do you want anything?"

"No. I'm fine. Don't have much of an appetite."

Maggie paused, unsure if she wanted to ask the next question, knowing it was tender ground to be walking on so soon. But she was a cop, and whatever it was that did this to Caleb was still out there. She had to find it before it attacked again. The next person may not be as lucky as Caleb. Looking at Caleb now, though, *luck* didn't seem an appropriate choice of words. She sat back in her chair. "What do you think did this to him?"

Joe ran his fingers through his hair and sighed. "I don't know. A coyote, some stray dog, maybe a black bear." He paused, looked at Caleb, and placed a hand on the boy's head. "Whatever it was must have been big…and Caleb must have put up a real fight."

"Was there anything in the cellar that might give us a clue as to what did it?"

Joe shook his head slowly. "Just some blood. There was an awful stench, though, like dead animal smell, but there was no carcass or anything. There was also a stray cat. Scared me half to death and scratched me up pretty good. Poor thing must have been down there during the attack and was scared witless. You might want to look for some fur samples, though. That would at least give us an idea of what kind of animal we're looking for."

Maggie noticed Joe said *we* but let it go. As soon as she found out what kind of animal it was, she would have it taken care of and Joe would be out of the loop. But she knew better than to try to dissuade him from getting involved. She knew *him*, and once he got his mind set on something, there was no changing it. Besides, it was his nephew who was attacked. Could she blame him for wanting to be involved?

"It's been too dark to do a good search. When the sun comes up, I'll head over to the Yates place and see what I can find." She made a mental note to look for fur, saliva, get some blood samples, anything that might shed some light on what kind of animal attacked Caleb. "You have a cell number where I can reach you?"

"Yeah." He gave her the number. "But I can't promise I'll answer. I don't like gadgets. Only have one because of work, and I have a habit of forgetting to turn it on when I'm not working. If I don't answer, just leave a message. I'll find it."

There was a long silence as Maggie watched Joe gently stroke Caleb's head. She marveled at how boyish Joe still looked, not much older than the teenager who left Dark Hills—and her—over a decade ago. "He's a good kid, huh?" she said.

Joe didn't take his eyes off Caleb. "The best."

CHAPTER 6

Mary Chronister was up early, milling around the kitchen in her orange housecoat and blue slippers, her silver, permed hair tucked carefully under a hairnet. She poured some coffee grounds into a filter, placed the filter in the coffee maker, and flipped the switch. "Coffee'll be ready in a few minutes, hon," she called to her husband, John, who, last time she'd checked, was comfortably seated in his recliner in the living room, scanning the Sunday paper while he dozed in and out of sleep. "Would you like some eggs?"

She waited, standing in front of the open refrigerator. "John!"

His voice, thick and husky, came from the living room. "Huh? What?"

"Do you want some eggs?"

"Uh…yeah…sure."

She shook her head and pulled the egg carton from the top shelf. As she turned toward the sink, something outside caught her eye—a movement in the field behind their home. The Chronisters had both lived in Dark Hills all their lives and had resided on Fulton Street for the past thirty years. Deer in the field was a common occurrence, especially this time of year, but Mary never grew tired of watching the gracefulness of a white-tailed deer as it nibbled on dried corn or bounded across the open ground, its white tail bobbing like a sailboat in rough water.

It was dawn and the sky was tinged with pastel orange, but the sun had yet to peek over the horizon. A light haze had settled over the field, washing everything in a subtle shade of gray.

She paused in front of the window and watched the field, waiting for the familiar outline of a deer to appear.

A movement snapped her eyes to the right. There. Something was in the field, by a line of maples running along the property line. But it was no deer.

John had just slipped into a deep snore.

Mary's eyes widened and her jaw dropped open. Her mouth silently formed her husband's name. Then again. Then, "John!"

John snorted and huffed. "For Pete's sake, woman, I said yes."

She lowered her voice. "Get in here."

The newspaper rustled and John grunted. "What in blazes are you hollering about?" he said, his slippers scuffing along the linoleum. "You can't make—"

Mary pointed out the window. "Look."

John peered through the glass, his eyes darting back and forth. "What? What am I looking at?"

"That," Mary said, pointing to the right in the general direction of the stand of trees.

John looked harder, squinting his eyes and leaning over the counter. "I can't see a blasted thing. It's too dark. What's gotten into you?"

"John, you old goat." Mary grabbed his chin with her left hand and yanked his head to the right. "There, by the trees."

John was quiet for only a second, then, "Jiminy Christmas! Is that—" He cursed, then apologized. Cursed again, then apologized again.

Mary kept her eyes fixed on the trees and elbowed John in the ribs. "Call Betty and Dick. See if they see it too."

"It's too early."

Mary elbowed him again. "Call them!"

"OK, OK." He grabbed the cordless from its cradle and punched in the number.

Betty and Dick Moyer had lived next door to the Chronisters for over two decades, and both couples would have agreed they were best friends. Dick and John golfed together every Friday morning during the summer while Betty and Mary canned vegetables. They regularly went out to eat together, went to church together, and played cards together every Thursday night—had for the past twenty-three years.

John held up fingers on his left hand, counting the number of unanswered rings. One, two, three, four. "I told you it was too—Betty, it's John, look out your kitchen window. Are you looking?"

There was a short pause, then John blurted, "Right in front of you!"

Mary grabbed the phone from John. "Do you see it?"

"Oh, hi, Mary. Do I see—Oh my stars! Dick!"

"Gotta go, Betty," Mary said. "I'm calling the police." Mary clicked the phone off and handed it back to John. "Call 911."

John took the phone. "That's for emergencies only."

Mary shot a look at John that could have burned a hole in steel. "You don't think this is an emergency?"

"Well—"

"John!" She said it slow. "There's a lion in our yard."

John paused for a moment, but only for a moment, then punched in 9–1–1.

Sundays were always trying days. Most of the working world—at least in small towns across rural America—had the day off, making it very unpalatable to be spending the day in a police cruiser.

Andy Wilt was on patrol when the dispatcher notified him of the Chronisters' odd call. He pulled up in front of their house, a small brick ranch house, shut off his cruiser's engine, and climbed out. Being a cop was something he'd always dreamed of. Now, at twenty-five, he was finally living his dream. Not many people could say that.

He'd grown up in Dark Hills and never imagined serving any other community. Sure, Dark Hills didn't have the action and adventure that big cities offered, and most of his days were spent sitting idly behind the wheel of his cruiser watching the hours tick by, but there was an honor and respect that went with being a small-town cop that the big-city boys would never know anything about.

But never in a million years did Andy think he would ever be responding to a call like this. Not in Dark Hills. Not in Pennsylvania. Not in America.

He padded up the front walk, muttering about senile old geezers seeing things, and hopped up the three steps to the concrete porch. The front door swung open and Mary Chronister greeted him in her orange house-coat and blue slippers. "Come in. It was right out back."

Andy stepped inside and was met by John Chronister. "Morning, Mr. Chronister," he said, dipping his chin. He removed a notepad from his coat pocket and clicked his pen. "So you say—"

"In here," Mary said, leading him by the arm into the kitchen. She pointed out the window. "It was right over there, by the trees. It stood there maybe, what"—she looked at John—"fifteen minutes? Then disappeared into the woods over yonder."

Andy looked out the window and saw nothing but an open field and a stand of old maples. "Uh-huh." He gave her a sideways glance. "And you say it was a lion?"

Mary nodded like a bobblehead. "Yes. I'm certain of it." She pointed to John, who was now also standing in the kitchen. "We both saw it, didn't we?"

John nodded. "I wasn't—"

"He saw it," Mary said. "The Moyers next door saw it too. Both of them, that's Dick and Betty Moyer. Write it down. I tried to get them over here, but they were scared to come out of their house, what with that young boy being attacked yesterday and all. Lord help us if it was a lion that attacked that poor boy. How awful! You can call the Moyers right now if you want to."

Andy started to write on his notepad, then stopped and looked at Mary. "Oh, I don't think that'll be necessary. You're sure it was a...lion? Big, furry, tan cat."

"Yes!" She pointed to the line of maples again. "It was standing right over there. Call the Moyers; they'll tell you."

"And did this lion have a mane?"

Mary looked surprised he would ask such an incredulous question. "I...well...yes, of course it did. Lions have manes, don't they?"

"Not all of them. Females don't, and I don't think all males do either."

"Well...well, this one did!"

Andy looked out the window again. "It's just that—" He paused. How do you tactfully tell someone she's off her rocker? "There're no lions in Dark Hills. I can assure you of that. Occasionally, there are black bears. And sometimes black bears are actually brown. You sure it wasn't a bear?"

Mary crossed her arms and wrinkled her brow. "Yes. I know the difference between a bear and a lion."

"Maybe it was a bobcat. They're tan. They're pretty shy and usually stay away from houses, but occasionally one will get brave."

Mary frowned. "How big is a bobcat?"

Andy held his hands about three feet apart. "About so big."

Mary shook her head. "No way. This was a lion. It was as big as a small horse." She looked at John. "Wasn't it?"

He nodded.

Andy sighed and studied the lines on his blank notepad. "It's just that—"

"Young man, look at me." Mary's tone caught Andy by surprise, and he jerked his head up. "I'm an old lady. I have arthritis in both my knees and shoulders and most of my spine. My hair is thinning, my hearing's going, and my skin is wrinkling, but do you see any glasses on this nose?"

Andy stared at her spectacle-less nose.

"Well, do you?"

"Uh, no, ma'am."

"No, because my eyesight is the only thing that hasn't failed me yet. It's still twenty-twenty." She leaned in and poked his notepad with her index finger. "Write it down. Mary Chronister saw a lion outside her window by a stand of maple trees. And now it's somewhere in those woods over there. Now what you do about it after you leave this house is your business. But I'm doing my civic duty by reporting it. Now don't second-guess me in my own house."

Andy smiled and double-clicked his pen. He liked the old woman's feistiness. "Yes, ma'am."

Maggie steered her cruiser off the rutted dirt road and stopped in front of the Yates house. It was a crisp, sunny, autumn day. A light breeze rustled what leaves were left on the trees. Beams of light reached through the porous canopy with thick fingers and mottled the leafy floor.

Maggie sat in her cruiser surveying the site. With the exception of her brief visit yesterday, she hadn't been to the old ruin in ages.

The clearing where the house sat was no more than fifty feet by fifty feet and, over the decades, was slowly being encroached by saplings and thickets. The house, what was left of it, was overgrown with moss. Vines had worked their way between the rocks in the walls, separating them and causing some areas to crumble. Around the right side and toward the back was the outhouse, leaning unsteadily to one side, the door still ajar from the previous night.

Maggie turned off the engine, grabbed her flashlight from the seat, and got out of the car. She slowly entered the house through the empty doorway and stomped on the rotting floorboards, testing their stability. Satisfied with their strength, she approached the concrete staircase that descended into the cellar and pointed her flashlight down the steps. There was a trail of blood going down the stairs and a spattering of blood on the

wall at the bottom—just as Joe had described it. She then swept the light
along the dirt floor as far as she could. She'd have to go down there sooner
or later. With one hand resting on her Glock and the other sweeping the
light back and forth, she descended the steps.

When she reached the bottom of the stairs she panned the whole
room—ceiling, walls, floor—leaving no corner untouched by the light.

Empty, except for a stack of old, rotted planks. But no sign of life.

Good. She could breathe a little easier now.

She turned toward the stairwell, squatted, and carefully inspected the
dirt floor, looking for anything the beast may have left behind. Something
glistened in the light. It was a clump of tan fur. Maggie picked it up and
held it under the flashlight's beam. Looked like cat fur. She set the flashlight down, beam pointing at the ceiling, reached into her coat pocket,
and pulled out a plastic bag. Shaking it open with one hand, she carefully
placed the clump of fur in the bag, sealed it, and returned it to her pocket.
Then, opening another bag, she held it against the wall and chipped some
dried blood off the rock and into the bag. She sealed that bag as well and
placed it in her pocket.

She then picked up the flashlight and continued scanning the dusty
floor, running the light along the ground at the base of the wall. The dirt
was obviously disturbed and clumped from dried blood, but there was no
lingering sign of any animal being in the vicinity.

Then, as if a cold breeze had blown down the steps, Maggie's skin quivered and broke out in goose bumps. She had the overwhelming sense she
was not alone. Blood pulsed through her ears like a river, and an eerie
numbness crept over her body like a shadow. The air in the cellar felt
heavy, thick with tension, as if the atmospheric pressure had just plummeted in anticipation of a monster of a storm.

Something rustled in the far corner. And by the sound of it, something
big.

Forgetting the flashlight, Maggie spun around and peered into the
darkness. The *something* moved again. She could just make out a faint
image on the other side of the cellar, moving slowly, quietly. Pacing along
the wall. Without taking her eyes off the image, she reached behind her
and felt for the flashlight. Her hand groped blindly. Where was it? C'mon.
C'mon! There. She whipped the light in front of her, pointing it in the
direction of the image. The light sliced through the blackness like a sword
and illuminated the corner.

Nothing. Nothing but the stone foundation and that pile of old lumber.

In a panic, Maggie pulled her Glock from its holster, holding it next to the flashlight, arms outstretched. She swept both the beam and the gun around the room, covering every square foot of space.

Still nothing. The cellar was clean…and empty.

Did I just imagine that? I must be losing my mind.

She slipped her Glock back in its holster and snapped it shut. She had to get out of there; the cellar was giving her the creeps.

CHAPTER 7

ROSA SAUNDERS KNELT by her son's hospital bed, hands clutching a black leather Bible to her chest, her head bowed low, lips moving silently. Prayer was where she found her strength, her hope. God was the only part of her life that never changed. Ever since she submitted her life to Jesus when she was in the fifth grade, He had been there for her. When her dad died of liver cancer when she was only fourteen—He was there. When her family moved to the States from Peru, leaving behind everything familiar and safe, and she was alone and isolated—He was there. When Rick died in the trucking accident—He was there. And now, with her precious son in a coma, his body battered and mauled—He was with her, taking every step stride for stride, carrying her when she could no longer find the strength to walk on her own. He was her God, her Savior, her Friend, her Rock. And it was always Him to whom she clung when life's storms raged.

She could feel Him with her now in the darkened ICU room. He was present, wrapping her in His arms of love, holding her like a mother coddles her child when he's sick or hurt or scared. And He spoke to her, whispering words of peace and comfort, promising to care for her, to lift her up—assuring her that she would once again hold Caleb in her arms, watch him run, hear him laugh.

She also prayed for Joe. She knew how hard he was taking everything. She knew how hard he had taken Rick's death. Joe blamed himself, hated himself. She knew. She could see it in his hollow eyes, hear it in the way his voice fell cold every time he talked about Rick. She prayed for him. She prayed that Jesus would draw him back and fill his life and wash away all the guilt and self-loathing. She prayed that Joe would let go and once again cling to the same rock to which she clung—the Rock that never faltered.

The glass door to the room slid open with a quiet *whoosh*, and Rosa looked up, her cheeks damp with tears.

"I'm sorry," Dr. Wilson said, diverting his eyes from Rosa. "I didn't mean to bother you."

"No, no. It's OK, Doctor," Rosa said. She rose to her feet and extended both her arms to shake the doctor's hand. "Thank you so much for what you have done for my son. You have been a blessing."

Dr. Wilson was a tall, lean man in his fifties with gaunt cheeks, deep-set, pale periwinkle eyes, and a shock of thin flaxen hair, clumsily parted to one side. His hand was large and warm, his grip firm and reassuring. Rosa liked him. She had spoken to him on only two occasions since Caleb was admitted yesterday, but she had a sense about people, and she could tell Dr. Wilson was genuine. He truly cared about her son.

"It helps that Caleb is so strong," Dr. Wilson said, a warm smile parting his lips. "How are you holding up? Are you getting enough rest?"

Rosa nodded. "I am doing fine. God gives me strength moment by moment."

Dr. Wilson motioned toward the chair. "Have a seat and we'll talk about Caleb."

Rosa sat, and Dr. Wilson leaned against the edge of Caleb's bed. "Good news and bad news," he said. Furrowing his brow, he studied the chart in his hand. "There's an infection in Caleb's arm. One of the grafts may need to be redone. We're increasing his antibiotics and will be monitoring his white blood cell count closely."

He paused and breathed deeply. "Rosa, I won't sugarcoat this. Sometimes these infections can get the devil in them. If it gets out of control, we'll have to take the arm. We can't let the infection spread to the rest of his body. There's a good chance the antibiotics will do the job, though. I know you're a praying woman. This is something to pray about."

Rosa nodded in silence.

Dr. Wilson paused and held Rosa's gaze for a second. "Now, the good news. Caleb's cranial pressure has been improving steadily, and we're hoping tomorrow to take him off the medication that's keeping him in the coma. It's up to him then whether he wants to wake up or not."

Tears welled in Rosa's eyes. She removed a handkerchief from her purse and dabbed at them. "Thank you, Doctor. That *is* good news. As for the infection—we will have to put it in God's hands. I am trusting Him to take care of my son."

Dr. Wilson smiled and reached for Rosa's hand. Taking it in his, he gave it a gentle squeeze. His voice was quiet and sincere. "I envy your faith. I can see it's what keeps you strong."

"God keeps me strong."

Miles away, in the tiny paper mill town of Dark Hills, the flame of a solitary oil lamp danced in the darkness of a small room, casting gyrating shadows on the walls. The globe had broken some time ago, exposing the flame to the cold drafts that blew through the decaying trailer home.

Stevie Bauer knelt in the middle of the room, crouched so low his forehead rested on the dirty, faded carpet. His shaggy hair fell around his ears and draped on the floor, the faint smell of body odor wafted from his unwashed shirt, and carpet fibers pushed through holes in his jeans and embedded in his knees. Before him sat the tan tabby cat, relaxed on its haunches, head tilted curiously to one side.

Stevie lifted his head, straightened his back, and sat back on his heels, facing the cat. He threw his head back and stared at the ceiling, eyes wide, hands resting on his thighs.

He glanced at the cat, making sure it hadn't lost interest. It remained motionless, watching him intently, obviously intrigued. Stevie giggled. He liked having an audience.

"I'm listenin'," Stevie said in a singsong way. The voice was speaking again. *Her* voice. And he had to listen carefully, follow directions, obey. Obey. He had to obey her voice. *Momma always knows best.*

His eyes darted back and forth along the ceiling, and a smile stretched across his face. "Caleb Saunders…finish the job. Dinsmore. Dinsmore. Dinsmore. Dinsmore. Shoulda left Stevie alone. Woody Owen…poor cripple. Glen Sterner. Eddie Hopkins. Naughty boys. Time to pay up. And Bob. Bobby boy. You thought you got away with it, Bob."

He paused, listening again. "Chief Gill, the old man. L-stone. Dirty pig. Last to go."

He began to laugh, louder and louder, his voice filling the small trailer, his body shaking, twitching, shivering.

Suddenly, as if a switch in his brain had been thrown, her voice stopped, and he fell silent. He looked at the cat; its eyes glowed large in the light of the lamp, reminding Stevie of two orange marbles. He tightened his vocal cords and made his voice high-pitched and childlike. "Soon, Momma. Soon. No one'll ever hurt us again."

Stevie leaned forward and put his mouth to the cat's ear. "You ready?" he whispered.

The cat growled low, pulled back, and took a swipe at his face. Stevie flinched and yanked his head back, reflexively covering his cheek with his hand. The skin under his fingers was wet and raw. He pulled his hand away and looked at his fingers—blood, bright and red, streaked across them. Stevie smiled. Blood tickled his cheek. The cat licked its paw.

"Oh, you're ready," Stevie hissed, breaking into wild laughter. "You're ready!"

Rosa was deep in prayer again. After speaking to Dr. Wilson and getting the latest on Caleb's condition, she felt compelled to take it to the Lord. Caleb was in God's hands now. There was so much damage to his little body—the head trauma, the shoulder, the skin grafts, the infection—only God could bring a full recovery.

He's Your child, Lord—

A soft knock came at the ICU room's door.

Rosa looked up to find Chief Gill standing in the doorway. She was dressed in her beige uniform, hair gathered in a tight ponytail.

Rosa's eyes widened with surprise. She got up, walked over to where Maggie stood, and took the younger woman's hands in hers. "Chief. What a pleasant surprise. Please, come in and sit."

"Hi, Rosa." Maggie looked Caleb over, then met Rosa's eyes. Concern wrinkled her brow, darkened her eyes. "How's the little trooper doing?"

Rosa shrugged. "He's alive, and for that I am thanking God, but he has a long way to go. He is fighting an infection now, where they did the skin grafts on his arm. But Dr. Wilson said they are giving him more antibiotics to hopefully take care of that." She sighed. "And then there is the brain swelling and the shoulder surgery." Rosa sat and forced a smile. "But I am trusting God to take care of him. And I know He will."

Maggie seated herself in the other chair and patted Rosa's hand. "You're a strong woman, Rosa. I don't know how I would hold up if I were in your shoes."

"You would do the same as me," Rosa said. "God, He gives strength when we need it most."

"Are you doing OK as far as work goes? If you need me to take care of anything—"

Rosa gave a little laugh and shook her head. "No, no, no. Thank you, but Mr. Bortner at the mill, he told me to take off as long as I need. He said they will hold my job for me. And Darlene, she is such a sweetheart. She said all the girls are practically fighting over each other to cover my shifts. I have been blessed to work for such great people. How many other bosses would be so generous?"

Maggie shook her head and smiled. "Not many. I'm glad they're all being so thoughtful."

"Joe told me you stopped by early this morning," Rosa said. "Thank you. That was very kind. Did you get a chance to talk to him?"

Rosa didn't miss the sparkle that touched Maggie's eyes. "Yes, I did. He seems to be holding up OK."

"*Seems*, yes. But there is a lot going on inside that heart of his, a lot that he keeps hidden away. He has never forgiven himself for his brother's death, and I know he partially blames himself for what has now happened to Caleb. He is very hard on himself."

Maggie frowned. "I'm sorry to hear that. I never knew he held himself responsible for Rick's death. That must be an awful burden to carry around."

Rosa cocked her head to one side and smiled at Maggie. She could almost read the woman's thoughts, as if they were written on her forehead. Rick had told her about Joe and Maggie's past relationship, and Rosa could tell Joe's sudden appearance last night had left Maggie shaken. She looked deep into Maggie's dark blue eyes and found the answer before she asked her next question. "You still love him, yes?"

The question obviously caught Maggie off guard. Her cheeks reddened, she fumbled with her hands, and she struggled to clear her throat. Rosa knew Maggie had come here to talk about Caleb, not Joe, and certainly not her feelings for him, but some things needed to be brought into the light. And Rosa was never one to shy away from honest talk.

Maggie cleared her throat again and ran a finger along her eyebrow. "I don't know. I feel something, but I don't know if I'd call it love or not." She dropped her eyes and studied her folded hands for a second. "I loved him once. Very much so. But that was a long time ago, and we've both changed so much."

Rosa leaned forward and placed her hand on Maggie's. "Joe still has feelings for you. I can see it in his eyes and hear it in his voice."

Maggie frowned and glanced away. "Well, I don't know about all that. It was such a long time ago."

"It wasn't *that* long ago. You should talk to him about it. I think he would open up to you."

Maggie straightened, and suddenly her face turned cool, professional. "Maybe I will, if I get the chance. But right now, I have other things on my mind."

CHAPTER 8

AFTER HER VISIT with Rosa, Maggie headed back to town for dinner. She strolled into Darlene's Diner, paused at the *Please Wait to Be Seated* sign, and waved at Darlene, who was coming straight at her, arms open wide.

Darlene's Diner was Dark Hills's watering hole. The locals gathered there for breakfast, lunch, and dinner to catch up on the town gossip, share the latest news, and offer their opinions on everything from politics to religion to sports.

Maggie never thought the small diner was much to look at. It was housed in a fifty-year-old building that began as Mack's Family Restaurant, was then The Dark Hills Restaurant, next Marco's Pizzeria, and finally The Johns Family Café. Darlene Slagle bought the floundering business from Pete Johns two years ago, closed the doors for two months while she gave the place a good scrubbing and new paint job, and reopened it under a new name and new management. It maintained its fifties era feel, though. The booths had red-topped tables rimmed with shiny chrome; the bench seats were red vinyl, cracked in places and held together with packing tape. There was a bar running along the left wall with red vinyl-topped chrome stools. Beyond the bar was the kitchen. "Always hoppin', never stoppin'." That's what Wayne Simmons, the stocky, dark-haired short-order cook said.

But the main attraction at Darlene's was Darlene. She had grown up in Dark Hills, worked as a cook in the high school cafeteria for forty years, retired two years ago at the age of sixty, and knew everyone—and every*thing*—in town. A large robust woman with bright red hair, green eyes, and a smile that could lighten the darkest mood, Darlene made sure to greet every one of her guests. She knew everyone in town by name and most of what was going on in their lives. She loved to talk, loved to laugh, and loved to hug. Even when strangers passing through Dark Hills would stop for a quick bite, they never left without first telling Darlene their entire life story and being the recipient of one of her locally famous hugs.

The diner was her pride and joy, her dream come true. Her husband died of a heart attack five years ago, and Darlene used the life insurance money and her retirement savings to buy the beat-up old place. She was slowly remodeling and updating, but it took time and cost money, two things she just didn't have in abundance.

"Maggie!" Darlene wrapped her arms around Maggie and just about lifted her off the floor. "Good to see ya. I was hoping you'd stop by soon."

Maggie laughed and politely loosened the larger woman's grip. "Why do you say that? Is something wrong?"

"Goodness, girl, I'm thinkin' of you. You've got a tough case, what with Rosa's boy and all. You doin' OK?"

Maggie smiled. "I'm doing fine. Thanks."

"Well, you give my best to Rosa next time you see her, OK? Tell her everyone here's thinkin' of her and prayin' for her and her boy."

"I'll make sure to do that. I'm sure she'll appreciate it."

Darlene put one arm around Maggie's shoulders, pulled her close, and gave her a gentle squeeze. "Now why don't you take a seat over there, and one a' the girls will be right with ya."

Maggie crossed the room and slid into booth number 17, glad Darlene hadn't asked for details about the mauling. She wasn't ready to talk about it and didn't want to add to the rumor machine that was gaining momentum. Moments later, Joann, a middle-aged waitress, appeared, pen and pad in hand. "Evening, Chief Gill. What can I get you?"

Maggie had no need for the menu; she ordered the same thing every time she stopped by for dinner. "I'll have the lasagna dinner with broccoli, Caesar side salad, and an unsweetened iced tea." Darlene's offered the best lasagna in town, hands down.

"Sure thing," Joann said with smiling eyes. "I'll be back with the tea."

"Thanks."

Maggie took her cap off and set it on the seat beside her. The bells jingled at the front door, announcing the arrival of another patron in need of a hug. Maggie looked up and felt her heart skip a beat. It was Joe. She almost laughed when Darlene grabbed him and swallowed him in a bear hug. The expression on his face was simply priceless.

So Joe Saunders was back. At least for a while. She watched him as he no doubt shared the thirty-second version of his life story with Darlene. He hadn't changed much in fifteen years. Sure, he'd put on a few pounds—mostly muscle, though, from the looks of it—and his hair wasn't quite as brown as it once was. But besides that, he held a remarkable resemblance to the Joe Saunders she once loved. Could love again. Maybe.

Rosa's words suddenly echoed through her head. *He still has feelings for you. I can see it in his eyes, hear it in his voice.*

Still had feelings for her? What was she supposed to do with that? Especially when she didn't know how she felt about *him*.

When Joe opened the glass front door he was pleasantly surprised by the change that had taken place in the old diner. The last time he set foot in the restaurant was as a teenager. It was The Dark Hills Restaurant then and probably inspired someone to coin the term *greasy spoon*. In fact, he was certain Scooter Koontz, the short-order cook who shared a remarkable likeness with Paulie, Burt Young's character in the *Rocky* movies, used the same grease to slick his hair and oil his mustache that he used to lube the burgers. It was no wonder the joint eventually folded.

"Well, well, well. Joey Saunders!" Darlene said, running at Joe, green eyes flashing like emeralds. She wrapped her arms around him and clapped him on the back with both hands. It was like being wrapped in a burrito with a bottle of Chanel Number 5. "It's good to see ya again, sweetie." She released her hug and stepped back, keeping her hands on his shoulders. "Let me look at ya. Wow! You've grown into quite a looker." If there was one thing Darlene lacked, it was tact. She said what was on her mind and didn't care much how it came out. "Where've you been all these years?"

Joe blushed at Darlene's sudden outburst of attention. "Living up in Huntingdon County—"

"Are ya married?" Darlene glanced at his left hand. "Girlfriend? Good-lookin' guy like you shouldn't be alone."

"No, no. Not yet. I do OK with alone."

"Aw, sure ya do. And ya got a bridge to sell me too, right? So what brings you back to Dark Hills?"

"I'm here visiting my sister-in-law, Rosa—"

The smile disappeared from Darlene's face. "That's right; I plum forgot you two are family. Ain't that a shame? How's the little guy doin'?"

"He's in a coma. It's kind of touch-and-go right now. He needed some pretty complicated surgery on his shoulder and skin grafts. But the doctors seem pleased that he's at least in stable condition."

Darlene shook her head slowly. "Poor boy. Sweet kid. How's Rosa holdin' up? How's she handling everything?"

Joe smiled politely. "She's hanging in there. She's a strong woman." He paused, feeling that familiar lump rise in his throat, then turned the conversation back to Darlene. "How are you?"

"Oh, never better. Never better. Look at this," she said, looking around the small diner as if it were Buckingham Palace. "I finally got my own place."

"It's beautiful, Darlene. Good for you. I'm so happy for you."

"Business is great too." She patted Joe's arm. "Hey, why don't you grab a booth, and I'll have Joann hook you up with some good grub—on the house. Our specialty is the broiled chicken. Absolutely delicious."

"Great. I'm hungry as a bear."

Joe turned to find a booth, but Darlene caught his arm and stopped him. "Joe"—she leaned in close, and Joe could smell the peppermint on her breath—"have you seen Maggie yet?"

"Yeah. She visited Caleb in the hospital. We talked a little."

Darlene tightened her grip on Joe's arm and motioned to where Maggie sat. "Why don't you two have some dinner together?"

Joe looked in the direction of Darlene's nod and saw Maggie sitting in a booth, smiling. She gave a little wave. He waved back. "That sounds like a good idea. Thanks, Darlene."

"And Joe"—she smiled and winked—"Maggie ain't married either; what a coincidence, huh?"

Laughing, Joe said, "Thanks for the heads-up. If I meet anyone interested I'll be sure to let him know."

He walked up to Maggie's booth and stopped beside it. "Hey. Mind if I join you?"

"Not at all," Maggie said. "Have a seat."

Joe sat down and the waitress appeared. He ordered the broiled chicken, then sat back and grinned at Maggie. "So are you on break?"

Maggie gave a quick laugh. "I'm never on break. A cop is *always* on duty, even when she's off duty."

Joe thought how appealing Maggie still was and how much she still resembled Ms. Hepburn. She didn't cake the makeup on like some women. She didn't need to. She had a natural beauty about her—large eyes, thin, straight nose, full lips, small chin. She was older now, that was evident, but she was the same Maggie Gill he knew way back when. Or was she? People can change a lot in fifteen years.

Harold Lippy cruised down Route 20, pressing his old pickup's accelerator closer to the floor. It was evening, the sun had just waved its farewell and dipped below the horizon, and the long, straight stretch of asphalt was abandoned. What did it matter if he was pushing sixty in a forty-five? He wasn't thinking about that anyway. His mind was on the conversation he had just had with Dick Moyer at the Legion. Harold smiled in the dark cab of his truck. A lion. What a crock. Did he really think he'd get an audience with that story? That kid getting attacked over the weekend had everyone a little on edge, jumping to conclusions, speculating, spreading rumors.

Still, something about Dick's retelling of the lion incident didn't sit right with him. He had fought side by side with Dick in World War II. They landed in France together on D-Day, dodged mortars, watched their peers die violent deaths, shook with fear, and cried for their mothers. They were only eighteen, and they went through hell together. For the past thirty years, they met at the American Legion every other Tuesday afternoon and swapped war stories with the other vets in town. Talking about the horrors they experienced and shared was therapy for all of them.

Harold was always impressed with Dick's memory and ability to recall events, battles, and people in such vivid detail. He made it all come alive again—the sounds of bullets whizzing by, the vibration of the earth when a mortar landed dangerously close, the screams in the night from the wounded, the smell of blood in the foxholes, even the twang of Sergeant Spivey's Tennessee draw. It was all there again, in vivid color, like a digitally remixed version of an early, black-and-white film. When Dick reminisced, the memories flooded back, so real, so intense, sometimes Harold would go home and cry. He didn't mind, though; it was good for him to recall those times, it gave his life some purpose, some meaning. He was a hero; that's what the kids down at the elementary school called him when he visited to talk about the war. He never got into too much detail, though. Their little minds didn't need to know about the blood and gore and death and fear, only about the heroics of the American fighting men.

But what was he to make of this lion story? Harold knew Dick was no liar; he had gone through everything Dick talked about, and the man didn't embellish a thing, told it just as it happened. But a lion? In Dark Hills? Impossible. Maybe Dick had taken one too many sips of his beer. He wasn't a drinking man and never could hold his liquor.

Suddenly, something stopped Harold mid-thought. He slammed the brake pedal to the floor and the pickup fish-tailed to a stop, tires screeching in the still night. Two glowing eyes peered at him through the darkness, straight ahead, in the middle of the road.

Harold closed his eyes tightly. No way. He had to be seeing things. He opened them and looked again. The eyes were still there, hovering just above the asphalt horizon.

Without thinking, Harold reached for the .22 in the rear of the cab, opened the glove box, and removed an ammo clip. He shoved the clip in the rifle and flipped the bolt up, back, and, forward, chambering the first round.

Opening the cab door slowly so it didn't squeak, he stepped out, staying behind the open door—just in case. The eyes were getting closer, growing larger, looming, floating.

It had to be Dick's lion.

Harold rolled the door's window down and propped the barrel of the rifle on the frame, holding the stock against his shoulder. *Not tonight, buddy boy. You picked the wrong soldier to hunt.*

Sighting down the short barrel, he aimed for the gaping space between the eyes. It would take more than one shot to bring the beast down. He steadied his hand by exhaling slowly and squeezed the trigger. The sound of the gun startled him, and his hand slipped off the trigger. He slammed the bolt up, back, forward, aimed, and fired again. The eyes swerved to the right, almost jumping the ditch alongside the road and heading into the cornfield. But they steadied again and headed right for him. His heart pounded, tightening his chest, shortening his breath. A throbbing ache had overtaken his left arm, and his vision blurred.

He rubbed at his eyes, reloaded, and fired again. This time he heard it—*Ping!* The sound of a bullet ricocheting off metal.

Suddenly, the eyes stopped, no more than fifty yards away, and a voice hollered, "Hey! Hey, man! What are you doing? Are you nuts?"

Harold dropped his rifle and clutched his chest, then collapsed to the asphalt. The rifle rattled to the ground beside him. He couldn't catch his breath. An unbearable weight had landed on his chest, paralyzing him, suffocating, pressing the life out of his lungs.

The last thing he saw before he blacked out was a man run up to him, curse loudly, then bend over, yelling something into a cell phone.

Maggie could hardly believe that after a decade and a half of not hearing a peep from the man she was once sure she'd marry, he was now sitting across the table from her and they were having dinner together. It was like something out of some cheesy romance movie. Girl and boy fall in love, grow up, go their own ways, lose contact, only to reconnect over a decade later, changed people, and fall in love all over again. Well, she didn't know about the falling in love all over again part. But maybe...

Maggie leaned her elbows on the table and smiled at Joe. "Where are you staying?"

"At the Dew-Drop Motel down the road. It's OK. Clean."

Maggie picked up a sugar packet and fingered it thoughtfully. "What have you been up to these past fifteen years?" She knew she might be rushing it, prying into his personal life a little too quickly, but she wasn't one to beat around the bush. He knew that.

Joe smiled and shook his head. "That's the Maggie Gill I once knew. Right to the point. Actually, I was wondering when you would ask. After the army, I was going to come back and try to pick up where we left off, but... it just didn't feel right. I don't know. I got into some bad things in the military and was really screwed up when I came out. For a while I worked for a trucking company making deliveries up and down the East Coast."

He hesitated, and Maggie could see by the pain in his eyes that he was once again fighting off the feelings of guilt. He swallowed and continued. "After Rick died, I took some time off, just wanted to be alone, you know, then started my own landscaping business. I've been doing that now for a little over nine years. Mags, I'm sorry I never came back for you, never even contacted you. Like I said, I was really messed up there for a while.

One day I woke up in a jail cell and realized I needed to change some things—even started going to church and praying and stuff. I had to start over completely. It was slow going because I had a lot to change, and change doesn't come easy for me, but I was getting there. Then Rick's...accident happened, and I sorta lost it. It was like climbing a difficult rock face and just as you're making some progress, getting a hang of it, you lose your grip and fall backward. I lost interest in everything, God, church, everything. Lost all the ground I had gained." He shrugged his shoulders. "But that's *my* battle. I'm sorry I hurt you."

Maggie smiled, and a gentle warmness spread throughout her body. Joe Saunders had sure grown up. She remembered the first time they met. It was in the first grade at Dark Hills Elementary. The school year wasn't even four days old when Joe lifted Maggie's skirt on the playground. Miss Munchin witnessed the crime and was on the scene in seconds. Grabbing hold of Joe's ear with a deadly pincher grip, she dragged him all the way to Principal Spotts's office. Spotts gave Joe a good clobbering on the behind and sent him home, where his mom gave him another clobbering. The next day Joe, walking a bit more gingerly than usual, found Maggie first thing and apologized. Don't ask why, but after that they were best friends and remained so all the way through high school.

Maggie smiled at the memory. The look on Joe's face when Munchin took hold of his ear was worth millions.

"I suppose all of us have battles to fight," she said. "It's not easy being chief of police and a woman."

"Seems like everyone likes you."

She laughed. "I don't know about that. They put on a smile and say 'Hi, Chief,' but I know there's plenty of them in this town who think I belong in a kitchen with a kid strapped to my waist. And I'm sure most of them think I'm too young to handle this job. Heck, sometimes *I* think I'm too young."

"Well, from what I've seen so far, you're doing a great job. Hey, how did it go at the Yates place this morning? Did you find anything?"

Maggie was glad for the change of subject. She wasn't ready to talk about domestic life with Joe. There was once a time when all she wanted was to be in a kitchen with a kid strapped to her. *Their* kitchen; *their* kid. "Just some clumps of fur. Looked like cat, but I wasn't sure. I sent it away for the lab to take a look." She paused, not sure if she wanted to tell

Joe about the eerie shadow. But what the heck, maybe he saw something similar. "There was something else, though."

Joe cocked his head. "What do you mean?"

"I—I don't know exactly. I got the feeling something was down there with me, watching me. And…I saw something in the corner. But when I shined the light on it, nothing was there but some old boards. It was probably just my overactive imagination playing tricks on me, but it really creeped me out." She sighed and rolled her eyes. "I was probably just seeing things. It's pretty creepy down there. I guess all the ghost stories about that place just got to me."

"Well, something *is* out there, something real. That was no ghost that attacked Caleb, and we need to find it before it attacks again."

Maggie frowned. "You think it will attack again?"

"It's only a matter of time. If not here, it will be somewhere else. It has the taste of human blood now, and who knows where it will turn up next."

Woody Owen backed his wheelchair away from the refrigerator, a can of Michelob and bowl of sour cream and onion dip on his lap. He wheeled over to the pantry, opened the door, and reached for the potato chips. Another quiet evening at home. Just him and the TV. Stephen King's *The Shining* was on tonight, and Woody was looking forward to settling into his recliner, snacks in hand, and enjoying the show. He spun his wheelchair around—it took him months of practice to be able to maneuver the chair in his tiny house—backed up a few feet, turned to the right, and headed into the living room, dodging stacks of newspapers and porn magazines.

Parking his chair at an angle to the recliner, he set his goodies on a TV tray to his left. He then lifted himself off the seat, spun his weight to the right, and landed softly in the oversized TV-throne.

He was ready; let the show begin.

The opening scene came on, and the TV flickered brightly in the darkened room. Woody reached for his beer, popped the lid, and took a long swig, wincing as the carbonation burned his throat. He then grabbed the bag of chips and tore them open. He'd seen *The Shining* a hundred times before, saw all of Stephen King's movies, but this was his favorite. This was going to be a great evening. Good snacks, good movie, nobody to bother him.

Right before the first commercial break, Woody's rottweiler, Cujo, began barking wildly outside. He was used to Cujo's ranting; the dog didn't know when to shut up. He'd bark at a squirrel in the yard. But this was different. The barking was continuous, intermingled with low guttural growls.

"Hey, Cujo," Woody hollered, not taking his eyes off the TV. "Shat up, will ya!"

But Cujo continued his ranting, a frenzy of barks and growls.

Probably some dumb kids messing around.

"Hey, boy, it's OK," he yelled again. "Settle down."

Still no break in Cujo's tantrum. The movie broke for a commercial. Cujo's barking increased.

"I'm gonna kill that dog," Woody muttered, lifting himself out of the recliner and lowering himself into his wheelchair.

Cujo growled, barked, let out a pitiful yelp. Then there was silence.

"What now?"

Woody wheeled over to the back door, winding his way back through the cluttered kitchen. He opened the door, leaned forward in his chair, and pushed the metal storm door open. "Cujo? Hey, boy, you all right?"

No answer.

Woody flipped the switch for the back floodlight and looked in the direction of Cujo's doghouse. "Oh, my—Cujo!"

CHAPTER 9

JOE EXTENDED HIS legs and stretched his arms overhead, yawning like a bear. The Dew-Drop Motel was certainly no Hilton; it wasn't even a Howard Johnson during a Buck Rogers convention. The room was small, furnished in seventies-style décor, had one queen-size bed, a small TV—with limited cable—and a small bathroom. The green shag carpet was mashed and worn in some areas, and the ceiling was stained with water marks. But the bed was comfortable. He'd slept well enough last night.

He reached for the TV remote and clicked on the morning news. Sitting on the edge of the bed, he rubbed the sleep out of his eyes and ran his fingers through his hair.

His cell phone rang.

He hit the mute button on the remote and flipped open the phone. It was Maggie. "Hey."

"Good morning. I wasn't sure if I'd get you or not. How'd you sleep last night?"

"Can't complain."

"Would you mind meeting me at Doc Adams's veterinary clinic? I want to show you something."

"Uh, yeah sure. What's up?"

"I'd rather you just see it for yourself. You remember where the clinic is?"

"Yeah. I'll be right over."

⚫

"Morning, Doc," Maggie hollered as she stepped into the small veterinary clinic.

Doctor Wells Adams emerged from a back room and shuffled down the hallway leading to the reception area. He tilted his head forward and peered at Maggie through the upper half of his bifocals. "Morning, Maggie. Is your friend coming?"

"Yes. He should be here shortly."

"Well, come on back when he gets here." He turned, walked back down the hallway, and disappeared into the last examination room on the right.

Doc Adams, part-time mayor and full-time veterinarian, treated everything from parakeets to horses, even performed a procedure on a python once. Seemed the snake had somehow swallowed a baseball and got itself one glory of an impacted bowel.

His practice was run out of his home—a large farmhouse just outside of town. The farm was sold in the eighties and subdivided for some new housing development that didn't look so new anymore. But Doc Adams had kept the house and about ten acres of land, enough on which to build a large kennel with plenty of roaming room for the animals.

When Joe entered the clinic, Maggie was seated in a chair waiting for him. She was dressed in her beige uniform, hair pulled back in a ponytail. She looked up and smiled. Dark circles cast ominous shadows under her eyes. "Hey, Joe."

"Hi, Mags. You look like you didn't sleep a wink last night."

"I got a couple hours in." She stood and smoothed the front of her shirt. "Come on in the back. Doc's waiting for us."

"So what's going on? Is this official business?"

"Just come with me. I want you to take a look at something and tell me what you think."

She led him down a narrow hallway lined with photos of Doc Adams and various dogs and cats—there was even one of him with a python—to a room in the rear of the house.

"Morning, Joe," Doc Adams said, shaking Joe's hand. His voice was thin and raspy, his grip weak. Doc was ancient with a pronounced hump on his back and thinning snow-white hair. His skin was thin, translucent as wax paper, and his eyes were a dull gray. He wore black pants, a white shirt with no tie, and a gray cardigan. He'd not aged very gracefully. So this is what became of Igor, Joe thought.

The room was small and painted white. The walls were decorated with framed certificates and more photos of Doc with his patients. In the middle of the room sat a stainless steel rolling table with a thick-bodied rottweiler lying on it. The dog's left shoulder had several deep gashes, and the back of its neck was badly mangled.

"Is this what attacked Caleb?" Joe asked.

Maggie crossed her arms and shook her head.

"Come here and take a look at this, Joe," Doc Adams said, pointing at the dog's neck. "Cujo here was brought in last night by Woody Owen and Maggie. Woody said the dog was attacked in his backyard."

Joe stood beside the large dog and bent over for a better look. It looked like bite marks on the back of the dog's neck.

"Tell him, Doc," Maggie said, nodding at Doc Adams.

Doc motioned toward the dog's neck. "You see those bite marks there?"

Joe looked again. "Yes. I'm taking it this wasn't the work of a maniacal Chihuahua."

"Not even close. See those claw marks on the front quarter?"

Joe looked at the deep gashes; the flesh was peeled back, curled at the edges like torn wallpaper, exposing the dog's thick shoulder muscles. So they were claw marks. "Yes."

"They're from something big," Doc said matter-of-factly, shoving his hands in his pockets and peering through the upper half of his glasses at Joe.

"Bigger than a Chihuahua."

"Much."

"Bigger than Killer here?"

"Cujo. And yes, much. The bite to the back of the neck here severed the spinal cord." He pointed to the deep puncture wounds on the nape of the dog's neck. "Whatever did this has powerful jaws. It cut clean through the vertebrae. And the claw marks"—he ran his finger along the gashes on the dog's front shoulder—"they measure ten inches in diameter." He looked at Joe, then at Maggie. "Now, Cujo's a big dog, but whatever attacked him was much bigger. And much more powerful. Its blow was quick and deadly. Cujo here probably didn't even have a chance to fight back."

"So what are we looking at?" Joe asked. "A bear?"

Doc rubbed his chin and shook his head. "No. This isn't typical of a bear attack. Bears usually take their time and gnaw a lot. This was quick and decisive. But I honestly don't know what else around these parts would be big enough to do this kind of damage."

Maggie cleared her throat. "Do—do you think it could be a lion?" She looked at Doc Adams, then at Joe, a tinge of red shading her cheeks.

Doc laughed. "I suppose so. But…this is Dark Hills, and I don't have to tell you the likelihood of a cougar roaming these parts is pretty slim."

"I mean a—an African lion. You know, king of the jungle."

Doc stopped smiling. "You're serious."

"What are you getting at, Mags?" Joe asked. He could tell by the dip of Maggie's mouth that she was serious—serious as a Russian playing roulette. "Why a lion of all things?"

Maggie shifted her weight uncomfortably and ran a finger over her eyebrow. "Yesterday, Mary Chronister called us swearing she saw a lion in her backyard. The Moyers next door to her said they saw it too. Andy responded to the call and said they were pretty worked up about it. There was no sign of anything. Ground's too hard and dry for tracks…but just the same, it makes you wonder."

Joe crossed his arms. "Doc? What do you think? Could this be a lion attack?"

Doc looked at the mauled body of Cujo again. He couldn't have looked more perplexed if Joe had asked him if he believed tiny green men from Jupiter were inhabiting the dog's colon. "Well, if I didn't know better, and if we were sitting in the middle of Africa, I'd say that's exactly what it was. Lions are actually pretty lazy animals. They don't want a fight, so they usually go for the spinal cord, paralyze the victim, then kill it. Quick and decisive. No fight." He looked from Maggie to Joe then back at Maggie. "But since I *do* know better and, last time I checked, there were no savannas—are we serious here? You're suggesting there's really a lion out there?"

Maggie held up both hands in mock surrender. "I'm not suggesting anything. If word got out that the police chief said there was a lion on the loose, there would be an all-out panic. Or they'd run me outta town. Either way, I don't want to be responsible for inciting trouble."

Doc removed his glasses and rubbed his eyes with his thumb and index finger. He shook his head and silently moved his lips as if arguing himself into playing along. "So what do you want to do?"

"I'm not sure," Maggie said. "But I'll start with calling around to the local zoos—Philly, Baltimore, Washington—and see if any of them have lost a lion or any big cats. I'll contact any circuses that have been in the area too." She nodded to Doc. "Thanks, Doc. I guess that'll be it."

Outside the clinic, standing by Maggie's cruiser, Joe had an idea. "Are there any big game hunters around here?"

"Only one I know of is Bob Cummings. He goes to Canada to hunt grizzlies every year and has been to Africa a few times. Why? You want to go after this thing?"

"Do you have a better idea? Those claw marks, they looked like the same ones that were on Caleb's arm when I found him. I'm betting whatever did that to Killer—"

"Cujo."

"—is the same animal that mauled Caleb. And if that's the case, then I know *where* it hunts. With a little bait, I'm sure I can lure it in. And when it shows, I'll be waiting. But first, I'd like to pay this Cummings a visit."

———

Stevie Bauer popped a can of cat food, squatted, and emptied the contents into a small bowl in the middle of the kitchen floor. "Here ya go, little buddy. You done real good. You earned it."

The tan tabby cat cautiously approached the bowl, sniffed, and crouched next to it, carefully biting off chunks of food.

Stevie held his hand over the cat's back for a few seconds, then gently placed his palm on its head and stroked down to the tail. Its fur was so soft. The cat began to purr.

"That's a good kitty," Stevie said, stroking the cat lightly. "You just be patient. Ole Woody ain't goin' nowhere. Momma always says good things come to them that wait."

The cat continued eating and purring, oblivious to the knife Stevie held in his other hand.

Stevie stopped stroking the cat and pushed up the sleeve of his right arm, exposing the tender, white skin of his forearm. With his left hand, he placed the tip of the knife on the skin and pressed. The tip dug in, and Stevie dragged it along the skin making an inch-long laceration. The sharp blade felt like it had been sitting in red-hot coals. Stevie grimaced under the burning pain. Bright red blood oozed out of the gash and ran down his forearm in one long scarlet ribbon. He held his arm over the cat's bowl and let the blood drip onto the food.

The tabby paused, startled at first by the intrusion of its bowl, then began devouring the food like a ravenous beast.

"Good, ain't it," Stevie said, smiling. "Soon you'll have all you want."

———

Bob Cummings lived in a large cathedral log house situated on twenty acres of meadow and woods just outside the town of Dark Hills. He'd been the town's only lawyer for years—handling everything from wills to mortgages to petty criminal cases—before calling it quits to take up a life of hunting and travel and seclude himself away in his wooden mansion. He was an impressive man—six three, barrel-chested, long gray hair pulled back into a tight ponytail, thick, mutton chop sideburns down to his jaw, a mustache that covered his entire upper lip, and steady, dark brown eyes. His voice was deep and gruff and his handshake like iron.

But Joe was more impressed by Cummings's choice of décor. The cathedral ceiling great room was stuffed full of mounts and souvenirs from his many hunting expeditions. The wall to the right, at least fifteen feet high, was decorated with several deer mounts, an elk, a bison, a mountain goat, and a caribou. And hanging above the massive stone fireplace was a huge moose head, keeping watch over the entire room. The opposite wall was adorned by a gazelle, a wildebeest, an antelope, an impala, and a kudu—trophies of Cummings's African adventures. In one corner of the room stood a nine-foot polar bear, arms outstretched, paws ready to take a swipe at anyone brave enough to wander within its reach. In another corner was a grinning cougar, crouched as if ready to pounce. But regardless of how impressive Cummings's purse was, the room held an eerie quality, as if it were a celebration of death, captured and frozen in the glass eyes of each victim. It was a shrine to make even Dr. Moreau mad with jealousy.

"This is my pride and joy," Cummings said, walking over to a fairly large leopard, sunning on a tree branch. He stroked its head as if it were alive. "Shot this pretty lady in Zambia. Hunted her for seven hours before she finally decided to take a nap." He laughed. "She never woke up."

Cummings walked across the room to a hyena, lips snarled, fur bristled. "I didn't want to shoot this guy," he said, patting the hyena's hind quarters. "But he charged me. I didn't have a choice. Got him in Zimbabwe."

Joe could envision Cummings, holed up in his big house all by himself, carrying on entire conversations with his dead companions, bidding them good night and good morning, and leaving the lights on at night lest they give in to their nocturnal instincts and start hunting each other while he slept. To rid his mind of the image, Joe eyed the mahogany gun case on the far wall of the room.

"You like what you see?" Cummings asked, not even trying to hide his glowing pride.

Inside the case were enough firearms to make any hunter envious. There were several .22s, a shotgun, a walnut-stock .30–06, and a .375 Remington 700 XCR. Joe recognized the .375 because he had just read about it in a hunting magazine. It boasted the latest technology in recoil padding and a hefty price tag that was well out of the reach of his bank book.

Cummings turned the key and opened the glass door. He reached in and removed the .30–06, handling it like it was a newborn. "This is what I used on that leopard and Snowball over there," he said, motioning toward the towering polar bear. So he even gave them pet names. He replaced the .30–06 and pulled out the .375, held it up to his shoulder, pointed it at the polar bear, and looked down the long barrel. "And this fella," he said, "well, I've been itching to use him. Next year I'm going to go to Zambia again and get me a giraffe. Maybe even an elephant." He looked around the cavernous room. "You think I could fit an elephant in here?"

Maggie, who had gone to Cummings with Joe to make the introductions, looked at Joe and raised her eyebrows.

"Well, anyway," Cummings said, placing the rifle back in the gun case and closing the door carefully, turning the lock, "what can I do for the two of you?"

"Do you mind if we sit?" Joe said.

"Of course. Have a seat and we'll talk. Would either of you like a drink?"

"I'm fine."

"No thanks."

Joe and Maggie sat on a comfortable taupe sofa, and Cummings eased his large frame into a black leather wingback facing them. The leather stretched and moaned under his weight. "Now," he said, leaning forward and resting his elbows on his knees, "let's hear it."

Maggie started, "Do you know Woody Owen?"

Cummings thought for a moment, then nodded. "I know Woody. A drunk and a pervert. What'd he go and get himself into trouble again? Drinking his sorrows away?"

"No. He's not in any kind of trouble with me, anyway," Maggie said. "Last night his rottweiler, Cujo, was attacked and killed. And I'm sure you know about Caleb Saunders being mauled—"

"How's he doing? Last I heard he was in a coma," Cummings said, looking from Maggie to Joe.

"He's still in a coma," Joe said. "He was pretty bad off when I found him. He's got a long road ahead of him."

Cummings wrinkled his brow and tightened his lips. "*Hmmm*, that's too bad. He's a good kid."

Maggie scooted to the edge of the sofa. "Bob, we think the same animal is responsible for both attacks. Doc Adams looked Cujo over and said that by the size of the bite mark and claw marks it's a big animal. Much bigger than the dog."

"And?" Cummings asked, eyebrows arched. Joe could tell his interest was aroused by the way he leaned into his question.

"And what?"

"Well, I'm bettin' Doc didn't just leave it at that. He's an opinionated man. What kind of big animal? The biggest predator around here is an occasional black bear."

Maggie looked at Joe, then took a deep breath. "Doc says there's a good chance it's a big cat."

"You mean a bobcat, 'cause that's the biggest cat in these parts, besides some old lady's fat housecat."

Joe wrung his hands and forced a smile. This was going to go over real well. He might as well be telling him his ninety-year-old osteoporotic grandmother went nose-to-nose with the dog. "No. Actually, more like a lion."

"A mountain lion? Around here? Naw, I doubt it."

Joe cleared his throat. "Well, uh, actually, we're thinking more African lion."

Cummings smiled and almost laughed. He sat back and looked between Maggie and Joe as if expecting a punch line at any moment. Interest lost. "Is this a joke? You know this is Pennsylvania, right? We don't usually have lions roaming our woods. Maybe it was a bobcat; they can get pretty big and ornery. They usually don't show their faces, and I doubt one would be brave enough to—"

"Bobcats don't get this big," Joe said, hoping he didn't insult the larger man. "Doc said this beast has to be big. It bit clean through the dog's spine, and the claw markings were ten inches in diameter."

Cummings's eyes widened and his Adam's apple rose and fell behind the loose skin of his neck. They had the old hunter's attention again. "Well, now. That's different...and interesting. Definitely rules out bobcat. Rules out mountain lion too."

Joe leaned forward. Cummings had taken the bait; now it was time to reel him in. "Bob, I don't know if there's a lion out there or not, but whatever it is, we need to get it before it attacks again. I'm going to hunt it, and I need your help."

Cummings looked at Joe and grinned like the stuffed cougar in the corner. "Count me in. When do we go?"

"Tomorrow morning OK?"

Cummings grimaced. "Hunt a lion during daylight? Good luck. Most likely, if it is a lion, it'll be sleeping somewhere cool during the day. Lions are nocturnal; they do most of their hunting at night. We'd have a much better time of baiting it after sunset."

"How 'bout tonight then?" Joe said.

"Perfect."

CHAPTER 10

USK HAD COME early, and the gray, clouded sky was quickly darkening. Joe leaned against his truck, waiting for Bob Cummings. They had agreed to meet at Harrison's Garage at five o'clock and hike into the woods together. But five had come and gone, and daylight was fading fast.

Joe had been a hunter since he was old enough to carry a gun, but he'd never been both the predator and the prey at the same time. The butterflies were already flitting about in his stomach. He thought about praying. He knew God was there. He'd known Him once, trusted Him, relied on Him, found comfort and safety in Him, and talked to Him. But that was years ago, an eternity, it seemed. The way he figured it, he didn't turn his back on God; God turned His back on him when He let Rick die and left Rosa and Caleb to fend for themselves.

Two headlights appeared, turning the corner onto McCormick. A large, royal blue Dodge Ram with oversized tires eased into the lot and stopped next to Joe's truck. The headlights winked out, and Bob Cummings opened the door and stepped onto the crumbling asphalt. The burly man straightened up, threw his shoulders back, and looked around as if awaiting applause. He was dressed in dark camo from head to toe. A bandana was tied tightly around his head; a wad of tobacco was nestled nicely in his lower lip. On one side of his thick leather belt dangled a survival knife with a ten-inch blade; on the other side hung a holster carrying what looked like a large revolver. Dirty Harry's .44 Magnum? From camoed head to booted toe, Cummings's whole ensemble and weapons load probably cost more than the GDP of Uzbekistan. If he was waging war against an irate horde of demented opossums, he may have been intimidating. But Joe doubted a lion would be all that impressed with his weapons cache, his attire, or his attitude.

"Evening, Joe," Cummings said, spitting a mouthful of thick brown juice at the ground. "Sorry I'm late. Wanted to make sure I had everything we might need." He reached into the backseat of his truck and produced three rifles: a .30–06, a break-action shotgun, and the sleek .375 XCR he was no doubt itching to use. The .30–06 and .375 both sported large scopes.

Tossing the .30–06 to Joe, he said, "Ever shoot one of these?"

Joe caught the gun and grinned. It was a Remington 750 Woodsmaster. "Sure have. I have one just like it back home, minus the scope." He studied the scope. "What is this, night vision?"

"Sure is. Gen 3. Ever use one?"

"Never even seen one. At least not up close."

Bob fingered some dials on the side of the scope. "This is your on/ off. And this is your focus. That's all you'll need to know in there. Just make sure you're looking through this before you shoot at anything." He gave Joe a wink. "Our target has four legs. Count 'em before you pull the trigger. I don't want any friendly fire coming my way."

Joe slung the rifle over his shoulder and shook Cummings's oversized hand. "Gotcha. I figure we'd do best to head down to the old Yates place. That's where Caleb was mauled, and Maggie—Chief Gill—swore she saw something there too."

"Sounds good. Let's do it. You got the meat?"

Joe held up a plastic bag with five pounds of bloody steak in it. Dark red blood pooled in the bottom half of the bag. If someone driving by happened to turn his head at just the right moment, Joe would no doubt have been mistaken for a bloodthirsty, wannabe vampire, looking for a cheap thrill with GI Joe's grandfather. "I asked the butcher to add extra blood. He looked at me like I was nuts."

Cummings laughed. "Maybe we are nuts." He then placed a heavy hand on Joe's shoulder and narrowed his eyes. "You nervous?"

Joe nodded. "I'd be lying if I said I wasn't."

Cummings clapped his shoulder. "Good. Overconfidence is a hunter's worst enemy. If that thing's in these woods, it's going to know we're here, and it'll be hunting us just the same as we're hunting it. Jitters will keep you awake and alert. And that will keep you alive."

A little over two miles away, in his beat-up, rusted trailer, Stevie Bauer was stretched out on his sofa, playing a handheld electronic Jeopardy game.

He always lost to the computer, but someday he would beat it. Someday he would shut up that little arrogant voice that jeered "INCORRECT" every time he thought he knew the right answer.

He scrolled through the categories and was surprised to see DINNER TIME flash on the little screen. Never saw that category before, he thought, and pushed the button for $200.

FEEDING TIME FOR KITTY scrolled across the screen.

What the—? Stevie sat up and looked around the room. His palms were suddenly damp with sweat.

WHAT IS:

A-THE YATES PLACE

B-THE YATES PLACE!

C-THE YATES PLACE!!

He knew this one! His pulse jumped into overdrive. There was no way he'd get this wrong. With trembling hands he punched the button for "C."

Pause.

"CORRECT!" The electronic voice was loud and forceful.

Stevie leaped into the air. The tabby cat, which had been curled up in a ball next to the sofa, jumped to its feet, arched its back, bristled its fur, and let out a low growl.

"Kitty!" Stevie shouted. He thrust both hands in the air and arched his back. "It's feedin' time!"

When Joe and Cummings finally arrived at the old Yates place, any daylight that was left had almost completely surrendered to the oppressive darkness that surrounded the house. The stone walls jutted out of the ground like ancient ruins, casting a dark shadow on whatever chose to find solace within them. The trees circling the clearing towered overhead, their twisted arms black silhouettes against the charcoal sky. There was no visible moon—it would be a black night.

After securing the meat five feet off the ground along the front wall of the house, Joe settled into a spot near a giant walnut to the left of the house, a forty-five degree angle from the doorway. Cummings headed for a fallen oak on the opposite side of the clearing. Both would have a clear view of the bait. And a clear shot when the beast showed itself.

Setting his flashlight and backpack on the ground, Joe crouched on his haunches, lifted the rifle, and peered through the scope. The still forest glowed an eerie green, like a Martian landscape. From where he sat he could see Cummings clearly, sitting on the oak, watching the house, rifle resting on his lap. Armed to the mutton chops and exuding arrogance, he reminded Joe of Jesse Ventura's character, Blaine, in *Predator*, just before the hunt ended very badly for Ventura and his fellow commandos. Joe hoped this hunt would have a happier ending, and he really hoped what they were hunting didn't turn out to be a self-cloaking alien bent on bloodshed and mayhem.

Regardless, if whatever was in these woods, whatever was in that old house came this way, somebody was going home with a new trophy.

It was getting chilly, and Joe was glad he'd decided to wear his long underwear. He opened his backpack and removed the handheld radio Maggie had given him. "Stay in touch," she had said. "I'm just a call away." Rosa had given Maggie the key to her house, and Maggie was going to stay there all night in case she was needed. Officer Wilt, who was patrolling the graveyard shift, would also be available.

Joe leaned his back against the rough bark of the old walnut and closed his eyes, listening, getting acclimated to his surroundings. Below him, not fifty yards away, Hunter's Creek bubbled. Further downstream, the creek opened into a small pool, almost seven feet deep. He and Rick used to swim in it. They'd tie a rope to a sturdy branch overhanging the pool and spend hours on summer afternoons outdoing each other's best flips and cannonballs. Rick would dangle from the rope and let out a Johnny Weissmuller jungle cry. To his surprise and great chagrin, no animals would charge to the scene offering their aid, no leopards, no tigers, no hippos, not even the ever-curious and oft-underestimated chipmunk.

To Joe's left a squirrel chattered, settling in for the night. Behind him some leaves rustled. No crunching, so Joe determined it must be something small—a chipmunk or mouse looking for an evening snack. Overhead, a light breeze moved through the tree tops. Branches creaked like arthritic joints.

The hospital was quiet, and the ICU was even quieter. Caleb slept peacefully, his chest rising and falling without the aid of the respirator. Rosa stroked his hair, remembering how, only days ago, she entered his bedroom at night and just watched him sleep. It was something she did often. Sometimes she would even pick him up and hold him in her lap, admiring his soft features and how much he was looking more and more like Rick. He was only one when Rick died. Poor boy, he never even had a chance to know his daddy, to play catch with him, hunt with him, ride bikes with him. But Rosa made sure to tell him at least one thing about Rick every day. It had become a ritual both of them looked forward to. She never wanted to let the memory of his father fade.

She knelt by Caleb's bed and started praying, something she did at least three times a day.

She prayed for her son, that God would heal his broken body and mend his wounds, that even in his comatose state, God would send angels to minister to him, comfort him, and protect him.

And she also prayed for Joe. *Father, Joe needs You.* Her heart was heavy for her brother-in-law and friend. *He knows You, I know he does. But he has lost his way. Bring him back to You; remind him of Your love for him.* She paused, letting that request linger in her mind. *And Lord, protect him now. Wrap him in Your arms; shield him from the fiery darts of the evil one. Set a hedge around him and preserve him. Show him Your might!*

———

At the edge of Yates Woods, just inside the tree line, Stevie huddled close to the ground, perched on all fours with his chest almost touching the leaves. He unzipped his thick wool coat and allowed the tabby to escape and land softly on the leaf-covered ground.

The cat looked at Stevie questioningly and tilted its head to one side.

Stevie giggled with excitement. "Well, go on," he whispered, shooing the cat with his hands. "Go get your dinner. I didn't bring you out here for nothin'."

The cat turned and bounded into the darkened woods, the sound of its soft footsteps fading quickly.

———

The temperature had dropped into the low forties, and Bob Cummings was feeling it. A quick shiver rippled through his heavy muscles. He looked at his watch and pushed the button for the light—twenty after one. His view through the scope showed Joe sitting against a tree, rifle balanced in his hands, eyes open. Good, at least he hadn't fallen asleep. His hunting instinct told him they were not alone in the woods, and he didn't want to make any sound. His shotgun was loaded and ready, leaning against the fallen oak. He'd use it only if he had to, preferring the .375 instead. If there was a big cat out there, and if he had the opportunity to bag it, he wanted to be able to mount it and show it off. Besides that, in these thick woods, and with it being so dark, he figured he'd only get one shot. With his .375, that's all he would need.

Slowly and silently, Bob unfolded his large frame and stood. His knees were stiff and sore, but that would soon pass. He had to focus, listen, smell, keep his eyes alert and his trigger finger ready. *It* was close; he could sense it. It probably knew he was there and had much better vision at night than he, so it would have the advantage. He clutched his rifle and scanned the luminous green woods through the scope, watching for any movement, any misplaced shapes.

This was a hunt. This is what he lived for. Advantage or not, he had to be ready. Tonight it was kill or be killed.

Joe's eyelids were growing heavier by the minute. He was fading in and out of a light sleep. Breathing in, he filled his lungs with the cold, moist air and shook his head. He looked at his watch—one-fifty. Leaning his head against the tree, he let his eyes slowly shut again. For some reason his thoughts went to God, and he again thought about praying.

No way. He wasn't going to be one of those people who pray only when they want something.

But the more he tried to get God and praying out of his head, the more he thought about it. Words ran through his mind. Bible verses he had read and memorized, sermons he had heard.

I will never leave you. I'm with you always. Call on Me. Fear not. Fear not. Fear…not.

His eyes popped open. What was that? A stick snapping? Was it real, or was his mind playing tricks on him while he lingered on the edge of sleep?

There. He heard it again. Definitely a twig snapping. Coming from Cummings's position. Was Cummings moving? Walking? Making that much noise? Surely he knew better.

Joe was fully awake now, eyes wide, gun to shoulder, sweeping the bright green surroundings for any movement. His ears were alert, listening, straining to hear even the slightest sound. He swept the scope's field of vision to Cummings's location. The big man was gone.

Did Cummings hear it too? Did he go after it?

Oh, man. This is it.

Joe stood slowly and shook the stiffness from his legs. His heart bounced in his chest.

Another branch popped, the sound echoing in the stillness like gunfire, ringing in Joe's ears. This one was closer, right on the other side of the clearing. Right where Cummings was. The hair on Joe's neck stood on end. His heart now hammered. Every nerve in his body was alert, ready to spring into action. But still there was no sign of Cummings.

He saw it before he heard it—the flash from the barrel of Cummings's .375 bursting bright white in the scope. Gunfire pierced the night air, exploding like a stick of dynamite in the darkness. Joe lunged into the clearing, rifle stock pressed into his shoulder, trembling finger resting on the trigger.

Something big blurred past, quicker than he could focus on it.

Cummings yelled, a hideous scream. Then a muffled groan. Then a rustling and crunching of leaves. Then nothing.

Joe's heart was in his throat. Adrenaline surged through his veins like jet fuel. He moved across the clearing in short, even steps. He didn't want to; he wanted to turn and run, run for his life. But something pushed him forward. Pushed him toward the sound of Cummings's scream. The woods around him fell still again.

Help me, God!

It was a prayer of desperation, of fear, but he didn't care.

When he got to the edge of the clearing, he paused and listened.

Nothing.

Nothing but a voice in his head.

Fear not.

Leaves crunched to his right. His hands buzzed.

Before he had time to react, something large hit him from behind, slammed into his back, and knocked him to the ground with a heavy thud. The smell of rotted meat assaulted his nose. His first thought was that Cummings had mistaken him for the beast or stumbled upon him in the dark, but he didn't remember the large man boasting such a ripe and interesting body odor. Reflexively, he squeezed the trigger of the .30–06— not really aiming at anything—and gunfire exploded around him.

He heard a snort over his left shoulder, followed by a short growl. Definitely not sounds Cummings would make unless in the middle of a deep sleep sans nasal strips.

Somehow, he was able to chamber another round, throw the gun over his shoulder, and pull the trigger again. Another explosion.

The beast flinched and retreated, disappearing into the darkness.

Joe jumped to his feet and scanned the clearing. Was it there? Hiding in the blackness, waiting to pounce again?

His heart raced so fast and hard it felt like it would burst right out of his chest. Then he heard it again, the popping of a dry branch, like when he was a kid and would break sticks over his knee. He chambered another round, squeezed the trigger, and fired off round after round, not even counting how many he discharged, aiming at nothing. He couldn't see the beast, but he knew it was there, waiting to strike and devour him.

He pulled the trigger again. *Click.* Nothing. He was out of ammo.

Quickly, instinctively, he ran to where Cummings had been and saw him lying prone in the leaves. He rolled the larger man over and moaned in shock and disgust when his hands found Cummings's face. Or where his face used to be.

No time to grieve. He groped about until he found Cummings's revolver, slipped it from the holster and listened, waiting for any sound, any indicator of where the predator could be. The woods were filled with silence, silence so deadening Joe could hear the blood pushing through his ears.

He heard something to his left that sounded like air moving. It was the thing, breathing. It had to be. In one quick motion, he spun to his left and fired off a round. The barrel exploded with a flash of light, and Joe could see the glow of the beast's eyes. He pulled the trigger again and again and again and kept squeezing off rounds, the gun bucking in his hands, until the revolver answered with an empty *click*. Silence filled the woods. Joe's head ached and echoed the loud retort of the handgun.

Adrenaline coursed through his arteries, and he did the only thing left to do—run.

CHAPTER 11

JOE CRASHED THROUGH the overgrown woods like a runaway bull, running, stumbling, groping his way through the darkness. In his panic he'd forgotten the flashlight, the radio, and the backpack. It was just him, an empty revolver, the darkness...and *it*.

He knew it was stalking him, toying with him, lurking just out of sight. He could sense it, smell it, and periodically, when he would trip over a fallen branch or rock and momentarily lie motionless on the ground, he could hear it, softly, quietly navigating the maze of undergrowth.

He had no idea which direction he was headed, but he knew sooner or later he would be out of the woods—if the beast didn't get him first. His mind argued with reason: maybe the predator was a self-cloaking alien bent on bloodshed and mayhem. He hadn't gotten a good look at it after it bowled him over. It was too dark and everything happened in a blur.

I'm going to die! The thought pounded in his head over and over. But beyond that voice—his voice—was another one, calm, soothing, confident. A voice from the past. Still and small.

I am with you always.

Then he saw it—a flicker of hope. No, a beacon of salvation. Was it a porch light? A lamppost?

The voice came again. Seeping through his mind like warm molasses.

I am the light. Follow Me.

The light hovered and swayed in midair, then it shined right in his eyes and he realized it was a flashlight.

"HEY!" he yelled, though he was so breathless and his lungs so paralyzed by the cold air filling them in huge gulps any call for help must have sounded feeble. He raced ahead, thickets and branches trying their hardest to pull him back into the beast's world where its knifelike claws could tear him limb from limb. The muscles in his legs screamed, begging for rest, but the adrenaline pushing through his arteries threw him forward, faster and faster, until the light was less than fifty yards away.

"Joe! What's wrong? I heard the shots." It was Maggie. Sweet Maggie. Joe was never so glad to hear her voice.

He burst from the woods, took the dirt alley in two giant leaps, and fell into Maggie's arms. He was frantic, panicked, soaked with sweat, and shivering uncontrollably. Maggie caught him, but his weight pushed her backward and they both hit the ground. The revolver slid across the grass.

Joe's mind was reeling. The beast was still there, had to be, just on the other side of the tree line, ready to pounce. He climbed to his feet, legs shaking, eyes wide and searching the darkened woods. "C'mon," he said, pulling at Maggie's arm. "We gotta get inside."

She must have seen the fear in his eyes and quickly figured out what he was running from. They both scrambled into Rosa's house. Joe shut the door, locked it, flipped the deadbolt. He then lunged for the trash can and emptied the contents of his stomach in it. He stood there awhile, leaning over the open mouth of the can, sucking air, wiping at his mouth. When he stood, his stomach was in a knot, still contracting. Walking to the back door, he peered out the window, watching the tree line. "It's out there," he said, his voice unsteady, eyes glued to the woods. "Get your gun."

Maggie's hand touched his shoulder. He jumped, looked at her, their eyes locking for only a second before he returned his gaze to the woods, panning the tree line for even the slightest movement.

"What—what happened?" Maggie asked. Her voice was low and calm, but Joe didn't miss the slight tremble in it. "Where's Bob?"

Bob. In his panic, Joe had forgotten about Cummings. The feel of sticky blood and mangled flesh was still on his fingertips, and his stomach turned. "Cummings is dead," he said evenly, his eyes still fixed on the woods. He was too fatigued to show any kind of emotion.

"Dead? You mean—"

"Dead, Maggie. He's dead. It got to him."

Maggie didn't say anything. Joe felt her hand slip off his shoulder and heard her footsteps retreat to the living room. He remained at the window, watching the darkness, waiting for those familiar glowing eyes to appear. But they didn't. He had no idea how long he stood there; it could have been hours or minutes or only seconds. It seemed like years. Finally, he turned and faced the living room. Maggie was slumped on the sofa, head in her hands.

"It's gone," he said.

She looked up, eyes wide. "Gone? How do you know?"

Joe walked to the sofa and lowered himself beside her. His back ached, and his legs felt like rubber. And for the first time, he noticed the tremor that had taken to both his hands. He clenched his fists, but it didn't stop.

"Joe, how do you know?"

He stared at a spot on the rug, a stain of some sort, maybe coffee. Rosa drank a cup every morning.

Maggie was saying something.

Cream and sugar. She liked cream and sugar in her coffee.

"—Joe."

He looked at Maggie. Her hand was covering his, but he didn't feel it. Her eyes were heavy. She looked concerned.

"Joe. Did you get a look at it?"

He shook his head slowly. "No. It all happened too fast. It—it was on me. Knocked me down from behind. I fired my gun. Must have frightened it." He remembered the weight of the beast on his back, its hot, putrid breath on his neck. "It's big."

"So you didn't see it at all? You didn't see what kind of animal it was?"

He blinked, irritation rising in his chest. "I said no," he snapped. "It hit me from behind. It was dark, and it happened fast."

"I'm sorry, Joe. It must have been terrible. It's just—I mean, you couldn't tell if it was a, you know, lion or not?"

Joe pulled his hand away from Maggie's. Anger flared inside him. "Maggie. I wasn't concerned with identifying it. I was lucky to get out of there with my life."

Maggie looked away for a second, then back at Joe. "I'm sorry. I didn't mean to upset you. It's the cop in me." After a moment she said, "Are—are you sure Bob's dead?"

Joe looked at her. *Was* he sure? It all happened so fast and it was so dark. His hands had found Cummings's face, he was sure of that, but there was no face. No breathing either. No movement. He was sure Cummings was dead. "Yes." His voice trembled, and he wished he could take the answer back, make it a lie. "I'm sure."

Maggie's hand went to her mouth. She closed her eyes tight and bit her finger. "Listen," she finally said, "why don't you go take a shower, and I'll make some phone calls."

"We need to go after it. We need—"

"Joe. Listen to me. Nobody's going back in those woods tonight. I'll take care of it. Go take a shower. Clear your head. I'll handle it from here."

Joe stood and removed his coat. His shoulders felt like someone had taken a baseball bat to them. "You'll tell me when you're going after it, right?"

Maggie stood and rubbed her forehead. "Joe, please, let me handle it. I'll keep you informed."

"Promise?"

She hesitated and bit her lower lip. Joe knew what that meant; she always bit her lip when she lied. "Promise."

He turned and headed for the bathroom. Five minutes later he was standing under the shower head, letting the hot water wash away the throbbing ache in his muscles.

Maggie waited for the sound of running water, then sat back on the sofa, dropping her head in her hands. Bob was dead, or so Joe claimed. But how could he know for sure? Maybe he was mistaken. Maybe Bob survived the attack and was lying in the woods now clinging to life. The simple truth suddenly hit her like a charging Mack truck, and her hands began to shake. If he wasn't dead, he might very well be by sunup, and it would be on her watch. *She* had arranged for Joe to meet Bob; *she* had approved the hunt. If Bob was dead and if word got out about this, it would be all over town in no time. She would be held responsible, of course.

She flipped open her cell phone and punched in the number to Andy Wilt's cell.

Andy answered on the first ring. "Is everything OK?"

"Andy, I need you to do something. When Gary gets there in the morning, the two of you go down to the old Yates place—"

"But it's my day off. Tuesday."

"Not anymore. Go down there and check things out. Something went wrong, and Joe thinks Bob didn't make it out."

There was a long pause, so long that Maggie thought she had lost her signal. Then, "Cummings is dead?"

"Joe thinks so."

"So they didn't get it?"

"No. And listen, if Joe's right, I'll call Larry. I'll tell him Bob was hunting and got mauled. That's what happened." She stopped and bit her lip. Larry Bowman, the county coroner, would be a hard sell, but she was pretty sure she could pull it off. She couldn't believe what she was doing. "And no one hears about this, OK? We don't need to get everyone riled up and scared to leave their homes. We're going to take care of this ourselves."

"OK, Maggie, whatever you say." Another pause. "Is Saunders OK?"

"He's all right. Shaken up, but all right."

"Maggie?"

"Yeah?"

"Is it safe to go down there? I mean, don't you think—"

"It's fine. There'll be plenty of daylight. Take your shotguns, though. Just in case. But be careful, OK? If anything looks or even feels off, you and Gary get out of there. OK?"

"Yeah, sure, Mag."

Maggie closed her phone and drew in a deep, slow breath. What was in those woods? A thought—theory, really—that was conceived after seeing the damage to Cujo and hearing Doc Adams confirm the big cat possibility now painfully birthed itself. Great-Grandpa. Philip Yates. The stories were real.

CHAPTER 12

COFFEE AT HER side, Maggie sat at her desk trying to concentrate on the morning's paperwork. First Caleb, then Bob. What in the world was happening? If it was what she thought it was...

She heard the double glass doors of the Dark Hills Borough Police Department slam open and footsteps on the ceramic tile floor. "Maggie. Mag!"

She ran out of her office, still holding her pen.

"He's gone," Andy said, coming around the counter. Gary hung back. "Cummings is gone."

"What do you mean, *gone*?"

Andy shook his head. "He's gone. We looked all around the Yates place and there was no body. No Cummings. Isn't that right, Gary?"

Gary stiffened, tightened his lips. "We circled the area twice. Nothing there but their guns and backpacks. If Saunders is right and Cummings was dead when he left him—*if*—he's guano by now. His truck was still parked at Harrison's. We swung by his place on the way over here, just to be sure, and it was a strike."

Maggie's mind churned quickly, digesting the events as they unfolded and formulating a new game plan. "OK. OK."

Andy sat at his desk, eyes fixed on Maggie. Gary leaned his elbows on the countertop.

"Look, you two remember the story that went around when we were kids? About Great-Grandpa?"

The two officers looked at each other and blinked, then at Maggie.

"Sure," Gary said. "The monster story. The one starring Crazy Yates."

Andy nodded. "I think so. I was pretty little when that was going around, but I remember something about some animal attacking people in town and weird voodoo stuff happening and Great-Grandpa taking care of it."

"Something like that, yeah," Maggie said. "No one hears about this, OK? Bob Cummings just went missing. We're looking for him. That's it. Understand?"

Andy looked at Gary, then back at Maggie.

"Understand?"

"Yeah, sure, Maggie," Andy said.

Gary gave a slight shrug. "As far as I'm concerned, that's what went down. How do we know Saunders didn't just go loco out there and imagine the whole thing? Heck, he coulda went Charles Manson on Cummings himself. We might have a homicide on our hands."

Maggie smoothed her hair with the palm of her hand. Her forehead was damp with a cool perspiration. Her mouth was like cotton. "Something's out there. Joe was terrified when he got out of those woods. Something was there. I believe him."

"Wait a minute," Andy said. "Are you saying you think that story was real? And it's happening again? The animal attacks? The monster thing?"

Maggie paused. She knew it sounded presumptuous, even ridiculous, but in her gut she also believed it to be true. "Yeah, I am."

"How can you be sure? It may just be—"

"Andy!" Maggie snapped. She paused and took a deep breath. Her world was starting to unravel. Heat rose beneath her collar. "Look, just go along with me on this, OK? Don't fight me."

"This is nuts," Gary said. "That was just a dumb story concocted to scare dumb kids. And we were dumb enough to fall for it."

"And Cujo? What do you make of that, Gary? And what about the Saunders boy and Mary Chronister?"

"Chronister?" Gary said. "You're honestly putting stock in what some old blue-hair *thought* she saw in her backyard? And whatever attacked the kid and the dog could be anything. For crying out loud, Maggie, next we'll be saying Bigfoot is roaming around crapping in people's yards and using their cats for toothpicks. Or maybe a horde of saber-toothed ferrets, that'd make a good—"

"Enough, Gary." Maggie held up her hand, silencing him. "That's enough. For now, we're going to assume the worst and figure out a way to deal with it. We just need to buy some time. That's it."

Gary held up both hands in surrender. "OK. Let's just say for argument's sake that the story was real and that there really is some *thing* roaming the woods looking to suck someone's blood. How are we gonna get rid of it? We don't even know what it is."

Maggie furrowed her brow and smoothed her hair with both hands. Her head was starting to hurt. "I don't know yet. I need some time to think this through, formulate a plan. But I think I need to have a talk with my dad first."

"Are you gonna tell Joe?" Andy asked.

Maggie drilled him with a cold stare. "No. He doesn't need to know all the details. And no one else does either. You two just stick to the story. Bob Cummings is missing. We don't know where he is. The last time any of us saw him was yesterday afternoon. Let me handle the rest. I'll file a missing person's report so it's all official and everything. And no talking about this over the radio. We use our cells."

Gary pushed away and headed for the glass door. "My money's still on Saunders," he said over his shoulder. "He's the one we should be investigating. Bigfoot's innocent."

Ignoring him, Maggie returned to her office, shut the door, sank into her padded desk chair, and rested her head in her hands. *Joe. Dear Joe. I'm sorry for getting you involved in this. This isn't your battle. It's mine.*

Suddenly, she was eighteen again, young and in love. Joe was there, his face youthful and handsome, his dark brown hair cut close to his scalp. He was facing her, holding both her hands, telling her he had joined the army and was leaving in a week, telling her he loved her, telling her he'd come back for her.

Oh, Joe. Why did you leave? Why didn't you come back? I've missed you so much. I'm sorry.

———

Until he entered the ICU room and saw Rosa sitting in the gray chair next to Caleb's bed reading her Bible, Joe had not decided how much of last night's happenings to tell her. But when she looked at him and their eyes met and he saw the fatigue on her face and the love for her son in her eyes, he quickly made up his mind—he would tell her nothing. At least not the truth. She didn't need to be burdened with that.

Rosa closed her Bible and set it on the table next to the hospital bed. She stood and gave Joe a firm hug. "Thanks for coming, Joe," she said. She released him and stepped back, looking at his face.

He knew he looked worn and tattered. His face was scratched, thin red lines crisscrossed his cheekbones and chin, and his eyes were bloodshot and ringed with dark circles. If she pressed for answers he'd just have to make something up, tell her he'd tangled with a gang of little people wielding miniature Swiss knives and sporting *Matrix*-like combat skills.

"What happened last night?" she asked, her eyes probing his.

Joe shrugged her question off and dropped his eyes to the floor. Better to keep it short and sweet and hope she didn't press. He wasn't sure she'd go for little people using *miniature* Swiss knives; they'd probably go for something a little higher on the intimidation scale, like a machete or scimitar. "Nothing really. It was uneventful." He absentmindedly lifted a hand to his tender cheek and ran his fingers lightly across the scratches. "We just got into some thick underbrush."

He paused, collecting his thoughts and giving his jittery nerves a chance to settle. "We got caught up in some brambles is all."

A twinge of guilt plucked at his heart, but he knew he wasn't hiding anything from Rosa anyway. She always could see right through him. He was a worse liar than Rick, and Rick never got away with anything.

Without prying, without pressing, Rosa sighed and patted his arm. "Well, I'm just glad you are OK. I prayed for you, you know."

Joe knew she had. He felt it. For the first time in ten years, he'd actually felt God's presence with him in the woods last night. "How's Caleb?" he asked, changing the subject to something other than himself.

Rosa sat down in the chair and looked at her boy. "This morning they took him off the drug that was keeping him in the coma, but he has not awakened yet. Dr. Wilson was in about an hour ago and said all his reflexes are normal, which means there is a good chance there will not be any permanent brain injury. And his white blood cell count and fever are both coming down, which means the antibiotics are working on the infection. He is breathing normally on his own, and all other vitals are normal." She forced a feeble laugh. "Listen to me, talking like a doctor. I'm learning so much." She reached for Caleb's limp hand. "He is just asleep and does not want to or cannot wake up. The nurse just told me they are going to monitor him for one more day and then release him."

"Which means?"

Rosa grinned. It was the first time Joe saw a genuine smile cross her face since Caleb's mauling. "Which means we can transfer him to a long-term care facility close to home. They already called Hillside Hall, and they have a room reserved for him. He will be just a few miles from home."

Joe touched Caleb's leg. Tears welled up in his eyes; one spilled over and ran down his cheek. His nephew in a nursing home—in a coma. He had to remind himself that it was progress, though, and any progress was good news. "That's great." It was all he could say.

Free of the ventilator, Caleb looked more like himself, but he was still attached to several machines via tubes. And he wasn't out of the woods yet. He was still battling that monster, fighting it off, wrestling for his life. Joe now knew what Caleb faced in that cellar in the darkness. He knew the horror of it, and the very thought of his nephew, his little buddy, experiencing it put a lump in his throat he could not swallow. He didn't want to cry in front of Rosa. "That's great," he said again, then turned to leave the room.

"Joe, wait." Rosa stopped him with her voice.

He stood at the doorway, his back to her, hiding the tears that now traced tracks down both cheeks.

He heard her stand and approach him, then felt the weight of her hand on his shoulder. "Don't leave yet. I need to tell you something."

He wiped his eyes dry with the sleeve of his sweater and turned around. He looked past her at the far wall, at a painting of a gently winding brook flowing under an arched stone bridge. Flowers bloomed on the banks and the sky was clear and blue.

Rosa sighed deeply. "I know you have been angry at God ever since Rick died, and I know you blame yourself for his death."

Joe didn't want to hear this; he didn't need her telling him again that Rick's death wasn't his fault and she didn't hold it against him. He had heard it before, and it was all just words—meaningless words. He set his jaw and braced himself. He would listen, that was the least he could do for her, but listen is all he would do.

"Joe, I need to tell you something," Rosa said. Her voice broke with emotion. "You *are* partly responsible for Rick's death."

Joe looked at her. Now she had his attention. But there was kindness in her eyes, not anger or blame.

"He was trying to save *your* job. He should have just let you fall on your face and learn from your mistake. But he loved you too much." She paused, took a deep breath, and wiped a tear from her eye. "But I forgive you, and so does God. He loves you, Joe, and I know He misses you. Let it go. The guilt. Trust God again. He will see you through." The tears then broke loose, spilling out of her eyes and down her cheeks. Both she and Joe began to cry. She hugged him again and buried her face in his shirt.

After a few seconds, Joe released her, turned, and left the room without saying another word. Her words had struck him with all the force of a charging bull, and he needed time to sort things out.

The sun hung high in the sky. Maggie looked at her watch—ten after three—then at Clark Martin. He looked grim. His sun-worn and leathery face was creased with deep wrinkles. His thick, wild eyebrows were pinched above his eyes, and his lips were pressed thin under a yellowing beard. He patted the rear seat of the four-wheeler and hollered, "Hop on, Chief. I'll show you."

Maggie climbed on, straddled the seat, and held on to Clark's coat. He had called earlier in the day saying there was something very interesting he wanted to show her. At first she had balked. Clark was known for his often eccentric behavior. A few months ago, Kevin the mailman told her Clark had brandished a shotgun and threatened to shoot him if he ever delivered junk mail again. Maggie had to spend half the day trying to calm Clark down and get him to promise never to shoot Kevin.

Then there was the cow leg incident. Clark ran a small dairy farm just outside Dark Hills and had about fifty cows. One day, Helen Carbaugh called Maggie in hysterics. Her dog had eaten a cow and brought one of the rear legs home. Maggie drove out to Mrs. Carbaugh's place and, sure enough, little Baxter was in the backyard chomping away on a cow's hind leg. After a little investigating, Maggie discovered that the cow had died a natural death, and Clark had removed the legs so his own dogs, all five of them, could "snack on 'em," as he put it. Baxter must have been drawn by the smell and stole himself a tasty snack.

So when Clark called her saying he had something "intristin'" to show her, she wasn't sure she really wanted to see. Knowing Clark, *interesting* may not be the right word. But her curiosity had been piqued, so she agreed.

One thing she quickly found was that Clark drove a four-wheeler with as much grace as a stampeding herd of buffalo. They flew through open field, bouncing over ruts and swerving around groundhog holes, jarring teeth loose when Clark didn't see one or didn't react in time. Every few seconds, he would turn his head and holler, "Sorry, Chief," but Maggie didn't want his apologies; she wanted him to watch where he was going...and *slow down*. She was sure she was going to be thrown from the vehicle and be pulverized by the ground whizzing by beneath them.

Thankfully, the death ride lasted only a few minutes. Clark stopped the four-wheeler beside what appeared to be the carcass of a cow and shut off the engine.

"Is that—," Maggie started to ask.

"Yup, it's a cow. What's left of her."

Maggie climbed off the four-wheeler and circled the carcass. The chest cavity had been ripped open and gutted, exposing bare ribs, picked clean of meat. The rear legs were missing, and the front legs were nothing but bones and tendons. The thick hide covering the back was shredded, the torn flesh curled around deep gashes. The cow's face was drawn and frozen in a look of panic, like it had given up the ghost in midscream. And then there was the odor—the nostril-burning smell of death after it had spent a morning and afternoon ripening under the sun.

"Sumptin' attacked this here cow," Clark said, crouching beside the cow's head and poking at it with his finger.

Maggie didn't answer.

"I told you it was intristin', Chief."

"Yeah, Clark, it sure is."

Clark looked up at her and squinted in the sunlight. For the first time Maggie noticed he was chewing on something. She couldn't tell what it was other than that it was black and was staining his teeth an odd shade of purple. "Any thoughts?" he asked.

Maggie shrugged. She wasn't about to tell Clark Martin a lion attacked his cow. She knew better than to throw gasoline on a fire. Word would be all over town before the day was over. "I don't know. What do you think?"

Clark stood and narrowed his eyes at Maggie. He ran a weathered hand over his jaw. "I've been hearin' word 'round town that there's a lion on the loose." He jerked his head in the direction of the cow. "Sure looks like sumptin' a lion would do, don't it?"

Too late. Word had apparently already spread through town.

Maggie forced a laugh. "Well, I know there are some rumors going around, Clark, but I don't know how much stock I'd put in them. This is Dark Hills, remember. America. Unless something's changed, I don't recall ever hearing that we have lions running wild in America. That's why they call them *African* lions. Now there are—"

"Chief—" Clark cut her off, holding up both hands and waving them like he was washing windows. "I don't know nuthin' 'bout what do and don't live in America. What I do know is that some folk say they seen a lion, and now I got me a dead cow that looks an awful lot like the work of one of them beasts."

Maggie nodded in consent. "I know, Clark. I know. I'm sorry about your cow. And as soon as I figure out what's going on around here, I'll let you know." That should hold him off for a little while, she thought. "Now, if you don't mind, I need to be getting back to the station. I know it's not the answer you were looking for, but I really don't have an answer yet."

Clark shrugged and climbed onto the four-wheeler. "If you say so, Chief," he said, turning the key and bringing the engine to life. "Hop on!"

Oh, brother. Maggie climbed on and tapped Clark's shoulder. "Go slower this time," she yelled in his ear.

"What?" And he gunned it.

CHAPTER 13

ELSTON GILL'S ROOM in St. Magdalene's Care Home was dimly lit and smelled like urine and sweat. Maggie stood in the doorway and watched her father, the former *Chief* Elston Gill, sleep. He'd spent the last four years of his life in this place, slowly deteriorating.

Maggie's mother, Gloria, died six years ago from cervical cancer, and Elston just couldn't function without her. He'd lost weight, showed up late for work, misplaced police reports, even wrecked his cruiser when he ran a stop sign, plowed into a pasture, and bowled over one of Clark Martin's heifers.

Maggie had moved in with him, thinking she could help him cope with the grief and make the life adjustment a little more smoothly, but a little over a year later, Elston suffered a major stroke and lost all control of his right side. His days as police chief were over.

Maggie tried to care for him on her own, wanted to keep him in his own home where she thought the memories of a life well lived might give him strength and purpose, but Elston only deteriorated further. It seemed without his beloved wife and without his beloved badge, he saw no reason to continue living and simply gave up trying. But fate was not on his side, and death was not ready for him. So when Maggie could no longer handle playing caregiver *and* newly appointed police chief, she put him in St. Magdalene's, a long-term care facility in Quinceburg.

Now, leaning against the doorjamb, hands shoved in her jacket pockets, she watched her dad sleep. He was wearing the light blue pajamas with navy blue trim she'd gotten him for Christmas two years ago. The bed covers were pulled up and neatly folded back at his waist.

The small room was nothing like home. A nondescript dresser sat against one wall, topped with a brass lamp, a framed picture of a young Elston in his uniform, and a small wooden jewelry box. Against the wall at the foot of the bed stood a coffee table with a TV. Next to the bed was a small table with a box of tissues, a clock, and a picture of Elston and Gloria at Maggie's graduation from the academy.

A twinge of guilt always jabbed at Maggie whenever she visited, which was never often enough. At times she felt as though she should have given up her position as chief to care for her dad. Family was more important than a job, wasn't it? But at other times she knew this was exactly what her dad had wanted her to do. Police work was Elston's life, his passion. And passing the family legacy on to his daughter was more important to him than maintaining his pathetic life. Those were his words. St. Magdalene's was his idea. He'd told Maggie he'd rather spend the rest of his life confined to a hospital bed and have her carry on the Gill name as police chief than be responsible for ending the Gill legacy because his only child had to stay home and change his diapers.

Maggie entered the room, sat on the edge of the bed, and placed her hand over her dad's. It was so thin and frail. Blue veins wove over and around stringy tendons, all clearly visible through the spotted paper-thin skin that clung to the bones. His cheeks were hollow, eyes sunken, hair thinning and greasy. The right side of his face sagged like melting wax, and a dribble of drool pooled in the corner of his mouth. No one would guess he was only sixty-five. He looked more like eighty-five. This man, father, daddy, who had given her so much confidence and pride, who had been her hero, her lionheart for so long, was now as frail as a bird.

Gently squeezing his hand, Maggie said, "Dad. Wake up, Dad. It's me."

Elston's eyes fluttered open and a dry tongue ran over his lips. The left side of his mouth lifted in a crooked smile. "Magpie. You...good?" The stroke had slurred his speech and left him with Broca's aphasia, a speech disorder that made speaking complex sentences all but impossible. At first, Maggie had a difficult time deciphering her dad's simple, child-like sentences, but years of guessing and filling in the blanks had honed her skill.

"I'm fine, Dad. Just fine."

Elston licked his lips again and swallowed. "How's house?"

Maggie knew he meant the police house, not their house. "Things have been interesting lately. Dad, I need to talk to you about something."

Elston's mouth dropped and the smile faded.

"I need you to just listen, OK? This is important."

Elston nodded and squeezed her hand. Maggie was surprised by how weak his grip had grown.

"Dad, do you remember Joe Saunders?"

He nodded again. "Nice."

Maggie smiled. "Yeah. You always liked Joe. A couple days ago his nephew was mauled by something in the old Yates place. Then Woody Owen's dog was attacked and killed. Doc Adams said it most likely was a large cat. Said it could very well be a lion."

Elston's left eye widened, showing the yellow sclera around the irises. His hand began to tremble beneath Maggie's.

"Dad, listen. Last night Joe and Bob Cummings went into Yates Woods to hunt it and…Bob was killed." She paused and fought back the tears waiting behind her eyes. "I don't know what to do, Dad. It's happening again, isn't it?"

Licking his lips, Elston tried to sit up, pushing his left elbow against the bed and grunting.

"Let me help," Maggie said, gripping him under the arms and hoisting him up to a more seated position. He was lighter than she expected.

She propped a pillow behind his head.

Elston reached out to Maggie, lifted his left hand, and stroked Maggie's hair. "No tell," he said, his voice strained and raspy. "No tell!"

"Why, Dad? Why can't I tell anyone, get some help?"

"No tell! Family…" He grimaced and dropped his hand. She knew what he was trying to say. Family legacy. To talk would be to expose the secrets her family had kept under wraps for generations, and it would taint the family legacy forever. The Gill name would be smeared, and everything three generations of Gills had worked for, sacrificed for, would be destroyed.

Finally, Elston gave up and relaxed his face. Tears formed in his eyes and trickled down his cheeks, catching in the creases around his mouth. He looked so pitiful. "Please," he said, "no tell. Please."

Maggie began to cry too. "Then what do I do, Dad?"

Elston reached up again and placed his hand on her cheek, thumbing a tear from below her eye. His face grew very serious, eyes intense. "Secret! Hide! No tell." His hand fell to the bed, and the left side of his lip quivered. "Please, Magpie, no tell. Please."

"OK, OK, Dad. I won't."

With jaws clenched, with eyes narrowed, Elston grabbed a fistful of sheet and said, "Promise!"

Maggie hesitated.

"Promise, Magpie."

"OK. I promise."

It was movie night again at Woody Owen's place on Fulton Street. Then again, every night was movie night. Woody was a loner of sorts. Ever since the roofing accident that left him paralyzed from the waist down, he had no need for company.

After the accident, he'd tried to resume his normal social life of going to McCormick's Bar every Friday night and partying Saturday nights. But he soon tired of the awkward stares he and his chair got, the gawking, the snickering, the people going out of their way to help him—*help the poor cripple*. He didn't need help. He didn't need anyone. He could take care of himself just fine, thank you. He didn't have a job, either, but disability paid the bills. He was doing OK.

His decision had cost him a lot of friends, even Evelyn, his girlfriend. She'd been there for him in the hospital, through the unsuccessful surgeries, the rehab, everything. But she'd have left him sooner or later. He knew it. How long could she keep up the sympathy act? How long could she pretend to love a cripple? He was doing them both a favor; at least that's what he'd told himself a million times in the dead of the night when the loneliness and remorse would sneak up on him.

But now he was used to the solitude. He even enjoyed it. He could do what he wanted, when he wanted, how he wanted, and there was nobody to tell him otherwise. He was a free man.

Over the years he'd become quite the movie connoisseur too. Every Sunday he would pore over the TV listings and plan his evenings. He would then go to Traynor's Video and rent a handful of movies for the week—usually horror or suspense. Tonight's selection was *Sleepy Hollow*.

Woody had gone through his nightly ritual of gathering snacks from the refrigerator and pantry, grabbing a six pack of brewskies, transferring himself from his wheelchair to the recliner, and settling in to his throne, remote in hand, snacks well within reach.

He was just about to push the start button on the remote when he heard a faint scratching noise at the back storm door.

He listened. There, the scratching again. And again. It was faint but persistent.

Can't be a stray, he thought, then remembered Cujo wasn't there anymore to chase the stray cats away.

Ignoring the scratching, he clicked the play button and the movie rolled. *It'll go away.*

Ten minutes later the scratching didn't go away, and a low, haunting meow started, first in short bursts, then in long, drawn-out, sorrowful howls. Woody finally decided that there was no ignoring the nuisance at the door. If he wanted to enjoy his movie night, he'd have to get rid of it.

He cursed as he punched the pause button on the remote and slammed it down on the TV tray. He then lifted himself off the recliner, swung around, and landed perfectly in the wheelchair. Dodging stacks of magazines and newspapers, he wound from the living room to the kitchen and positioned himself in front of the back door. He pulled the door open, and there, on the other side of the storm door, was a tan tabby cat, sitting on its haunches and shivering, looking wide-eyed up at him.

"Go away!" Woody hollered. The cat cocked its head and looked at him as if trying to decipher the strange sounds coming out of his mouth. "Go on, git!"

But the cat didn't budge. It only stared at him longer, let out a long, mournful meow, and pawed at the door.

Woody leaned forward and banged on the metal bottom half of the door. The cat flinched but didn't leave its perch on the back stoop. It meowed again and pawed at the door some more.

"OK, OK." Woody opened the door a few inches to allow the stray access to the warm kitchen. "There. Happy now?"

The cat began to purr and rub its head and neck against the large rear wheel of the chair. Woody bowed and stroked the cat's head, which led to more leaning and deeper purring.

Sighing, patting his lap with both hands, Woody said, "C'mon, you little devil. C'mon up here, and let me take a look at you."

The cat crouched, wiggled its bottom, then leaped onto Woody's lap. He slid his hand down the cat's back, starting at its head and ending at its tail. The fur was slick and soft, and the cat pressed into his touch, purring even louder.

"You're a friendly fellow, aren't you?" Woody said, stroking the downy fur of the cat's cheeks. "You wanna join me for movie night? I'll even share my snacks with you."

CHAPTER 14

THE PLAYGROUND HAD seen better days. The swing set was still sturdy, but the poles were covered with chipped paint, rust taking over where the paint had bailed. The cracked-rubber swings were supported by creaky, rusted chains. The merry-go-round was lopsided and rusty, like Sylvester Stallone in *Rocky Balboa*; the sliding board, once the mightiest structure in the park, was slightly warped, dipping in the middle as if it had received a gut-shot and lost its will to fight. The grass was patchy, the mulch old and crusty. On the other side of the open area stood an old oak, half its branches rotted, brittle, and leafless. Somebody had neglected this park for far too long. Joe leaned back against the smooth wood of the only park bench and sipped his gas station coffee from a Styrofoam cup.

Behind the swings, the horizon glowed pink, the opening act of what was promising to be a glorious sunrise, nature's grandest performance, much grander than even Rocky's attempted comeback.

Joe had risen early, hoping to catch the sun's arrival. He needed some time alone before starting the day. After visiting Rosa at the hospital yesterday, he'd returned to his motel room, tried several times to call Maggie (which had resulted in leaving awkward messages on her voice mail each time, which had resulted in him feeling like a pimply teenager calling for a first date), then fell asleep in front of the TV. He didn't awaken until after five o'clock, tried Maggie again (more voice mail, more pimples), and spent the rest of the evening hunkered down in the Dew-Drop, watching old western movies where the villains all had names like Snake-Eye Joe and Cactus Will.

He awoke this morning feeling exhausted and drained. He hadn't slept well. Most of the night was spent battling images of a self-cloaking, sharp-clawed, six-shooter-sporting little person named Rattlesnake. He would awaken, go in the bathroom, splash water on his face, then return to bed, only to engage in another battle with his diminutive adversary.

Morning had come too soon, and giving up on peaceful sleep, Joe got up and headed to the Mobil station, grabbed a coffee, and walked to the park. He was hoping to clear his mind and settle his nerves before meeting Rosa and Caleb at Hillside Hall at ten o'clock.

"Good morning," a voice behind him said.

Joe recognized it right away and turned to see Maggie approaching. She was wearing her beige uniform and black jacket. Her cruiser was parked along the street.

"Mind if I join you?"

"Mornin', Mags. Have a seat," Joe said.

Maggie sat next to him on the bench, keeping a foot of space between them. "Glorious morning, isn't it?" she said.

"Beautiful." There was a moment of comfortable silence between them as they both watched the sky above the horizon lighten its shade of pink. "We used to ride our bikes here all the time as kids," Joe said. "Do you remember when Tommy Stambaugh fell out of that oak and broke his arm? Said he could climb to the top of it."

Maggie smiled. "I remember. It was smaller then, and healthier, but it was still a long fall. I thought for sure he was going to die."

Joe laughed. "The place sure has changed. The whole town's changed so much in some ways, and then in other ways it hasn't changed at all."

"Such is life in a small town. Change happens, but with resistance. Sometimes for the better, sometimes not." Maggie looked at Joe. "You've never come back since you left?"

"I've come back. To visit Rosa and Caleb. But I stayed away from coming in town, just…I don't know." But he did know, and he knew that Maggie knew too: to avoid seeing her.

There was another moment of silence, this time uncomfortable.

Joe said, "Why hasn't anyone kept up with this place? We used to love to come here as kids."

"No money. The borough can barely afford to pay me and Gary and Andy. The budget's tight and stuff like this"—she waved her hand around the rundown playground—"is expendable. Besides, kids don't play outside much anymore; they have TV and computers and video games now."

Joe held the coffee cup to his chin and let the steam warm his nose. "Why didn't you call me back yesterday?"

"I did," Maggie said. "I tried calling you a couple times in the afternoon, like around two o'clock or so. I didn't want to leave a message."

"You didn't call the room?"

"Were you there?"

"Most of the day. I visited Rosa and Caleb in the morning, then went back and crashed. I was probably asleep and didn't hear the phone. Dead to the world."

"Poor choice of words."

"Yeah. I guess. Sorry."

Maggie shifted on the bench so she was facing Joe. "How's Caleb doing?"

Joe shrugged. "He's stable. He's coming home to Hillside Hall in a couple hours. I'm supposed to meet Rosa and the ambulance there. Ten o'clock."

"That's great. So he's improving?"

"Improving, yes. He's breathing on his own, and the infection in his arm is almost gone, but he's still in a coma."

Maggie placed her hand on his shoulder. Her touch was gentle and welcomed. "I'm sure he'll come out of it. He's a tough kid."

Joe could feel a lump surfacing in his throat, the same lump that surfaced every time he talked about Caleb. He needed to change the subject to something more light-hearted, something other than Caleb. "So what are you doing this morning? What does a small town cop do when there's no one to lock up?"

Maggie laughed. "There's never anyone to lock up. I haven't arrested anyone in over a year. This place is like Mayberry. I probably don't even need to carry my weapon."

"There're no troublemakers in Dark Hills? No redneck rowdies? I remember Friday nights at McCormick's used to get pretty wild."

"Oh, they still do, but most of the time all it takes is for one of us to show up, give a warning, and things settle down pretty quick."

"Does anyone ever give you a hard time because you're a woman?"

Rolling her eyes, Maggie said, "Sometimes. But it's usually outsiders. Last month we had a guy down at McCormick's trying to pick a fight with Tom Newsome, a machine operator at the mill. I showed up and told him to settle down or I'd have to do it for him. He turned on me and tried to shove me."

"What'd you do?"

"Well, let's just say I'm pretty handy with my baton. He left town limping like a dog with his tail between his legs and hasn't been seen since."

Joe smiled and shook his head. "Even you've changed. I'm sorry, but I just can't see you doing that. Not the Maggie I knew."

"Change isn't all bad, you know," Maggie said. "Everybody changes. We grow up, adapt to the road life has laid for us. Do you think I've changed for the worse?"

"No, no. It's just…you're different, that's all. More confident, more in control."

"Agreed. Being a police officer does that to you. Being the chief of police does it even more."

"Look at that," Joe said, pointing at the sky behind the swing set. Tendrils of pink streaked across the sky, originating from the horizon and climbing upward and out like a fan.

"It's beautiful," Maggie said, a quiet, reverent tone to her voice.

After several seconds of silence, Joe turned toward Maggie. "How's your dad?"

Maggie gave him a questioning look.

"Rosa's been keeping me updated on town news." He knew his knowledge of her mom's passing and dad's stroke made him look like a jerk. He'd never called to offer condolences, never even sent a card.

Fortunately, Maggie didn't lay on the guilt. "He's been better. He's in St. Magdalene's over in Quinceburg. He's been really going downhill for the past six months or so."

"I'm sorry." And he was. Sorry for not calling, sorry for not visiting, sorry for not being there when she needed someone. Sorry for not caring.

"Yeah." That was all Maggie said.

Another moment of uncomfortable silence passed. Half of Joe wished Maggie would get up and leave, let him wallow in his guilt alone, and half of him wanted her here, by his side.

He took another sip of coffee and said awkwardly, "What happened with Cummings? Were you able to reach any of the family?"

Maggie had pulled over and approached Joe with the single intent of feeling him out, seeing how he was coping with the events of the other night. She knew sooner or later the question of what she did with Bob's body would come up, and she wanted to be prepared. She'd learned some time ago to plan ahead and anticipate what direction a conversation may take. And she had come prepared. But this conversation had taken a wrong turn. It had turned personal and dredged up feelings she'd not dealt with for years. She had once given her heart—and future—to Joe, had fallen head-long into the abyss of adolescent love. She had waited for him, clinging to the remnants of her fading dream as if her very life depended on it. And he had failed her.

But once again she found herself falling for him.

She pushed aside the sentimentality of the moment, told herself to stick to the plan, and said in as confident a voice as she could muster, "No, I'm going to wait on that. I sent a hunting team into the woods to recover the body and flush the...animal out. But they didn't find either. So—"

"Wait a minute," Joe shifted his weight on the bench. "You went hunting that thing and didn't tell me?"

"I didn't go in there. I assembled a team. Gary, Andy, and some local hunters—"

"And didn't tell me."

Maggie felt herself tense. Deep-seated frustration over Joe's neglect clashed with the guilt of her premeditated lies. She was prepared for this, though. She swallowed and composed herself. "You didn't need to know."

"You promised."

"I made a judgment call. I'm sorry. I was looking out for your own good. After what you went through, I thought the last thing you needed was to go down there again."

Joe turned his head away from her, toward the rising sun. "Maybe you should have let me make that call."

"Next time I will."

Seconds of awkwardness. Finally, "They swept the whole woods and didn't find anything?"

"Nothing. No body. No predator of any sort."

"And they checked the Yates house, the cellar."

"Of course they did. There was nothing there."

Joe lifted his cup to his mouth, then lowered it without taking a sip and asked, "So what are you doing about Cummings?"

"I'm writing him up as a missing person until we find something that will prove otherwise." She knew that wouldn't go over well, but it was the story she'd decided on, and that was that. She braced herself for his rebuttal.

Joe stood and drilled her with wide eyes. "Missing person? What do you mean? He's dead. I saw him."

"That's not the way it works, though. The coroner has to pronounce someone dead. If there's no body, he can't very well do that, so . . . I don't really know he's dead. I don't want to notify the family of something like that if I'm not sure it's true."

Joe tried to speak, but Maggie held up a finger to stop him. He turned his back on her. "Look," Maggie said, "I know it doesn't make sense, but we—I—have to follow procedure. If I pronounce him dead, notify the family, they have a funeral, and so on and so on, then he turns up alive somewhere in some ditch or some hospital's ICU, that wouldn't go over so well. Would it?"

Turning back around, Joe said, "That *sounds* good, but why don't you tell me what's really going on. You've been chewing on that lip of yours like you haven't eaten in days." He drained the rest of his coffee and walked toward the metal trash can by the merry-go-round.

The conversation had wandered down a bad road. She had to end it. Quickly, Maggie slipped her cell phone from her belt and paged Andy. *C'mon, Andy. Make it quick.*

Joe returned and sat again. He looked at Maggie with tired eyes. "What's going on, Mags? I want the truth."

Maggie sighed and forced a smile. "Nothing's going on. I'm a cop, and not just any cop; I'm the chief of police. I have to follow procedure."

"Maggie, you're forgetting something. I was there, remember. And he was dead. That *thing* probably went back and finished off what was left of him. I think his family should know."

"How do you know he was dead? It was dark, Joe. You were scared, panicked. Do you—"

"Are you saying I imagined the whole thing?"

"I don't know what to say—"

"Well, I do. I didn't imagine it, Maggie. And I didn't imagine that *thing* pouncing on my back. Cummings was dead."

"Did you check for a pulse, breathing, anything? Or are you just assuming he was dead because of the condition of his body? I've seen people survive some pretty bad stuff, trust me."

Joe flinched.

A battle was raging inside Maggie. She could only imagine the nightmare Joe had lived with since the incident. It was ripping her apart inside to put him through this. But she had to. It was her job. Her dad's words came back to her: *Please, Magpie, no tell. Please.* How could she let her dad down? How could she disrespect him by ignoring his wish, quite possibly his final wish? No, she had to stick to her story. It was the only way.

"He didn't have a face!" Joe said, struggling to keep his voice low. "I know dead when I see it, and he was dead." Joe sat back and took a deep breath.

Maggie sighed and slumped. She was pushing too hard. She had to defuse the situation. "Joe, I'm sorry. I didn't want this to come between us. But I just can't do it. I know you were there. I'm not second-guessing your testimony, but people have survived some pretty horrendous things. Without any confirmation of his death, I just can't go around saying he's dead. I have notified the family that he's missing, though. I hoped you would understand my predicament. I have a mauled boy, a survivor, thankfully, a dead dog, and a missing—"

"Dead—"

"—*missing* man. I'm at my limits here. I can only do what I'm legally allowed to do. I have protocol to follow."

Joe's shoulders slumped too. Finally, she'd broken through to him. She knew if she stood her ground long enough he'd look for a compromise. "I do understand, Mags," he said. "I just know what I saw or felt or whatever, and it was horrible and gruesome. There's no way anyone could survive that. But I wouldn't want you to do anything that could get you in trouble."

Maggie smiled and reached for his hand. "Thanks."

"But what are we going to do about this *thing*, lion, or whatever it is running around out there?"

"I'm not sure. All the zoos and circuses got back to us, and no one's missing any lions or anything else for that matter. It seems our beast is still a mystery."

"Well, we have to do something. We can't just wait around for it to strike again. Can't you call the Game Commission or National Guard or something? Get some help down here?"

Maggie's stomach knotted. More lies. But consistency was everything now. *Where are you, Andy?* "I did. The game commissioner said until we know what we're dealing with, he can't afford to send any men. There's a lot of bureaucracy and red tape involved with something like this. It can become a real hot potato. It's frustrating, I know, but there isn't much more we can do."

Joe pulled his hand away, obviously annoyed. "This is ridiculous! We have a predator roaming the woods, killing people, yes, *killing*, and no one seems to care." He tapped his thigh with his finger. "Well, I care, and I'll hunt the thing down on my own if I have to."

"I care too," Maggie said. She knew the moment the words left her mouth that they didn't sound totally convincing. "I'm going to do all I can to make sure whatever it is, is taken care of. Please, Joe, don't do anything stupid."

Just then the cell phone on her belt chimed. *Finally.* She unhooked it, flipped it open, and held it up to her ear. "Chief Gill."

"Maggie." It was Andy. *Thank you.* "You paged me?"

"*Mm-hm.* OK, be right there."

"What? Maggie, why did—"

She flipped the phone shut and reached for Joe's hand, squeezing it gently. "Gotta run. We'll talk later."

———

Joe watched Maggie walk away, get in her cruiser, and drive off. She gave a weak smile and a little wave as she pulled away.

It had been over thirty hours since Cummings's death. Yes, death. He didn't care what Maggie wanted to call it—Cummings was dead. As a doornail. Period. He wasn't off playing peek-a-boo with Smokey the Bear or being nursed back to health by Goldilocks. He was expired.

Thought of the incident still sent a shiver through Joe's bones. Whatever was in those woods was in no way indigenous to the area. It *ate* the indigenous. Joe knew how fortunate he was just to escape with his life, let alone unharmed. As much as he hated to admit it, God was looking out for him. No question about that.

And then there was Maggie and her politically correct mumbo jumbo. Sure, she was the chief of police, but didn't that come with the responsibility to uncover the truth, not conceal it? What was she hiding, anyway? He knew she was lying, but about what, he wasn't sure. What part of her story was fact and what was fiction? He'd have to do some digging to find out.

What's going on around here, Mags? There were so many things about Dark Hills that were so familiar to him, but something suddenly seemed very unfamiliar, strange even, like there was a part of this small community that he had never known. And never would.

CHAPTER 15

J OE ARRIVED MINUTES after Caleb was wheeled into his new room at Hillside Hall, a skilled nursing facility just outside the Dark Hills borough line. The facility was new, owned by one of those healthcare megacorporations that were throwing up assisted living homes and skilled nursing facilities like an ADHD toddler with Legos. They had broken ground a little over a year ago and had been open for business only about three months. The building sat on a sprawling campus surrounded by fields brown with dried cornstalks.

Joe parked his car and entered the building through the automatic sliding glass doors. The lobby was a wide open room with a twenty-foot cathedral crystalline ceiling, finely upholstered sofas and chairs arranged around a colorful Persian rug, and lots of potted trees and plants. The place smelled of new carpet and furniture polish. The receptionist, seated behind a large sliding glass window, looked comfortable and friendly.

"Can I help you?" she asked Joe when he stepped in front of the window.

Joe returned her smile. "Hi. Yes. I'm looking for the honeymoon suite."

The receptionist, a twenty-something, brown-haired woman with small oval glasses and a name plate that read Christy, gave him a blank look.

"Never mind," Joe said. "I'm looking for Caleb Saunders's room."

Christy hit the keyboard lightly and stared at the monitor. "Room B-13. That's B Wing, down the hall, to your right. Room 13."

"Thank you," Joe said and turned to follow the directions he'd just been given. He looked around again at the lobby. It was impressive, indeed. At least Caleb was in a nice place.

He headed down the hall and turned right down the corridor marked *B Wing*. Caleb's room was halfway down the hall, on the left. It was small but nicely furnished with a hospital bed, two maroon padded chairs, and a small round oak table. A bathroom was located just inside the door.

Rosa was there, as was a nurse, hooking up Caleb's feeding tube and IV line. The boy was comfortably situated in a hospital-style bed, blanket pulled up to his waist. He looked like he was merely asleep and would awaken at the slightest noise, glad to see his uncle had come to visit him. But Joe knew that wouldn't be the case. The Brooklyn Tabernacle Choir could sing the "Hallelujah Chorus" in his ear and he wouldn't wake up.

"Joe, we just got here," Rosa said, rising from her chair when Joe came through the door. "It's nice, yes?"

He smiled. "Real nice. Impressive. I'm so glad Caleb can stay here."

Rosa motioned to one of the chairs. "Sit down. Can you stay a little while?"

"I was planning to."

Outside, in a far corner of the parking lot, just inside the first row of corn, Stevie Bauer paced back and forth, methodically rubbing his hands.

"Gotcha," he hissed. "You can't hide now. Sticks and stones. Sticks and stones. Shoulda left Stevie alones."

He giggled at his own absurd attempt at rhyming.

The thing was out there, just beyond the protection of the hole, lurking in the darkness, pacing, waiting.

Caleb wanted to push back further into his sanctuary, melt into his hole, lose himself forever in the darkness. But something was drawing him out; something was wooing him toward the opening.

He inched closer, running his hands along the dirt floor and rough wall, feeling for the opening. There. There it was. He listened. No sound of anything but his own steady breathing.

He leaned forward almost enough to poke his head out of the hole.

Thump! Something whizzed by his head and landed heavily on the floor beside him. In a panic, he pushed back into the hole and shriveled as far from the opening as he could.

It was there. He couldn't see it, but he could hear its claws pawing at the floor, scratching, tearing at the dirt, like a cat groping for a mouse hidden in a wall.

Terror overwhelmed him, and he panicked. He tried pushing back further, but his hands and heels slipped in the loose dirt. This was it. This was how he was going to die. He would never escape the darkness.

Inside Hillside Hall, room B-13, Joe leaned back in his chair, swung his left leg over his right, and smiled. "So how'd you land Caleb in this place?"

"Dr. Wilson has been wonderful. He was able to pull—" Rosa stopped mid-sentence and whipped her head around to look at Caleb. "What was that? Did you see that?"

Joe looked at Caleb, sleeping peacefully, then back at Rosa. "See what?"

"He moved. I saw it out of the corner of my eye. Like a shudder or a shiver or something."

Suddenly, Caleb's whole body spasmed—not a violent seizure, like a thousand volts of electricity had surged through it, but a gentle shiver as one may do when suddenly struck by a blast of arctic air—then relaxed.

Rosa jumped out of her chair and stood beside his bed. "What was that?" she said, looking at Joe, wide-eyed.

"I don't know. Why don't you get one of the—"

It happened again, this time more violently. Caleb's body began to quiver and shake, muscles spasmed, locked up like dry gears, then relaxed, then spasmed again. Neck muscles bulged like taut cords ready to snap, muscles throughout his arms and legs, abdomen and chest rippled and contracted. This was an electrocution sans electricity.

"Oh, God, help us. What is happening?" Rosa cried.

Joe burst into the hallway. "Nurse! Nurse! Come quick."

A young, heavyset nurse ran down the hall and into Caleb's room. Caleb's body shook one last time, like the gentle aftershock of an earthquake, and relaxed.

"He—he was seizing or something," Rosa said.

Joe added, "It looked like he was being electrocuted."

The nurse fingered some dials on the machines by Caleb's bed, checked all the tubes, then put her fingers on Caleb's right wrist and checked his pulse. After a few seconds she said, "His pulse is a little high, but other than that everything checks out OK. Sometimes patients who are in a coma will have involuntary muscle movements, even spasms. It's quite normal. I'll document it, though, so when Dr. Montgomery gets here, she can check it out as well." She patted Caleb's hand. "I'm sure he's just being feisty. If it happens again, let me know."

"Thanks," Joe said as the nurse left the room.

Rosa patted her chest and took a deep breath. "That scared me. We need to pray right now, Joe. I don't know why, but I just feel this over-whelming need to pray." She bowed her head without even waiting for him to reply and started to pray. "Dear Lord, protect my son..."

Joe leaned against the wall next to Caleb's bed, his head bowed, eyes open, watching Caleb as Rosa prayed. He wasn't thinking about what she was saying; his mind was elsewhere, with Maggie and wondering what she was hiding, why she was acting so strange. In some ways she was the same old Maggie he once knew, loved...and left, but in some other way, a way he couldn't quite put his finger on, she was much different. She had become an enigma of sorts.

Rosa continued praying, "...his body is frail and wounded..." Her mind was on her heavenly Father. She was in *His* presence, before *His* throne, interceding for her young son, who was in *His* hands now. There was nothing she could do but pray. It was frustrating at times. She was a problem-solver, a fixer, but this was one problem she could not fix. She had to let Caleb go and put him in God's hands. All she could do was pray.

And so she *would* pray; night and day she would fervently plead with God.

A light appeared, not bright or brilliant in any way, just a pinhole, high above Caleb, like the first star to appear against a black velvet sky, piercing the darkness like a sword, illuminating his hand and nothing more.

Peace surrounded him, dispelling the fear and panic that had gripped his body.

Warmth penetrated his flesh. Starting at the top of his head, it slowly spread down the back of his neck, over his arms, torso, then legs and feet, seeping into his bones and internal organs.

Then a voice, deep and full, like waves crashing on the surf, shook the dungeon and vibrated in his chest. Oddly, he was not afraid. In fact, he found the voice comforting.

"Speak for Us."

Caleb opened his mouth and tried to respond, form words, but no sound came.

"Speak for Us."

How?

The light turned a warm orange, like the glow of smoldering coals and burning embers after a fire has been left unattended for too long. The glow hovered above him, moving closer, descending slowly until it rested in his hand.

He flinched, expecting fiery pain to send his nerves screaming, but none came. He could smell the pungent odor of burning flesh, see the light searing his hand, but there was no pain, no sensation at all.

"Speak for Us, child. My child."

Yes. I will.

———

"...he is in Your hands now, Lord," Rosa prayed. "Even in this lifeless state, use him to glorify Yourself—"

She heard Joe calling her name. "Rosa. Rosa."

She stopped praying, opened her eyes, and looked at Joe questioningly. He motioned with his eyes toward Caleb. Her son was lying perfectly still, peaceful, like he was sleeping, but his eyes were open—wide open, like saucers. He stared blankly at the ceiling.

Rosa stood and approached Caleb's bed. She leaned over and looked into his eyes, searching for recognition, for awareness, for *life*. "Caleb? Caleb honey, can you hear me?"

There was no reply, only a vacant stare. His eyes were hollow—lights on, nobody home.

Suddenly, his right hand began quivering, slowly at first, then more rapidly.

"Look," Joe said, pointing at his hand. "Look at this."

Caleb's body was completely relaxed except for his hand. It closed so his fingertips touched as if holding a pencil and moved in short, swift movements up and down, side to side, clockwise, counterclockwise.

Joe started to head for the door to call the nurse, but Rosa stopped him. "Wait, it's OK. Let's just see what he does."

The hand jumped back and forth for less than a minute then stopped. Caleb's eyes slowly closed, his hand relaxed, and he was once again resting quietly, chest rising and falling as if to the steady rhythm of a metronome.

Rosa looked at Joe. He frowned and shrugged, obviously just as perplexed as she was. "God is doing something here," she said. "I don't know what, but He is doing something."

CHAPTER 16

AFTER HER NOT-SO-productive talk with Joe in the park, Maggie made her usual Wednesday morning rounds of Dark Hills. She traveled the length of Main Street, then circled around the perimeter of town, weaving in and out of side streets lined with small, dirt-dusted, single-family homes and rental units, and slowly worked her way back to the center square along High Street.

The town "square" was actually a circle, and there wasn't much there to attract any kind of outside attention. On one corner was McCormick's, the hub of the Dark Hills nightlife; across from it and traveling counter-clockwise was a Mobil station, Finnigan's Hardware, and M & T Bank. High intersected Main at the circle, and just outside of town, about a mile down East High, sat the Dark Hills Paper Company, founded in 1870 by the town's father, Andrew Adams.

The paper mill consisted of several colossal gray buildings, all faded and streaked with rust stains and decades of dirt and grime. The mill overlooked the town like a giant dragon huffing out huge billows of thick white smoke. Most of the buildings were abandoned now, left to rot knowing they'd never be used again. Broken-down, rusted truck cabs and logging trailers, partially hidden by waist-high weeds, littered the crumbling and faded asphalt area around the mill. Three railroad tracks passed through the complex, weaving through the countryside like steel arteries. One was still in use. The others had long ago been relegated to the task of storing dilapidated, vandalized boxcars.

Like the rest of Dark Hills, the paper mill had lost its vitality.

At one time, in the early and mid-1900s, the mill was bustling with activity that spilled over into the town. Population within the borough had soared to over ten thousand and looked like it would continue to climb. But in the sixties the mill lost several large contracts, business plummeted, jobs were cut, and the town of Dark Hills slipped into the dark ages. The population shrunk to just under four thousand and never recovered.

It usually didn't take Maggie long to make her rounds. The town's perimeter had also shrunk over the years to barely twenty-five square miles surrounded mostly by open fields and small wooded areas on the south and west sides, and the thickly wooded Dark Hills to the north and east. When she finished her tour, she'd drop by some of the local businesses, shoot the breeze with some of Dark Hills's old-timers, refill the cruiser at the Mobil, and run any errands that couldn't wait.

Things happened at a crawl in a small town, and at times being the chief of police was downright boring. But it was in her blood; it was part of her family's legacy. Her father was chief, as were her grandpa and great-grandpa. She wasn't about to be the Gill that broke the cycle. But she knew she would be. At thirty-three, single, and childless, the chances of her passing on the family birthright were getting smaller and smaller every year. The legacy would no doubt stop with her.

Maggie steered her Crown Victoria cruiser onto East High and headed back toward town. She'd circled the plant a few times and found nothing out of place. She never did. She reached for her coffee, took a long sip, and momentarily thought about spending some time cleaning the clutter that had accumulated on her dash.

Her cell phone rang. Flipping it open, she checked the display. It was Gary. "Yeah, Gary. What is it?"

"Maggie, I'm at Woody Owen's house. You'd better get over here right away."

By the sound of Gary's voice and the quiver that vibrated through each word, she could tell something was wrong. Gary wasn't shaken easily. She asked the first, most obvious question that jumped into her mind. "Is it what I hope it's not?" Now *her* voice shivered.

There was a pause so long that Maggie thought she'd lost him.

"Yeah. I'd say so. I don't know what that loser Owen got himself into. Just get over here. OK?"

"I'm on my way."

When Maggie stopped in front of Woody's house, she took one look at Gary standing on the front porch—hat off, hair disheveled, face ashen and drawn—and knew the worst had happened. Gary liked to put on the tough-cop appearance, but Maggie knew there was more to him than that. Everyone had their weaknesses, their tender spots.

She got out of the cruiser, leaving her own hat on the passenger seat, shut the door, and walked across the small lawn to the porch. Built in the fifties during the population boom, Woody's house was a yellow, two-bedroom rancher with a wide concrete porch and bay window. It sat on a barren, one-acre lot backed by a small wooded area that connected with Yates Woods about a half-mile away. Beyond the woods was the five-hundred-acre farm owned by Josiah Walker.

"You OK?" Maggie asked Gary. "You look like you're gonna puke."

Gary didn't smile. His face was white and expressionless, like cold stone. "Already did. I'm OK."

Maggie reached for the doorknob of the storm door.

"I'd put something over your nose before you go in there," Gary said. "Unless you want to taste your breakfast again."

She reached in her pocket, pulled out a white handkerchief, and held it over her mouth and nose.

As soon as Maggie opened the door, she realized the handkerchief would do no good. The stench hit her like a truck and pushed her back outside. The house was saturated with the smell of death—stale blood and rot. Bile rose in her throat, and she had to swallow hard to keep from vomiting. She turned her head away from the open door, sucked in a deep breath of fresh air, put the handkerchief back over her mouth and nose, and stepped back inside.

The first couple breaths of the stale air in the house burned in Maggie's nostrils. She had to fight the bile pushing its way up her throat and the growing urge to gag.

At first glance it looked like a break-in. A lamp was broken on the floor, pictures were knocked off the wall, shards of glass scattered across the carpet. The TV tray was lying on its side, popcorn and chips crushed into the rug. She peered into the kitchen and noted the splintered back door, hanging by one hinge like someone—or some *thing*—very large had muscled through it.

But where was Woody? Where was his wheelchair? Maggie turned to Gary, who had followed her into the house, and gave him a questioning look.

He nodded, keeping his mouth clamped tight, and motioned toward the hallway.

Maggie stepped through the living room, carefully avoiding toppled furniture and broken glass.

At the far end of the hall, where it cornered and led to a bedroom and the bathroom, the wheelchair lay on its side.

But still no body.

Maggie walked down the hall and hesitated at the corner. Instinct told her what awaited. She didn't want to look, couldn't imagine the horror she would find. And yet she had to look; she was a cop, and this was part of her job. It was her duty.

She made one more attempt at swallowing the acid in her throat, rounded the corner, and hesitantly looked in the bathroom. Bile shot up her gullet like a rocket, and she doubled over and vomited on the carpet. Her stomach twisted and contracted, her nose burned, eyes blurred with tears. There, on the floor in the middle of the bathroom, was Woody—or what was left of him. The body lay face up, ripped open from pelvis to neck. That was all that registered in Maggie's mind before she turned away. That was all she needed to see. It was more than she needed to see.

She turned, stumbled, and fell into Gary, who was able to steady her again. "Nice welcome, huh?" he said, holding her by the shoulders.

She heard his voice, faint and muffled, but didn't focus on it. "I—I need to get out of here." It was all she could say. Her head was spinning, her stomach churning. A wave of bile burst from her throat.

Maggie staggered down the hallway, through the living room, and pushed through the door into the outside world. She ran to the edge of the porch and breathed in, filling her lungs with cold, crisp air, cleansing her nostrils of the putrid odor that burned in them. Oxygen rushed her brain, and she suddenly felt very light-headed. Bending over, she rested her hands on her knees and breathed in again. Long inhale, fill the lungs from the bottom up.

Gary was right beside her, his hand on her back. "Owen was never a pleasant sight, but I've seen him looking better. You OK?"

She nodded and sucked in another deep breath. The cool air burned in her nostrils, but it was a welcome burn, purifying. "You believe me now?"

Gary folded his arms and scanned the open field across the street. "Do I have a choice?" He was silent a moment, letting Maggie catch her breath.

"It gets weirder. I got an anonymous call this morning. Said, 'Woody Owen needs your help.' That was it. So I dropped by and knocked on the door. When there was no answer, I looked in the window and saw the living room. Looked like a bomb went off in there. My first thought was break-in, right? So I walked the perimeter and found the back door busted like you saw. That's when I searched the place and found *that* in the bathroom."

Maggie straightened her back and inhaled again. The smell from inside the house was wafting out onto the porch. "Shut that door, will you? Check and see if the neighbors saw or heard anything."

Gary swung the front door closed. "What do you want to do with Owen's...remains? We can't just leave 'em there. In a few days the whole place'll stink to high heaven. We'll have every scavenger in a five-mile radius showing up to check out the new raw bar."

Maggie pressed her lips together and held her hand over her nose and mouth. Could the smell get any worse? Unfortunately, she knew it could...and would. In a couple days, the neighbors would smell it in their homes. She brought both her palms to her forehead. Her head felt like an overinflated balloon that would at any second reach its maximum capacity and burst wide open. "I don't know. I wish this whole thing would just go away. Just...just get rid of it. Everything. For once, Gary, do something on your own!"

Gary stared at her but didn't say anything.

"Sorry," Maggie said. She glanced at the house; the smell was still there. "I'm sorry. Just take care of it, OK? And I don't want to talk about this again."

She turned to leave when Gary said, "It was that nut job, Bauer."

Maggie gave him a sideways look. "What was Stevie?"

"The caller."

"How do you know?"

"How could I not know? You know Bauer's voice when you hear it. Definitely one of a kind."

Maggie dropped her brow and pressed her lips together. "Let's pay Stevie a visit, see if he's in the talking mood."

Maggie slowly navigated her cruiser down the rutted dirt lane that led
back to Stevie's abode. Gary followed her lead in his cruiser. They parked
side by side in front of the trailer and climbed out of their cars.

Stevie's trailer looked different in the daylight—it looked worse. The
corrosion was more pronounced, a stark contrast to the dirty white and
faded green exterior. The blue tarp on the roof was held in place by fraying
rope that wrapped underneath the trailer and up the back. Torn garbage
bags, bulging with refuse, were piled waist high, and rotting food and soiled
containers were strewn around the small yard. Knee-high weeds grew up
around the trailer, hiding the skirting that was falling off in some places
and torn completely away in others. It wasn't much to look at, but Maggie
knew it was all Josiah could afford. After all, it was out of his own benevo-
lence that he'd taken Stevie in and raised him, then gave him a place of his
own. Josiah paid all the utilities and taxes on the trailer, drove Stevie to
doctor appointments, and brought him groceries every week. He was a real
saint, that Josiah, even if he was a little unusual himself.

Stevie was waiting for them at the front door. As they approached,
he opened the storm door and stepped outside onto the wooden steps,
shoved one hand in his pocket, and shifted his weight from leg to leg, back
and forth, back and forth.

"Howdy ho, Chief Maggie," he said, giving Maggie a quick smile and
flick of the wrist. His eyes darted from Maggie to Gary and back to Maggie
again. "What brings you to my neck of the woods?"

He looked nervous. But then again, Stevie always looked nervous around
other people. He suspected everyone of plotting some grand conspiracy to
have him arrested or kidnapped or "knocked off," as he called it. Everyone
was the enemy—except Maggie. She was his friend. That's what he called her.
She was the only one who protected him and chased away his pursuers.

"Hi, Stevie. Is it OK if we come in and talk?"

Stevie looked at Gary again and narrowed his eyes. "Does *he* have to
come too?"

Maggie looked back at Gary and nodded. "Uh, no. He'll stay out here
and wait for me."

Stevie straightened his back and clicked his heels together, motioning toward the opened doorway like a ritzy hotel doorman. "Then right this way."

When Maggie stepped inside Stevie's trailer, she quickly surveyed the kitchen area. Not much had changed since she last visited. The trash can was still overflowing with empty milk cartons and cat food cans. The place still reeked, and the clutter had only grown worse.

Stevie let the storm door slam shut behind him. "C'mon in and have a seat."

"That's OK," Maggie said, following him into the living room. "I can stand. I've been sitting in my car all morning."

Stevie sat in his recliner and smiled a big open grin at Maggie. His teeth, what were left of them, were yellow and black and rotting. "Question?"

"Stevie, I'm going to be straight with you. Officer Warren said you called him this morning and told him Woody Owen needed help. Is that true?"

Stevie's smile vanished like a puff of wind had kicked up and blew it away. He shifted nervously in his chair, his eyes darting about the room like he was following the path of some invisible leaves blown about by the same wind. His face twitched, and he raked his fingers through his shaggy brown hair. "Uh, no, I don't think so," he said, trying desperately to avoid eye contact with Maggie. "The good officer must be mistaken."

Maggie put her hands on her hips and looked down at Stevie like a mother would her rebellious child. "Don't lie to me, Stevie. I'm your friend, remember? I'm here to help you. I just want to know how you knew about Woody, that's all."

"I, uh, I, uh, don't know what you're talkin' about."

"Stevie." Maggie's voice was now stern and commanding. "How did you know Woody was hurt?"

Stevie pulled his knees to his chest and began to tremble. "I ain't seen nothin', Chief Maggie," he yelled. "And I ain't talkin' anymore 'bout it."

"OK, OK. Don't get all upset about it. Must have just been a misunderstanding, that's all." She knew he was lying. Stevie was one of the worst liars she'd ever seen, and she'd seen her fair share. But arguing with him would do no good; she knew that from experience. When Stevie had enough, he'd shut himself off and hide somewhere within himself that no one else could get to. "I'll just be leaving then."

She spun around to leave, stopped in the kitchen, and turned to face him again. "How's your cat, Stevie?"

Stevie peered at her from behind his knees. "What cat? I ain't got no cat."

"Well, then, you've really taken a liking to cat food, huh?" She glanced at the trash can.

He followed her look, and she knew she'd pushed a button.

"Have a good day, Stevie."

CHAPTER 17

T HE LIGHT IN Caleb's room was dim and soft, like the early morning glow just before the sun peeks above the horizon. But the dimness was not caused by the light of dawn but merely by the heavy curtains drawn over the large glass windows. Only a single shaft of sunlight snuck between the fabric, throwing an illuminated bar across Caleb's bed, but allowing enough residual light to cast the room in a muted blush.

Sometimes, Rosa would pull the curtains, turn off the lamp, and enjoy the peace and serenity of the dim room. It reminded her of Caleb's bedroom at home with only the soft shine of the night-light to polish the sharp edges. At times, sitting here next to her son's bed, she could almost convince herself that they *were* home and he *was* only sleeping, tired out after a full day of school, homework, and play. She told herself that in a matter of hours he would awaken, stretch, yawn, and pad downstairs, hair disheveled, pajamas wrinkled, face sheet-creased, and enjoy a breakfast of eggs and toast with her before she went to work and he to school.

Reality would then lift its misshapen head, and the room would lose its softness, its innocence, and become the sterile, clinical place it was, a place where her son lay in a coma, the victim of a heinous act of violence, with no guarantee that he would ever awaken.

Rosa leaned back in the chair and closed her eyes. The room was warm and quiet, as still as a summer morning. Beyond the closed door, only the occasional squeak of a sneaker or muted voice disrupted the calm.

A soft knock came at the door.

Rosa opened her eyes and said, "Come in. It's open."

The door opened, and a pudgy man with a round face, smallish eyes, upturned nose, and full lips crowned by a thin mustache entered the room. In one hand he carried a clipboard, the other he put over his heart. "Good afternoon, ma'am. I'm Roger Lipinski, your boy's physical therapist."

Roger's voice was high and nasally. Rosa guessed he was in his fifties.

"Hello, Roger. I'm Rosa, Caleb's mother."

Roger smiled, his eyes almost shutting, and bowed theatrically. "It's a sincere pleasure to meet you, ma'am." He then turned, placed the clipboard on the table, clicked the lamp on, and stood beside Caleb's bed. Placing a hand on the boy's forehead, he glanced at Rosa, then said, "Howdy, pardner, I'm Roger, your Wild West therapist, and I'm gonna get you moving a little, keep you nice and limber so when you wake up you can just hop outta this bed and jump on your horse and ride the range."

"He loves cowboys," Rosa said.

Roger nodded. "All boys love cowboys. There's something about riding a free range on the back of a horse that's mesmerizing to a boy. Do you talk to him? Tell him stories?"

Rosa smiled. "All the time. I talk, sing, pray, anything so he knows I'm here."

"He ever talk back?"

Perplexed, Rosa said, "Talk back? I didn't know—"

"Oh sure, some of 'em—sleepers, I call them—they talk like parrots. None of it makes sense, mostly just jumbled words. The poor family hangs on every word, but they don't mean anything of course, just words."

Rosa had never heard of such a thing. "No, he's never talked."

"Well, it's probably for the best. Like I said, the family usually takes it too seriously and sets themselves up for disappointment." He wrapped his hand around Caleb's heel and pressed his forearm against the ball of his foot, pushing the toes toward the knee. "This stretches the calf muscle, the gastrocnemius. For instance, Mr. Gutswald, down the hall. He's been in a com—I mean, asleep for six months. Last week he started talking. He's been saying, 'The sea tastes of chocolate,' over and over again. His family is going nuts trying to figure out what it means. But it doesn't mean anything. They said themselves, he never even liked the water, was scared to death—I'm sorry, bad choice of words—was scared witless—no—scared, just scared of it, and he's allergic to chocolate. Go figure."

—■—

The light was there again, piercing the darkness, hovering high overhead but slowly descending in a spiral movement. The orange glow stopped just above Caleb's head and filled the hole with warmth.

Suddenly, a tiny book was there, hovering before his face. It wasn't much of a book—no more than two inches by two inches and just a few crisp, worn pages.

"Take and eat," the voice said.

Eat?

"Eat the words, My child."

He reached for the book, snatched it out of the air, and placed it in his mouth. It tasted sweet, like honey, but quickly dissolved on his tongue.

"Speak for Us."

He didn't answer, but savored the sweet aftertaste of the strange book.

"Speak Our words."

I will. I'm Yours.

Releasing Caleb's foot, Roger rounded the bed and proceeded to stretch the opposite calf, the gastrocnemius. "Anyway," he continued in his nasally, high voice, "Mrs. Gutswald, who's there every day, has something against me. Maxie, one of the night nurses, said Mrs. G complained about my physique. Said I'm too outta shape to be a therapist. Can you believe that?"

He paused as if expecting an answer, but when Rosa opened her mouth to protest, he continued. "I thought that was pretty bold of her. Outta shape. I'm in shape. Round is a shape. I was just telling Maxie the other day—"

He stopped and let go of Caleb's foot. "Hey, Mrs. Saunders, look at this." He was pointing at Caleb's right hand.

Rosa stood and rounded the bed. Caleb's hand was twitching and jumping about, fingertips pressed together. "It did that this morning," she said. "It lasted a little while, then just stopped. The nurse, she said it was normal."

"Normal?" Roger said, his eyebrows rising as if operated by hydraulics. "I wouldn't say it's normal. There's nothing normal about a coma, being asleep." He reached for his clipboard, placed a pencil in Caleb's hand, and held the board under it. "I saw this article once about patients like Caleb here who actually created art. They put pens, pencils, even paintbrushes in their hands when this happened and watched to see what happened. The article said they even sold a bunch of the art, donated the proceeds to medicine."

In Caleb's hand, the pencil whispered across the paper, scribing circles and lines, angular markings and fluid scribbles.

When his hand finally stopped and his fingers relaxed, the pencil fell from his grip. Roger glanced at the sheet of paper, slipped it from the clipboard, and handed it to Rosa. "There you go. A Caleb Saunders masterpiece. Hold on to that; he'll want to see it when he wakes up. A real keepsake."

Rosa looked at the markings. At first glance they meant nothing, just a tangle of flowing lines and dashes and spirals. But the longer she looked, the more it started to make sense. She noticed the *E*s first, then an *h*, then an *s*.

Then whole words formed.

Then the picture cleared and it made perfect sense.

Did her eyes deceive her? Her heart skipped, and the soft hair on her nape prickled. Written behind the scribbles was a message, clear as a flashing neon sign.

Jo hold sEcrE.

Joe rushed to Hillside Hall after receiving a call from Rosa saying she needed him there right away. She wouldn't tell him why, even after he repeatedly tried to pry it out of her. She said he had to see it for himself.

When he walked into Caleb's room, he was fully expecting to see the boy awake and sitting up in bed, smiling at him with that crooked grin that made him look so much like his father.

But when Joe saw Rosa sitting in the chair that now seemed to be a permanent part of her anatomy, and Caleb lying in the same place he was the last time Joe was there, his heart deflated like a punctured balloon.

He looked at Rosa and twisted his face into confusion. "What's going on?"

Rosa smiled wide. She held up a sheet of paper. "This. Look at this. It is a miracle, Joe."

Joe took the paper and studied it. It looked like nothing more than a bunch of scribbles. Something a two-year-old may have done. "What am I looking at? Who did this?"

Rosa stood. "Caleb. Remember when you were here this morning and his hand was jumping about and we thought it was spasms?"

"Yeah." Joe looked at the paper again. Were the scribbles beginning to make sense now? Or was his mind getting so scrambled he was making sense where there was no sense to be made? He shook his head, trying to untangle the wires.

"Well, Roger had an idea to put a pen in his hand. And this is what he wrote. It's amazing. They were not spasms at all. My son was communicating, Joe. It's a miracle."

"Wait a minute." Joe was confused. "Slow everything down. Who's Roger?"

"Caleb's physical therapist."

"And you're saying Caleb *wrote* this...while he was in the coma?"

"He did. It's amazing, yes?"

Joe looked at the paper again. Now he could see letters and they formed words: *Jo hold sEcrE*. Incredible! But how could Caleb— "What does it mean?"

Rosa pointed at the words as she interpreted the writing for Joe. "Joe holds secret."

"What secret?" Joe was now really confused. His head felt like Jaws, the metal-mouthed villain of James Bond fame, was squeezing the noodle out of it with a garrote. What did Caleb's mauling have to do with him? What secret did he hold? Wait a minute! This came from a kid in a coma! Was it chance that random scribbles not only formed letters but words as well? A message?

Rosa said, "I was hoping you could tell me."

Joe rubbed his temples. Metal-mouth hadn't loosened any on the garrote. "Honestly, Rosa, I have no idea what this means. I don't have any secrets, especially regarding Caleb." He studied the paper closer. "This is incredible. How did he do this?"

Rosa put her hand on Joe's arm. "Joe, have you reconciled your differences with God yet? I know you don't like to talk about it, but I care about you, and I care about your walk with God."

Joe's defenses were suddenly raised. "What does that have to do with this?"

Rosa lifted her chin and looked Joe in the eyes; her hands fell to her side. "Please, Joe."

He sighed and dismantled the barricade around his heart. He knew his question had hurt her. "Rosa, I...I, uh—" He let his shoulders slump and head drop. She'd respected his privacy long enough; now it was time to come clean. She deserved that much. "I'm sorry. I haven't. I know He's there, and I know He wants me to come back to Him, but I just don't feel I'm ready. That's it. That's the only excuse I have."

"It's OK," Rosa said. Her voice was soft and soothing and put Joe at ease. "I understand. Just do one thing for me?"

Joe looked at her but didn't say anything.

"Do…" She paused and swallowed. "Do you remember when Caleb was born? You came to the hospital."

Memories of the day flooded Joe like a tsunami. He did visit the hospital. They were all so happy. Rosa's little room was jam-packed with friends and family, and they were all talking and laughing so much a nurse had to ask some of them to leave. After about an hour, everyone had left except Joe. It was just him, Rosa, Rick, and little Caleb. He remembered holding Caleb for the first time. He had never realized how heavy a newborn was—and how fragile. Holding his brother's son stirred something deep inside him, and he remembered well how the tears streamed down his cheeks as he watched innocence sleeping in his arms. Before he had left the room, Rick stopped him. "Joe, I want you to promise me something."

"Anything," he had said. *Anything*. His heart was right, but he should have known he could never deliver on *anything*.

"If anything happens to me, I want you to be like a father to Caleb. Take care of him. Teach him how to be a man, but more importantly, teach him how to be a man of God."

Now, back in the present with Rosa and the invisible can-crunching Jaws still trying to squeeze pasta out of his head, Joe's cheeks were once again wet with tears.

Anything.

He hadn't kept his promise. He would have been better off just keeping his big mouth shut.

Anything.

That word had haunted him for ten full years.

Rosa placed a hand on his cheek and turned his face toward hers. Her dark eyes were moist and filled with compassion and concern. "It's never too late, Joe. You can still keep your promise. Start with talking to God about this message. It has to be important, but I have no idea what it means. Pray about it, Joe, and God will shed some light on it for you. I know He will. Pray, Joe…for Caleb's sake."

Joe left without saying another word, but as he walked down the hallway leading back to the lobby, one thought echoed in his mind over and over again: *for Caleb's sake.*

CHAPTER 18

GERALD HELLER'S LIFE had taken a new direction.

A little over six months ago, his wife, June, discovered a lump in her right breast and immediately scheduled an appointment with her family doctor. Mammograms were ordered and a mass was detected, confirmed by subsequent ultrasounds. A biopsy followed, and after that the one word she'd dreaded from the moment she'd found the lump—*malignant*.

Her family doctor had referred her to a cancer specialist in Chambersburg who wanted to remove the mass. But June hadn't been thrilled about the idea of surgery, and with her husband Gerald's reluctant support, decided to pursue a natural remedy, but the shadow on the ultrasound only grew larger.

Weeks turned into months, and finally, after much encouragement from Gerald, she'd agreed to the surgery. It was scheduled for a Monday morning, and by Monday night Dr. Sinahara was delivering the bad news: the cancer was extremely aggressive and had metastasized to lungs and brain.

He gave her only months to live.

Gerald reached over and patted his wife's hand. They were determined to make the most of their remaining time together, but the impending fate hung over both of them like a storm cloud, darkening their mood and suffocating their happiness. He pressed on the accelerator, sending their Olds Cutlass speeding down Route 20 farther and farther away from Dark Hills. "How are you feeling?"

June shrugged and looked out the window. "OK, I guess." She turned her head and faced her husband. The whole ordeal had aged her considerably. Her face was gaunt, eyes sunken, skin parched. Lines had appeared around her eyes and mouth that weren't there just a few months ago. "I'm not sure I'm up for this, Gerry."

They were on their way to Gettysburg to enjoy an afternoon of shopping and roaming the battlefields, something they used to enjoy doing.

He knew what she meant. He knew the pain and depression she'd fought every day since the surgery. He patted her hand again. "You're alive now, babe. Let's just focus on that. We'll take it one day at a time."

She turned and looked out the window again. Gerald glanced at the cornstalks whizzing by on the other side of the glass. Life was so much like those graying stalks, flying by in a blur. He thought of his kids, all grown and raising their own families. How fast the time had flown—

Something bolted from the corn on the right side of the road, and Gerald had to yank the steering wheel to the right to avoid hitting it. The car swerved and fish-tailed, wheels screeching on the asphalt, before coming to a full stop.

"What are you doing?" June hollered, gripping the dashboard with both hands.

"Did you see it?" Gerald still had a white-knuckled death grip on the steering wheel. His face suddenly felt cold.

"See what?"

Gerald looked at June and gasped. "It just ran across the road. I almost hit it. Didn't you see it?"

June's face had drained of color, and she looked at Gerald with wide eyes. "See what?"

"The—the…lion."

"Lion? What lion? Honey, you're not making sense."

Gerald finally released the steering wheel. "On Sunday both the Chronisters and the Moyers said they saw a lion, then Harry Lippy shot up Mike Little's car before having a heart attack, said something about thinking it was a lion, then just a couple days ago, a cow was mauled and half-eaten on the Martin farm. And…I don't even want to think about that boy who was attacked last week. What if…June, there's a lion around here, and I almost hit it!"

June sat back in her seat, closed her eyes, and drew in a long breath. She pursed her lips and shook her head from side to side.

Gerald thumped the steering wheel with his palms. "That does it. I'm going to Maggie and demand she do something about this."

———

The TV was off; the lights were dim, curtains drawn. Joe sat back in his bed at the Dew-Drop Motel, room number 5, pillows propped up behind him. He stretched out his legs, rested his head against the headboard, and shut his eyes. It was just him and God now. He could do this...for Caleb's sake.

OK, God. It felt awkward talking to someone whom he'd ignored for the past ten years, knowing all along that *He* knew his every thought, every desire, every emotion. Who was he trying to kid? He obviously wasn't hiding anything. Maybe he was trying to punish God. Give Him the silent treatment. He didn't even know. It had been so long since he prayed he'd forgotten why he had stopped.

He tried again. *God, You know I haven't talked to You in some time. Too long, maybe. I don't deserve any favors from You. Or maybe it's the other way around. I don't know. This isn't about me, though. Rosa needs You, and so does Caleb.*

As he prayed, the words came easier. A familiar feeling began seeping into his heart, his soul. It was a feeling of oneness with God. Even though he'd abandoned talking to God, he knew he was still one of His children—that would never change.

As he talked honestly and openly with his Father, a warm sensation filled his body. Was it peace? He didn't know, but it was familiar...and comforting. Something he thought he could get used to again.

Please, God...Father...protect Caleb. Bring him out of this coma so Rosa can have her son back. And show me what this message means, if it means anything at all. If I'm hiding a secret that will help Caleb, show me what it is.

Joe paused to be still, be silent.

Suddenly, a voice filled his head. It was quiet, like the gentle whisper of wind through a willow, but so clear he almost opened his eyes to see if someone was in the room with him.

Nothing is secret that will not be revealed.

It was one of those Bible verses from his past, hidden somewhere in the convoluted twists and turns of his brain.

Joe smiled, his eyes still closed. *Thank You.* He didn't know what it meant. He didn't know what any of this meant, but with the voice came peace, definitely peace. This time there was no mistaking it.

Now he'd just have to wait.

—◆—

"Now, everybody just calm down." Officer Gary Warren stood behind the counter at the police station, both hands resting on the Formica top, and raised his voice above the murmur of the group of angry citizens who had poured into the small lobby. "Chief Gill will be here in a few minutes."

He picked up the phone and called Maggie's cell again.

"I'm on my way," she said. "I'll be there in about a minute; just try to keep everyone calm. Last thing we need is a riot breaking out."

Gary placed the phone back in its cradle and hooked his thumbs in his belt. He looked over the crowd of locals, pursed his lips, and sighed. He used to wonder what he was doing in this dead-end small town. Dark Hills wasn't exactly in need of a crime fighter. It needed a babysitter. Heck, in the past seven years, he'd only used his handcuffs four, maybe five times, and had never unholstered his gun, until Woody's the other day. The most action he'd seen in this hole-in-the-wall town was an occasional speeding ticket. He actually found himself longing for one—just one—young punk to cop an attitude with him, take a swing at him, anything that would warrant a little justified police force. After the navy, he'd entered the police academy with every intention of joining the force in Baltimore or Philadelphia. He even entertained thoughts of going across the country, maybe Vegas or LA. He wanted big-city action—homicide, burglary, car chases, hostage situations, stakeouts, maybe even hunting down some terrorists. He wanted to be where the action was, where the real crime fighting took place. But then Maggie talked him into spending a few years in Dark Hills. "Hone your skills, your instincts," she said, "then move on to a big city." Well, this recent string of events wasn't exactly big-city crime, but it was *something*; it was action, and it had his adrenaline charged. Maybe after this was all over he'd move on to a bigger—

The front door of the station opened.

Maggie burst through the door and the crowd hushed. "Good evening, everyone," she said, picking her way through the gathering of about twenty people.

She stepped behind the counter and surveyed the group. The Moyers were there, as were the Chronisters and the Hellers. Clark Martin was standing near the back, stroking his hairy chin. Mike and Bernadette Little were next to him. Others were there as well; no doubt they'd heard about the lion stories at Darlene's or McCormick's. Small towns...news travels quickly.

Maggie straightened her back and scanned the crowd. "What seems to be the problem here?"

"You know what the problem is, Chief," Gerald Heller said. He put his arm around June's waist. "This afternoon I almost hit a lion that ran in front of my car. And others here have seen it too."

"We saw it in our backyard," Mary Chronister said, her voice squeaking.

"So did we." Dick Moyer spoke up.

Clark Martin piped up next, his voice low and steady. "And you saw my cow, Chief. It all makes sense."

"We just want to know what you're doing about it," Gerald said. "We don't want to wake up some morning hearing about another child, or anyone, getting mauled...or worse."

"Now, now, settle down," Maggie said, holding up both hands for silence. "I'll have you all know I've already taken measures to look into the problem."

"Problem?" Mike Little said. "You call a rogue lion roaming our woods and fields a *problem*? You think bullet holes in my truck is a *problem*? That's quite an understatement, don't you think?"

That brought a roar from the small crowd. "Yeah!"

"It's more than a problem, Chief!"

"Someone's gonna get eaten!"

Maggie raised her voice and slapped the countertop. "Quiet! Now, I've contacted all the zoos in the area, and none of them are missing a lion. I've also contacted all the circuses that have been in the area or have passed through the area in the last year, and none of them are missing any lions. *If*, and I say *if*, there is a lion out there, we have no idea where it came from, but I assure you we're doing all we can to protect our citizens."

"Like what?" Clark's voice rose from the back of the lobby.

Maggie hesitated. "Like…like having both my officers, Wilt and Warren, patrolling the town and outskirts. Like contacting the proper authorities and notifying them of the sightings."

"Did you call the Game Commission?" Clark asked.

"As a matter of fact, Clark, I did. And I'll have you know it took a lot of convincing to get them to look in to the matter. They think we're all a little nuts down here. Look, you all have to believe me that we're doing all we can. I know what you all want, but I'm not about to let a bunch of hunters go traipsing around Dark Hills shooting at anything that moves, especially since we really don't know for sure what it is."

"Then I'll take my gun and hunt it myself," Clark hollered, his voice cutting through the murmur of the crowd.

Others in the room joined in. "Me too."

"I'll help ya, Clark."

"Count me in."

Maggie held both hands in the air and clapped them three times. "Now hold on. Hold on!" When the room had quieted, she continued. "Nobody's going to do any such thing. You all can leave your guns and macho attitudes at home and try to calm down. If I catch anyone hunting without a license, or hunting at all, for that matter, I'll haul you in, you hear? Look at yourselves, all ready to form some posse and go hunting *something*, and you don't even know what the something is."

"It's a lion!" someone yelled.

"Oh, really," Maggie said, resting her hands on her hips. "You're all so sure about that. Mary, what time was it when you thought you saw a lion in your yard?"

Mary looked around the room before answering. "I'm not sure, it was dawn."

"Was the sun up yet?"

"Well, no, not fully up. But I know what I saw."

"Really? What direction was it facing? Was it standing or sitting? Was it male or female? Did it have a mane? Some lions don't have manes, you know."

Mary looked around the lobby again, a hint of red touching her cheeks. "Well, I don't know all that. I—I didn't get that good a look at it before it was gone. I'm…I mean, I'm pretty sure it had a mane."

Maggie shot a glance at the Moyers. "How 'bout you, Dick, Betty? Did you get a clear look at it?"

They were standing in the middle of the crowd, no more than ten feet from the counter. Dick shot a furtive glance at Mary Chronister, then lifted his chin and said, "Sure did."

"You did, huh? And you were wearing your glasses?" Maggie knew for a fact that Dick and Betty didn't wear their glasses unless they left the house. She'd had that conversation with them before.

Dick shrugged. "Well, no. We only wear them when we go out."

Maggie held up a small placard that read, *DUI Doesn't Pay.* "Can you please remove your glasses and read this for everyone here?"

Dick slipped his glasses off his nose and squinted, Betty blushed, but neither of them could make out the words. They both shook their heads.

Maggie continued to make her point. "And, Gerald, you say it ran across the road, right in front of your car, right?"

"That's right," Gerald said, nodding emphatically.

"Did you notice if it was male or female? Did it have a mane?"

Gerald looked at June, then back at Maggie. "Well, no. It all happened so—"

"If you had to testify in court, to a judge and jury, swearing on the Holy Bible to tell the truth, that you were 100 percent sure what you saw and almost hit was a lion, would you be able to do it? *So help you God?*"

"I, uh—well, when you put it that way…" He paused and swallowed, his face bright red. "No. I suppose I wouldn't."

Lastly, Maggie looked to Clark Martin. "Clark, all you have is a dead cow. It could have been a bear or a pack of wild dogs. You know it, I know it, and everyone in here knows it. None of us can say for sure that it was a lion."

Clark offered no comment. He stood by the door, leaning against the wall, arms crossed, staring defiantly back at Maggie.

"People, I've taken every necessary measure I can with what we have. Now if you don't mind, I'm going to have to ask you all to clear the lobby. This meeting's over."

There was a hushed grumbling as the crowd made their way out of the station. When all had left, Clark Martin stood by the door and paused. He then turned to Maggie and said, "Chief, when someone dies, it's gonna be on your conscience. You know that, don't you?"

Maggie didn't answer. It was already on her conscience.

———

Later that evening, long after the sun had bid its final farewell and surrendered to the encroaching night, having left his car parked a quarter mile away on an empty stretch of road, Gary Warren crept through the darkness, stealing from moon shadow to moon shadow. Holding his breath, he entered Woody Owen's house through the back door and turned all four knobs on the stove as far as they would rotate to the left. The flameless ranges hissed. He then dialed the thermostat down to fifty-five degrees.

The house would fill with natural gas, and when the temperature inside dropped to fifty-five, which should happen sometime in the early morning hours while he was home fast asleep, the furnace would kick on, and then...well, Maggie said to take care of it, didn't she? It would be taken care of. By the time the fire department arrived, there would be nothing left of poor Woody or his house. An investigation would be done, and Bob Foster, the fire marshal, would conclude that it was a tragic accident caused by a gas leak.

After arriving home, Gary downed two beers and fell asleep on the sofa. At exactly 3:17 a.m., according to the clock on the DVD player, Andy called, informing him that Woody's house had exploded. The fire department was there now putting out the resulting inferno.

CHAPTER 19

AT NINE O'CLOCK in the morning, room 5 of the Dew-Drop Motel was still dark. The shades were drawn, lights were off, and Joe Saunders was just stirring out of a restless sleep. He forced his eyes open, rubbed the sleep from them, rolled over, and lifted his head to look at the clock—9:17. He then noticed he was still in his clothes from the previous day—must've fallen asleep while praying last night. With a grunt, he fell back into the pillow and allowed his heavy eyelids to close again.

He had dreamt a lot last night. Most of the images were now cloudy, some of Caleb, some of Rosa, some of Rick. Fortunately, none contained sharp-clawed little people with a thirst for blood. But one remained vivid in his mind's eye. He could still see the images flashing on the inside of his eyelids like an old silent movie reel. It was in black and white and seemed to happen in varying speeds—fast, then slow, then fast again.

Maggie was there, pinned to the gray leafy ground by two huge, blood-stained paws resting on her shoulders. There was fear in her eyes, heart-stopping fear. She was panicking, screaming, writhing, and thrashing, trying to free herself from the beast's hold. Then her eyes fell on him—Joe—and she began yelling his name, begging for help. He couldn't hear her, but her lips formed his name over and over again.

Her face was twisted and distorted by the fear, her lips dry and cracked and bleeding.

Joe ran to her, fighting off the branches and thickets that pulled at his flesh. His skin tore and ripped, but he felt no pain. He didn't care anyway; he had to get to Maggie. Finally, he made it to where she had been, but now she was gone.

Then his ears were opened, and he heard it—laughter. Not happy, jubilant laughter, as might be induced by a troupe of costumed poodles performing flips and somersaults at a circus, but mocking, tormenting howls of demented laughter. The kind produced by malevolent funhouse clowns just before the ax falls.

He looked around. Where was it coming from? What happened to Maggie? The laughter continued, growing in volume and intensity. It struck him then—it was Maggie laughing.

From his right, he felt something large and heavy brush against him. He spun around, but there was nothing, only darkness.

Joe began to panic. His heart raced; the hair on his nape bristled. He tried to move. He had to get out of there, but it was as if his feet were glued to the ground. He tried to yell, but no sound would rise out of his throat.

Suddenly, two glowing eyes appeared in the blackness, hovering in midair. They stared at Joe, bore holes right through him as if those huge paws had ripped him wide open, exposing his soul. He tried to move again, tried to lift his feet, but it was useless.

Funhouse Maggie, unseen, continued laughing, mocking.

The gleaming eyes jerked, and the beast lunged, its razor claws splayed, ready to tear him to shreds.

The room phone rang, and Joe jumped. His eyes flipped open like taut window blinds. His heart hammered in his chest, lungs heaved. Was it real? Was it a dream? He was in a fog.

The phone rang again.

He looked around the room. Everything was as it should be. The TV sat quietly. The curtains hung silently, motionless. No evil-grinned, ax-wielding clown lurked in the corner. All was as it had been when he fell asleep, except another day had expired. It was Thursday, five days since the attack.

The phone rang again. His cell was on the dresser, plugged into the wall socket recharging.

Joe drew in a deep breath and exhaled slowly, then reached for the receiver. "Hello?" His throat felt raspy and dry.

"Good morning, Joe. Did I wake you?" It was Rosa.

"Uh, yeah. I guess you did. But it's OK. I needed to get up anyway." He looked at the clock—9:43. "Wow. I overslept."

"Are you OK?"

He was still trying to climb out of his fog. "Um, yeah. Yes. I'm fine. I didn't sleep well, that's all. Had some bad dreams."

"Do you want to talk about it?"

"Uh, no. Not really. I'm fine…I am."

"OK. I was wondering if I could ask a favor of you."

"Sure. What is it?"

"I need to run some errands and was wondering if you could come sit with Caleb for a little while. I think it would do him good to hear your voice."

Joe didn't hesitate. He'd wanted to spend more time with Caleb anyway. "Sure. Just let me get showered and ready, and I'll be right over."

"Thanks. I'm going to leave now, so when you get here, just come in and pull up a chair. OK?"

"Got it."

There was a short pause on Rosa's end, then, "Joe, are you sure you're OK?"

"Yeah, I am. Really."

Stevie Bauer looked like a new man. His hair was neatly parted to one side, his face cleanly shaved. He wore a pressed pair of khakis and a pale blue button-down shirt. His fingernails were clean and trimmed, and his eyes sparkled.

Dress to impress, that's what Momma always told him. People judge a man by his clothes.

Stevie had awakened early and spent the better part of the morning preparing himself and ironing his clothes. He had to figure out how to use the iron Josiah had given him a few years back—he'd never used it before. But when he had dressed and groomed himself, he looked in the mirror and liked what he saw. *Dapper!* That was another one of Momma's words.

Stevie strolled up to the double glass doors of Hillside Hall, his shoulders back, chin up, sunglasses in place. It was a cool, sunny day, and he thought the shades would add nicely to his *dapper* outfit. A blue and tan canvas duffle bag dangled from his hand, swaying back and forth.

He stopped in front of the doors and waited for them to slide open. He glanced at his watch—10:38. "Sticks and stones," he muttered. "Sticks and stones."

———

Joe removed his sunglasses, leaned to his right, and looked at his reflection in the rearview mirror. He brushed a few loose strands of hair off his forehead and smiled at himself, checking his teeth for leftover granola. The clock on the dash read 10:39. He had made good time.

After hanging up from his conversation with Rosa, Joe had jumped in the shower and let the hot water run down over his head, face, and shoulders, slowly, gently, waking him up. The images of his dream, the sound of Maggie's laughter, the feeling of panic that had crept into his chest, eventually faded, becoming mere shadows, like figures in a fog.

He had tried to pray again too. He remembered he used to pray in the shower a lot, and the feeling of last night's prayer was still vaguely familiar. But the words hadn't come so easily this time.

As his mind cleared of the cobwebs from his restless sleep, it began to churn, like gears of an old car slowly creaking to life after years of sitting idle. Was the beast still at large? Would it attack again? And when? Where? Who? There had to be more Maggie could do. She was the police chief, for crying out loud. She had to have connections.

He had decided there in the shower that he would talk to her soon, pick her brain a bit, apply some pressure if needed.

———

Stevie waited until the glass doors slid open with a mechanical hum. He stepped inside the tile-floored breezeway, lifted the duffle bag, and patted it gently. Something inside moved and let out a low growl.

"Soon enough, little one," he whispered.

He walked across the lobby, trying to look confident and casual at the same time, his heels clicking on the tiled floor. Passing the receptionist's desk, he made eye contact with the young brunette behind the glass window, dipped his head slightly, smiled, and gave a little wave with his free hand.

She smiled and nodded in return.

Easy as pie. This was cool!

Stevie shoved his free hand in his pocket, pulled his shoulders back, and headed down a corridor marked *A Wing*.

As he clicked down the long hallway, he quickly read the names posted outside each door. Baublitz…Linford…Sanchez…Dubbs. The names went on and on, but none of them were familiar. When he reached the end of the corridor, he turned right and walked down a narrow hall that came to a door marked *B Wing*. He swung the door open and proceeded down the long hallway, reading off each name in his head.

Joe got out of his truck and squinted in the sunlight. There was a nasty glare reflecting off the gold-lettered *Hillside Hall* emblazoned across the stucco façade of the building. He shielded his eyes with his hand as he crossed the parking lot.

The dream he'd had about Maggie was the second such dream. The first was the one about Caleb tumbling over the cliff. And Caleb had been in trouble, hadn't he? So, was this most recent dream some kind of premonition? Joe tried to shove the thought aside. Ridiculous. Coincidence, that's all. But what if there *was* something to it? Did that mean Maggie was in trouble now too? And if it meant she was in trouble, did it also mean he was in trouble? He now wished the dream *had* contained Rattlesnake, the pint-sized self-cloaking outlaw. He would certainly be easier to handle than the mysterious beast.

The double glass doors hummed open and Joe entered, once again admiring the luxurious appearance of the lobby. It was not unlike a high-end hotel lobby, complete with brass trim and mahogany woodwork. Someone had spared no expense. He passed the receptionist, gave a wave and a smile, and proceeded down the hallway to B Wing.

Stevie stopped at the room with *Saunders* posted beside the door. He looked up and down the hallway. Nothing but rolling metal carts, an IV stand, and a plastic laundry bin. The coast was clear.

Lowering his knees to the floor, he set the duffle bag down and unzipped it. The sound of the zipper echoed off the bare walls and startled him. He looked around again.

The IV stand smiled back at him. A metal cart laughed.

Stevie giggled and tilted the bag sideways. Kitty crawled out and looked around. Stevie gently nudged the cat toward the open door leading to Caleb's room. "In there," he whispered, restraining his voice. He was so excited his hands trembled. He wanted nothing more than to bolt down that long corridor hollering and whooping until his face was blue.

Patience, Stevie, patience. That's what Momma would have said.

The cat growled and slinked into the quiet room without making a sound, its ears folded back, tail hanging low.

Seconds later, Joe rounded the corner and pushed through the doors leading to B Wing. A middle-aged nurse was just coming out of a room to his right; she nodded and gave a polite "hello," and he returned the pleasantry. He walked several feet farther and stopped in front of Caleb's room. The door was open, and the curtains across the large window were pulled back, allowing natural light to brighten the room.

Joe felt the sudden urge to say a quick prayer. Ten years ago the words would have come easy, flowing out of his heart and landing on the ears of God. He prayed a lot then; it was his lifeline.

While in the military, he had gotten involved with some guys that led him down the twisted path of alcohol abuse. Alcohol had become his god, his savior, the safe haven to which he ran when the pressures of life boiled up. But then, sitting in a jail cell for trying to rob a convenience store while he was intoxicated, he had found Jesus, or rather, Jesus had found him, broken, needy, and in dire need of a rescuer. That's when he fell in love with a new God, a new Savior. Life was different then; there was purpose and meaning. God was close, so close Joe had felt he could reach out and touch Him sometimes. Praying came easy.

But then Rick died, and all that changed. A wall was erected, a moat dug. The words didn't come so easy anymore...

He stood in the doorway for a full thirty seconds before deciding to enter without praying. Suddenly, from inside the room, he heard what sounded like silverware clinking on the floor. Was someone in there? A nurse, maybe? Or the physical therapist, What's-his-name? He entered the room and looked around. Nobody was there except Caleb, resting quietly, looking the same as he did the last time Joe saw him. A metal clamp lay on the floor beside the bed.

Joe looked in the bathroom. Nobody there either.

He reached down to pick up the clamp. When he stood, he started, let out a shout, and jumped back against the wall. "Oh, man!"

A tan tabby cat was crouched between Caleb's knees, ears laid back flat against its head. The cat hissed and eyed Joe, daring him to move.

It looked like the same cat that had used his head as a scratching post at the Yates house. Couldn't be, though. Never a cat lover, preferring a dog's humble outlook on life to the high-and-mighty divalike arrogance of a cat, Joe took the dare. "Get out of here," he shouted, and, executing his best John McEnroe backhand, minus the headband but with all the attitude, swatted it off the bed. "Go on, get outta here!"

The cat launched off the bedcovers and landed on its feet, tail puffed out like cotton candy, and bolted for the doorway. It turned left as it exited the room, slid along the newly waxed floor, and scrambled down the corridor.

Joe followed the now-humbled cat out and looked up and down the hall for a nurse. There was nobody but a duffle bag-toting man in a blue shirt hurrying the other way. The man pushed through the doors on the far end of the hall, and the cat slipped past him.

Joe shook his head and went back into the room. His pulse had spiked during the encounter but quickly resumed its normal rhythm. He pulled the maroon chair next to Caleb's bed and eased himself into it.

After a moment of silence, he said, "Well, buddy, it's just you and me here." It felt awkward talking to a sleeping boy.

<hr />

A familiar voice, deep, masculine, filtered through the darkness. It was muffled and distorted...but familiar.

Along with the voice came warmth and comfort. Memories tried to surface. Images smeared in Caleb's mind and fluttered past like pictures on a Rolodex. None of it made sense, none of it was recognizable...except the voice, now echoing in his ears, stirring up emotions, some familiar, some strangely foreign—joy, contentment, love, confusion, anger, hate.

And hope—he was not alone in the hole. Someone was there with him. But there was no face, only a voice from the past—a man's voice.

Caleb tried to call to him, but his mouth seemed to be fused shut, his jaw locked, tongue plastered to the roof of his mouth. He tried to move, but he was stuck fast in his hole. He had to warn the man about the beast. Surely he hadn't encountered it yet. *Oh, please, please, let the words come.*

Joe looked Caleb over. He looked like the same Caleb with the exception of the gauze bandage wrapped around his left arm from the shoulder to the hand. Only the fingers protruded, swollen and red like five little sausages. The doctor had told Rosa that the infection was gone and the skin grafts were healing nicely. Progress was slow, so any good news was always welcomed with wide smiles all around.

Joe felt Caleb's index finger. It was warm and smooth. He again regretted not spending more time with his nephew. The poor boy didn't have a father, and Joe was the next closest thing. He knew he was nothing like Rick, never would be, but was certainly better than nothing.

"Caleb, I promise you, when you get better, we'll do more things together. I'll take you camping and to baseball games. Maybe even take you hunting, if your mom agrees."

He swallowed hard. A lump had swelled in his throat, and he fought back tears. "I know your mom tells you about your dad all the time, but I never have." He paused. Memories of Rick swarmed into his mind, and a sudden rush of guilt and sorrow and remorse brought the tears to his eyes. "He was a great guy, you know. Much better person than me. He loved you and your mom and God. Those were the three most important things in his life. I was the big brother, but so many times I felt like he was. He was the responsible one, always looking out for me, trying to keep me on the straight and narrow."

He paused again and wiped the tears that were now falling from his eyes, blurring Caleb's form. "Boy, did I make it hard on him. I was useless, Caleb, an irresponsible wart that depended on his little brother for everything."

Joe wiped at the tears with both hands now. "Buddy, I never told you how sorry I am for your dad's death. He was looking out for me, as usual, and it got him killed."

The memory of that day rushed into Joe's mind. He had been out late trying his best to impress Kristy Rinaldi and totally forgot about the delivery he'd told his boss he would make. When he got home, well past midnight, he had checked his answering machine and found a message from Rosa saying Rick had been in an accident and was flown to the nearest shock trauma unit. He died three days following that message. Only later did Joe find out what had happened. His boss had called Rick and Rosa's house looking for him. He said if Joe didn't show up and make the delivery he would be fired. Rick had no idea where Joe was, so he volunteered to make the run for him. Twenty miles down the road the front axle snapped, and the twenty-year-old truck spun out of control. The vehicle veered off the road and tumbled down a steep embankment, rolling over and over. The driver of a car behind Rick had seen the whole thing unfold and went for help. With a crushed pelvis and fractured skull, Rick clung to life for three days before it all came to an end.

Joe laid his hand on Caleb's leg and wept. Years of grief and guilt poured out of him, spilling down his cheeks. "It should have been me. It should have been me. You'd still have your daddy. I'm sorry. I'm so sorry." His voice trailed off, and he sat there next to Caleb, holding the boy's leg, weeping until there were no more tears to shed.

Then he forced himself to pray...for Caleb's sake. *God, heal this boy. Rosa needs him, and I need him.*

That was it. That was all he wanted to say, all he could say.

CHAPTER 20

J OSIAH WALKER UNZIPPED his sleeping bag and sat on the edge of the sofa. The air in the living room was chilly. He had gotten into the routine of turning the thermostat down to sixty degrees at night. Three years ago, after his wife, Ginny, passed on, he began sleeping on the sofa, unable to cope with a bed empty of her warmth, her smell, her company. For months he wrestled with night sweats and had taken to turning the thermostat down to combat the waves of heat that rushed him during his restive nights. Both the sofa sleeping and the cool air were habits he now found hard to break. Besides, sleeping on the first floor saved his arthritic knees from climbing stairs.

He looked at his watch—2:15. Slipping from the sofa, he slid his feet into the worn slippers that waited on the braided carpet. He had heard the voice again—*His* voice. For the past three nights at exactly 2:15 he had heard the same voice, clear as day, just after awakening from a sound sleep. But this night was different; an image had accompanied the voice, an image of a dark-haired man sitting in a booth at Darlene's. His face was drawn and sad, maybe confused; Josiah couldn't tell exactly. He looked like he had a question to ask but couldn't remember what it was.

Josiah stood erect, feeling a pop in his lower back, and rubbed his arms. His knees were stiff, as usual, but that would diminish soon enough. He shuffled across the floor to the hallway and on into the kitchen. When he'd heard the voice before, he'd gotten up and fixed himself a nice cup of hot tea—Earl Grey was his favorite. Tonight would be no different.

Following Ginny's death, he'd thought about selling the farm and the old farmhouse but never seemed to get around to it. Bottom line was, he just didn't want to leave. There were too many memories on the farm, memories he didn't know how much longer his mind could maintain without the prompting of *being* there. Besides that, no one would want to buy the property. No one was moving *into* Dark Hills; it seemed everyone was moving *out*. Now, three years later and older, he sometimes wished he could sell it. It was getting to be too much for one old man to keep up with.

After pouring himself a steaming cup of Earl Grey, Josiah lit an oil lamp in the living room, lowered himself into a wingback chair, and propped his feet on a caned stool. In the quiet of the night, he preferred the soft glow of a flame over the harsh light of a bulb. This was his time to meditate, to focus on the voice and let its baritone echo resonate in his soul.

Tonight, though, he would focus not only on the voice but on the face too. The face of a man he knew only as "Joe."

Across town, Maggie was awake as well. She'd tossed and rolled and flipped and wrestled with sleep for three hours, trying to get comfortable. But comfort seemed like a distant memory tonight. She had lied to Joe, lied to the townsfolk, and lied to herself. So this was how it started, huh? This is what her great-grandpa wrestled with, her grandpa and her father as well. This was the Gill family lie, the Secret, as it had come to be known among those who knew.

As a child, she'd heard the stories passed around schoolyards, slumber parties, and, occasionally, from the mouth of her own grandpa, but thought they were just that—stories, the ramblings of a small town's over-active imagination. Her father never spoke of the tales, never mentioned the Secret, and never answered her questions about either. Would it get worse for her as it did for her great-grandpa? Would she end up like him? Controlled by the Secret? Consumed by it until it determined her every move, her every decision? She shuddered at the thought, and then swept it out of her mind.

No, it wouldn't.

She was different from Great-Grandpa and Grandpa and Dad. She wouldn't lie as they had. But she already had, hadn't she? It was happening again, just as it did decades ago, and she had no idea how to stop it. She was scared. Bob Cummings may very well be missing, or his attacker, the thing in the woods Joe claimed to have seen, may have been a rogue black bear or coyote. But Woody Owen's death was obvious. If she had any doubt at all, it was quickly dispelled the moment she walked into Woody's house. No animal native to Dark Hills would, or even could, do what she saw. Fear crept over her like a million black spiders, filling every safe place she ever ran to.

She thought about calling Joe, telling him everything, but the three green numbers on her clock reading 2:32 advised against it.

She needed to talk to someone, seek help, get advice, anything. And the only person she trusted outside her family was Joe. At least she thought she could trust him. She did at one time. Maybe she would call him in the morning. Then she remembered it *was* morning. She needed to get some sleep. She'd call him when she woke up.

It had turned out to be a dreary morning. The sky was slate with a ceiling of dense, low-hanging stratus clouds. The air was cold and heavy with a damp humidity, the kind that penetrated skin and sinew and settled in the bones. Joe had entered Darlene's intending to enjoy a quiet breakfast and read the morning paper. He had grabbed a booth in the corner, hoping for some privacy, and sat with his back to the door. The waitress, Sam, according to her nametag, had promised to be back "in a jiffy" with his food.

Joe snapped open the weekend edition of *USA Today* and scanned the headlines for anything that looked new and interesting. The president was getting slammed for some kind of alleged scandal again. Things in the Middle East were still looking grim. The Senate was fighting over some immigration bill. Nope. Nothing interesting. Well, at least nothing new.

Across the aisle, in the booth opposite his, he heard an elderly man with thick glasses and yellowing gray hair jawing to his wife about "that kid who got attacked." Apparently he thought that Maggie wasn't doing enough.

Sam appeared again, holding a dish full of pancakes and a small pitcher of syrup. "Here ya go," she said with a wide smile and a quick wink. "Enjoy."

"Thanks," Joe mumbled. He folded the paper and set it aside.

He was in the middle of cutting into the tall stack of pancakes when an elderly man walked up and stood beside his table.

Joe looked up and stared blankly at his visitor, not recognizing him. He was at least eighty, with gray eyes, deeply creviced face, thinning snow-white hair, and a mouth that curved downward like it was stuck in a permanent frown. His hands were tucked into the pockets of his baggy blue-jean overalls.

Either the old-timer was a bum looking for a handout or the American Hillbilly Society had adopted a new recruitment technique—*I ain't leavin' 'til you join up.* Maybe the army should take notes.

The man invited himself to sit across from Joe and crinkled his eyes in a smile. "Well, Joe, you're not exactly what I expected, but I'm sure I got the right guy." He had an amazingly clear voice for a man his age.

Joe blinked. Was this guy crazy? "Excuse me?"

The old man laughed, showing a mouth full of large, stained teeth. "Oh, I'm sorry. You don't even know who I am." He extended a large, weathered hand across the table. "Name's Josiah Walker, but my friends call me Jo."

An electric shock bolted up Joe's spine and buzzed along his skull. *Jo holds secret.* He stared at the man, unable to speak, holding his fork in midair like a pronged diving board.

Josiah pulled his hand away and laughed. "Well, I can tell by the way your mouth is hangin' open that I got the right guy. I s'pose this must seem awful strange to you, 'cause it is, you see. I've never had anything like this happen to me before."

Joe shut his mouth and just stared at the old-timer. What was he talking about?

"I said I've never had anything like this happen to me before."

Joe blinked. "Like—like what?"

"There you go. I've been hearin' a voice for the past few nights, and then last night I had a vision that accompanied the voice. It was you, Joe, sitting right in this here diner in this here booth looking just like you are now. It was a vision."

Great, the Hillbilly Society was a front for a nutty religious cult. Next thing, Uncle Jesse here would be pulling out a variety pack of Kool-Aid, asking Joe what flavor he fancied. "Really," Joe said, not trying to hide his skepticism. "And my voice too?"

Josiah laughed. "Oh, no. It was God's voice, all right. There was no doubt about that. No mistakin' the voice of the Lord."

Now Joe laughed. "God's voice. You mean God has been speaking to you at night." He went back to cutting his pancakes. "Maybe you were dreaming. Bad scrapple or something."

Josiah shook his head. "Nope. Woke up first, then heard the voice. Always happens at two-fifteen in the a.m."

Great, not only was the quiet breakfast ruined, but now he had to share it with Rev. Redneck here who thought he was some kind of prophet from the R2-D2 Gamma System. "Why two-fifteen? What's the significance of that?"

"Beats the buffalo chips outta me. Tell you the truth, I don't think there is any." Josiah folded his hands and looked Joe square in the eyes. "You don't believe me, do you?"

Joe put his fork down and sat back. "Kinda hard to, don't you think? I don't even know who you are. You come up to me, somehow knowing my name, and tell me God talks to you at night, or in the morning, whatever, and you saw my face in your dream. I'm still waiting for the Raelians-want-you pitch. And that's when I tell you to get lost."

"There will be no pitch, I promise, and it wasn't a dream," Josiah corrected. "It was a vision. There's a difference. And you do know me. I just introduced myself. By the way, what is your surname?"

Joe cocked one eyebrow. "You don't know? Didn't God tell you that?"

"No. He just said 'Joe.'"

"What did He tell you about me?"

"Well, now. I can't tell you that 'til you believe I actually heard from God."

"OK. I believe."

Josiah laughed. "No, you don't. I know you're one of His children, He told me that much, but like most Christians nowadays you've put God in a safe little box and told Him what He can and can't do, or should and shouldn't do." He leaned on the table with both elbows and narrowed his eyes at Joe. "Son, God can do anything He wants to do so long as He doesn't contradict Himself, and He's very careful not to do that. If I were you, I'd let Him out of that box you've got Him in and see what He'll do. Why can't God talk to someone? I mean, audibly like talk to someone. Even an uneducated, farm-raised old geezer like me? That's what you're thinkin', ain't it? Is He not capable of it?"

Joe didn't know how to answer. He remembered the voice he'd heard in the woods and while he prayed the other night. Sure, it wasn't audible, but it was real enough, and he knew it was God's. As much as he hated to admit it, the old farmer was actually making some sense. "Uh, sure He is."

"So why won't you believe? I mean, really believe?"

"Look, Mr. Walker—"

"Jo. I said my friends call me Jo. And I count you as a friend now."

"OK. Thanks. Look, Jo. I do believe that God can do anything. But like I said, I don't even know you. Yeah, I know your name, but I don't know anything else about you. For all I know, you could just be some loony jerking my chain."

Josiah sighed and shrugged. "Well, that's reasonable. At least you believe it is *possible* for someone to hear God's voice. Maybe this will help. He told me 'Joe needs answers.'"

Joe's heart thumped in his chest. Maybe this guy wasn't as cuckoo as he appeared. Maybe he really did hear God's voice. It was unbelievable, yes, and yet somehow, strangely, totally believable. Joe turned both hands palm up. "OK. You've got my attention."

"And you've got mine. What kinda answers do you need?"

Joe pushed his plate aside. He wasn't thinking about his appetite anymore. He wanted to see what kind of secrets this overalled hillbilly had to reveal. "My nephew was mauled by something a week ago and is in a coma. A few days ago his hand started spasming, and the physical therapist put a pencil in it. He wrote words. They said, 'Jo hold secre.' Jo holds secret. I thought it meant me, but now I think it means you. You hold the secret to something, but I'm not sure what."

Josiah furrowed his brow and lifted a hand to his chin. "That *is* interesting. A boy in a coma who I met but a couple times writes about a secret I hold. Let's talk some more, and maybe we'll stumble upon the answer. I'm assuming you don't live here in Dark Hills. What's happened since you've been here?"

Joe looked around and lowered his voice to almost a whisper. "Did you know Bob Cummings?"

Josiah looked surprised. "Did? I *do* know him. Went hunting with him a few times. Mainly whitetails. Good hunter too."

"Yeah, well, he and I went hunting the thing that mauled Caleb, and—" Joe swallowed. It was still hard to talk about Cummings's death. "He was killed. The beast, we didn't even know what it was...killed him."

The blood drained from Josiah's face, and it fell a pasty white. Joe definitely had his attention now.

"Joe, my boy," Josiah said, leaning back. He swallowed hard, his Adam's apple jerking up, then slowly falling. Looking around conspiratorially, he said, "I think I know the secret you're after. Has Maggie Gill looked into this?"

"That's just it. She won't lift a finger. Her officers went back to get Cummings's body and said it was gone. She wouldn't even admit he was dead; she wrote him up as *missing*. Had all kinds of excuses too."

"She won't be any help to you," Josiah said. He was as matter-of-fact as if he were commenting on his brand of denture adhesive.

"Why not?"

"First of all, let me say one thing, make the waters a little clearer, then you'll have to do some homework on your own. Her *officers* are her cousins. The Gills—"

"Wait a minute," Joe said, cutting Josiah off. "Cousins? I dated Maggie in high school and met most of her family. I never met them."

Josiah held up a hand. "Let me finish, and then you'll understand. Most people 'round here don't know the history of the Gills, and if they do, they chose to forget about it a long time ago. Makes life a whole lot easier. But I've been around long enough—seventy-eight years to be exact—and I can follow the family tree. Your secret, the secret I hold because I may be the only one in Dark Hills that knows the real story of the Gills, is the Gill family secret—*the* Secret. You know that since the early 1900s the police chief has always been a Gill?"

"Yes."

"You know why?"

Joe shrugged. "No."

"Because of the Secret. All the police officers have been Gills. Sure, they don't all claim the Gill name, but they all have Gill blood. Decades ago they stopped associating with one another on an extended family level so people wouldn't know who was part of the family and who wasn't. Gives them a sense of privacy. It's so twisted and convoluted now nobody even cares anymore. And they wouldn't know unless they kept track of the family tree."

"And you have?"

"Not intentionally. But I know who's who and what's what."

Joe lifted his eyebrows and leaned forward on the table. "So what's the secret?"

At that, Josiah laughed and held up a finger. "Not so fast, young man. It ain't that easy. I need to ask you something. You said you dated Maggie in high school. Was it serious?"

Joe sniffed. "What's that got to do with—"

Josiah held up a hand again, stopping Joe in his tracks. "Answer the question, then you'll get your own answers. Was it serious? Your relationship with Maggie."

"I guess. Yes. We were serious. Even talked about marriage."

"Do you still have romantic feelings for her?"

"Look Mr. Walker—Jo—I'm sure you think you're getting to the bottom of something, but I really don't see how my feelings for Maggie have anything to do with what almost killed Caleb and did kill Cummings."

Josiah sighed deeply and wrinkled his brow. "You're gonna have to trust me on this, Joe. It has everything to do with what you're about to find out. Just answer the question. And be straight with me."

Joe hesitated. His feelings for Maggie were none of this guy's business. He'd answered his first question, however absurd and irrelevant it was. What more did he want? Maybe he should tell him about all the other girls he'd been interested in too. Tell him about his hobbies, favorite book, color, waist size, boxers or briefs—a regular truth-or-dare session. But Josiah had done a good job of convincing him that he did indeed hold the secret Caleb wrote about. And now Joe's curiosity was aroused. If Walker held the secret, he wanted to find out what it was. He *had* to find out what it was. He nodded his head slowly. "Yeah, I guess on some levels I do."

"What do you mean *on some levels*? Either you do or you don't."

"Yes. I do...I think."

"Good enough. Then you'll have to do some homework first. The Gill secret goes back to the 1920s. I want you to read the Gills' side of the story first; then I'll tell you the truth."

"The truth? And you know what the truth is?"

A light twinkled in Josiah's eye, a spark of confidence. "I'm fairly certain I do."

"OK. What do I have to do?"

"Go to the library and look up the old *Dark Hills Gazette* from 1922. It was a weekly paper they printed up, and the library has all of them. Read 'em, and then we'll talk."

"Nineteen twenty-two. Read all of them? What am I looking for?"

"You'll know it when you see it."

"How can I reach you?"

Josiah pulled a napkin out of the chrome napkin holder, then a pen out of the front pocket of his overalls, and wrote a phone number on the napkin. "When you're done, call me."

———

Maggie Gill awoke at 8:30, still tired after six hours of restless sleep. Now she wrestled with the thought of whether to tell Joe about the family secret or not. Seeing him again and having him back in her life had brought feelings to the surface that she thought she'd long ago buried. His sudden appearance had changed everything. She now thought of the life they could have had together. They would be married, two or three kids in school, and busy running around to basketball games and school concerts. Maybe it could still happen. Sure, they'd be a little behind schedule— fifteen years behind—but it's not like it had never been done before. They could still be happily married. She could rid herself of the Gill legacy, the Secret, and Dark Hills forever. Live the rest of her life in peace.

She still had feelings for Joe; she knew that much. And she had been doing a lot of thinking about where her life was headed, and her conclusion was simple: in a word, nowhere. She was thirty-three, single, childless, living in a small town getting smaller, with no social life to speak of. She had no friends, her mother was dead, and her father, her dear father, was only a misshapen shadow of the man he once was.

Her father. Chief Elston Gill. As a child she thought her dad was a real-life Lone Ranger. He was her hero, her idol. She wanted to be just like him. Now, his pleading eyes and raspy voice came back to her: *Secret! Hide! No tell.* But she had to tell, didn't she? She couldn't bear this burden. Over the years she'd done some of her own research and learned more and more of the family secret. The Secret that was protected by the legacy. Gill blood had enforced the law in Dark Hills for the last century. It was what her dad so desperately wanted to preserve. It was his legacy, his father's legacy, and *his* father's legacy. And now it was her legacy.

But she could trust Joe. She knew she could. She had to. She was tired of lying.

She would call him and ease into it, see how he responded before fully disclosing her family's past.

Picking up the phone, Maggie punched in the number for Joe's cell phone.

The phone rang.

But how could she ever explain all that had happened? Simple, she wouldn't. But that would be protecting the Secret. And she wanted to rid herself of the Secret. Or did she? After all, it was part of her family history. Part of who she was, imprinted on her genetic makeup. But if she and Joe were ever going to have an honest relationship, she'd have to be just that, honest.

Again, her dad's voice was there: *Promise, Magpie.*

And she had. "OK. I promise." That's what she'd said. And she had meant it.

The phone rang three more times before Joe's prerecorded voice came on instructing her to leave a message.

Maggie slammed the phone into its cradle. *Dumb idea, Maggie. You promised Dad. Joe would never believe you anyway.* And even if he did, how could anyone love a crooked cop who lied to protect her family legacy? No. It would never work. Dad was right. Protect the Secret. Protect it at all costs.

CHAPTER 21

THE MEETING WASN'T exactly a meeting of the minds. No one claimed it was. It was more a meeting of the wills. Clark Martin had organized an "emergency" meeting to discuss with some of the men of Dark Hills what they would do to rid themselves of the beast stalking their town. Someone had to take action, and Clark saw himself as the only someone willing to do it.

Fifteen were invited. Three showed up. Four total. It seemed after the gathering at the police station, the witnesses had lost some of their credibility around town. *Well,* Clark had thought, *they'll believe us when we march through town with a lion carcass in our pickup.*

The men had gathered at Clark's farmhouse. Besides Clark, there was Mike Little, Gerald Heller, and Dick Moyer—the Fearless Four. Not exactly what Clark had hoped for. Not what any of them had hoped for. But it would do. It would have to do. It would only take one shot anyway, right?

"Thanks for comin', guys," Clark said, caressing the stock of his pump-action shotgun like it was the family pet as he sat on a wooden chair. He stood and eyed the three men in his living room. Mike Little, dressed in full military camo, was impatiently shifting his weight in the middle of the room. Gerald Heller was wearing a camo jacket and hat and stood by the door. Dick Moyer, clad in a tree bark camo jumpsuit, was seated on the sofa. "I guess you know why I called this here meetin'. It's time somebody takes action and does sumptin' about that beast that's out there. If we sit around on our *behinds* like Chief is doin', people are gonna start dyin'. I hear the Saunders boy is hanging on, but he coulda just as easily been…well, you know. We don't want anyone else…look, somebody's gotta protect this town, *our* town, and it looks like the job has fallen on us."

"I say we go now," Mike Little said. He was a red-cheeked, fiery young mill worker always in the mood for a good fight. Down at McCormick's he'd gotten quite a reputation. Some of the guys had given him the name "Sparky" because of his short fuse. "We're only wasting time sitting around here talking about it." He looked around the room. The redness in his cheeks was spreading down his neck. "And it looks to me like we all came with the same thing in mind. Let's go get us a lion."

"Now hold on," Dick said. He stood up and ran his palm over his head. "Let's not go rushing into this. There's a few things we need to understand. First, we'll be breaking the law. Chief said no one was to hunt this thing, not to mention the fact that we'll be trespassing on Walker's land. We all need to make sure we're ready for the consequences if we get caught. Second, remember what it is we're hunting. This is a lion we're talking about, not some Bambi hopping around in the woods. This is a killer in its own right. A hunter. And third, by my count and expectation"—he looked around at each man—"we're a little short-manned. I think all of us were expecting a few more guns. Now, I'm ready and willing to go with what we have, but I want to make sure we all understand we go in as a team, we stick together, we cover for each other. No solo jobs out there. No heroes."

Clark looked at Mike Little as Dick finished. If anyone was prone to play hero and go it alone, it would be Mike. Fortunately, the younger man nodded in agreement.

Clark cleared his throat and rubbed the stock of his gun. "Dick's right. We gotta stick together. There's only four of us and"—he looked at Dick and Gerald—"three of us are past our prime. You guys up to this?"

Gerald nodded. "I know what I saw. I don't care what Maggie tries to make it seem like. I saw a lion, plain as day."

Dick nodded once without saying another word.

"Well, then," Clark said, a smile stretching across his face. "What are we waitin' for? Let's move out."

Minutes later Clark eased his dual-cab Ford pickup off Pheasant Run Road and ground it to a halt in the loose gravel along the shoulder. To his right was an open field that had lain fallow for the season and rose in a gradual slope for about four hundred yards before bumping up against Yates Woods. It was the same field that bordered the Chronisters' and Moyers' backyards a quarter mile away.

All four men swung open their doors and stepped out. They all met in front of the truck, weapons in hand, and Clark looked up at the gray sky.

Some clouds were starting to part, and it looked as though the sun would peek through any minute. It might turn out to be a nice day, after all.

A nice day for a kill.

"OK, gents," Clark said. He turned his head and spit a wad of black juice on the gravel. "This is it. We'll head through the field here and enter the woods over yonder. That beast has got to be in there somewheres."

He studied the tree line for several seconds before looking at the three other men. "Keep your eyes peeled, you hear? And we stick together."

A palpable tension had settled on the small group. The others firmed their jaws and silently nodded in agreement.

"Men," Clark said, "remember, we're doin' this for the good of our town, our people. It's kill or be killed. That simple."

They hadn't walked twenty yards when a *wooup-wooup* pierced the morning stillness. The men froze, then turned in time to see Maggie's cruiser skidding to a stop behind Clark's truck.

Clark slumped his shoulders and cursed. To his left, Mike kicked a wad of dirt and cursed loudly, and to his right, Gerald and Dick leaned on their guns, wagging their heads.

Maggie climbed out of her car and stood along the side of the road, hands on her hips. She tilted her head to the left. "Morning, fellas. What brings you out here on this fine day?"

"You know what we're doin'," Clark yelled. "We're doin' *your* job."

Maggie smiled, not that she was humored at all by the four's brazen disregard for her orders, but simply to hide the anger that had boiled up inside her. "I'm doing my job too, Clark. I'm protecting you. You go in there"—she nodded toward the woods—"and chances are, not all of you will be going home tonight."

"We all know the chance we're taking," Mike said. "It's for the good a'the whole town. Maybe you should think about that."

"Well, unfortunately for you, I'm the one who calls the shots around here. So let's go. Party's over. Everyone go home."

The four didn't budge. They stood their ground and eyed Maggie like a pocket of outlaws from some old western movie.

Maggie waved them in. "I said let's go. Come on, guys. Go home and cool off."

Still nothing. Only firmed jaws, clenched fists, and stares of defiance.

Maggie was growing impatient. "Guys, I really don't want to have to arrest anyone over this. Now come on. Dick, Gerald, what would your wives say if they knew you were doing this? Or if they had to come down to the station to bail you out? It's not worth it. Gerald, think about it; is this what you want? For June to have to deal with? Come on. Let's go."

Clark snarled his upper lip. His eyes were like flint behind those bushy eyebrows. "Chief, it's gonna take more than empty threats to stop me. You're gonna have to shoot me."

He shouldered his gun and turned to head for the woods.

"The same goes for me," Mike said, and followed on Clark's heels.

Dick and Gerald stayed where they were, bolted to the ground. Dick made a quick glance at Clark, then back at Maggie.

"Clark, Mike, stop right now." Maggie was doing her best to remain calm, but the situation was quickly spiraling out of control. She grabbed her radio and called for backup. Gary would be there in minutes. Then she quickly surveyed the situation. Gerald and Dick were caving; she could see the doubt in their eyes. They wouldn't be a problem. Clark and Mike were a different story. They were approximately twenty-five yards away now. Clark shouldered a pump-action 12-gauge shotgun. Mike cradled what looked like a .30–06 in the crook of his left elbow. She had to stand firm. For her safety and theirs.

"Guys, stop now or I'm gonna shoot." Maggie heard herself say the words but didn't believe them herself. She could never shoot Clark Martin or Mike Little. Yes, they were armed and ignoring her order, but they were *her* people, the people she'd sworn to protect. But her anger had gotten the better of her, and their defiance had pushed her over the edge. And lately, that edge wasn't so far away. Whether she would actually shoot them or not, she didn't know.

But she had an eerie feeling she was about to find out.

When they ignored her threat, she slipped her Glock out of her holster and leveled it on Clark's back. Time seemed to stand still. A hawk screeched in the distance. "Clark Martin, stop where you are or I'll shoot."

Stop, Clark. For heaven's sake, stop!

In her peripheral vision, Maggie saw Dick nudge Gerald in the side. "I'm done," he said, and headed toward Maggie.

Gerald looked back at Clark, then hustled to catch up with Dick.

"Clark! Mike! Darn it, guys. Stop now!" Maggie said. Her arms were shaking, and her breathing was rapid. If they didn't stop she'd have to—

Clark stopped and turned around. "Maggie Gill," he hollered. He and Mike now stood about thirty-five yards away from Maggie. "Are you really gonna shoot me? 'Cause if you are, do it now and shoot me in the chest. Don't shoot me in the back like some kinda yella coward. But either way, you're gonna have to shoot me 'cause I'm goin' in those woods, and I'm gonna kill that lion." He looked at Mike, who nodded in agreement. Both men faced Maggie and stood perfectly still, drilling her with narrowed eyes.

It was a dare, Maggie knew. They were testing her, calling her bluff. This was a showdown, western style. She refused to back down. Not now. No way. She lowered her pistol a half inch, moved it a quarter inch to the left, and squeezed the trigger. A loud crack sliced through the air. The handgun kicked back against Maggie's arm, and a puff of dirt exploded not five inches from Clark's right foot.

Clark flinched and took a quick step to the left. He looked at the ground where the bullet had hit, then at Maggie. His eyes were wide in obvious disbelief.

Mike shifted his weight back and forth—right, left, right, left—and clenched his free fist. He glanced at the woods behind him.

"Don't even think about it, Mike," Maggie hollered. A trail of sweat broke from under her cap and pooled in her left eyebrow.

Mike looked at the woods again and motioned to his left.

Maggie shifted the pistol an inch to the right and squeezed the trigger again. Another crack, another kick, another puff of dirt, this time within inches of Mike's left foot.

Now Mike flinched and took one step to his right so he and Clark were now side by side, shoulders touching.

"Now," Maggie said, keeping her pistol at an arm's length, pointed at the ground in front of Clark and Mike, "do as I say and get back here." Her voice was like hard, cold, edgy steel.

Clark eyed Maggie for a long time before a smile parted his lips. "You won't shoot me. You ain't got it in you."

Just then, Gary's cruiser appeared and skidded to a stop; the front tires jutted into the field. Gary swung the door open and jumped out. Andy climbed out of the passenger seat, dressed in street clothes. Both were double-clutching their Glocks at arm's length by the time they reached Maggie.

"Clark Martin and Mike Little," Gary hollered, using his *don't-mess-with-me* voice and pointing his pistol at Clark, "you are under arrest. Lay your weapons down and put your hands behind your head."

Neither Clark nor Mike moved.

"Do it now!" Gary barked, his voice deep and commanding.

Finally, after a long, tense pause, Clark cursed and let his shotgun fall to the ground. Mike did the same. The showdown was over.

Maggie took a deep breath and lowered her pistol. Her hands were trembling, and the emotional release brought tears to her eyes. She saw Gary and Andy rush Mike and Clark and handcuff them. She heard the hollers, the curses, the Miranda rights, but her body felt numb. The hawk screeched again in the distance. She had almost shot Clark Martin. And over what? She was losing control. She was losing her mind.

"Chief?" It was Gerald Heller, standing next to her, his hand on her shoulder. She turned her head toward him.

"Are you OK?"

She blinked and swallowed hard, dashing a stray tear that had slipped from her eye. "Yeah, I'm fine." She sniffed and forced a smile. "Thanks, Gerald."

Gerald patted her shoulder. "I'm sorry, Chief. I don't know what came over me. I shouldn't have been out here."

Maggie drew in a deep breath, clearing her head. Gary and Andy were walking Clark and Mike back to the cruiser. Dick was sitting on the ground, his head in his hands. "It's OK. I know we've all been under a lot of stress lately. I'll give you and Dick a lift home."

CHAPTER 22

J OE STEERED INTO one of the five parking spots next to the Dark Hills Public Library, shut off the engine, and got out of his truck. The building really wasn't much of a library. It was located in an old house, one of the oldest in town, and shared the building with the historical society. The century-old building was a two-story, gray, stone colonial that sat atop a small green slope midway down West High Street and, like most of the homes in Dark Hills, was in desperate need of repair. The blue paint on the windows and front door was faded and peeling from baking in the sun for the past century. The shutters dangled from the window frames like autumn leaves ready to release their grip and blow away. Some clung to one hinge; others sagged and drooped, submitting to the forces of gravity. The roof was the worst, though. Decades ago, the old slate had been replaced with shingles, and now the shingles were at the end of their lifespan. Some flapped in the breeze, some curled like burnt paper, and some hung on by one nail, dangling precariously. Over the years, the foundation had shifted, giving the house an odd shape, almost as if the whole structure was frowning, begging to be renovated.

The building looked the same as it did fifteen years ago. As a kid it had reminded Joe of a haunted house where ghouls and specters hid in every shadow, waiting for the unsuspecting bookworm to stumble upon them. Being no bookworm and therefore avoiding the library like an eight-foot ogre with an appetite for amphibians, he'd considered himself safe.

Joe rounded the house on the narrow concrete walkway and stepped onto the wood-plank porch. The porch moaned under his weight, and more than one board sagged when he stepped on it. Rotted through and through. He jiggled the brass doorknob—which was loose—and pushed open the door, half expecting said giant ogre in platform boots to welcome him and offer a snack of newt's eyes and salamander toes.

Thankful the library housed no super-sized fiend, he entered and looked around. The interior was not much better than the dilapidated exterior. The wide-planked, pine floorboards were rough and gray; the walls were an odd off-white, muted by years of dust and road dirt that had made its way through the front door and open windows in the summer; and the plaster ceiling was cracked in so many places it was beginning to look like a road map.

The downstairs housed the library. There was a desk to the left, a small wooden table with three uncomfortable-looking wooden chairs to the right, and the rest of the main room was occupied by overstuffed, dusty bookcases arranged in narrow aisles.

There were no smoke alarms, at least not any in sight, no emergency lights, no exit signs, no overhead sprinklers, and no visible fire extinguisher. A building inspector would find himself in dire need of a Valium within seconds of beginning his examination.

The floor creaked as Joe walked across it, the pine boards alerting any other occupants that someone had entered the old wreck.

An elderly woman with gray hair pulled back in a tight bun poked her head around the corner of one of the bookshelves and tucked her chin at Joe. "Morning."

"Good morning," Joe said.

"You need any help just let me know." She smiled and held Joe's gaze for a moment.

"Thanks. I do need some help, actually."

The woman stepped out from the aisle. She was short and round and wore a white dress with little blue flowers, thick nylons, and black leather shoes. Round wire-rimmed glasses sat nicely on her nose and partially hid a pair of thin gray eyebrows. "What can I do?"

"I need all the copies of the *Dark Hills Gazette* from 1922."

The woman dipped her head and peered over the rims of her glasses at Joe. "They're upstairs in the historical society. I'll go fetch 'em." She turned and disappeared behind a wall that hid the staircase ascending upstairs.

Joe looked around while Library Lady *fetched* the papers. He could hear her walking around on the second floor. Every footstep sounded like the floor would give way. He imagined her crashing through the floorboards and plaster, landing in his arms, toppling both of them to the floor.

Moments later, the woman appeared toting a large green cardboard binder in both hands. "Here you go, 1920 to 1929," she said, deep creases forming around her eyes as she smiled. She handed Joe the binder as if it were the Gutenberg Bible and stood there staring at him for several seconds. "Are you a reporter?"

"No, not exactly," Joe said. "Just doing some research on the history of the town."

She raised her eyebrows. "Do you live here in town?"

"Used to," Joe said. "I grew up here but moved away after high school." He didn't say any more, hoping she'd get the hint that he wasn't there for conversation. He just wanted the newspapers, thank you.

Apparently, she got the hint. "Oh. Well, if you need anything else, just give a holler."

He said he would.

Joe seated himself in one of the wooden chairs—and yes, they were uncomfortable—placed the binder on the table in front of him, and cracked it open. The *Dark Hills Gazette* was hardly a newspaper. Each weekly edition was four eighteen-by-twelve pages. There were no photos, and the typeset was clumsy and unprofessional. Obviously, the paper was a homegrown tomato that didn't get much financial support from the town.

Across the top of the front page of each edition, in large bold font, were the words *Dark Hills Gazette: A Weekly Newspaper Serving the People of Dark Hills, Pa.* In the upper left corner, in much smaller font, were the date, volume, and issue numbers, and in the upper right was the price— two cents. The paper was distributed on Sundays and contained the news of the previous week.

Joe fanned through the crisp, brittle pages and turned back to the January 3, 1922 edition. It was volume 3, issue 1. He scanned the headlines but saw nothing of much interest. He flipped through week after week but headline after headline was nothing more than the mundane news of a small hick town. So-and-so was marrying Nobody Special; what a wonderful wedding it will be. Harry Someone was awarded such and such award; how splendid. The spring ball will be held at the home of Joe You-Know-Who. A new building was built on this street; a new shop is going in on that street. Growing up, Joe had never thought Dark Hills a dull town; now he realized just how dull it was and always had been. Is this what Josiah wanted him to see? How ordinary and run-of-the-mill this tired little town was?

He flipped the page to the September 10 edition, and the first headline caught his attention, tightening the skin behind his ears: *Local Boy Killed in Bear Attack*. He ran his fingers over the black, faded words as he read.

Joseph Kline, 19, was found dead in Yates Woods as a result of a bear attack, Monday, September 4.

His body, which had been terribly mauled by the bear, was found by Mr. Philip Yates. The funeral was held on Wednesday with family and friends in attendance.

Chief Gill said there were no witnesses, but from the condition of the body, the culprit was most likely a large black bear.

A hunting party of five men was dispatched to kill the beast, but it could not be located.

The attack was the first of its kind in Dark Hills' history.

So sleepytown finally woke up and found itself in a nightmare. An oddly brief account, though.

Joe turned to the next edition—September 17. His heart banged against his ribs, and heat crept down the back of his neck. *Local Man Mauled by Bear*. He looked around. Library Lady was nowhere to be found. Probably had her nose in a book somewhere. He dropped his finger to the page and traced the words.

Mr. Roger Bixby, 45, was mauled by a black bear Wednesday, September 13. The bear apparently attacked him while he was gardening in his yard on Jackson Street.

Mr. Bixby's neighbor, Mrs. Audrey Martin, found his body late Wednesday night and reported the incident. There were no eyewitnesses to the attack.

Mr. Bixby was an employee of Dark Hills Paper Company and has no known relatives. The funeral was held on Thursday.

Chief Gill said this was the second mauling in as many weeks, and residents are being urged to practice caution while outdoors.

So Yogi Bear had gone postal and was roaming the town mauling people to death. Interesting. Unfortunately, the accounts in Dark Hills's little newspaper didn't shed much light on the mystery.

Joe flipped to the next week—September 24. No major headlines on the front page. He turned to page two and ran his eyes through the headlines. There it was. *Two Killed in Animal Attacks.* The subject matter was beginning to seem redundant.

> Mr. Max Gregory, 51, and Mr. Alvin Billet, 35, were victims of more animal attacks.
>
> Mr. Gregory was found dead in his home on Sunday, September 17. Chief Gill said it could not be determined if the incident was another bear attack or not. He would not comment on the condition of the body.
>
> Mr. Gregory was an employee of the Dark Hills Paper Company and has no living relatives. His funeral was held on Monday.
>
> Mr. Alvin Billet was reported missing on Monday, September 18, by his mother, Mrs. June Billet. Two days later his body was found, apparently mauled by an animal, in the field behind their Fulton Street home. The field is owned by the Rev. John Claybaugh.
>
> Chief Gill said an investigation is underway.
>
> Mr. Billet is survived by his mother only. His funeral was held on Friday.

So now it's just an *animal attack.* What happened to Yogi? Why no comment on the condition of Gregory's body? Chief Gill is suddenly getting clammy.

Joe turned to the next edition, fully expecting to see another headline announcing yet another *animal attack.* Instead he found only the same old mundane news. No attacks. No reports. No updates. Nothing. Everything, it seemed, was back to normal.

Until the following week—October 8. The headline jumped out at him like a jack-in-the-box: *Member of Hunting Party Mauled by Mystery Animal.*

An odd headline. He quickly read the article.

Mr. Leonard Toomey, 44, was the fifth victim in a string of animal maulings resulting in death. Mr. Toomey was a member of Chief Gill's hunting party dispatched to investigate what nature of animal was responsible for the previous four attacks.

On Saturday, October 7, the party was surveying Yates Woods when, according to a member of the party who wished to remain anonymous, a loud roar was heard, followed by screams from Mr. Toomey. When the other members of the party finally reached Mr. Toomey, he was dead and badly mauled.

Chief Gill had no further comment on the tragedy.

Mr. Toomey was an employee of the Dark Hills Paper Company and is survived by one daughter living out of state. His funeral is scheduled for Monday, October 9.

There will be a town meeting held by Chief Gill in Adams Hall on Wednesday night, October 11, to discuss precautions residents should take.

Why did the witness wish to remain anonymous? Why did Gill pull a *no comment*? A roar was heard? Joe's heart thumped louder now, and he was certain Library Lady could hear it. No, she was upstairs. He could hear her heavy footsteps pounding on the floor above him, threatening to fall into his lap.

He turned to the next edition. There were no mauling stories, but one headline did stand out among the other humdrum ones: *Gazette Reporter Dies in Tragic Accident*. He couldn't help but read on.

Mr. Luke Gibbs, reporter for the *Gazette* who had been investigating the animal maulings, died October 12 as a result of injuries he suffered from a fall down a flight of stairs the previous day. According to Chief Gill, Mr. Gibbs was alone in his home on Poplar Street when he slipped and fell headlong down a flight of stairs, suffering a broken neck and multiple other broken bones.

Mr. Gibbs was 25 and served Dark Hills as a *Gazette* reporter for two years. He is survived by his mother and father. The funeral was held on Saturday.

Gill was singing like a songbird after that one. How did he know Gibbs was home alone? How did he know he slipped and fell *headlong*? There was something very fishy about the article, and Joe was starting to get some idea about the Gill family secret.

He turned to the next edition, but again, nothing was out of the ordinary, just small town life as usual. It was in the October 29 edition that his heart nearly stopped. Buried at the bottom of page two was a short article bearing the headline, *House Fire Claims One Life*. Things were getting ugly now.

The home of Mr. Philip Yates, 76, was destroyed by fire Friday, October 28. Chief Gill said the blaze started in the chimney of the home around 10:30 Friday night. The alarm was sounded, and eight members of the Dark Hills Volunteer Fire Company responded.

According to Chief Gill, the fire quickly raged out of control, and the volunteers were unable to extinguish it.

Mr. Yates, owner of the woods surrounding the home, was presumed dead. He was trapped inside the house while it burned. Yates is survived by one daughter and a grandson.

Old Man Yates. So the tales about an angry mob and a devil worshiper weren't true after all. It was just a chimney fire, and poor Yates was stuck inside. So much for all the ghost stories.

Joe turned to the next edition, but there was no mention of any animal attacks. He flipped through the rest of 1922 and found no headlines declaring bear attacks or any other kind of attacks. No deaths of any kind. It seemed the incidents stopped after the Yates fire. He quickly flipped through 1923. Nothing. 1924. Nothing.

Joe closed the binder and sat back in the chair, rubbing his eyes. Library Lady clunked down the stairs behind him, holding a stack of old papers. "Find everything you were looking for?" she asked.

Joe pushed away from the table and stood. "Yeah. Yes. I did. This town has some interesting history, doesn't it?"

Library Lady smiled. "It sure does. Did you know Teddy Roosevelt stopped here once?"

Joe shook his head. "No, I didn't."

"Sure did. Took a tour of the paper company. From what I understand, he was real impressed too." She set the papers down on the desk with a thud. A cloud of dust floated into the air.

"Well, that is interesting," Joe said. He handed the binder back to Library Lady. "Thanks again for all the help. It was a real eye-opener." Then he turned and got out of the old library before the woman could bend his ear anymore.

Maggie steered her cruiser into a parking space alongside the Dark Hills Library and Historical Society and shut off the engine. When she had passed by the library on her way back from her confrontation with Clark Martin and friends and noticed Joe's truck parked in the gravel lot, questions immediately started floating through her mind. Whether because of some underlying nagging guilt that occasionally saw fit to knock on her conscience or mere police intuition, a flash of panic had hit her when she saw his truck, and she'd decided then and there to do a little snooping of her own.

Now, sitting in her cruiser, the same questions resurfaced. Why was Joe visiting the local library? Was he snooping around in Dark Hills's closet? Looking for long-lost skeletons? She brushed the questions aside. He was probably just checking out some books to pass the time. There was no way he could know about Maggie's family history. No one knew, outside the family, that is.

She thought again of Joe and hoped he had indeed just picked up some light reading. He was never a heavy reader. At least the Joe Saunders she used to know wasn't. This new Joe was different, not all that different, but enough so to be intriguing—and possibly threatening.

She had finally admitted to herself that she still had feelings for him. How could she not? She had never stopped loving him. She had waited for him for almost five full years before facing the awful fact he wasn't coming back. And what a bitter pill it was. Everything reminded her of him. His image was everywhere. At the park, near the lake where had they shared dreams of what their future held. At the Dark Hills Treat, where too many times to count they had shared a booth and a milkshake. At the elementary school playground, far corner behind the swings, where they had shared their first kiss one hot spring day. And at her house, which was then her parents' house, on the front porch, where they had shared a pledge to love each other forever. That was right before he left for the army. So much for promises.

So much for forgetting about him.

But she had tried. For several years, she had dated a few guys, nothing serious, mere platonic relationships that never materialized into anything more than cordial short-lived friendships. But they were no match for Joe. Even while she was with the other guys, memories of Joe constantly bobbed to the surface of her mind, bringing with them a flurry of emotions. She simply could not escape his mark on her life.

Now he was back, and there was a part of her that wanted to fall into his arms, tell him how much she loved him and missed him and wanted him. But another part of her, the rational part, told her that emotions were dangerous. She had to send her feelings to the rear of the line, ignore the palpitations that fluttered her heart every time she saw him, even thought about him, and listen to reason. She had a job to do now, a big job, bigger than her or Joe—protect the family legacy. If the Secret was exposed, if Joe ever found those skeletons placed so carefully in the darkest corner of the Dark Hills closet and she took a fall, the family legacy would be flushed right along with her.

That couldn't happen. She'd have to make sure it didn't happen, regardless of her feelings for Joe Saunders.

CHAPTER 23

J OE WAS SEATED on the edge of his bed in the Dew-Drop Motel trying to piece together what he'd read earlier in the day. It was bizarre at best, downright sinister at worst. First, a string of animal attacks resulting in deaths. Gill tries to pass them off as the handiwork of a black bear. Then more attacks, and deaths, and the attacker is suddenly no longer a bear but an animal, a *mystery animal*, and the good Chief Gill suddenly clams up. The reporter covering the cases finds an *anonymous* witness willing to tell at least some semblance of the truth, and less than a week later the reporter falls down a flight of stairs and dies. Odd coincidence. Guess that's what happens when a reporter does his job in Dark Hills. Joe could hear old Gill now: *Poor fellow. Oh, well, accidents happen.* Then, strangest of all things, Old Man Yates's house burns with Yates in it, and the attacks suddenly stop. What gives? Obviously Yates was somehow tied to the attacks—maybe it *was* witchcraft—and Gill knew something he wasn't sharing with the rest of Dark Hills. Fire? Again, odd coincidence. And wasn't there a house fire in Dark Hills just the other day? Wednesday, was it? He'd heard some guys at the gas station talking about it, said Woody Owen—the guy with the dog, Cujo—died in the fire. A gas leak or something. Was there any connection? He'd have to ask Maggie about it next time he saw her.

Hopefully, Josiah would be able to shed some light on the mystery, put the pieces together.

He reached into his pocket and retrieved the napkin on which Josiah had jotted his phone number. He picked up the phone and punched in the numbers.

"Hello?"

"Josiah?"

"Yes."

"This is Joe…Saunders." He couldn't remember if he had even told Josiah his last name.

"Oh, hi, Joe. I take it you done your homework. Did you find anything interesting?" Josiah asked.

"Puzzling would be more like it."

Josiah snorted. "Puzzling don't even begin to cover it. There're more pieces to uncover, though. Can you do breakfast again tomorrow?"

More to uncover? The plot thickens? "Uh, yeah, sure. Darlene's again?"

"That'll do. How's seven sound?"

"Works for me."

"OK. See you then."

"Wait a minute…" Joe pressed the receiver closer to his ear. "Josiah? Are you there?"

"What is it?"

"You can't just leave me hanging like this. What does it all mean?"

Josiah sighed, filling the receiver with static. "Patience, Joe, patience. We'll talk more over breakfast."

"But—"

"Breakfast, Joe. Tomorrow. Darlene's. Seven o'clock. I'll see you then."

The phone went dead.

———

"Afternoon, Ruth," Maggie said, shutting the door behind her.

Ruth Stoltzfus, the Dark Hills librarian, poked her head out from behind a stack of books. "Oh, hi, Chief."

Maggie left her hand on the doorknob and jiggled it. "This could use some attention, and so could that porch."

Ruth laughed and looked over her glasses, raising her eyebrows at Maggie. "There's a lot around here that could use attention, including my knees. But the library isn't exactly at the top of the town budget, and one little old lady can hardly keep up with everything."

"No, I suppose you can't. I'll see what I can do about getting someone out here to help you."

Ruth stepped out from behind the books. "Well, what can I do for you? I know you didn't stop by to inspect the doorknob, and I'm fairly certain you've not come for small talk." She narrowed her eyes and studied Maggie. "And you didn't come for a book either, did you?"

Maggie removed her cap and held it with both hands. A slight smile parted her lips. This old bird was intuitive. No use beating around the bush. "No, I didn't. Did Joe Saunders come by here this morning?" She knew full well he had but didn't want to appear like she was snooping— even if she was.

Ruth smiled as though she had known the reason for Maggie's unexpected visit all along. "Well, I don't know about his name, but there was a man here this morning, young fellow, dark hair and handsome." She tilted her head to one side. "Is he in some kind of trouble?"

Maggie shook her head. "No, no. He's an old friend, and I've been trying to track him down, you know, catch up on old times." She forced a smile hoping Ruth wouldn't see past her veneer. "If I may ask, just out of curiosity, what was he looking for?"

Ruth raised those thin gray eyebrows again. "He asked to see the 1922 issues of the *Gazette*. Said he was researching the town's history."

Maggie felt her face flush and warmth radiate down her neck. Nineteen twenty-two. The Secret. The legacy. The skeletons. Joe was on to something. She suddenly realized her mouth was hanging open and snapped it shut. She donned her cap and smiled politely at Ruth, who had no doubt noticed her strange reaction.

"Thanks, Ruth. Have a good day, now, OK?" She turned, jiggled the doorknob, pushed the door open, and nearly fell onto the porch. Collecting herself, she turned back toward Ruth. "Uh, make me a list of everything that needs to be done around here. I'll be back tomorrow to pick it up."

With that, she turned on her heels and, leaving the door hanging open, bolted off the porch. When she reached her cruiser, she placed both hands on the roof, dipped her head, and drew in a long, deep breath of cool air.

Relax, Maggie. Think.

The rules of the game had suddenly changed. Which meant it was no longer a game, was it?

Which meant she had to come up with a new strategy. But first she needed to know the truth, and that meant another visit to see her dad.

It was time for some honest talk.

—

Stevie sat on a fallen tree in the woods. His jeans were dirty, his flannel jacket torn, hair disheveled, face unshaven. He was back, and it felt good.

He liked the woods. The trees understood him; they accepted him. Never did a tree laugh at him or hit him. Never did they mock him or treat him like some kind of retard. They respected him. And he respected them.

He ran a dirty hand through his hair and inhaled deeply, letting his eyes roll back in their sockets. Sounds of bullets hitting the metal exterior of his trailer banged in his mind. Again and again. *Bang. Bang. Bang. Bangbangbangbang.* He was under fire. They had come back for him, come back to finish the job. He had been the only witness. He hid in a closet, *under* the closet, in a hole, holding his ears shut with his hands, until the shooting stopped. Then there was laughing. The sound of children's voices laughing and calling his name.

Calling him a retard.

Stevie snapped out of his trance and breathed. He was trembling. Not to worry, though. Things were going as planned; justice would soon be served. What goes around comes around. He'd heard Momma say that once and it sounded cool. The taste of revenge sat on his tongue like a piece of candy. And he liked it.

Through the trees he could see the Dinsmore boys playing in their backyard. After-school fun. There were four of them, throwing a football, calling plays, running patterns, hollering and laughing.

That laughing.

Stevie hated that laughing. But they wouldn't be laughing for long.

"Enjoy it while you can, boyssss," he said, letting the final syllable drag on like a hiss. He laughed at himself, thinking how cunning he was, just like a snake. A snake, yeah. Hiding in the tall grass.

Kitty sat on the ground next to him and watched with interest as a couple of sparrows played a game of tag. Stevie stroked the cat's head. "We'll have to take this one day at a time. Lure them in, real cunnin'-like. Sneak up on 'em like a snake in high grass and then...strike!"

He gave Kitty a little pinch on the back of the neck, gripping the loose skin between his fingers. The cat growled. "Go make friends now, Kitty. But be nice. Nice is how you be, see?" He laughed again.

The cat slinked off toward the yard, weaving gracefully in and out of the thick undergrowth. Stevie watched as it navigated the leafy terrain, crossed the dirt alley, and pranced into the backyard right up to the tallest Dinsmore.

Tall One stopped his arm midthrow. "Hey, guys. Look at this." He bent down and extended a hand, open-palmed, to Kitty. "Here, kitty, kitty. Come here."

Their voices carried over the dry leaves like a stone skipping across water. Stevie held perfectly still, slowing his breathing, so he could hear every word.

The other three brothers gathered around Tall One, and Kitty lowered its haunches to the grass.

"Cool!" one of them said.

"A cat!" exclaimed another.

Tall One laid his hand on top of Kitty's head and gently stroked down its back. "It likes me. Friendly, huh?"

The shortest Dinsmore ran his hand over Kitty's smooth, silky fur. "So soft. You think we ca–ca–can k–keep it?"

No! You can't keep Kitty. Stevie mouthed the words as he thought them. *Stupid kid! Kitty's mine.* He thumped his chest silently.

One of the other brothers, the pudgy one, shook his head emphatically. "No way. You know what Mom and Dad say about pets." He dipped his head and rounded his shoulders and said in a low, mock-adult voice, "Four boys are enough to take care of without an animal runnin' around, gettin' under my feet."

The other boys laughed and continued petting Kitty, stroking its back and rubbing its jowls.

Stevie didn't like the attention Kitty was receiving. It made him a bit jealous, but it wasn't about him anymore. His plan was working, just like Momma had said it would.

"Do you think he has a home?" Pudgy asked.

"I don't know," Tall One said, rubbing Kitty's cheeks between his thumb and index finger. "It doesn't have a collar. Maybe it's a stray."

"It's awful friendly, though," Pudgy said. "I wish we could have a cat. This one would make a perfect pet."

Stevie rocked on his fallen tree, holding a hand tightly over his mouth to muffle his untamed laughter. His eyes were wide with excitement. "Good job, Kitty," he mumbled into his hand. "You're doin' great. Make those friends." He shut his eyes tight, clenched his free hand into a fist, and squealed.

Kitty suddenly pulled away from the boys' touch and bounded through the yard, over the dirt alley, and back into the woods. Back to Stevie.

Pudgy said something, but Stevie missed it.

Tall One shrugged and picked up the football. "I dunno. But listen, nobody says anything to Mom or Dad about it, OK?"

"Yeah."

"OK."

"Now go long!"

———

Elston Gill was reclined in his bed, covers up to his waist, watching CNN when Maggie arrived. She knocked on the doorjamb and startled him.

Elston smiled and widened his eyes. "Magpie! You visit again. Why?"

Though she knew he meant nothing by it, his question stung. She knew she didn't visit him enough. The fact that he was surprised she would visit twice in one week bit into her conscience. He wouldn't be around much longer, and she should be spending as much time with him as her schedule allowed.

Maggie entered the room. It was dimly lit and too warm. Nothing out of the ordinary. She sat on the edge of the bed and patted her dad's hand. "You mind if I turn the TV off so we can talk?"

Elston lifted the remote in a shaky hand and clicked off the TV. Smiling, he said, "You good?"

"I'm fine, Dad. Really. But...I've been thinking about something." She paused to collect herself and shore up her resolve. She wasn't leaving without answers. "I need to know what happened between Great-Grandpa and Philip Yates. I need you to tell me the whole story."

Elston's countenance fell and his mouth dipped at the corners. "Can't do, Magpie. You...no need to know. It over. Forget."

"I can't forget about it, Dad. I'm in it. I'm dealing with it right now. And I need to know what it is I'm up against. The more information I have and the better I understand what happened then, the better my chances of dealing with it now and keeping it under wraps. Or getting rid of it."

Elston reached for Maggie's hand. "Magpie. Gary good?"

Maggie pulled her hand away. "Don't change the subject, Dad." That was his classic technique for avoiding any talk of the past. When Maggie was young she'd hear stories about her great-grandpa or Yates and run home to verify them with her dad, the police chief. But Elston would never give her a straight answer. He would either sidestep the question or change the subject altogether. It wouldn't work this time, though. "I need answers this time. I need you to tell me everything you know. People are dying, just like back then, and if you want to protect me and the family, I need to know what's happening. You can't protect me by not telling me. Ignorance won't help me anymore."

Elston grimaced and clenched his fists. He shut his eyes tight, then relaxed and opened them. Sadness washed over his face. "It bad, Magpie."

Leaning in close, Maggie ran a hand over his thin hair. "I don't care, Dad. It's my family too. My legacy. My history. I'll keep it safe. I promise."

Releasing a long sigh, Elston nodded once and blinked slowly. "OK. I tell. Hard though."

"I know it is. I'll help you find the words." And she did.

CHAPTER 24

FRIDAY EVENING, ROSA was deep in prayer, seated next to Caleb's bed. Her hand rested lightly on his leg. Her head was bowed low, eyes closed, lips moving silently.

This was her time with God.

She normally interceded for Caleb, bathing her son in prayer, begging God to revive him. But tonight she prayed for Joe.

Early that morning, before the sun had showed its face, she had awakened trembling uncontrollably, her sheets soaked with sweat. A man's voice had startled her awake. Slowly, like tea steeping in hot water, the memory of the dream had replayed in her mind. It was more auditory than visual. She was in a dark room, groping blindly through the blackness, trying to find her way out. In the distance, maybe another room, she could hear Joe calling her name. He was trying to find her, looking for her. Or was he asking her to find him? Maybe he was lost. She wasn't sure. It continued for what seemed hours before a voice from someone, a man standing right next to her, whispered in her ear—*Pray for Joe*. She turned and felt the darkness, hoping to take hold of the voice's owner, but there was nothing. No one. The voice came again—*Pray for Joe*. She continued probing the dark, feeling for anything human, but the room was empty.

Then she heard the deep voice, bold and clear, from outside her dream, somewhere in her bedroom. "Pray for Joe."

She had roused with a jolt, reached for the lamp on the bedside table, and turned it on. She was panting and sweating like she had just run a mile. The voice still rang in her ears. She climbed out of bed and walked through the house. Of course, it was empty. It had just been a dream.

So now she prayed for Joe. She wasn't sure how she should intercede; the voice simply said *pray*. But God knew; after all, it was His voice. She was sure of that. She'd heard His voice before, and it was quite unmistakable. It spoke not only to the ears but to the heart also.

How much time had passed, Caleb could not tell. Time seemed to be irrelevant here. The darkness made everything stand still while he floated in
nothingness, suspended in timelessness.

He wanted to give up, give in to the oppressive darkness, succumb to
the beast that loomed somewhere in the shadows. Put an end to it and be
done with it. Hopelessness had begun its awful attack. Slow and calculating. Patient. Sooner or later he would give in to it and allow the beast to
have him. He couldn't take much more of this.

Then the light was there again, the orange glow high above him,
hovering, circling, floating toward him, illuminating his face in a warm
blaze. For the moment, the hopelessness was dispelled and comforting
warmth seeped through his body.

"Speak for Us."

He reached for the light.

"Write for Us, child."

I will. Use me.

Rosa felt a quiver run through Caleb's leg. She stopped praying and lifted
her head. The bed was trembling now, the headboard rattling against the
wall like a machine gun. She stood and looked down at her son. His right
hand was jerking about again, as if writing. It *was* writing! Quickly, she
grabbed the clipboard and pencil Roger had left on the table, slipped the
pencil between Caleb's thumb and index finger, and held the clipboard
under his hand, steadying his arm with her free hand.

The graphite scratched along the surface of the paper. At first it was
just scribbles, circles and lines, dots and dashes. Then letters started
appearing. He was frantically writing, like a scribe desperate to get it all
down before the inspiration left him.

S S S S S S. Over and over again, overlapping, intersecting, small, large,
his hand stuttered out the letters.

Then more appeared. A *t*, an *e*, a *V.* And more followed.

Then, just as suddenly as it had started, his hand stopped and went limp. The pencil slipped out from between his fingers, rolled the length of the clipboard, and clinked to the floor. Rosa turned the paper and studied the scribbles.

SteV No.

She didn't have the slightest idea what it meant, but it definitely spelled *SteV No.*

A chill spread down Rosa's back. This was incredible. If she hadn't witnessed it with her own eyes, she would never have believed it. From somewhere in his deep sleep, Caleb was trying to communicate. But what was the poor boy trying to say? First it was *Jo hold sEcrE*, and now *SteV No.*

She cupped Caleb's soft face in her hands and kissed his forehead. "I am getting your messages, my son. But what do they mean? Please wake up and tell us. Please, son. Help us understand."

Then she called Joe.

Unbelievable. That was all he could think.

Joe stood in Caleb's room and stared at the paper. A penetrating buzz reached through his arms all the way down to his hands. His heart fluttered like the wings of a butterfly. He was still trying to get over the first message, find some way to process it that made even a little sense. And now this. Another cryptic message.

The paper he held in his hands looked the same as the first one. There was a maze of scribbles, confusing marks, but in the midst of the disorder it was there, plain as day: *SteV No.*

Rosa sat in her chair, hands folded across her lap. She eyed Joe with a steady gaze. "What do you think it means?"

Joe looked at the paper again and shook his head in disbelief. "I don't know. But I found out what the first message meant."

Rosa's eyes widened and a smile lifted the corners of her mouth. "You did? What? What did it mean?"

Joe pulled the other maroon chair around the bed so it faced Rosa and sat. "*Jo* wasn't me at all. He's an old farmer named Josiah. Josiah Walker. I met him in Darlene's this morning. He said God told him to find me and share the secret. You know, *Jo holds secret.* Apparently, the secret is something the Gill family has been hiding from the rest of Dark Hills for decades. I'm not sure what it is yet. He had me reading old newspapers from 1922, and I'm supposed to meet him again tomorrow to talk more about it. It's got something to do with animal attacks and some kind of cover-up Henry Gill, Maggie's great-grandpa, was involved in. There may have even been a couple of murders."

Rosa looked confused. Her brow was firm, lips slightly parted. "But what does that have to do with anything? And how would Caleb know about—" She lifted a hand to cover her mouth. "Oh, my, Joe. God is speaking to Caleb. Giving him these messages. God is moving Caleb's hand. My son is a writing instrument in the hand of God."

Now Joe was confused. "God? Are you serious?"

"Absolutely!" Rosa looked at him with scolding eyes. "Joe, God is moving here. He is speaking to people, to Caleb, to this farmer, to me. I heard him last night, clear as if He were standing right next to me, telling me to pray for you. Something is happening here, and God is intervening."

Joe was still skeptical. He wasn't sure why—what Rosa said did make sense—but he just wasn't ready to believe that God was talking to people, or through people, or whatever. Especially a comatose boy.

＊

Rosa didn't miss the look on Joe's face. She knew he was having a hard time accepting the truth. His faith had taken some hard hits, and he was struggling to resuscitate it.

She leaned forward and placed a hand on his arm. "Joe, God *does* speak to people. Yes, most of the time it is through the Bible. But sometimes He chooses different ways, like using a donkey or a burning bush or writing on a wall, and sometimes it is just that still, small voice that speaks directly to our heart. But He does speak to people. You have to believe that. You have to believe that He can even speak to us through Caleb."

She stared at Joe for a full five seconds before laying the argument in his lap. "Do you believe that?"

Joe dropped his eyes to the floor and twisted his hands. "In my heart I do. But my mind says He just doesn't work that way. It isn't logical, isn't rational." He looked at her. "If God's going to speak, why does He do it in riddles like 'Jo holds secret'?"

Rosa took his hands in hers and looked deep into his brown eyes, past the façade, past the *I'll-be-OK* act, and into his soul where he was tender and vulnerable, hurting and lonely. She had to reach him. She had to help him believe. Belief was the only way he would ever return to God.

"Do you understand everything you read in the Bible?" She didn't give him time to answer, not that he would have, anyway. "No, you don't, and neither do I. So what do we do? We study it more, we pray, we ask God to give us understanding. We rely on Him to show us what it means. It is called faith, Joe. Faith is the key to everything. When you think about it, nothing this world has to offer makes any sense. It is meaningless. It is a riddle. But faith does make sense. Because with faith we stop trying to figure everything out and just put it in God's hands and let Him figure it out for us."

Tears were pooling in Joe's eyes, and he quickly dashed them away. "OK. So what does *SteV No* mean?"

"Why don't we pray about it?" Rosa gave Joe's hands a gentle squeeze and bowed her head. "Heavenly Father, give us wisdom and understanding to see what it is You are telling us. We acknowledge the difficulty is with our understanding, not Your message, for You are truth. Give us the ability to see clearly what it is You want us to see."

When she was finished she looked up. Joe was staring at her with a look of anticipation on his face.

"Anything?" he said.

She squeezed his hands again and lifted up onto her toes so her face was closer to his. "Give it time, Joe. Give it time. God is in no hurry."

"Time. That's something I'm not sure we have a lot of."

<hr>

Maggie looked at the clock on her wall. It was a round, 1940s' style, analog stainless steel clock with bold black numbers that she'd picked up at a flea market—9:45. Surely, Joe would be in his motel room by now. She had been trying to contact him all day, leaving message after message, without any luck.

She picked up her phone and dialed the Dew-Drop Motel. Nancy answered.

"Hi, Nancy, it's Chief Gill. You working a long day, or are you just covering for the evening?"

"Hi, Chief. I've been here all day. Bill's sick, so I have front desk duty until ten, then Amy will take the overnight."

Maggie chuckled. "Well, tell him I wish him well."

"Thank you. I will."

"Can you connect me with room 5, please?"

"Sure."

The phone in Joe's room rang only once before he picked it up. "Hello."

"Hi, Joe, it's Maggie. Your cell's been off all day, hasn't it?"

"Oh, hi, Mags. Uh, yeah, sorry 'bout that. Told you I hate those things. What's going on?"

Maggie swallowed, hoping Joe wouldn't notice her hesitation. "Not much. Hey, I don't have long to talk, but I was wondering if you'd be interested in coming over to my place tomorrow night for dinner, say sixish?"

Now Joe hesitated, and there was no missing it. "Uh, yeah. Sure. Six is fine."

"You sure, I mean if it's—"

"No, no. I mean yes, I am sure."

"OK then. You know where I live?"

"In your mom and dad's house, right?"

"Yeah."

"OK, see you then. Bye."

"Bye."

Joe put down the phone and sighed.

He wanted to see Maggie, he really did. He missed her, even longed for her company. It had been years since he last held her in his arms, but it seemed like mere days. He could still feel the pressure of her body against his, smell the lavender in her hair, taste the sweetness of her lips. Some things are never forgotten. But a voice screamed in his mind, or was it his heart—*Danger-Danger-Danger*—warning him like a fire alarm.

He didn't have any hard evidence that Maggie had done anything wrong yet. Sure, she acted a little strange about Cummings's death, but maybe she *was* just being cautious, following protocol. But she was a Gill, and she had Gill blood flowing through her veins. That meant she was part of the Secret. Or did it? He ran both hands through his hair and rubbed his temples. This whole thing was giving him a headache.

He reached for the bottle of Tylenol on the nightstand, popped the lid, and tossed two pills in his mouth, washing them down with a swig of lukewarm water.

He'd have to be careful, but maybe he could get some information out of Maggie without her even knowing what he was up to.

He'd have to set his feelings for her aside. Some things were more important than feelings.

CHAPTER 25

JOE SAT IN a booth at Darlene's, red-eyed and foggy-minded. He didn't sleep well last night. A million thoughts had scattered in his mind, and now he was trying to corral them again. But it seemed as fruitless and futile as trying to lasso a pack of wild Chihuahuas. First, there was the attack on Caleb, then Cujo, then Cummings. Then there was Maggie's strange behavior, the Secret, the newspaper articles, Caleb's cryptic writings, Josiah's voices, Rosa's prayers. His mind couldn't take much more, but somehow he knew there was much more to come.

He sipped at a cup of black coffee, letting the steam moisten his upper lip and nose. It was a cold morning, and a light rain had begun falling. He hated this kind of weather. It was raw, like an open wound, and he'd rather just spend the day inside. Maybe that's just what he would do. After his meeting with Josiah, he'd head over to Hillside and visit Rosa and Caleb, then go back to the Dew-Drop and relax until it was time to meet Maggie. Maybe he'd take a nap before going over. Yeah, he could use a good nap.

A young, blonde-haired waitress named Becky had come by with a menu, but Joe had waved her off. He wasn't hungry. Coffee would do, and keep the refills coming.

The door jangled, announcing the arrival of another hungry customer drawn to the smell of frying lard and Darlene's overpowering Chanel. Joe looked up just in time to see Darlene pull Josiah into a hug and give him a dose of aromatherapy, Number 5 style.

When she released him, Josiah nodded politely, found Joe, and headed toward him.

"Mornin', Joe," he said, looking a little sheepish and embarrassed about being caught in Darlene's arms. He slid into the bench across from Joe and removed his coat. "Ugly mornin', ain't it?"

"Sure is," Joe said. "But you're smelling beautiful. A real dandy."

Josiah blushed. "Darlene's a fine woman. A real sweet spirit." He looked Joe up and down. "You, on the other hand, look awful. Not a mornin' person, huh?"

Joe shook his head. "Didn't sleep well last night. Too many things running through my head."

Becky came by and asked Josiah if he'd like a menu. "No thanks. Cup of caffeine will do just fine." He looked at Joe. "You ready for more?"

"More of what? Information? Yes. Mystery? No."

Josiah reached into his pocket and pulled out a piece of paper. "Check out these editions of the *Gazette*." He slid the paper across the table to Joe.

Joe took the paper and read it. *March 7, 1995. April 2, 1995.*

"What's this? More Gill family secret stuff? Look, I—"

"Hold on, there," Josiah said, holding up a hand. "I know. I know. You don't know why I don't just come right out and tell you all about it. You don't know why I'm sending you on these goose chases. And you're tired of the mystery cloud hanging over this town. I have my reasons."

"And they are?"

Josiah stroked his rough face. "If I were to just come out and tell you what I know, you probably wouldn't believe me. As a matter of fact, if I was a bettin' man—which I ain't—but if I was, I'd bet the family farm, literally, that you wouldn't believe me. You'd think I was just some old coot who didn't know a rat's nose from his behind and was listening to too many stories or watching too many TV movies. I need you to see this stuff for yourself so you'll believe it. So you'll get a firsthand picture of what the Gills have been hiding and how it's affected this town."

Joe wasn't in an arguing mood. Besides, the *old coot*, if that's what he wanted to call himself, had a point. "OK. So is this all? Just these two editions?"

"No, it ain't all." Josiah fumbled around with his coat for a few seconds and finally revealed a small, brown leather-bound book. Its cover was worn and faded, and the edges of the pages were browned. He slid the book across the table to Joe. "Read this. I bookmarked the important pages."

Joe picked up the book and opened its worn cover. There was a man's handwriting, neat and flowing, on every crisp page. The writing had faded over the years and in some places had almost vanished.

"It's a journal," Josiah said, answering Joe's question before he could ask it. "Have you ever heard the story about how the Yates place burnt down? Not the one the newspaper told"—he leaned forward, resting on his elbows—"the *real* story. The one that says Chief Gill and a minister visited Yates, and he threatened them with a shotgun, and later that night the townsfolk burned the house to the ground?"

Joe nodded. "Sure. But—"

"*Shh*. Listen!" Josiah looked around Darlene's like he was sharing information he'd stolen from the CIA. "The minister was Reverend John Claybaugh, pastor of the Methodist church here in town, and he was a good friend of my father. Now listen. Claybaugh lost his wife when he was only fifty somethin', had no children, and spent the rest of his thirty years alone. On his deathbed, my father was the only true friend the man had. Right before he died, Claybaugh told my father everything that really happened back in '22. Guess he needed to 'fess up and clear his conscience before meetin' the good Lord. And he told my father where his journal was. He had to hide it so Gill and his cronies never found it. If they did, they woulda destroyed it sure as bats are deaf, and probably arranged for some unfortunate accident to happen to the reverend. That book you hold is the reverend's journal. It speaks the truth about the real Gill family secret. If you want to know what happened and what it is Maggie Gill is hiding, spend some time readin' through that book."

Joe set the book down and took a long sip of coffee, keeping his eyes on the faded cover. He tapped the leather with his index finger. "So this journal holds all the answers to my questions?"

Josiah snorted. "You got a lot of questions, young man. I don't know if any book outside the Bible can answer *all* your questions. But this one here will give you some real insight. By the way, how's your nephew doing?"

Joe snapped his head up and set his coffee down. "Oh, yeah. I forgot to tell you. He had another writing or whatever you want to call it. Another message."

Josiah leaned forward and widened his eyes.

Joe tapped the table once with his palm. "*Stev no*."

"*Stev no*? That's it?"

"*Stev no*. I have no idea what it means, if it means anything at all."

Josiah's face went gray and his mouth popped open. He leaned back in his seat and gripped the edge of the table. "Could it be Stevie knows?"

"I guess. Makes as much sense as anything. Why? What's the matter? Who's Steve?"

Joe waited for Josiah to continue, but no further information came. "Well, are you going to tell me?"

Josiah's Adam's apple bobbed, and he cleared his throat. He paused as his eyes shot back and forth over the table as if he were looking for the answer to be hidden somewhere in the stains on the Formica. Finally, he swallowed again, looked at Joe, and spoke. "Stevie Bauer is a boy my wife and I cared for after his momma died. He's part of the Gill secret, and so is his momma's death. Now, what he actually knows and what he *thinks* he knows are two different things. Stevie is schizophrenic. He sees things that ain't there, hears voices that ain't there, and imagines whole events that never happened. But he'll swear it's all true. He witnessed his momma's murder thirteen years ago, when he was eight. He was the only witness. And that's true."

Josiah paused and took a sip of coffee, and Joe wondered if he was finished. Then he shook a finger as if debating with himself whether to divulge any more information. With the matter settled, he continued. "I might as well tell you now, and then you can read *their* version in the newspaper dates I gave you. Stevie used to get teased somethin' awful when he was in school. He wasn't diagnosed with schizophrenia until he was ten, but he was always a little...odd."

He paused and raked his fingers through his thin hair. "The other kids used to torment him terrible. When he was eight, he was outside playing in his yard when some high school kids passing by decided to have some fun with him. They beat up on him some, but when Stevie started fighting back, they really took it out on him. Whipped him with a rope over and over until the poor boy's back and shoulders was raw. His mother heard the commotion and came runnin', but the three punks shoved her inside and locked the door. Stevie watched from outside as they beat her and had their way with her...if you know what I mean.

"She died that night in the hospital. Of course, Stevie was the only witness and pointed the finger at the punks that did it. At first, Elston Gill made the arrests, routine stuff, but later dropped all charges against 'em. Said Stevie's testimony was no good because the boy was crazy. After that, my wife and I took him in and raised him the best we could. Ginny's been gone just three years now, and I've had an awful time keepin' up with him on my own. He's twenty-one now, and I've set up a trailer on my land for him to have a place of his own. He does OK, I guess. Still hears voices, though, and thinks people are out to get him all the time."

Joe shifted in his seat and kept his eyes on Josiah. "So that's what Stevie knows? The truth about his mother's death? What does that have to do with Caleb or the beast that's out there? For that matter, what does the whole Gill thing have to do with the beast?"

Josiah shook his head. "So many questions. Don't you see what the Lord's doin' here? He's opening the blinds a little bit at a time. Slowly letting the light in, revealing the truth. Just be patient and pay attention. Nothing is secret that will not be revealed."

Joe shuddered. Goose bumps freckled his arms. "What did you say?"

"Nothing is secret that will not be revealed. It's in Luke. I've taken it out of context, but it's one of those sayings I like to quote. My point is, be patient. In time—God's time—He will reveal what we're supposed to know."

"God said that to me."

Josiah continued nursing his coffee. "Said what?"

"A couple nights ago. I was praying—trying to, anyway—and God spoke those words to me. 'Nothing is secret that will not be revealed.'"

A smile curled Josiah's lips. "So there you have it. God is speaking to you too. Do you see what I mean now? He's slowly bringing everything into focus. We just need to be patient."

"Meanwhile that thing's out there," Joe said, suddenly feeling a wave of anxiety fall over him. "My nephew is in a coma, and Cummings is dead. And who knows when or who it will attack next."

Josiah tapped the table with his finger. The thump seemed to echo in Joe's ears. "Young man, you got a lot to learn about God's sovereignty. Don't you think He knows what's going on here in Dark Hills? He's got it under control, and I see Him workin' things out. Sure, it's not all at once like we want it, but it's happening. And what are you planning to do about it? Go hunt the beast? Put yourself out there in the middle of those woods, some John Wayne attitude, and shoot at the first thing that moves? I don't think the answer is in guns and bullets."

"Well, what do you think it is, then?"

"Don't know. But I betcha God's gonna show us," Josiah said, winking at Joe. "Just wait and see. Meanwhile, read that journal there, and you'll get yourself an education."

Eddie Hopkins cruised down Route 20 in his late-model, maroon Buick LeSabre. It was raining steadily, and the water blurred his windshield. Time for new wipers. But it didn't matter; he knew this stretch of road like he knew his own living room. From here to the next stop sign where 20 intersected with Route 117 was a straight shot. Asphalt cut through cornfield like a scalpel making a precise incision.

His foot slowly depressed the accelerator, and the car's engine moaned a little louder.

Eddie was running late for work…again. His boss at the paint shop in Rhoads told him the next time he was late it would be his last. He'd be looking for another job. So Eddie was determined to cover the eight-mile stretch from Dark Hills to Rhoads in record time.

As long as no cops pulled him over, he might make it just in time.

Gripping the steering wheel tighter, Eddie pictured his boss's angry face, beet red, bulging eyes, yellow teeth peeking from behind fat lips as he yelled obscenities. What a jerk. Making him work on a Saturday. Eddie should be late on purpose just so he could be fired and have a reason to give that porker a piece of his mind. He'd been working for the paint-mixing shop ever since his wife left him five years ago. The only time he was ever late was when his old Buick clunker wouldn't start. Maybe if Porker would pay him more, he could afford a new car.

His foot fell a little heavier on the accelerator. The clunker pressed on, slicing through the rain. Dried, beige cornstalks whizzed by like fence posts, blurred in the rain.

Suddenly, something lunged at the car from the field on the right side of the road. Eddie caught it in the corner of his eye.

He yanked the steering wheel to the left and stomped on the brake. The car's wheels locked, sending the vehicle into a tailspin. Eddie pumped the brake and tried to turn the wheel back to the right, but the car was out of control, sliding toward the shallow gully that separated asphalt from cornfield.

The car lurched off the road, jumped the gully, and slammed into the field, bowling over stalks as if they were toothpicks. *Whap! Whap! Whap!* The wet stalks slapped against the car's windshield and side panels.

The car bounced along the rutted field, rattling everything inside it, including its driver. Eddie held the steering wheel in a vice grip and leaned heavy on the brake, pressing his body into the seat. The car finally slid to a stop in the mud twenty yards into the field.

Dazed and shaking, Eddie opened the car door and stumbled out. His forehead burned. He lifted a hand to feel it. *Ouch!* He must've hit it against the window or maybe the steering wheel. He couldn't remember. His legs felt like rubber, and his vision blurred. He shut the door and leaned against it, letting the cold rain spatter his face. It felt good on his forehead.

Eddie rubbed the water from his eyes and blinked—still blurry, and his head now throbbed. He looked behind the car but could barely make out the swath of flattened cornstalks that cut through the field from the vehicle to the road. He made a fist and pounded the roof of the car. "Stupid deer!"

His stomach contracted and a wave of sudden nausea overcame him. Leaning on the car, bent at the waist, he retched violently.

A rustling in the corn to his right caught his attention. He righted himself, wiped his mouth and shivered, then rubbed his eyes again. Maybe he hit the deer and it was wounded, flopping around on the ground somewhere in the corn.

He began making his way through the corn toward the sound of the rustling but stopped dead when he saw a blurry shape moving amongst the stalks a couple of rows ahead of him. Water ran off his head and into his eyes. He ran his hand across his face, top to bottom, but it was useless. It was raining too hard and the jolt in the car had done something to his vision. He looked closer at the object in the corn. He couldn't make out what it was, but it was big and blended in with the color of the dried stalks. It was no deer. He knew that much.

"Hey!" he hollered, waving his arms, hoping to scare away whatever it was. He wiped the water from his eyes again, squinted, and peered into the rows, looking past and between the stalks. Maybe it was a dog. No, too big. Maybe a horse. That made sense. Someone's horse had gotten loose and was roaming the fields.

It moved again. He could now make out the size of the beast. It was at least five feet in height and eight feet in length. Had to be a horse.

He swiped at his face, took another step forward, pushing cornstalks out of his way.

Then he heard it. A low growl.

Not a dog's growl. Deeper and more guttural, like the supercharged engine in the '69 Charger his dad used to have.

He froze. He'd never heard a horse make a sound like that. Come to think of it, he'd never heard a sound like that, period. He tried to think, but his mind had been invaded by a thick fog. The only thing that stuck was a line his mind latched on to from a newspaper article he'd read a week ago: *...young boy attacked by a mystery animal is in critical condition.*

Attacked by a mystery animal.

Attacked. Mystery. Animal.

Slowly, carefully, he took a calculated step backward, avoiding a stalk that was directly behind him and keeping his eyes on the large shape. It stood motionless for several seconds, then, in a sudden burst, quicker than a blink, it was gone.

Eddie's pulse quickened. He scanned the thick maze of corn looking for anything that moved. The rain intensified, beating at his face like gravel. He heard the animal again, rustling the stalks as it moved, first behind him, then to the right, then in front, then behind. He spun around and around trying to get a bearing on the location of the sound. It was behind him, definitely behind him. He turned and realized the car was also in that direction. The thing had positioned itself between him and the car.

It growled again, this time louder and more guttural. A low roar.

Eddie panicked and turned to run. It was the only thing his clouded mind could register—*Get out of here!*

He ran through the rows as fast as he could dodge the stalks. They slapped at him like long wet arms, and he shoved them out of his way. His ankles turned in the loose soil; his head pounded, pulse raced, stomach knotted. He could hear the beast hot on his heels, grunting in pursuit, bowling over stalks as if they weren't even there.

Eddie scrambled through the field, not thinking, just running, left, then right, then left again. His heart throbbed, frantically trying to deliver oxygen to his screaming muscles. His lungs burned like fire, heaving for air, precious air.

He was slowing down. His legs were turning to lead, his diaphragm spasming. Rain pelted his face harder, blurring his already fuzzy vision even more. When he could go no farther, he collapsed to the muddy ground, sucking in huge gulps of air.

The thing was still there, just beyond his sight, pacing in the corn, waiting to attack. Its raspy panting was like gravel in a bucket.

Eddie tried to scramble to his feet again, but his legs wouldn't have it and collapsed under his weight. This was no way to go. If that thing was going to attack, get it over with.

"Well, c'mon!" Eddie hollered. "Bring it on." He was easy prey, he knew, but he wouldn't go without a fight.

Suddenly, faster than Eddie's sluggish mind could even record what had happened, the beast was on top of him, its huge paws digging their daggers into his chest, cutting through his coat, shirt, and flesh. He stared up at a huge mouth. Five-inch canines glistened with saliva, ready to rip him limb from limb. And that tongue...

Fear paralyzed him, numbed every nerve in his body. He tried to scream, but nothing came out. The weight of the thing was almost enough to crush him.

It snarled its lips, then growled again, definitely a roar. Hot, putrid breath surrounded his face.

The beast curled its toes, digging its claws further into Eddie's flesh. The huge head reared back, the mouth opened, hideous tongue curled.

Eddie closed his eyes and grimaced. He didn't want to see what would come next.

CHAPTER 26

J OE HAD PROPPED up some pillows on his Dew-Drop bed, slipped off
his shoes, and settled in for an afternoon of relaxation and perusing
the journal of Reverend John Claybaugh.

He had stopped by the library after his meeting with Josiah, and once
again, Library Lady was very accommodating, retrieving the *Gazette*
editions Josiah had suggested. She handed them to Joe with a smile and a
wink and said, "I'll be in the back cataloging some new books. If there's
anything else you'll be needing, just let me know."

What Joe found did not surprise him. The article in the March 7, 1995,
issue covering the murder of Gail Bauer was short and lacking any important details. The three boys who were charged were listed by name: Glen
Sterner. Woody Owen. Eddie Hopkins.

Nothing was said of the beating Stevie endured or the fact that he
watched, helpless, as his mother was raped and murdered.

Chief Elston Gill had no comment on the alleged murder.

Interestingly, the article in the April 2 issue stated that all charges
against the boys were being dropped and the case was being closed.
Again, Chief Gill had been infected with a sudden case of *no-comment-
itis*. Surprise, surprise. Getting information out of him was about as easy
as coaxing a pro wrestler to a tea party. But the bombshell was that the
article mentioned the name of the boys' lawyer—Robert Cummings.
Cummings! He was involved in the Gail Bauer case.

Now, sprawled on his bed at the Dew-Drop, Joe flipped through the
leather-bound journal, scanning the pages Josiah had not bookmarked.
The reading was interesting, to say the least. The good reverend must have
been a notable figure in the town of Dark Hills. It seemed he was involved
in almost everyone's life in some way or another.

But it was when Joe got to the bookmarked pages that the reading got
really interesting. The first marked page was dated September 4, 1922. Joe
scanned the handwritten entry.

Joe Kline was found dead today. Henry said he was mauled by a rogue black bear. I have my doubts, though. I've seen what a bear can do to a deer, a dog, even a cow, and the condition of the poor man's body was far worse than anything I have ever witnessed—too gruesome to put into words. I have no idea what nature of beast could maul a man so viciously.

Henry and three other gentlemen went hunting for the beast but returned without success.

Joe flipped to the next bookmarked page, dated September 20.

There have been three more deadly attacks in the past week, Roger Bixby, Max Gregory, and Alvin Billet. The most stunning and saddening was the death of Alvin. He had always been slow and depended on his mother to care for him. The beast showed no mercy. I cannot even bring myself to pen the details of his attack, but the images will remain with me for the remainder of my time in this earthen vessel. My heart aches for his mother who is now alone.

Henry is becoming more and more secretive and reclusive regarding the animal attacks. He seems to know something but is divulging no information. None that is helpful, anyway. The citizens are becoming restless and frightened. Today, when Alvin's body was found, there was widespread panic in town. Nobody leaves their homes after dark anymore. Many have come to me seeking spiritual comfort. I've done the best I can.

Even more disturbing is the behavior of Philip Yates. He's been seen wandering the streets of downtown ranting about a "devil lion" ushering in the Day of Judgment. He mentions vengeance often. People are beginning to say that he is involved in devil worship. I must speak with him regarding this matter.

Joe's interest was hooked. There was turmoil in Dark Hills: savage murders, a rogue beast, a reclusive cop, and a nutty hermit ranting about the devil. The *Gazette* had left out some of the best parts. He read on.

October 1, 1922

I went to the home of Philip Yates today. He is an odd man, indeed. As is his home. His grandfather was a plantation owner in South Carolina, and the Yates home is furnished with a variety of African carvings and idols the slaves produced in their free time. Philip showed particular interest in and was especially proud to tell me about a severed lion paw. He said his grandfather accepted the paw from one of his slaves as a gift. Apparently, the lion was a man-eater that had eaten upwards of ten men in a remote village. The slaves called the beast Simba Mfu, a devil lion. Philip then spent the rest of my visit ranting about the wrongs committed against him by the people of Dark Hills. He never mentioned the nature of the wrongdoings, nor did he mention the names of the wrongdoers, even after my repeated questions, but he promised revenge on all of them.

I am concerned Philip may be dealing in witchcraft. He insists he is not, but his behavior has grown so bizarre I can draw no other conclusion.

So the folklore was right. Old Man Yates was dancing with the devil. Joe fanned through the pages to the next marked entry.

October 7, 1922

I was involved in a hunting party dispatched to Yates Woods to track and kill the beast that has been terrorizing our town. Two hours into the ordeal, all of us heard a bellowing roar, like a lion's, then a hideous scream. We ran to where the scream had sounded and found Leonard Toomey mauled and dead. The image of his faceless head will forever be seared into my memory. Only God knows what took his life.

When we returned to town carrying Leonard's body, Philip Yates was waiting for us, ranting about the judgment that had befallen Dark Hills, the vengeance that was rightly administered. I must admit, he has the whole town fearful. Henry warned him, but Philip only became more insistent.

Was Yates just playing on the town's fears, or was he really involved in witchcraft? Or was he just plain nuts? There was one more page marked.

October 29, 1922

God forgive us for what we have done. Last night Henry and I went to the home of Philip Yates to speak with him. It was our intention to be forthright with him and inform him of the fear and hysteria he was planting in the hearts and minds of the townsfolk. He wanted nothing of our visit and threatened to shoot us if we did not leave his property.

Henry and I returned to town, and Henry promptly organized a posse to run Philip out of his home and out of Dark Hills. A mob of about thirty men was soon assembled. Most had guns, and I noticed some carrying gasoline containers. I urged Henry to reconsider. I told him force was not the way to handle the problem. But he pushed me aside and led the mob into Yates Woods.

By the time I caught up with them, the posse had worked themselves into a frenzy, accusing Philip of being a devil worshiper and calling upon an evil spirit. They demanded he come out of his house and face his due punishment. After some time, Philip fired what sounded like a shotgun into the air. Henry then ordered the house be doused with gasoline, and it was promptly set to fire. As the home burned, the screams of Philip could be clearly heard. This only seemed to inspire the mob more, and they began discharging their weapons into the blazing house.

It took only about thirty minutes for the house to be totally engulfed in flames. At the fire's fiercest point a loud roar could be heard coming from inside the home. I do not know what

Philip had in the home, only that his screams and that roar will not soon leave my ears. I pray God will forgive us, but I do not expect any mercy for the sin our town has committed.

So much for the chimney fire story. The ignorant folks of Dark Hills were incited. And Henry Gill was behind the whole thing.

There was only one more entry in the journal.

October 31, 1922

I write this final entry with much fear and trepidation.

Henry met me at my house today and urged me neither to speak of what happened in Yates Woods nor to speak of the animal attacks. When I hesitated, he became very obstinate and threatened to punish me if I ever spoke or wrote of it. His demeanor has changed since the burning. He has become very reclusive and ill-tempered. I fear he will not hesitate to harm me if I do not heed his request.

So this will be my final entry in this journal. I can only pray that God will know the condition of my heart and see the contrition of my soul.

Joe closed the book slowly and ran his hand over the smooth leather cover. His heart was beating fast, and his palms were moist with sweat. *So that's the Gill family secret.* No wonder they'd kept it under lock and key for so many decades. Not exactly a history to be proud of.

He looked at the clock—4:40. He'd have to go to Maggie's soon.

Maggie. What should he do about her? He'd confront her, that's what he'd do. Lives were at stake. One had already been lost. This was no time to keep secrets if she had information that could save more lives from being taken. One question still remained, though: What was that thing that mauled Caleb and killed Cummings? Was it really a lion? Or was it a *devil*, a Simba Mfu, as Old Man Yates called it? Yeah, right. The guy was nuts. Maybe Maggie knew. Maybe she'd known all along, and it was all part of the Secret.

Then it hit him like a lightning bolt to the chest—*Stevie knows.*

Maybe that's what Caleb was trying to say. Stevie knows the answer. He made a mental note to call Josiah in the morning and arrange a time to talk to Stevie.

For now, though, he had Maggie to deal with.

CHAPTER 27

MAGGIE LEANED TOWARD the mirror and put the finishing touches on her face—hazelnut eye shadow, seashell lipstick. She smoothed down a few rebellious strands of hair that had decided they would not conform to the style she had chosen for the evening, stepped back, and looked at herself. Her lips glistened, eyes sparkled. Her hair hung loosely over her shoulders—not bad for an old maid.

She then set about to putting the finishing touches on the house— lighting candles, votives, and a fragrant oil burner, cinnamon.

She glanced at the clock on the wall—5:35. Joe would be there soon. Butterflies flitted about in her stomach, and she wished she could open a door and just let them escape. She was looking forward to her meal with Joe, but questions had been swirling in her head all day, and she wrestled with the answers. What was Joe doing reading papers from 1922? The answer was obvious, wasn't it? He was looking for something. People didn't just walk into the Dark Hills library and ask for the 1922 editions of the *Gazette*—the 1922 editions. Hardly light reading. But what was he looking for? And how did he know where to look?

Relax, she told herself for the hundredth time that day. *Relax*. He can't know anything and wouldn't find anything reading some old newspapers, anyway. Great-Grandpa made sure the historical account was what *he* wanted it to be. He was thinking about future generations, planning ahead. But someone knew. Of that she was sure. Someone had to tell Joe where to look. She'd have to keep an eye on him, find out who he'd been talking to.

But it's Joe, Joe Saunders, she reminded herself again, not some two-bit snoop trying to ruin her career.

But it's your family, Maggie. Your legacy. Your daddy. And if the truth surfaces, it will ruin your career and ruin what little quality of life Dad has left. He'll go to his grave with nothing. The reality of that truth pressed against her heart like a tumor.

She went to the kitchen, opened the oven, and checked the chicken. A wave of heat carrying the aroma of rosemary, bacon, and pearl onions floated past her. What if he started asking questions? Started getting all nosy, wanting answers?

Relax. Just stick to the story in the *Gazette*. That was history, the only historical record there was.

But why not just tell him the truth? She could trust Joe, couldn't she? She was once ready to trust him with her life. Couldn't she trust him now?

No! No way. He would never understand. Things had gotten too complicated already. No one could know what really happened. Not even Joe.

She swallowed hard and tried to will those butterflies away. *Please, Joe, don't ask questions.*

A knock at the door startled her.

Joe. He was early.

Maggie took one last look in the mirror, wiped some mascara from her cheek, scolded those rebellious locks, and drew in a deep breath. It felt like there was a jackrabbit in her chest trying to thump itself free.

Relax. It's just Joe.

She swung the door open and smiled. Joe stood before her, a vision from the past. His hair was neatly combed, his face cleanly shaven, and the brown coat he wore brought out his milk chocolate eyes. He looked just like that eighteen-year-old boy who stole her heart so long ago, but his broad chest and thick shoulders were definitely those of a man.

"Hello, Maggie," Joe said. It had stopped raining, the clouds had parted, and the evening light cast a soft glow on the sloping angles of his face.

"Hi, Joe." She opened the door wider and stepped aside. "Come on in. Dinner's almost ready."

Joe stepped inside and removed his coat. "Smells great. What did you make?"

"Rosemary chicken. It's something new I'm trying. Hope it turns out OK." She took his coat and hung it behind the door as she closed it. "I gotta go check on it, so"—she motioned toward the living room—"have a seat and make yourself at home."

"Is there anything I can help you with?"

"No. You just sit and relax."

Joe sat on the sofa, and Maggie returned to the kitchen to finish preparing the meal and setting the table.

"I like your place, Mags," Joe said from the living room. "It's got real personality. I like the retro forties look."

"Thanks." Maggie leaned against the doorframe between the kitchen and living room and looked around. A lot of the furniture was her parents', but she'd spent a lot of her off time scouring antique shops and flea markets for glassware and accessories from the thirties and forties. She liked the era; life was simple then, slow-paced. "I like it. It's home, you know. It's me."

Joe smiled and nodded, looking around. "Yeah. I can see that."

Maggie returned to the kitchen and put the chicken on a glass platter. "So…how's Caleb doing?"

She didn't miss Joe's hesitation. Her police experience red-flagged it: he was hiding something. "Uh, he's not much better. The doctors say there's progress, but nothing we can really see. He's getting good care, though, physical therapy and everything."

Maggie moved into the dining room and busied herself with setting the food on the table. "I'm sure he'll come around. How's Rosa holding up?"

Joe laughed. "Oh, you know Rosa. She's incredible. I don't think she has ever doubted that Caleb will make a full recovery. Her faith is inspiring. I feel so small whenever I'm with her."

"She is an incredibly strong woman," Maggie said. She made a few trips back and forth between the kitchen and dining room and finally said, "OK. It's ready."

For the next thirty minutes, Joe and Maggie intermingled talking with chewing. The conversation was mostly small talk, reminiscing about old times, trading gossip about old friends and schoolmates, and generally just catching up on the last fifteen years. Maggie was careful to keep the conversation on comfortable ground and avoid any talk of the attacks. It was like doing a conversational waltz—going through the motions while staying out of each other's way.

Joe set down his fork, propped his elbows on the table, and rested his chin in his hands. "So why did you become a cop? What happened to being a vet?"

Up until that point, Maggie was happy with where the conversation was going—and not going. If they could just steer clear of her family, police work, and Dark Hills history, she might just make it through the evening unscathed. But Joe had asked the question and now sat staring at her with wide eyes, waiting for an answer. She'd have to play it safe. For now.

She forced a shaky laugh and finished chewing her chicken. "Too much college. After you...left." She paused and noted the shift of his eyes. She'd made him uncomfortable. "I took some courses at Penn State Mont Alto, general ed stuff, but the more I took, the more I realized college wasn't for me. You know I never was a bookworm."

"But you always got good grades."

She gave him a look that scolded. "Not *good*. Better than you, but not good enough for veterinarian school. That's when I decided to enroll in the police academy in Harrisburg." She held her fork in midair, letting her mind wander back to the day she announced she'd be attending the academy. Her mom and dad were sitting at the table in this very room, finishing their dinner when she barged into the house all smiles and giggles.

"How were your classes today?" Mom asked.

Maggie sat down at the table next to Mom and across from Dad and smiled a grin that took up half her face. "Classes were terrible."

Dad looked at her with one eyebrow cocked. "So why all the smiles?"

Maggie slapped the table. "Mom, Dad, I have an announcement to make."

"Oh, boy," Mom said, rolling her eyes and lowering her fork. "I don't know if I'm ready for this. You're not pregnant, are you?"

Maggie held a hand over her mouth and laughed. "Mom! No way! You two know I'm not really cut out for this college stuff, don't you?"

Her parents just looked at each other, neither saying a word but both wearing a look that said they knew what was coming.

"Well, I decided to drop out," she paused for effect while her parents exchanged glances, "and join the police academy. I want to be a police officer!"

Dad jumped up so fast he nearly knocked the table over. "My baby's going to be an officer," he shouted, then wrapped her in a bear hug so tight she thought she'd never catch her breath.

"—Maggie."

Joe was saying her name. She blinked the memory away and stared at Joe.

"How did your dad take the news?"

A gentle smile tugged at the corners of Maggie's mouth. "As you could guess, my parents, especially my dad, were very pleased when I told them I wanted to become a police officer. He actually cried." Her eyes drifted from Joe's and focused on some distant memory on the far wall. "It was the first time I ever saw him cry."

"You were carrying on the legacy."

Maggie snapped her eyes back to meet Joe's. The legacy. He'd mentioned the legacy. Her mind was in the present again. "Yes. That's right. My family's been in law enforcement here in Dark Hills for generations."

Joe picked up his fork again and speared a piece of chicken. "Did you feel any added pressure to carry on the torch?"

"No. Never." Maggie was quickly erecting walls around her and knew Joe could tell by the tone of her voice. "I mean, I knew my dad wanted me to be a cop. It was no secret. But I also knew he would have supported me wholeheartedly if I'd chosen to do something else outside law enforcement."

"Are you happy with the choice you made?"

Maggie paused and let her mind wander for just a moment. She always thought she liked her job—she was doing some real good in the world, at least in Dark Hills—but now sitting in her home with Joe across the table made her think twice about whether she'd made the right choice all those years ago. "Yes and no. I love being a cop, helping people, making sure they feel safe, doing some right in a world that seems to have so much wrong with it. I have the power to make a real change. It may only be in this little community, but for the people who live here, this is their world. And I can help make their world a safer place. I like that." She stopped, satisfied with her answer.

"And the no?"

Maggie looked at Joe and raised her eyebrows.

"The no. You said, yes and *no*."

"Oh, yeah." She paused again and put her fork down, giving herself time to gather her thoughts. "Being a cop, especially the chief, can be pretty lonely at times." A mild warmth touched her cheeks. "It seems nobody wants to get close to a female cop."

Joe cocked his head to one side. "Have there been any guys you wanted to get close to?" he said with a mischievous smile.

"No." She said it so quickly she surprised herself. "I mean…no." Joe had succeeded in flustering her. She needed to change the subject. And quick. "So how about you? Why landscaping?"

Joe shrugged. "I love being dirty."

Maggie laughed at the double meaning, and Joe joined her when the humor obviously struck him. It was nice to have some comic relief.

"No, no, no. Not like that," he said, waving his hands back and forth. "Goodness. Talk about a poor choice of words. You know what I mean."

She laughed some more. "Do I? Remember, Joe Saunders, I knew you when you were a young buck strutting your stuff. Remember the time we snuck away during the senior class trip. They looked for us for hours, and when they finally found us I think everyone knew what we'd been up to. I think they were more embarrassed than we were."

Joe chuckled and tilted his head. "That was such a long time ago, wasn't it? We've both changed so much."

Maggie shifted in her chair. It *was* a long time ago. Too long, and they'd both changed too much. "Yes, we have, and you wound up in land-scaping."

"Oh, yeah." Joe shrugged. "I love working outside and getting my hands dirty. In high school, I was thinking about going to college for botany or agriculture or something like that."

"I remember. That's why it surprised me so much when you showed up that day with a buzz cut saying you were joining the army."

———

Yes. That day. He had joined the army.

Joe thought back to the day. He remembered it all so vividly, the smell of Sergeant Wickham's cologne, the scratch of the pen as he signed his name, the sound of the clippers as they ran over his head, the seemingly endless drive to Maggie's house to tell her the news, the beating of his heart so fiercely he thought for sure it was going to bust right out of his chest, the look of shock on Maggie's face, the tears, the questions, the smell of her flowery perfume and softness of her body as they hugged, the feeling of finality even though he had promised to return.

He knew he had hurt her, but he also knew his life was going nowhere. He'd never make it in college. Sure, it was nice to dream about such things, but the reality of it was that he wasn't smart enough to coast through and wasn't determined enough to work hard. He'd have flunked out anyway.

And what kind of husband would he have made? He would have wound up a college dropout working twelve-hour shifts at the paper mill, hating his job. Miserable. But if his life had taken a different direction, Rick would still be alive and Caleb would most likely not be in a coma. So it *was* all his fault.

Forcing aside the rising wave of guilt that suddenly threatened to overcome him, Joe sighed. "Yeah, I know. I guess it surprised me too. It was an impulsive thing. I guess all the talk about college and how serious we were getting just kind of scared me, and I ran. Unfortunately, I fell into the wrong arms."

Maggie propped her elbows on the table and cradled her chin in her hands. "So why landscaping, though? Why not forestry or farming or something else that's outside and"—she smiled and never looked more like Audrey Hepburn—"natureful, if that's a word."

Joe smiled. "I don't think it is, but I'm sure Mr. Webster would be proud of you for coining a new one." He grew serious. "After Rick died, I ran again. Seems to be the story of my life. Maybe I should have trained for a marathon."

Maggie smiled politely.

Joe continued. "I moved north, rented an apartment, a real dive, and started a three-week wallow in my own guilt and shame. I don't think I left the apartment once. Then, one day, I woke up and looked around. The floor was littered with crumbs. Empty pizza boxes and Chinese cartons were everywhere, even in the bathtub. The kitchen sink was piled high and overflowing with dirty dishes. I looked in the mirror and saw a man with bags under his eyes, a scraggly beard, and greasy hair. I didn't even recognize myself." He paused, remembering the painful moment of the awakening. "It was at that moment I realized what I really was, what I had become—a loser. I was everything I had once despised, everything I had told myself I would never become. And at that moment, standing in the bathroom, looking at that stranger in the mirror—that loser—I determined to change. So that very day I cleaned that apartment so good it sparkled.

"There were plenty of older people in the neighborhood who needed help around their yards. So I made up some fliers and went door-to-door offering my services: mowing, pruning, trimming, sheep shearing, whatever. Within a week I had five clients—no sheep to shear—and the rest, well…"

They both smiled and finished his thought in unison, "…is history."

Maggie laughed again, not a polite or forced laugh, but a genuine laugh that reached all the way to her eyes and bent them into little crescents that warmed the room. "I'm proud of you, Joe."

There was an awkward moment of silence until Maggie looked at her plate and must have noticed her food was gone. She set her fork down and sat back in her chair. "Wow. I'm stuffed."

Joe smiled. Maggie *was* beautiful. She put that Hepburn lady to shame. The way the candlelight glowed on her soft face and danced in her endless blue eyes made him wish he'd never left Dark Hills, made him wish all this business about her family and the attacks did not exist. It made him wish it was just the two of them, here, now, together, with no barrier between them so they could pick up where they had left off fifteen years ago and fall in love all over again.

He would do it right this time. They'd get married, move away from Dark Hills, start a new life somewhere else. Maybe up north. New England. He'd always wanted to live in New England.

"It was delicious," he said, placing his napkin on the plate. "Well done." He wanted to say more, so much more, but something prevented him. Maggie's next question would reveal why.

"So what have you been up to?" she asked.

No! Don't ask that. I don't want to lie to you.

And it was at that moment, staring into her blue eyes, feeling emotions that had been buried for fifteen years, that Joe decided what he had to do. He wouldn't lie to her. He would tell her the truth. "Maggie," he said, leaning his elbows on the table and meeting her gaze. "I need to be honest with you. I was at the library yesterday and—"

The phone rang.

Joe glanced into the kitchen as if willing the thing not to ring again. He had to get this out, and this may be his only chance. "I, uh—"

It rang again. Maggie slid her chair back and stood. "I'm sorry. Let me answer it and get rid of whoever it is."

She ran into the kitchen.

Joe heard her say "Hello."

CHAPTER 28

MAGGIE, WE GOT a situation." It was Andy. He was covering the evening shift.

"OK." Maggie found it hard to hide her annoyance at the untimely interruption.

"Um, I'm gonna need you to come out here."

"Where's *here*?"

"'Bout a mile outside of town, off Route 20."

"I'm kinda busy right now. Can it wait?"

There was a loud sigh on the other end. "Eddie Hopkins ran off the road and into the cornfield. Um, it looks like another... attack. And... there's something here you'll want to see."

Maggie's throat constricted. *Another attack.* The words pounded through her head like a semi.

She needed to get rid of Joe.

"OK. I'll be right there."

"Everything OK?" Joe asked when Maggie returned. Her face looked like someone had turned a valve and drained the blood out of it.

She stood by her chair, fingering the ring on her right hand. "Um, I'm sorry, Joe. I have to run. That was Andy. There's been an accident out on Route 20 and I need to check it out."

"Oh." Joe pushed his chair back and stood up. "I'll come with you—"

"No," she said, cutting him off. "You don't need to do that. It may wind up being a late night. Besides, there'll be tons of paperwork to do afterward. Just a bunch of boring police stuff. It's gonna be a late night."

"OK," Joe said. He could tell by Maggie's behavior that something was going on, something more than just a car accident. He decided not to press the issue, though, knowing it would do no good and not wanting to ruin what had turned out to be a pleasant evening. "Well, thanks for the meal and the company. It was nice, Mags. Real nice. I'm glad we got to spend this time together."

Maggie smiled and reached for her coat. "I enjoyed it too. Thanks for coming over."

Then came the moment of awkwardness. They stood face-to-face, no more than two feet apart, staring at each other while an uncomfortable silence hung in the air between them. Finally, Joe clumsily put out his hand and took Maggie's in his. He smiled awkwardly and said, "Thanks again, Mags. Maybe we can do it again sometime soon."

"OK." That was it. That was all that came out. He wanted her to say more, but her mind was obviously not on him.

It was on Andy's phone call. It was on Route 20.

When Maggie arrived at the scene of Eddie's accident, Gary and Andy had already marked the area off with yellow police tape and were waiting by the road for her.

She eased her car to a stop and opened the door.

Gary was right there. "Maggie, this is some weirded-out stuff."

She grabbed the flashlight from the passenger seat and clicked it on.

Gary led the way, keeping his light on the glowing rear reflectors of Eddie's Buick. Andy and Maggie followed, stepping carefully over the flattened stalks and scanning the rows of corn with their lights.

"I was driving by and noticed the corn down," Andy said. "I took a closer look and noticed a car sitting in the field. I ran the plates, and it came up Eddie's. At first I thought he'd just lost control and ran off the road. But then I noticed the trail."

Maggie looked at him. The flashlight was bright enough that she could clearly make out the lines of his face. She knew Andy well enough to know that when he was disturbed the lines at the corners of his mouth dipped downward and deepened. And he was disturbed. "What trail?"

They arrived at the car, and Gary pointed his light at the corn. "There," he said, pointing past the first row of stalks.

Maggie looked hard, but all she saw were a few illuminated shoots of corn against a black backdrop. "I don't see it."

"Show her, Andy," Gary said.

"Here." Andy pushed two stalks to either side and stepped past the first row. He pointed his flashlight where a row of stalks had been flattened, broken at a right angle three inches above the ground.

Maggie leaned in and pointed her light in the same direction. "OK. You got my attention. Did you follow it?"

Andy nodded. "I called Gary and waited for him, then the two of us followed it."

"And?"

Andy looked at Maggie with wide eyes. "Well…I think you better see for yourself."

Maggie stiffened her back. "Andy, I'm not in the mood for surprises. What's down there?"

"Eddie."

"What's left of him," Gary added.

Maggie took a deep breath. Dread gnawed at her gut. Andy's words swam through her head: *another attack.* If it was anything like the attack on Woody Owen, she would almost certainly lose her dinner. She wondered what the rosemary chicken would taste like a second time. An odd thought. She swallowed hard and braced herself. "OK. Let's go."

Gary led the way, followed by Maggie, then Andy. The ground was soft from the rain, and their shoes sank into the soil as they walked. The trail of broken stalks wound through the field for maybe thirty yards before it finally ended.

Gary stood in a small clearing and pointed his light at his feet. "Eddie."

Maggie pointed her light at Gary's feet. Bile surged into her throat, and her skin went cold.

It was a hand, severed at the wrist.

"That's it," Gary said. "That's all we found. We circled the perimeter maybe ten, fifteen yards out but found nothing. The rain must have washed away any blood trail."

Maggie held her light steady on the muddy hand. Its fingers were curled around something. It looked like a piece of paper. "What's that in the palm?"

"I'm not sure," Andy said. "We didn't want to touch anything until you got here."

Maggie stooped and carefully pulled the paper from the rigid fingers, causing the hand to shift. She turned the paper over. There was writing, blurred and smeared, but decipherable. An icy rush started in her hands and crept up her arms, through her neck, and settled in the back of her head.

She read the words aloud: "An eye for an eye."

Now she had three dead. And this. A note.

Was the killer a person after all? Some serial nutcase roaming Dark Hills? But Joe saw a beast of some sort in the woods. And Doc Adams said Cujo's killer was most likely a large cat, a lion. And no human could possibly do what was done to Woody Owen.

And didn't Great-Grandpa say something about Old Man Yates ranting and raving about Judgment Day? About vengeance? They were pieces to a puzzle, but where did they all fit? And how did they fit together? Maggie had a growing feeling that she wouldn't like the picture the pieces made.

She crumpled the paper and stuffed it in her pocket. Her hands were shaking, and her stomach was roiling. "OK. Nobody hears about this. Eddie drove off the road, and nobody's seen him since. Andy, get rid of the hand. Gary, get rid of the tape, and call Carl Summers to tow the car."

Andy moved his light away from the hand. "What do you think the note means? Who do you think wrote it?"

Maggie pressed her molars together. The pressure in her head was building again. "I don't know. I need some time to think this through."

Not more than thirty feet from the hand, Stevie crouched close to the ground, still, silent, listening and watching as the cops discussed their next move. He was dressed in black and felt invisible among the thick rows of corn.

He smiled. The glow of the flashlights reflected the fear in Chief Maggie's eyes—they glowed red with terror.

Wilt and Warren were trying to be tough guys, but he could see the fear in their eyes too.

So far things were going as planned. They had found the hand, which was good. And they had found the note, which was better.

He waited patiently for them to leave. Chief Maggie left first, then Wilt bagged the hand and waited with Warren until the tow truck came. It took all of thirty minutes to hook the car up and drag it out of the field. But all the while, Stevie crouched, smiling in the darkness.

When the last flashlight winked out and their headlights faded out of view and the field was once again dark and quiet, Stevie let out a hoot and ran through the corn like a crazed animal.

"Momma!" he yelled. "It's happenin', Momma. I didn't forget. Three down, two to go."

He pushed through the stalks to the clearing and collapsed to the ground, lying spread-eagle on his back.

A voice hammered in his head. It was Momma's. Over and over it begged, *Avenge my death! Avenge my death!*

"I will, Momma."

His eyes rolled back in his head, and a charge of electricity raced through his nerves. His body began to quiver and shake, muscles spasming and writhing. His heart pumped like a piston at full throttle, and his breathing grew raspy and labored.

A minute later he stopped, opened his eyes, and stared at the velvet sky spattered with tiny pricks of light. A wide smile bunched his cheeks, and he began to laugh hysterically. He chuckled, hooted, and snorted for a little over a minute before stopping to compose himself. He tried to harness his laughter, but it soon broke through his closed mouth in a spray of saliva, and the hysterics resumed. Another minute later, he finally wound down and lay exhausted on the wet ground, breathing heavily.

"Glen Sterner," he said between breaths. "Time to pay the piper. Then L-stone."

CHAPTER 29

T HE AIR IN the house was as cool as a mid-autumn morning. But when Josiah Walker sat straight up in his sleeping bag, eyes wide, mouth agape, sucking air, he was drenched in sweat.

He'd had a dream. Not a vision—this time it was just a dream.

No voices this time, either; just images. Gruesome images that struck terror in his mind. In his dream, he had panicked at the sight of the corpses. There were two of them, floating in shallow water, just below the surface, concealed in a stand of cattails. Their bodies were naked and torn to shreds, like someone had run them through a farming combine. And they were faceless. Not faceless as in no features, but faceless as in no face, like it had been chomped clean off.

But in spite of not seeing their faces, he knew who they were.

"Oh, God," he whispered into the darkness. "What are You doing here?"

He unzipped his sleeping bag and swung his legs over the edge of the sofa. He sat there, wiping at his sweat and feeling a chill run through his body as the moisture evaporated in the cool air.

He needed some tea. He needed to think. He needed to pray.

Josiah slipped off the sofa and into his slippers and padded across the living room, ignoring the pain in his knees.

Though he knew his way around the kitchen and had no need for the light, he flipped it on anyway. He put a pot of water on the stove and turned the knob to the left. The gas range clicked a few times and ignited into a blue flame.

"Lord," he prayed aloud, leaning against the counter, arms folded across his chest, "what's happening in this old town? I ain't sure of what You're doing, but I trust You. Lead us."

He paused and thought about how simple his prayer was. But it had to be simple—God was keeping him in the dark and only allowing pinpoints of light to filter through to him. He knew God was working, but it was behind a veil, hidden from man's eyes and understanding.

The teapot whistled like a faraway steam engine. Josiah sighed. "You may have to help us out a little more, Lord. We are an ignorant people."

He took the pot off the heat and poured a mug full of steaming water, steeped his tea bag, and tossed it in the trash can. Holding the mug to his lips, he shuffled down the hall and back into the living room. After putting a match to the oil lamp, he found his favorite wingback chair. He was still trembling from the dream and couldn't shake the images of the dead bodies. Every time he closed his eyes he saw the gray, bloated, faceless corpses. What did it mean? Somehow, he knew exactly what it meant.

Gotta call Joe. The clock on the mantel read 1:25. *Better use his cell phone.* He reached for his cordless and dialed in the number Joe had given him. The phone rang four times before a recorded message—Joe's voice—came on instructing the caller to leave a message.

That won't work. He retrieved the phone book, found the number for the Dew-Drop, and called the front desk. He was then connected to Joe's room.

Five rings later the phone picked up and a groggy voice on the other end mumbled something incoherent.

"Joe?"

"Yeah—yeah. Who's this?"

"It's Jo. Josiah...Walker."

There was a pause and Josiah could hear a click on the other end of the phone, then some rustling. "Josiah. What are you calling me at one thirty for? Is everything OK?" Joe sounded a little irritated. Understandable, though. After all, it was the middle of the night, and Josiah had obviously roused him out of a sound sleep.

"You awake, Joe?"

"I'm talking, aren't I? Yes. I'm awake. What's going on?"

"I had a dream." Josiah waited for a response, but when none came he continued. "I dreamed I saw two mauled corpses. Faceless corpses."

"OK. And?" Things didn't seem to be registering for Joe.

"And I know who they were."

"I thought you said they were faceless?"

"They were." No response again. "But I just knew. God, He told me."

There was a breath of static on the other end. "Maybe it was just a bad dream. People have them, you know."

"No. It was more than that. Remember our talk? God is showing us little by little. This is another clue."

"A clue?"

"Yes. A piece of the puzzle. When we put all the pieces together, we'll have the total picture. It's like we're putting the puzzle together, and God is handing us one piece at a time. You know, like you do a child."

There was a pause again, and Josiah imagined Joe thinking hard about what he'd just said.

"So who were they?" Joe asked.

"Eddie Hopkins and Woody Owen. I think they're dead."

Another pause. More thinking. "They were two of the guys involved in the murder of that woman...Gail—"

"Bauer. Stevie's mother. Right. I think they're dead."

"Owen *is* dead. I heard some guys talking the other day that his house exploded and he died in the fire."

Josiah scratched at his chin and rubbed an eye. "True. But that fire ain't what killed him."

"How do you know?"

"Joe, wake up. Jumpin' George, son, shake the dust outta your head. Are you awake? I just told you. God told me. I believe Owen's death was the same as Hopkins's. If we find out how Hopkins died, we'll find the truth about Owen's death."

"You really think Hopkins is dead? I mean, you're sure about it."

"Sure as a bloodhound's nose."

"Um..." Another pause. "OK. I have an idea. Meet me along Route 20 tomorrow morning. I want to check something out, and it'd be nice to have someone else there."

Josiah took a sip of his tea. The heat brought some warmth to his body as it settled in his stomach. "What's on 20?"

"Last night I was having dinner with Maggie, and she got a call that there was an accident on Route 20. I offered to go with her to check it out, but she got real weird and acted like she didn't want me anywhere near the place. I got the feeling it was more than just a routine accident. There was something there she didn't want me to see. So tomorrow morning I was going to check it out for myself. I'm not sure where along 20, but I'm hoping it will be obvious enough."

"I'm game. How's seven?"

"Sounds good. And Josiah, no more one-thirty calls, OK?"

Josiah laughed. "No problem."

It was a beautiful Sunday morning. The air was cold and sharp, the sun was just peering over the eastern ridge of the Dark Hills, coloring the sky with long ribbons of pastel pink and orange. A thin layer of dew had settled on the grass, glistening like crystal.

The sleepy town of Dark Hills was just beginning to climb out of its slumber at 6:50 in the morning. Rusty pickups and late-model sedans flowed in and out of the paper mill, signaling the changing of the guard from third to first shift. And Darlene's was slowly filling with bleary-eyed patrons, filing in like caffeine-starved zombies drawn by the aroma of sizzling grease and the lullaby of hardening arteries.

Joe parked his truck in the small Mobil lot and walked into the empty mini-mart. After filling a 16-ounce Styrofoam cup with coffee, he muttered "Morning" and "Thanks" to the cashier and headed down Route 20.

He had hardly slept after Josiah's call. He'd spent the rest of the night tossing and rolling in bed, wrestling with unanswerable questions that, nonetheless, begged for answers, or at least something that made sense. But nothing did. Maybe it was because he was tired and not thinking clearly. Or maybe it was because he was just tired of chasing the unknown. There were too many questions and no answers.

But there *were* answers, weren't there? Josiah was right; answers were coming slowly, one at a time. It was as though God *was* feeding them morsels of information, testing their faith, their patience, their resolve. Compared to what he knew when he had first arrived in Dark Hills after hearing of Caleb's mauling, he had gained a ton of knowledge. But where was it all leading? How did it all fit together? Only time would tell. Hopefully.

About two hundred yards up the road, Joe saw Josiah's beat-up blue and beige Dodge pickup sitting on the gravel shoulder, and Josiah leaning against it. He steered his truck off the road, gravel grinding under its tires, and stopped behind the Dodge.

Josiah met him at his door, a stainless steel travel mug in his hand. "Mornin' to ya."

"Cold one, huh?" Joe said, stepping out of his truck.

"Sure is. Beautiful, though."

Josiah motioned toward the car-wide corridor of crushed cornstalks cutting a straight path through the field. There were deep tire tracks in the soft ground, either the work of a tow truck or Maggie and her deputies had spent the evening joyriding a John Deere. "I assume this is where the accident happened."

Joe eyed the path. It cut about twenty yards into the corn, then stopped. "Sure looks like it. Let's go have a look."

They headed down the trail of fallen stalks, stepping over and around the debris. When they came to the end, Joe looked around and shrugged. "Nothing seems out of the ordinary. Looks like someone just ran off the road."

Josiah shook his head. "No. There's somethin' here. I can feel it. Like a tickle in my bones. This place has somethin' to do with my dream last night."

"The dead guys?"

"The dead guys. Let's split up and walk around a bit. You go that way"—he motioned to the rows of corn on Joe's left—"and I'll go this way." He motioned to the corn on his right. "We'll circle around and meet back here. If you find anything unusual, give a holler."

Joe nodded. "Will do."

Joe entered the corn to his left and immediately found a trampled path that led farther into the field at an angle. He followed the trail to where it stopped and looked around, studying the ground and the stalks. It was a small clearing of broken stalks, no more than six feet by six feet. Some lay flat on the ground, and some leaned at odd angles, twisted and fractured. The ground was disturbed, and some of the stalks were streaked with a dark brown color. Something had definitely happened here.

Joe squatted for a closer look. He examined a stalk and realized it wasn't dark brown at all; it was deep red—dried blood. He looked around the small clearing and now noticed the blood smeared on almost every stalk. It was smudged in places and diluted by the dew in other places, but it was on everything. Pushing one of the fallen stalks aside, he examined a large indentation in the ground.

His heart beat out a staccato rhythm. "Josiah! Jo!"

"Yeah. Over here." Josiah's voice was muffled by the corn.

"I got something. You better take a look."

It took almost a minute for Josiah to work his way through the corn to where Joe was kneeling on the ground. "What is it?"

Joe ran his finger in a circle around them. "Look around. Blood all over the place." Then he pointed at the ground in front of him where he had moved the stalk. "And look at this."

Josiah crouched next to him and ran his hand over the indentation. "Looks like a paw print."

The print was only a partial one, but the pads and three toes were visible.

Joe placed his hand over the print. The large paw extended at least two inches past the tips of his fingers. "It's about eleven, twelve inches long." He looked at Josiah, who only bit his lower lip and stared at the indentation.

"What do you think?" Joe asked.

Josiah narrowed his eyes and looked at him. "You really want to know what I think?"

"I wouldn't ask if I didn't want to know. Let me have it."

Josiah ran his fingers over the paw print again. "I'm no tracker, but this is definitely a cat print." He looked at Joe and caught his gaze. "A big cat. And I think someone died here last night. Hopkins. Which means Owen didn't die at the hand of any fire." He shifted his gaze to the corn around them, looking around as if watching for the unseen predator.

Joe rubbed the back of his neck and twisted his face. "So Owen's death in the fire was a cover-up. Maggie intentionally..." He didn't finish his thought. It was absurd, he knew, but totally possible. Still, he felt like some conspiracy theory junkie looking for that next grand cover-up. What would be next? Lincoln's assassination? JFK? Elvis in leotards hugging it up with Darlene?

Josiah ran his hand over the print again. "Whatever it is, it's hunting us."

"Us? Or them?"

"What do you mean?"

Joe stood and looked around at the corn. "If your dream is right and Owen and Hopkins are dead as a result of animal attacks, that makes three dead total. And all three were involved in the murder of Gail Bauer. I know it sounds crazy, but if they're the only ones who have died so far, it seems the beast, or cat, or whatever it is, is only going after those involved in the case. It's only hunting *them*. Some kind of revenge thing. Like with Yates."

Josiah stared at him for a few long seconds before speaking. "And Caleb? How does he play into this revenge theory?"

Joe tightened his lips. "I don't know. Unless it was just a case of mistaken identity."

"But..." Josiah frowned and shook his head as if debating with himself again. "It's possible, though. Yes. Very possible. Just as God is working through people, maybe Satan is working through an animal." He nodded slightly. "Good and evil playing a game of chess. Possible."

Suddenly, Joe's heart quickened again, and he felt a tingle in his neck. He looked at Josiah. "Stevie knows."

Josiah's head shot up. "Then I suggest we have a little sit-down with Stevie."

"We will," Joe said, tunneling a hand through his hair. "But first I need to pay Maggie a visit. Seems she's been keeping secrets."

CHAPTER 30

JOE PUSHED THROUGH the glass door of the Dark Hills Police Station and stood in the small lobby. There were some questions he needed answered. Questions that could not wait.

The lobby wasn't very inviting. A few empty metal folding chairs lined the wall to his left; an information board littered with wanted posters and public notice announcements hung on the wall to the right. The counter in front of him was unmanned at the moment, and a small metal desk bell sat on it with a handwritten sign, *Ring for Service*. Beyond the counter was an open-doored office with *Chief* painted on the frosted glass—Maggie's office. A single black coat hung from a row of metal hooks on the wall to the left of the office door.

Joe rang the bell twice and stepped back from the counter, half-expecting a bug-eyed Barney Fife to materialize.

In a matter of seconds, Maggie appeared from her office wearing her beige uniform, hair pulled back in a loose ponytail. Her eyes widened when she saw Joe, and she smiled. "Joe. This is a pleasant—"

"Why didn't you tell me there were more attacks?" Joe was in no mood to be cordial. He tightened his jaw and gave Maggie a look that could burn a hole in steel, waiting for her response.

Maggie froze, and the smile on her face disappeared. He had succeeded in catching her off guard. That was good. Joe had figured the Gills were well rehearsed in protecting the family skeletons. Maggie would have an answer for everything; he hadn't realized it at the time, but he'd already experienced that with the Cummings incident. His only hope was the element of surprise, catch her off guard and maybe, just maybe, she'd slip up and divulge some important information.

Maggie glanced around as if looking for someone who obviously wasn't there, then peeked at her watch. "Come into my office." Her voice was low and authoritative.

Joe followed her, and she shut the door behind them. He kept his eyes on her as she casually strolled behind the large wooden desk and sat in her swivel chair.

Motioning toward a padded metal chair across from her, she said, "Have a seat, Joe."

He knew she was stalling for time, and, with each second that passed, he was losing his advantage. "I'd rather stand." He paused and glared at her, waiting for an answer to his question. Finally, he said, "Maggie? Why didn't you tell me?"

Maggie shrugged. "Tell you what?"

Joe's blood began to bubble in a hot boil. No way. He wasn't going to let her play ignorant. "You know what I'm talking about. There've been more attacks, more deaths. Why didn't you tell me?"

"I don't know what you're talking about." Maggie was trying to appear calm, but from the almost imperceptible quiver in her voice, Joe could tell he had rattled her. She may look like Audrey Hepburn playing a tough-cop role (something unimaginable to Joe at that moment), but inside she was more Barney Fife than she'd like to admit. "The only attacks I'm aware of have been Caleb and Bob. And I haven't verified any deaths yet. And since there haven't been any attacks since Bob's, I'm assuming the animal has moved on. Heck, for all we know, maybe one of the shots you fired the other night hit it, and it just crawled away and died." She stole another glance at her watch.

Joe clenched his fists and firmed his jaw. So that was the Gill way, deny everything. Well, he wasn't going to let her off the hook so easily. Time for plan B. He was taking a chance, he knew that, but if Josiah's dream was right, he'd really have her cornered. Then again, maybe it was just that—a dream—and he'd look like a fool. But it was all he had. He'd take his chances.

Joe met Maggie's eyes and held her stare for what seemed minutes. "Eddie Hopkins and Woody Owen." He said it using his best Clint Eastwood voice, even and unwavering. He felt like an outlaw dropping a challenge on the local lawman. Eastwood versus Fife.

By the way Maggie's jaw dropped and face turned an odd shade of off-white, Joe knew he'd struck an artery.

But Maggie's surprise was only brief. She quickly shut her mouth and regained her composure. "What about them? Do you know something I don't? Unfortunately, Woody died Thursday in a home fire. And that accident I told you about on Route 20? It was Eddie's car, but no Eddie. He was probably drunk, ran off the road, and staggered away somewhere to nurse his wounds." She shrugged. "It wouldn't be the first time. Now if you have any more information, I suggest you speak up, or you'll be the one keeping secrets."

She was doing her best to put up a front of casual confidence and quell the tremble that shivered through each word. Henry Gill would be proud if he could see the effort his great-granddaughter was putting forth now.

But Joe had had enough. He slapped the top of Maggie's desk with an open hand; the sound echoed in the small office. "C'mon, Mags! It's me, Joe. You don't have to lie to me. I know about your family's secret, about the corruption and cover-ups. Just level with me. There's a man-eater out there roaming around, and we need to stop it. We need to kill it before it kills again."

Just then the back door of the building shut. Seconds later there was a knock on the door of the office.

Maggie kept her eyes on Joe. "Come in."

The door opened, and Gary Warren stood in the doorway, his large frame filling the empty space. "What's going on? I heard yelling."

Joe turned his head and followed Gary's arm down to where his hand rested on his belt just above his sidearm.

Gary motioned with his head toward Joe. "Is everything OK, Chief?"

Maggie shot a look at Joe, then back at Gary. "Uh, yeah. Everything's fine. Joe was just leaving." She looked at Joe and arched her eyebrows as if to admonish him and suggest he accept her gracious gift and leave before Gary tossed him out.

Joe snapped up, straightened his spine, and threw his shoulders back. He kept his eyes on Maggie as he said, "Yeah, I was just leaving." Then he turned and left, walking out of Maggie's life—again.

—————

A twinge of regret poked at Maggie's heart, but she quickly brushed it aside. No place for silly emotions now. This was serious. She waited until she heard the front door shut, then looked at Gary, her lips tight. She had a headache. "He knows."

"What do you want to do about it?"

Maggie hesitated, staring at a blank spot on the wall. Her mind was wading through a pool of glue. Her hands were shaking, and a cool sweat beaded on her brow.

Joe, please don't make me do this.

Finally, she met Gary's eyes again. "Just keep an eye on him. Let me know who he talks to."

Stevie was stretched out on his green vinyl sofa, a pillow pushed under his head, a bowl of popcorn balanced on his stomach, watching an old Bugs Bunny video, when something hit him like a wrecking ball in his chest. He flipped, turned, and rolled off the sofa, landing with a hollow thud on the plywood floor. Popcorn scattered across the carpet.

Then it hit him again.

And again.

And again.

He looked around, eyes wide, chest burning, looking for the source of the abuse.

The crushing blow came again, this time sending him into a full body spasm. His back arched off the floor, arms and legs rigid like wood. When it stopped, and his body relaxed, he scrambled to the side of the sofa and cowered like a wounded animal.

Someone was there, in the room with him. *They* had come for him, come to finish what they started.

First Momma, now him.

Wham! It hit him again and pushed him back against the wall. His chest ached now, throbbed like a fresh bruise. Sweat poured down from his forehead and stung his eyes.

"Get out!" Stevie screamed, a blood-chilling screech. "Leave me alone!"

He crouched behind the sofa and peered over the arm, scanning the room. His lungs were working overtime; his pulse tapped like a woodpecker in his ears. He swung his head to the right. He heard footsteps...in the trailer. Not just one pair, but two, maybe three. He heard them but saw nothing. His eyes darted around the room—back and forth, back and forth—searching every corner, probing every shadow. No one was there, but he heard *them*. Running now. Heavy footfalls thumping on the plywood, banging in his ears.

Then, as if the invisible runners weren't enough, the trailer began to vibrate like a locomotive. Was it an earthquake? A bomb? A stack of magazines toppled over, sliding across the floor. The popcorn bounced on the carpet as though it were still in the popper. A glass spilled over, soda soaking the rug, leaving a dark stain. Like blood.

Then, as quickly as it started, it stopped, and there was silence. No vibrating, no footfalls, no chest thumps. Silence...except for the sporadic, tinny sounds of a cartoon.

Stevie looked around the room trying to decide if it was safe to venture out of his crouched, defensive position. He listened for the footsteps, but all he heard was laughing, wild laughing. Deep, raspy hysterics filled the room, growing in volume.

He turned his head toward the source of the laughter—the TV—and almost choked on his own saliva. Yosemite Sam was jumping up and down, turning in circles, kicking up dirt, firing his pistols into the air, laughing, laughing, laughing.

Stevie narrowed his eyes and pursed his lips. "Stop it!" he hollered at the TV.

But Yosemite kept right on laughing, mocking Stevie.

"Stop it!" he hollered again.

Yosemite suddenly stopped laughing and holstered his twin six-shooters. His face grew larger on the screen until only his eyes, nose, and mouth, all framed by bright red hair, were visible. "Kill Gill," he said in his low, throaty voice. "Kill...Gill!"

Stevie stepped back and stumbled over the arm of the sofa, landing on his back on the soft cushions. He lifted his head and looked at the TV.

Yosemite was still there. "Kill Gill!"

Stevie reached for the remote, grabbed it, fumbled it, dropped it, picked it up, and clicked the TV off. The screen went black. He sat up and swung his legs off the edge, planting his feet on the floor. He rested his elbows on his knees and took a long, deep breath. Sweat-soaked hair clung to his forehead. His heart was rapid-firing like a machine gun. He rubbed his chest and looked around the room. A flashing light on the microwave caught his eye. The LED blinked: KILL...GILL. KILL...GILL. Again and again the same message.

"No!" Stevie shouted, "I won't! That ain't part a'the deal."

KILL...KILL...KILL...KILL.

Stevie grabbed two handfuls of hair and pulled hard. "No. No. No!"

A voice then started in his head. Not Momma's voice, but a man's, deep and firm. It was Yosemite Sam again. Not on TV, but in his head. "Kill Gill. Kill Gill. KillGillKillGillKillGill."

Stevie clapped his hands over his ears, batted at his head, ground his teeth. "NO!"

There was a knock on the door.

Rosa didn't go to church Sunday morning. She was right where she needed to be, right where God wanted her to be—with Caleb. She had arrived at Hillside at eight o'clock, chatted with Gloria, the morning nurse attending to Caleb, sang a few praise and worship choruses, and cracked her Bible. The building was quiet. Only the occasional squeak from a nurse's sneaker on the tile floor broke the silence.

For most of the morning Rosa read from 1 Peter, sticking with her normal routine of intermingling prayer and meditation with the reading of God's Word—read, meditate, pray; read, meditate, pray. It was a slow process but well worth it. God's Word was a delicacy to be chewed slowly and thoughtfully, every flavor enjoyed, every taste savored. It was during those moments, moments of quietness before her Lord, with His words fresh in her mind and heart, that He spoke to her, illuminating His message and giving her understanding.

A few days ago, she had started reading aloud. If Caleb could hear, he might as well be hearing God's Word.

Now, Caleb lay quietly as Rosa read. She hoped her voice would have a soothing effect on her son. It filled the small room with the poetic rhythm of Peter's exhortations.

She finished reading several verses in chapter 4, closed her eyes, and let the words soak into her mind, whispering them as they settled. "Do not think it strange concerning the fiery trial which is to try you...but rejoice...when His glory is revealed...exceeding joy...If anyone suffers as a Christian...glorify God."

She then fell into prayer, communing with her God, standing before Him, open and bare, her heart and soul exposed. "Father, thank You for the trials we are now enduring." The words came easily. She was thankful,

thankful for His arms enveloping her in His love, protecting her, whispering comfort to her heart. "Thank You for the assurance that Your glory will be revealed in Caleb's life. I glorify You. I glorify You."

The glow was there again, bringing comfort and warmth.

The darkness had grown colder, and Caleb found himself longing for the soft light of the orange glow and the baritone rumble of the voice that accompanied it.

Occasionally, he would hear familiar voices somewhere on the other side of the darkness, but they were always muffled and garbled, unintelligible. But they brought some comfort nonetheless—like a salve on an open wound. In the black hole where he hid, anything even slightly familiar carried with it a sense of hope.

He reached for the light again, accepting it, welcoming it, ready to be used by it, deliver its message. He didn't understand what the messages were or what they meant; they were just letters to him, symbols, lines, shapes. But someone was receiving them; of that he was sure.

The light hovered above his right hand, and he could feel the intense heat radiating from it.

"Write, My child."

I'm ready. Use me.

Rosa opened her eyes and noticed Caleb's body twitching, not violently, but gently, like some unseen hand was trying to nudge him awake. His right hand began to move, slowly at first, then increasing in speed. She knew what to do. Though she'd seen it two times before, she still could barely believe it. Her pulse increased, and her own hand began to tremble.

She rounded the bed, took the pencil off the bedside table, and slipped it between Caleb's thumb and index finger, holding the clipboard under his hand.

His hand began to move frantically, writing and tracing the same letters over and over. The writing was clear this time—no scribbles, no errant lines, just letters, dark and bold.

When Caleb's hand finally relaxed, Rosa turned the clipboard around and stared at it.

Her blood ran cold.

The words hit her like a shotgun blast—SAVE GILL.

—

The knock came again, this time louder.

Stevie slunk away, shaking, sweating, panting. Then a familiar voice: "Stevie? You OK?" Josiah.

Stevie approached the door, trembling. What if it was a trick? *They* could make their voices sound like anyone they wanted.

Cautiously, he slipped his index finger behind the curtain on the door and pulled it aside just enough to catch a glimpse of the knocker, the owner of Josiah's voice.

A familiar face stared at the door.

"Stevie. Open up, son."

Stevie turned away from the door. "Uh, j–just a minute." He reached for a dishtowel and wiped the sweat from his brow, took two deep breaths, and held out his hand, palm down—it was still shaking.

He looked around the trailer and found Kitty hiding under the TV stand, resting with all four paws tucked under its body. "Go hide, Kitty. Go."

The cat jumped up and ran into Stevie's bedroom. Good Kitty.

Stevie turned the doorknob and opened the door.

—

Josiah had heard the commotion coming from inside the trailer as soon as he and Joe climbed out of his truck. But that was not odd in itself. Stevie often talked to himself. Even hollered at himself. Sometimes the voices in his head could be very demanding.

Over the years, Josiah had learned to deal with Stevie in a very patient, gentle manner. The boy was easily agitated, and stirring him up never accomplished anything.

When Stevie opened the door, Josiah could tell right away that the voices were again getting the better of him. His hair matted against his forehead. His sweat-stained shirt clung to his chest. His cheeks were blushed, his eyes wide. He was no match against his own paranoia.

"Hi, Stevie. Are you OK?" Josiah said. "I heard hollering."

Stevie looked around as if the answer was to be found somewhere in the cluttered trailer. "I, uh, was just yellin' at the TV."

"Oh, well, can we come in?"

Stevie's eyes looked past Josiah's shoulder and fell on Joe. He shot a questioning glance at Josiah.

"It's OK, Stevie," Josiah said, reading the confusion and fear on Stevie's face. He gestured toward Joe. "This is Joe Saunders, a friend of mine."

Stevie eyed Joe carefully, looking him up and down.

Josiah nodded at Joe, and Joe smiled at Stevie. "Hi, Stevie."

Stevie pushed a sweaty lock of hair off his forehead. "O–OK. Come on in."

He went into the living room and sat in his recliner. Stepping carefully over the popcorn that littered the floor, Josiah and Joe followed. They both sat on the sofa.

"I—you startled me when you knocked, and I dropped my popcorn." Stevie smiled and gave a little chuckle. "Sorry."

Josiah forced a laugh. He could tell something else was going on, something more than just the routine battle with the voices. Something more sinister. He could feel it. There was a weight in the room, a dark weight. "That's OK. Happens to all of us."

Stevie sat on the edge of the chair. "Would—would either of you like a drink?"

"No, thanks," Joe said.

"No," Josiah added. "I'd like to ask you a few questions, though, if that's OK with you."

Stevie glanced at Joe, then back at Josiah. His knee bounced like a silent jackhammer. "I guess."

Josiah could tell Stevie was uncomfortable with their intrusion. His paranoia was in high gear. His behavior was more erratic than Josiah had seen in years. But why? What had triggered it? He knew Stevie hated strangers in his home. And he knew Stevie hated questions. But it was more than that, wasn't it? It was the weight, the oppression. Stevie could no doubt feel it too, and it was spinning his brain in circles.

"Stevie," Josiah said, his voice calm but firm. He maintained eye contact while he was talking. "I need you to tell me the truth now. Can you do that?"

Stevie glanced at Joe again, then nodded. Beads of sweat dotted his forehead and upper lip.

Josiah smiled. He'd have to tread lightly. After Joe's debacle with Maggie earlier, Stevie may be their only source of information. Their only chance at finding out the truth. "Good. I know you like to go walking in the woods—"

Stevie tensed.

"—and that's OK," Josiah said quickly. "It's OK to walk in the woods. Have you ever seen any big animals in there?"

Stevie gripped the arms of the chair. "Why are you askin' me? I ain't never seen nothin'. I just go walkin'. I like lookin' at the trees and watchin' the squirrels."

Josiah held up both hands. "I know, I know. And that's great, Stevie, really it is. But I need to know if you ever saw anything in there that scared you."

"The devil."

The answer came so quickly and so matter-of-factly that Josiah almost missed it. *God, give me wisdom.* "The devil. What do you mean by that? An animal that looked like the devil?"

Stevie didn't answer. His face went blank as if he was listening to some faraway voice.

"Stevie. Stevie."

Stevie started and looked at Josiah, eyes glazed.

"What did you see, son?"

"I—I can't say. They won't let me."

Josiah kept his eyes on Stevie. "OK. That's OK. Stevie, I don't know if you know it or not, but there have been several attacks around here lately. A large animal, maybe a lion, is roaming Dark Hills." He watched for Stevie's reaction.

The young man's body tensed, and he glanced quickly at the bedroom doorway.

Josiah caught the look, noted it, and continued. "A little boy, Caleb Saunders, was one of the victims."

Stevie now stole a fleeting look at Joe as if making the connection.

"Stevie," Josiah said, leaning forward. "This is very important that you tell me the truth. Tell me whatever you know. I won't be mad at you. I won't tell *them* about it. Three people are dead. Did you know Bob Cummings?"

Stevie shook his head and pressed himself back into the chair like he was trying to melt into it.

"He was mauled to death. The others were"—Josiah paused for effect—"Woody Owen and Eddie Hopkins."

Stevie twisted his face as if in pain and dug his fingers into the arms of the recliner. "Ohhhh! It's the devil...the devil. He's out there. He's in here. He's here. Momma! Momma!" He hit his palms against his forehead, both at once, then alternating, rapid-fire. "I have to help Momma. I hafta!"

Josiah got up and placed his hands on Stevie's shoulders and patted them gently. "*Shhh.* It's OK, son. Calm down. No one here is gonna hurt you. We're all friends here."

Stevie lowered his hands and looked at Josiah. There were tears in his eyes, but beyond the tears there was something else, something dark. Josiah saw it and stepped back, startled.

"I hafta help Momma, Mr. Walker," Stevie said, fear streaked across his face. "I hafta help her."

CHAPTER 31

URINE AND SWEAT.

Maggie was back in Elston's room at St. Magdalene's, and the smell was almost nauseating. The stroke had robbed him of not only his badge and livelihood but his dignity as well. She'd have to talk to one of the nurses about keeping him cleaner, changing his bed linens more often.

The room was dark save for the muted spasmodic light of the TV, the one-eyed monster keeping watch over its invalid prisoner. Elston was fast asleep, breathing heavy and even, whistling through his nose on every exhalation.

After finding the note yesterday, Maggie had to talk to him again, find out what it meant. If anyone would know, it would be her dad.

An eye for an eye.

She approached his bed on light feet, stealing through the darkness like a phantom gliding on a cushion of air. Sitting on the edge of the bed, she reached for his hand and gave it a gentle squeeze. "Dad. Dad."

Elston stirred, snorted, wheezed, but did not wake.

Maggie smoothed his hair and shook his skeletal shoulder. "Dad. Wake up. Hey, Dad."

Elston's eyes fluttered open, then shut again. He pursed his lips and grunted.

"C'mon, Dad. Wake up. I need to talk to you."

With a stir and a moan, the former police chief's eyes slowly opened, and he looked at Maggie and half smiled. "Magpie."

"Hi, Dad. I'm sorry to wake you, but I need to talk to you about something again."

"How Gary?"

"Gary's fine. He's a good cop."

"Andy?"

"He's a good cop too. You had your doubts about him, didn't you?"

223

Elston smiled and nodded. "Good boy. Soft cop."

"Not soft, Dad. He cares. Andy has a good heart. But that's not what I'm here about. Last night, Eddie Hopkins ran his car off the road and...um"—an image of Eddie's curled and stiff hand, as white as paper, jumped through her mind—"all we found was his hand. There was a note in it that said *an eye for an eye*. Do you know what it means?"

Fear widened Elston's left eye. "No."

"Think, Dad. I need answers. Bad things are happening, and you're the only one I can turn to. You have to help me."

"No," he said quietly, almost a whisper, and shook his head.

Maggie placed the back of her hand on her dad's cheek. "Lay it all out, Dad. This has to be the end of all the secrets. Tell me everything, OK?"

After a few seconds of silent contemplation, Elston finally nodded and blinked slowly.

"Bauer. Mur-murder."

If Maggie had swallowed an anvil, she couldn't have felt a heavier weight drop into her stomach. The Gail Bauer murder. She remembered hearing about it, reading about it. She was in the academy at the time, and Elston had filled her in on the details. Bauer was raped and murdered in her home, and Stevie, who was also beaten, was allegedly the only witness. Stevie pointed the finger at three Dark Hills High seniors. Charges were pressed and an investigation begun, but Stevie's testimony was so fragmented and full of holes that the charges were eventually dropped against the boys. The real murderer was never caught.

She gripped her dad's hand—it was dry and cold and fragile—this the hand she reached for when she was a frightened child, the hand that promised protection and comfort, the hand that was always there, bigger and stronger than her fears. "The Gail Bauer case. I remember. What about it?"

Tears puddled in Elston's eyes and spilled over. The left side of his mouth quivered. "Guilty." He clenched his jaw and his eyes darkened. "Boys guilty."

"Owen, Hopkins, and Sterner?"

Elston began to shake, whether with fear or anger, Maggie couldn't tell. "Guilty. Mur-murder."

"They did it, didn't they?" Regret, anger, disappointment, and sorrow darkened Maggie's vision and constricted her throat. She suddenly found it difficult to breathe and longed for the fresh, clean air of the outdoors.

Now the tears formed two rivulets from Elston's eyes. He made no attempt to wipe them away, as if allowing them to flow freely would somehow cleanse him of culpability. He opened his mouth to speak, but the words seemed stuck in his throat. He tightened his grip on Maggie's hand. "Mi–Mickey...threat–threatened. Hurt you and Mom."

Understanding dawned on Maggie like a black sunrise. Glen Sterner was the son of the recently deceased Mickey Sterner, former mayor of Dark Hills, bosom buddy of Bob Cummings, and hobnobber of both state and federal legislators. Everyone knew Dark Hills was just a training ground for Sterner; he was bound for Washington, and there was no way he'd let his son's sullied reputation stop him. Two years after the murder he left Dark Hills and won a seat on the Pennsylvania state legislature. His next move was going to be Capitol Hill. But fate had different plans, and four months ago Sterner was dropped dead by a massive aneurysm.

"Did Mickey threaten you? That if you didn't drop the charges on his son and the others he would hurt me and Mom?"

Elston closed his eyes, nodded, and wept like a thousand-pound weight had been lifted from his chest. He kept his eyes closed while he talked, as if that would lessen the humility, the shame of facing his daughter with the truth. "Lose job. Hurt you."

Disappointment and sorrow gave way to anger. Her dad had been blackmailed. If he didn't drop the charges and keep quiet about the murder, he'd not only lose his job (and Mickey Sterner was powerful enough and had the right connections to make sure he never served in law enforcement again), but he'd also live with the fear of retaliation against Maggie or Gloria. The pieces were falling into place now. The beast. Stevie. Vengeance. *An eye for an eye.* Maggie ran her hand along her dad's cheeks, wiping the tears. "I love you, Dad. Thank you."

Joe sat against the headboard of his bed back at the Dew-Drop, legs pulled up, wrists hanging over his knees, fingers interlocked. After his and Josiah's very brief and very bizarre visit with Stevie, he'd come back to the motel to think and plan his next move. He had finally resigned himself to the fact that he wouldn't be getting any information out of Maggie. She had been well rehearsed in the ways of the Gills: when the heat was on, the best—and only—answer is always, "No comment." Henry Gill had taught his family well.

Joe had all but gotten over the disappointment in Maggie. He was frustrated, yes, even angry, but she had only become a product of her environment. He would have turned out the same way under the circumstances. But she definitely was not the same person he'd walked away from fifteen years ago. That person was in there somewhere, he was sure of that, past all the Gill family stuff, past the chief of police stuff, past the cover-ups and secrets. Unfortunately, that person hadn't seen the light of day for decades, buried under years of brainwashing and *legacy building*.

Then there was the enigma that was Stevie. If Stevie knew anything, which Joe and Josiah were both convinced he did, he didn't even know what he knew. It was confusing, yes. But then again, Stevie was a bucket of confusion. He was so steeped in his own paranoia that he was helpless to separate reality from his psychoses. His ranting about a devil in the woods proved that much.

Well, if Stevie was a dead end and Maggie was going to play games, Joe would just have to appeal to a higher authority. No, not *the* Higher Authority, though he knew he should. Prayer—the idea of it, that is—had been on his mind a lot lately. But he still couldn't bring himself to be on conversational terms with God. While enlightening, his prayer time the other night had been a fluke, a one-time showing with no replays. He had strayed too far, grown too bitter, for time like that to be a normal occurrence. His journey back would have to be a slow one, like a wayward son regaining his father's trust.

But he *should* pray, shouldn't he? Yes, he should. What was happening here in Dark Hills was bigger than him and his wounded spirit, bigger than Maggie and her precious legacy, bigger than this run-down little Mayberry town. People were dead, souls lost forever, and Caleb was still in a coma, hanging onto life in some dreamy fog. It was time to set his pride aside and go before his Father.

It was time to pray.

So, like a man testing a rotting tree limb to see if it would hold his weight, Joe shut his eyes and inched his way into God's presence. Immediately, he felt a warmth welcoming his soul like that father running down the dusty road to greet his prodigal son. There was a sense of comfort, of acceptance, of familiarity, and then he realized what it was—he was home. This was where he belonged. Hot tears flowed freely from his eyes, making wet tracks down his cheeks. He opened his heart to God and prayed, just prayed. It was a short prayer, asking for help and guidance—and answers—but it was a powerful prayer, not because of the words spoken or because of the man who spoke them, but because of the God who heard them.

When "Amen" finally passed over his lips, Joe opened his eyes and wiped the tears from his cheeks. He reached for the yellow phone book on the bedside table and opened to the blue pages. Running his finger down the page, he stopped midway and tapped a number. He flipped open his cell phone and glanced at the digital screen. He had a message from Rosa. She'd have to wait. He punched the numbers on the phone's keypad.

A woman's voice answered. Short and curt. "Pennsylvania State Police, Troop H Station. How can I help you?"

"Hi, yeah, I have a crime to report."

"What's the nature of the crime, sir?"

"Well, it's, uh, it's a string of animal attacks—"

"Have you contacted the Game Commission?" Very curt.

"No, I—"

She cut him off cold. "Sir, the state police generally don't deal with wildlife issues. It is a wildlife issue, isn't it?"

Joe stumbled. "Well, I—I, uh, I guess so."

"You'll have to call the Game Commission and report it."

"But can't I just speak to someone about it? There's more to it than just some animal attacks."

"One moment, please."

Boy, someone was having a bad day. And Joe wasn't off to a good start. This was going to be harder than he'd expected.

There was a quiet pause, then the sound of Michael Bublé crooning the lyrics of "Home" filled the earpiece. After a few seconds there was a click, and a man's voice came on. "Lieutenant Patrick, what can I do for you?"

Joe swallowed. Make it a good one. "Hi. My name's Joe Saunders, and I'd like to report a crime in Dark Hills."

"Have you contacted the local authorities about it?" Patrick's voice was big, and Joe imagined the man behind the voice was also big. Big head, big gut, big meaty hands...and big ego.

"Yes, and—I—I think they're in on it, covering it up."

"What's the crime?" Patrick didn't sound convinced.

"Well, the crime is actually the cover-up. You see, there've been several animal attacks leading to deaths, and no one on the police force here is doing anything about it. They're hiding the whole thing, even the deaths."

"If they're hiding it, how'd you find out about it?"

Joe paused. Good question. He wasn't expecting to be interrogated, and his mind was beginning to unravel. He should have planned this better. Well, here goes nothing. "I saw one of the victims. Bob Cummings. He and I were hunting, and he got mauled and—"

"Wait a minute, Mr. . . . ."

"Saunders."

"Saunders. Is this a wild animal, like a bear or something?"

Oh, boy. "I'm really not sure what it is." This was only getting worse. The more Joe talked, the more he realized how ridiculous his version of the story sounded. He might as well be telling the lieutenant he saw Big Foot dressed in a sundress hiding Easter eggs in the middle of the woods.

"What were you hunting?" Now Patrick sounded condescending. He wasn't buying it. Nope. For all he knew, Joe was just another lunatic with a grand story looking for attention.

Joe tried to recover. "Again, I'm not sure, but—"

"Mr. Saunders. Let me just stop you right there. I'll tell you what. Anything involving wildlife and hunting is usually an issue for the Game Commission. Why don't you call them and get them involved. If they think there's a crime or conspiracy or other foul play going on, and if they deem it necessary to include us in the investigation, I can assure you they'll contact us. OK?"

Joe gave up. Patrick would never take him seriously enough to investigate. "OK, sir. Thanks for your time." Wave the white flag. Save the sundressed, Easter egg–hiding Big Foot story for some other time.

He flipped back one page in the phone book and quickly found the number for the Franklin County office of the Southcentral Region of the Pennsylvania Game Commission. He punched in the number.

After two rings, "Pennsylvania Game Commission. Franklin County. May I help you?" It was a woman's voice again. She sounded pleasant enough.

"Hi. I'd like to report a series of animal attacks in Dark Hills."

"What's the nature of the attacks?"

Joe stumbled. Not again. "Well, I, uh…can I just talk to someone in charge?"

There was a long pause on the other end, then, "I'll put you through to a wildlife officer. May I ask who's calling?"

"Joe Saunders."

There were a few seconds of silence, then a man's voice squeaked across the line. "Hello. This is Officer Ferguson." His voice was high-pitched and whiney. Not at all what Joe would have expected from a wildlife officer.

"Hi. I'm Joe Saunders. Um, I'm calling from Dark Hills, and we've had four animal attacks and three deaths here in the past couple of weeks."

"I don't remember hearing anything about that. Has local law enforcement been involved?"

"I wouldn't say involved. They—"

"What kind of animal attacks?" Joe could hear a hint of disbelief in Ferguson's voice. He was losing him already. And if he told him the truth, the officer would probably have him locked up, or at least fined, for making a prank call.

"I'm not sure, really. But something big."

"Something big, huh? Where did you say you're calling from?"

"Dark Hills. Maggie Gill, the police chief, said she reported it."

"I don't recall hearing about any calls from Dark Hills." Joe heard the sound of computer keys clicking. "I'm looking here, and…nope, I don't see that anyone filed any reports—"

"How far back did you go? The first one would have taken place—"

"A month."

"A month? And no calls?" Maggie had lied to him. "Are you sure?"

"Computers don't lie, Mr.…?"

"Saunders."

There was a brief moment of silence while Joe heard more keys tapping in the background, then, "Look, Mr. Saunders, we're short-staffed. I don't have anyone to send out there now, but I can get a deputy wildlife officer out there first thing in the morning. He'll interview you, you tell him your story, and we'll go from there, OK?"

"Can't I just give the report now?"

"That's not how it works," Ferguson said. "Are there bodies to examine? Remains? Any other evidence?"

Joe swallowed. "Well, that's part of the problem; not exactly, you see—"

"Mr. Saunders, I really think it would be best if you wait to speak with the wildlife officer in person. First thing in the morning, OK?"

"OK." Not what Joe was hoping for, but it would have to do.

"Where are you staying?"

"The Dew-Drop Motel, in Dark Hills."

"Good enough. I know it. Tomorrow morning."

The line went dead, and Joe set his cell phone on the bed and flopped back, combing his hands through his hair. What did he expect? His story probably sounded totally contrived, totally unbelievable, and totally the product of a very ill mind. He'd be surprised if he got a visit from a Boy Scout, let alone a wildlife officer.

CHAPTER 32

MAGGIE SAT AT her desk, head in her hands, reviewing the conversations she'd had with her dad, sifting through each unbelievable detail, each chilling event. She needed to formulate a plan. On one hand she had a mystery animal (a lion?) and three deaths to deal with; on the other hand she had this Gail Bauer case and her dad's cover-up. And the two hands were joined. The common denominator? Stevie Bauer. All three of the deceased played a role in Gail Bauer's murder; all three were killed by the mystery animal. Was Stevie using the animal to get revenge? Absurd. How? And what about Caleb? How did he fit in?

One thing she was certain of, she couldn't let anyone know about her dad's role in the Bauer murder. If it got out now that he was responsible for letting three murderers walk, it would be the end of him. There would be a media storm, investigations, inquisitions, charges brought up…where would it end? With his death. It would kill him. She couldn't let that happen. She would have to deal with things herself, and she knew where to start: Stevie.

Just then Gary came in and sat in the metal folding chair across from her desk. Maggie could tell by the way he dropped his large frame in the chair and blew out a forced sigh that he had news of some importance to share.

She lowered her hands, arched her eyebrows, and forced a smile. "Yes?" Even on the gloomiest days she found some humor in the sight of Gary's large, six-four, two-hundred-forty-pound frame swallowing the tiny metal chair. He got his size from her mother's side of the family. Uncle Dick was six-two, and Uncle Ned was six-three. From what she understood, size ran in the family as far back as anyone could remember. *Built for intimidation.* That's what Uncle Ned used to say.

Gary shifted in the chair. "I trailed Saunders to Crazy Bauer's hole."

Maggie sat back. "Stevie's trailer?"

"Yeah. He and Old Man Walker went in. The pow-wow lasted fifteen minutes, then they scattered." He cracked his knuckles against his jaw. "You think that clown knows something he isn't telling you about?"

Maggie frowned. "Yeah, I do. I think he knows a lot more than he's telling us."

Gary leaned forward, his eyes burning with all the intensity of a gasoline-fueled fire. The chair moaned. "You want me to bring him in?"

"No. He's not a threat to talk. Who would believe him anyway? Everyone in town knows he's out in left field. Making up stories about conspiracies and the FBI hunting him. It'd just be another one of his paranoid delusions." She had decided she wouldn't tell Gary about Gail Bauer's tainted murder investigation and how her dad had been blackmailed and threatened into playing along with Mickey Sterner's sick ambition. The less he knew, the better for him and her dad...and for her. When the opportunity presented itself, she would, however, tell him about their family history with the beast, Great-Grandpa's monster. He deserved to know that much.

Maggie reached for her notebook, opened it, and started to jot down some notes. When several seconds ticked by and Gary had not moved, she looked up and held him in a steady gaze. "What's wrong?"

Gary rubbed the back of his neck. "You got any plans?"

"For what?"

"For *it*."

Maggie shoved the notebook aside and sat on the edge of her chair. She ran a finger along the smooth wooden desktop, making circles. "I'll get some guys on standby. Seasoned hunters. If it shows up again, I give them a call, and we all go take care of the problem."

"What hunters? Who?"

"I was thinking Mike Kline, Dan Berwager, Barry Wagman."

"Are you going to tell them what's happened?"

Maggie shook her head. "No way. Only that I may need them to hunt our rogue animal. I'll have their numbers in the top drawer here, so you know. I'll tell Andy too. Just in case." She paused and traced another circle on the desk. "Do you remember any of the stories that used to go around?"

Gary shook his head. "Not a whole lot. I was a runt then. I remember the part about an animal killing people, about the Yates place, and that's about it."

"There's a lot more to it than that." Maggie reached for her coffee mug, tipped it toward her mouth, and quickly pulled it away. Coffee was cold. "Phil Yates and Great-Grandpa were once good friends, before all the mess with the...*thing* started." She hesitated and gave a nervous chuckle. "Look, I always thought this was just made-up stuff kids used to pass around, handed down by parents who wanted to scare them. Or at the very least an embellished version of the truth. You know, small town looking for notoriety, beefing up a few animal attacks to make them into something much more sinister. But when the Saunders boy was mauled and then that dog, it got me thinking. Wondering. Cummings pretty much convinced me, but Owen's body sealed the deal. I had a couple difficult chats with my dad and finally got him to tell me the whole story. At least everything he knows. It isn't pretty."

She set her mug on her desk and went back to drawing imaginary circles with her finger. "Anyway, somewhere along the line Yates got his hands on a lion's paw, I think it was his dad's or something, and he got involved in some kind of African black magic stuff. No one's sure exactly what it was. But he got so deep in it that it started to freak Great-Grandpa out. That, and the fact that Yates's behavior was becoming more and more bizarre. Apparently, he was a little odd to start with but became even more erratic. Well, shortly after that, the *thing* started showing up, and people started dying. Now, I don't know where it came from. Seems nobody did. And I don't know what kind of animal it was—presumably a lion, but from what Dad said, nobody who ever saw it lived to talk about it.

"Eventually, something went down between Great-Grandpa and Yates, and there was bad blood. My dad said it was because Yates somehow got the upper hand, said he was controlling the beast, having it kill whoever he wished—he was all worked up about some revenge thing or something—and Great-Grandpa was jealous, not to mention scared that Yates would turn the thing on him. Next thing you know, an angry mob is burning down Yates's house with Yates in it. Nobody knows exactly what happened or how it happened, but Great-Grandpa knew, and it haunted him the rest of his life. Did you know he committed suicide?"

Gary shook his head. "News to me."

"Yeah. Dad said that toward the end there the old man was always talking about the *devil lion* coming after him. Said he'd seen it in the fields, heard it in his house. Really weird stuff. It eventually drove him crazy, and he offed himself."

Gary sat still, massaging his knuckles. "So crazy runs in our family too. Man, this whole town is whacked out. Does Andy know about any of this?"

"Only what he's heard along the way. He doesn't need to know."

Gary nodded. "So what's your call?"

Maggie sighed and spun a pen on her desk. Her call was to pay a visit to Stevie. If she pushed him hard enough, he might just crack and spill whatever it was he knew. But she had to handle it right, slowly, and she wanted to do it alone. If she told Gary her plan, he would insist on joining her. She couldn't have that. Stevie trusted her as long as she was alone. Maybe trusted her enough to let her inside his head. "Right now we sit tight and wait for this *thing* to make another appearance. If it even does. Maybe we'll get lucky. Now you need to get back out there on the street."

Gary stood and arched his back. "If you need anything, holler. And if you decide you want me to bring Loony in, let me know."

"I will. Go." She waved him off.

Gary left, and Maggie dropped her head into her hands again. What had she gotten herself into? She had to see Stevie; he was the answer. Stop Stevie and she stopped the attacks, the beast. How? She had no idea and wasn't sure she wanted to know. If the story her dad had told her was true, it had something to do with powers she didn't understand, couldn't understand, and had no desire to understand. One thing she did know—and it put the fear of God in her—was that if she failed, her dad would eventually meet a gruesome death. He and Glen Sterner were the only two left.

A knot seized her throat at the thought of her dad at the mercy of such a beast, helpless to even attempt to fight back. She balled her hands into fistfuls of hair. She just wanted this to be over. She wanted her dad to be safe, and she wanted her small-town life back.

CHAPTER 33

MAGGIE SLOWED HER cruiser to a stop in front of Stevie's trailer. The egg-yolk sun was just starting to ooze into the horizon, and the western sky was awash with fiery hues of orange and pink and purple. Long shadows stretched across the clearing where the trailer sat. Maggie thought how out of place this rusty, battered box looked sitting in the middle of a cornfield, woods behind it, a pond so still it looked like glass situated not twenty yards to the right. Under better circumstances, she'd take a few moments to enjoy the sunset, but this evening she was in no mood for such things. She just wanted to get this over with.

She'd changed into her street clothes and skipped out of work early, leaving Andy to cover the desk and answer the phones. Gary was on patrol, not that there was really anything to patrol, but it gave him something to do while he calmed down. Maybe he'd bag some hothead trying to break the sound barrier along Route 20. She'd left without telling Andy or Gary where she was going. They'd just want to tag along, and she wanted to do this alone.

She shut the engine off and climbed out of her cruiser. A light was on in one of the trailer's cloudy windows, and the curtain was pulled slightly to one side. Was that a face peering out the window at her? She looked again, and the curtain fell back into place. Stevie was home.

Climbing the three wooden steps to the storm door, she made a fist and knocked on the metal door.

Inside, Stevie was beside himself. The voice in his head, Yosemite's voice, was pounding away—*Kill Gill. Kill Gill.* He didn't want to obey it; he wanted it to shut up and go away forever. But that wasn't going to happen. It would only get more and more persistent, louder and louder, more forceful, more demanding, until he finally gave in and appeased it. He couldn't live like this. But he also couldn't do what the voice was demanding of him.

Kill Gill. KillKillKill. The voice kept echoing through his brain. It filled every cavity of his head, vibrated through his skull, finding no resting place.

He wouldn't answer the door. She would think no one was home and go away.

Maggie knocked again. "Stevie? It's Chief Maggie; can I come in?"

Shhh. Just keep quiet, and she'll go away.

Kill Gill. Your chance has come. The voice was getting louder. She'd hear it. She had to hear it. How could she not hear it? It screamed in his ears, ran through his body like electric shocks, pierced his eardrums like nails.

Kill...Gill.

Shhh. Just keep quiet. Quiet. Shut up!

Maggie could hear movement on the other side of the door. She tried the doorknob. It was locked.

"Stevie. I know you're home. Are you all right? It's OK, I just want to talk. I'm alone."

Ohhh. She knew he was home. He couldn't ignore her forever. She was a cop. She had ways of breaking into homes. And she would do it too.

With the voice still ringing through his head, Stevie stood up, smoothed his clothes, and opened the door.

Chief Maggie stepped back and nearly fell off the steps. "Oh, hi, Stevie. Is everything OK?" She was wearing normal clothes—a green jacket and blue jeans. Not normal. She always wore her uniform. The tan uniform. The one that said she was a cop, a protector. A friend.

Stevie smiled and willed the voice in his head to shut up. She had to hear it. "Sure, I was just doin' some straigtenin' up. Sorry to keep you waitin'."

He stood in the doorway staring down at her until Chief Maggie finally spoke. "Do you mind if I come in for a minute? I need your help with something."

Heat stung Stevie's cheeks. *No, don't come in.* "Oh, uh, yeah, sure."

He stepped out of the way and allowed Chief Maggie to enter.

The inside was no different from any of the other times Maggie had been in there. Clutter was piled waist high; the sink was full of dishes, crusted with days-old food. The trash can was overflowing, and that smell of sour milk and rotten meat still hung in the air like a toxin.

Straightening up, huh? Doubtful. He was hiding something. The shifty eyes and quivering chin gave it away every time.

Maggie had an idea. "Stevie, why don't you let me help you clean up a bit? We can start here in the kitchen."

Stevie's heart nearly lodged in his throat. "Oh, no, Chief Maggie. You don't have to do that. Mr. Walker, he—"

"Stevie, I insist. Look at this place, it's filthy. I'll start with the dishes. Where's the dish soap?"

Stevie was growing more agitated. His face twitched, his eyes wouldn't stop blinking, and a steady trickle of sweat ran down his temple.

And the more agitated he grew, the louder the voice in his head shouted. *Kill Gill. Kill. Kill. Kill.*

"Ohhh, I think maybe you should leave, Chief Maggie." Stevie raked his fingers through his hair and rubbed his cheek. He paced back and forth, scrubbing harder at his face. "This ain't good. You should definitely leave."

"Oh, stop it, Stevie. I just want to help, that's all. I'm your friend, remember?"

Stevie shook his head. *Kill Gill.* "Nooo. You should leave."

"Where's your dish soap? Is it down here?" She opened the cupboard under the sink and squatted.

The voice pounded like thunder in Stevie's head. *KILL GILL. Kill her, retard! She's a Gill. She let Momma's killers go free. Now! Do it! Kill Gill!*

He could resist it no longer. He had to give in; he had to let the voice have its way. He reached for a ball-peen hammer that was on the counter, clutched it in his right hand—the wood was cool and smooth—lifted it above his head, and brought it down on the back of Maggie's skull.

Crack! It sounded like a gun went off in Maggie's head. Then blackness.

Stevie felt the jarring impact of the hammer with bone, saw the blood spurt, turning her blonde hair crimson.

The voice had ceased, and everything was quiet now.

Chief Maggie's body went limp and collapsed to the floor, facedown; her head rested in a growing pool of red. Stevie stood over her, his heart thumping wildly in his chest, his lungs struggling to fill with air. He let the hammer slip out of his hand and fall silently to the floor.

He killed her. She was dead.

He fell to his knees beside her lifeless body and began to weep. "No. No. No. See what you made me do? See?"

Wait. What was that he heard? A faint wheezing sound. He lifted his head and looked at Chief Maggie's face. Her head was turned toward him, eyes closed, lips slightly parted, cheek bunched against the floor. Her face was pale and still—the look of death. But her back was rising and falling. It was moving. She was breathing. She wasn't dead.

Immediately, the voice was back in Stevie's head. *Kill Gill. Finish it. Finish it. Retard!* His eyes fell on the hammer, resting on the floor. The hammer called to him, begging him, ordering him, pleading, commanding. *Kill Gill Kill Gill. Finish it. For Momma.*

"NO!" Stevie shouted. He clapped his hands over his ears. "I won't. I won't!"

Across town, Joe entered B Wing of Hillside Hall and strolled along the tile floor. He hadn't talked to Rosa all day and had decided he would surprise her and meet her for dinner. They could eat in the small cafeteria in C Wing. He'd eaten there only once before and found the food more than edible. It was pretty good, actually.

He came to Caleb's room, knocked once, and poked his head in.

Rosa was pacing back and forth and snapped her head around at the sound of his knock. "Joe!" she said, half angry, half panicked. She held a piece of paper above her head and waved it back and forth at him. "Where have you been? Why did you not return my calls?"

Joe turned a palm up and shrugged. "What calls?" But before he even finished his question, his hand was flipping open his cell phone. "Oh, man, I had the ringer turned off. You left a message, and I was going to call you back." He looked at her, then at Caleb. "What's the matter? Is Caleb OK?"

Rosa came at him like a bull, intensity raging in her eyes. "I tried and tried to reach you, but all I got was your voice mail. And the phone at the motel was busy, busy. I was going to try to find you, but I didn't want to leave Caleb in case he wrote another—"

"Rosa." Joe laid both hands on her shoulders. "I'm sorry, OK? I was making some phone calls. What's the matter?"

"This!" Rosa shoved the paper at his face. The bold, handwritten letters screamed at him—SAVE GILL.

Joe knew right away it was one of Caleb's writings. He took the paper from Rosa and stared at it. *Save Gill.* What does—? Oh, no. Maggie was next. The blood drained out of his face and could have pooled in his feet for all he knew; his body was numb. His mind seemed to be stuck in mud. He tried to think, tried to process, but some soupy fog had floated into his head and clouded his brain. Maggie was next. Maggie was next. Maggie…was…next!

He looked at Rosa. She was looking at him. "Maggie's next. The next victim."

Without saying another word, he turned and bolted from the room. He didn't know what he would do, had no plan, but he had to do something.

He heard Rosa calling after him, but he had to run. He had to hurry. No time for explanations. He ran down the corridor, through the lobby, out the sliding glass doors. The darkening outside world spun around him. *Maggie's next.* His own words echoed in his ears. *Maggie's next!* He had to do something. Think. Think. Think. Where would Maggie be? How would it happen? His mind was a black void, an empty abyss. "C'mon," he shouted, banging his forehead with his fist. "Think!"

He flipped open his cell phone and punched in the number for the Dark Hills police.

After two rings a man's voice answered on the other end. "Hello. Dark Hills—"

"Is this Gary?"

"Uh, no, this is Officer Wilt. Who's this?"

Joe ran for his truck as he talked. "Andy, it's Joe Saunders. Is Maggie there?"

There was a short pause. "Are you OK? It sounds like you're breathing heavy."

"I'm running. Is Maggie there?"

"No. She, uh, left for the evening. Can I take a message? Are you OK?"

Joe reached his truck, opened the door, and slid in behind the wheel. "Did she go home?"

Another pause.

C'mon, Andy, we don't have time for this. "Did she go home?"

"I don't know. What's this all about? Are you OK?"

Joe started the engine and shifted into gear. "I'm fine. Andy, Maggie's the next victim. Do you know what she was gonna do after her shift? Where she was going?"

Andy was beginning to sound skeptical. Just like Lieutenant Big Head. "Wait a minute. Did you say victim?"

"Yes!" Joe hollered into the phone as he tore out of the Hillside parking lot, rubber squealing. "I'm heading over to her house now."

"Of what?"

"The beast, lion, animal…whatever. She's next."

Andy blew out a breath of static. "How do you know this?"

Joe caught himself. Telling Andy that a warning came from a comatose boy who writes messages given by God would not go over well. "I just know; that's all I can say. This is serious, Andy. We need to find her. She's the next victim."

Now Andy sounded very skeptical. "Yeah, you said that already. And I'm supposed to believe you because you have some feeling, right? You just know."

C'mon, c'mon. Not now. Joe took a left-hand turn at thirty miles an hour. The tires of his truck screamed against the asphalt. "Andy! It's real. Just believe me. Call Gary and tell him; maybe he knows where she was going or what she was gonna do. Wait a minute. Hang on. I'm almost at her house."

"Joe, let's just say what you're telling me is—"

"She's not home."

"Come again?"

Joe said it louder and slower. "She's not home. Her car isn't in her driveway, and all the lights in her house are out. I'm gonna knock on the door." He jumped out of his truck, ran up the front walk, and knocked on the wooden front door. "Andy, you still there?"

"Yes." Andy was sounding more and more impatient.

"She's not home." He looked in the windows. "All the lights are out. The house is empty. Looks undisturbed. She never came home. What time did she leave?"

"About five, maybe quarter of. Maybe she had some errands to run or went over to someone's house for dinner. I really don't—"

"Andy! Just call Gary; maybe he knows where she went."

"Joe—"

"Please, Andy. How would you feel if, by some freak chance, I'm right and something did happen to her? How would you feel?"

Andy sighed. "OK, OK. I'll ask Gary if he knows anything."

"Thanks. Call me at this number, OK?"

"Yeah."

CHAPTER 34

GARY RUMBLED DOWN the dirt lane that wound its way through Walker's fields. His cruiser bounced over deep ruts, sometimes bottoming out, kicking up a cloud of dirt. He'd just gotten off the radio with Andy. He didn't want to give too much credit to Saunders's odd call, but Maggie did say she was going straight home after work, and Andy said she wasn't there. Maybe, just maybe, she had stopped by to pay Psycho a visit. If anyone could get information out of him it would have been Maggie. Bauer trusted her. Sort of.

The cruiser slid to a stop, gravel spitting up around the tires. Gary swung the door open and jumped out, leaving the headlights on to illuminate the trailer. A light was on inside, and he caught a glimpse of a shadow dart past the window.

Gary tightened his jaw and clenched his fists. He wasn't going to play games with this nutcase. Bauer would give him some straight answers or—

He hopped up the three steps, opened the storm door, and knocked hard. "Stevie Bauer, open the door. This is Officer Warren."

The soiled curtain slid to the side, and Bauer peered his grimy face out the window. Then the curtain fell back into place.

Gary knocked again. Harder. "Bauer, if you don't open this door I'm gonna bust it down. Open up!"

The door cracked open no more than six inches, and Bauer poked his nose out. "What do you want?"

Gary shoved the door and jerked it open. It creaked on its hinges and knocked Bauer off balance.

Gary caught him, placed a hand on his chest, and drove him into the kitchen. "Was Chief Gill here?" He towered over the smaller man and knew how to use his size to his advantage. *Built to intimidate.*

Bauer cowered away, stumbled, and caught himself against the counter. "N–no. Not recently. Why are you askin' me? I ain't done nothin'."

Hands on his hips, Gary scanned the disheveled kitchen and living room. "It stinks in here. Don't you ever take the garbage out?"

Bauer didn't say anything. He only leaned against the counter and eyed Gary suspiciously.

Gary asked again, slow and demanding. "Did Chief Gill stop by here?"

Eyes wide with fear, Bauer shook his head, his shaggy hair flip-flopping back and forth.

Gary reached out, grabbed a handful of Bauer's shirt, and yanked him closer, so close their noses were only inches apart and he could smell the smaller man's stale breath. Bauer was like a rag doll in his hands. He could break him so easily if he wanted to. It was actually very tempting. He never did like this freak. Gary wrinkled the bridge of his nose and looked right through Bauer's wild eyes. "Don't lie to me, Stevo. I don't like liars."

⁓

Muted sounds. Somebody talking. A familiar voice. And footsteps. Miles away. Somewhere on the other side of...of what?

Maggie was facedown in darkness, surrounded by it, smothered under it, lost in it. It pressed down on her, pinning her to the ground. She tried to lift her head, but it was filled with cement. And it throbbed like a jackhammer.

The warmth of her body had faded and a damp chill had set in, seeping into her bones, sending her muscles into violent shivers.

She tried to open her eyes, but the darkness was so thick, so oppressive, maybe they were already open; she couldn't tell.

There. The voice again. Familiar but muted. Her mind was a cloud, teetering between consciousness and unconsciousness. Fading in and out of reality. Was this a dream? No. Reality was greeted by the cold throbbing in her head, distanced by the warmth and comfort of sleep.

Maybe she was in hell.

She tried to open her mouth, but it was sealed shut, her lips fused. There was something in her mouth, something that carried an awful taste. She tried to swallow, but her throat was like sandpaper, her mouth like cotton.

This must be hell.

Slowly, the dream cleared and consciousness began its painful return. Her hands were bound, as were her feet. She was in a hole of some sort, lying on the ground. The back of her head began to burn, bringing with it the memory of a gunshot. Was she shot? Was she supposed to be dead? Maybe she'd been buried alive. Maybe they—who?—she didn't know—*they* thought she was dead and buried her. Panic gripped her chest like an icy hand, and she tried to scream. It was useless. Whatever was in her mouth muffled any sound coming from her throat.

She heard the voice again. Coming from above her. It was closer now. Think. Whose voice?

An image appeared in her mind. Gary. It was Gary's voice!

She wasn't buried. Couldn't be.

She tried to holler his name, but only a muted, hoarse "Mmmm" came out. She tried to move, but her body refused to obey.

She would most certainly die here. It wasn't hell. No, but it was a grave.

She was buried alive.

Bauer hung limp in Gary's grip and began to quiver. "No—no sir, I ain't lyin'. You gonna kill me?"

Gary released him with a shove, sending him back against the counter. "Don't give me a reason to. I'm going to look around." He pointed to a metal chair in the kitchen. "Sit."

Hooking his thumbs in his belt, Gary walked to the middle of the living room and looked around. Something wasn't right, something was...off. His police instincts were screaming, his senses acute. He scanned the room, letting his eyes rest momentarily on every corner of clutter, every piece of furniture, every empty glass, every inch of carpet, looking, searching for that one scrap of evidence, that one clue—a blonde hair, a spot of blood, a sign of struggle. He breathed in slowly, testing the air for any trace of Maggie's scent. But there was nothing. If it was there it had been long masked by the sharp odor of rotting meat and Bauer's body.

But she was there; he knew it. His physical senses didn't pick it up, but his raw instinct couldn't miss it. He could *feel* her.

He turned and glared at Bauer, warning him with a steady look that said *don't try anything stupid*, then headed into the short hallway leading to the only bedroom.

———

Heavy footsteps—Gary's footsteps—closer to her, pausing almost directly above her.

"Mmmm!" *Gary!*

———

Gary froze. What was that sound? A moan. To his left, just inside the bedroom, was a closet. He opened it, unclipped the flashlight from his belt, clicked it on, and used it to push the clothes aside. No sign of Maggie.

———

"Mmmmm!" *Help!*

———

There it was again. He shut the closet door and turned around, listening, searching, studying the room. The sound didn't come from anywhere, but it was there. Just there. Odd. He lowered himself to his knees and looked under Bauer's bed. Two glowing yellow eyes stared back at him. He shined the light at the tabby's face, and it gave a low growl—a moan—then hissed.

Idiot cat.

Gary clicked the flashlight off and stood up.

Bam!

An explosion sent a numbing shockwave through his head and down his neck. He crumpled to the floor in darkness.

Was he shot? He tried to scramble, but his arms and legs were in quicksand.

He'd been shot.

That demented lunatic shot him in the back of the head. Slowly the light came back, and he focused his eyes just in time to see Bauer charging him, ball-peen hammer high above his head, howling like some banshee outta hell. Gary slid to one side, his throbbing head screaming in protest, and kicked at Bauer. His boot connected with Bauer's knee. Letting out a primal cry, Bauer's leg collapsed under him. Gary reached for his sidearm, but Bauer was like a bobcat, pouncing, clawing, biting. Gary tried to free his right arm, get his hand around to his Glock, but the smaller man's sinewy strength was deceptive, his wiry muscles like steel cables.

The two rolled on the floor, punching, grabbing, twisting, cursing, slamming into bedposts, knocking into walls, toppling a floor lamp, a chair, and a mirror. Hands groped, teeth grit, sweat sprayed. They were fighting for their lives.

Boom!

Both men stopped and slumped to the floor, panting heavily.

Maggie flinched when she heard the gunshot. What was happening? She was fully aware now. Her head still throbbed, and her body still felt like lead, but she was alive and coherent.

Somebody above her wasn't.

Please don't be Gary. Please, please. She stayed motionless, held her breath, and listened, listened for those familiar footsteps. But they never came.

Stevie rolled over and faced Warren. Blood spurted out of a gaping hole in the cop's abdomen, pooling on the floor beside him. His face had drained itself of color, and his lips quivered. He blinked and looked at Stevie with wide, frightened eyes. He reminded Stevie of the fish he used to catch in the pond. He'd hold their wriggling body, looking into their scared eyes, until their mouth stopped moving and gills stopped searching for water.

Kneeling beside Warren, Stevie placed the barrel of the Glock against the cop's forehead and whispered, "This ain't what I wanted."

Warren's lips moved in one final silent plea, then his eyes blanked into an empty stare, a camera shutter capturing one last image.

Stevie dropped the gun and began to cry.

His wailing grew louder and louder, filling the tiny trailer.

Maggie wept silently, tears spilling out of her eyes and running down the bridge of her nose, puddling on the floor. Her sobs were choked by whatever was stuffed in her mouth.

She knew Gary was dead, shot by Stevie. It was over. He would kill her next. She was sure of it.

CHAPTER 35

MAGGIE FADED IN and out of consciousness. The chills and shivers would melt into comfortable warmth, starting in the back of her head and spreading like liquid through the rest of her body. Then she would fade out. It was always the same, though. She was falling, falling, falling, through a black tunnel. The heat was intense and hands grabbed at her, trying to slow her descent. Then a familiar voice would call to her, gentle and calm, but sorrowful—*Maggie, Maggie.* Joe. He would call to her over and over.

Then she would come to a sudden jolting stop. Hands held her fast, suspending her above the bottomless pit, groping at her, grabbing, pawing. Joe's voice would echo through the darkness in one painful question—*Why?* She would try to answer, call out to him, explain, but no answer would come. Someone had stolen her voice, fused her lips, sutured them tight. Slowly, slowly, the chill would revisit, crawling over her body like tiny spiders, and she would begin to shiver. Consciousness would gradually return, and she would remember where she was.

The best Maggie could tell, she was somewhere under Stevie's trailer. Her mouth was stuffed with a cloth, lips sealed, maybe taped. Wrists and ankles bound, she was lying prone on a blanket that reeked of body odor. She thought of her cell phone. If she could only reach it and make a...no, she'd left it on the passenger seat of her car.

The blackness was oppressive, and with each passing minute, the temperature dropped, bringing a whole new wave of violent shivers.

For the past half hour, she listened to Stevie's footsteps crisscrossing the trailer. She heard something heavy being dragged across the floor, then the storm door open and slam shut, a car door slam, then the rumble of the police cruiser's motor. Wheels rolled over dirt. Then, faintly, a splash. Stevie must have ditched Gary's cruiser in the pond. He probably ditched hers there as well.

She assumed Stevie was disposing of Gary's body too. Maybe there was a chance he was still alive. After all, Stevie had apparently meant to kill her and failed.

Some time later the door opened and shut again, and the footsteps returned. Water ran, the toilet flushed, lights clicked on and off. Then there was silence.

Maggie was fading out again and fought to remain conscious.

Focus, Maggie, focus.

She thought of Joe, his voice calling her name, questioning her, always *Why?* Why couldn't she answer him? She knew what he was asking. Why had she turned on him? Why had she lied to him? Why had she betrayed his trust? Why, why, why? Why had she committed fraud, forgery, been so deceptive? Why had she chosen this path of corruption?

She faded, enveloped in a shroud of guilt and remorse. Maybe she would just let herself fall through the endless darkness, plummet into nothingness for eternity. She was wretched, corrupt, evil.

She deserved hell. She blacked out.

Suddenly, she was snapped back into consciousness by the sound of Stevie's muffled voice. How much time had passed? Minutes? Hours? She had no way of telling.

Stevie lay flat on his back in the middle of the living room, legs straight, arms outstretched in a crucifix form. His breathing was heavy, his brow damp with sweat. He'd done it. He'd obeyed the voice, and now it owned him. It was the lone proprietor of his soul, digging its hands into his chest and wrapping its bony fingers around his heart. It was his master now; he was the slave.

He'd done what was necessary. Chief Maggie was safe and her car was hidden. No sign she was ever there. Warren and his car were both taken care of, as if they never existed.

Momma's voice was gone now, drowned out by the constant drone of the deep, throaty tone. And it had an urgent command—*Do Sterner.*

Stevie shut his eyes and concentrated on slowing his breathing. In and out, nice and slow. Relax. In and out. Just like Momma had taught him. When he was little and the darkness would chase him, Momma would cradle him in her lap, stroke his hair, and repeat over and over, "In and out. In and out," until his breathing settled into a steady rhythm.

Momma would be proud of her son. No, she wouldn't. There were still two left. Sterner and L-stone. The names taunted him, mocked him, dangled just out of his reach. Sterner and L-stone would get away with what they'd done to Momma. They would walk free. *No!* The voice shouted. *Sterner dies, then L-stone.*

But Stevie concentrated on a different name. He had a score to settle first. Momma would understand.

But the voice only grew louder and more obstinate—*Sterner. Sterner first!*

Stevie's breathing spiked again, his diaphragm working overtime to fully inflate his lungs.

"Dinsmore first," he whispered.

Then it hit him again, the blow to the chest, like an anvil dropped from the ceiling. The weight pressed down on him, suffocating. He gasped for air, tried to move his arms, but they were pinned to the floor; he tried to sit up, but the weight on his chest was just too much.

Sterner. Sterner.

"No!" His voice was strained, his breathing labored. The weight was unbearable, threatening to crush him. The room started to darken. Darker, darker, darker, only a tunnel of light.

"OK. Sterner."

The weight lifted, and Stevie swallowed a huge gulp of air. His lungs were working frantically, filling with precious, life-sustaining oxygen.

"OK. Sterner first, then Dinsmore. Then L-stone. L-stone deserves to be the closin' ceremony."

He sat up, taking long deep breaths. The stale air of the trailer never tasted so sweet.

Kitty climbed out from under the sofa and sauntered over, climbed up on to his lap, and rubbed its head against his chest, purring like a Bentley.

Stevie stroked Kitty's head. He ran his hand over the cat's ears and around its jowls. "Kitty, we got work to do." He pushed up the sleeve of his left arm, exposing the soft, white skin of his forearm, dug the nail of his index finger into the flesh, and dragged it to midway up the forearm. The trail of torn skin blanched, then filled with bright red blood.

Stevie smiled, ran his finger across the line of blood, and put it to his lips. He then extended the arm in front of Kitty. "Here, Kitty. We hafta become one...blood brothers, you know."

Kitty looked at him curiously, its head cocked to one side, as if contemplating his strange behavior, sniffed at the blood, and ran its sandpaper tongue over the crimson scratch.

Stevie laughed and let out a yelp. Kitty startled, scolded him with a low growl, then went back to lapping at the thickening blood.

"Good Kitty," Stevie said, trying to restrain himself from letting loose with another yelp. "It's just you and me now. Just us two...brothers."

Maggie heard the whole thing. The world above her had come crashing down. All she could do was listen. The sounds were everything to her, her only connection to the world.

It was starting to make sense now. Like so many pieces to a puzzle floating in space, finding each other and joining themselves together to complete a picture. Bob, Woody, Eddie, and now Glen and Dad. All victims. Images rushed through Maggie's head, painful images. Nineteen twenty-two. The Secret. Great-Grandpa. Philip Yates. The attacks. Gail Bauer. Stevie. The pieces rushed together, crashing into one another, smashing the reality she knew, or at least thought she knew.

The lion. Stevie.

Stevie is...the lion! It's all an elaborate hoax. There never was a real lion. It was Stevie all along.

No. He couldn't be. Could he? How could he pull that off? It didn't make sense. But it *did* make sense. Steve wrote the note—*an eye for an eye*. Stevie wanted revenge. That's why she had come here, to talk to him, probe his mind. He was behind all of it. But what about Caleb? Why—? The stones. The Dinsmore boys said they used to throw stones at Stevie's trailer. He's going after the Dinsmore boys! But what did he say? Sterner first, then Dinsmore. Glen Sterner is next. Then the boys. Then Dad.

Oh, God, no. No. No. Please, God. NO!

If Glen Sterner was a religious man he would have prayed, but since he wasn't, he wrote off the feeling he was having as just a bad case of nerves. He needed a beer.

He went to his refrigerator, pulled out a Bud, cracked the top open, and indulged in a good long swig. *Mmm. That was more like it.*

At thirty years old, Glen felt like he'd already lived three lifetimes. He'd been in the marines, married, divorced, had two kids he never saw, an ex-wife who hated him, no friends, and was plagued every day by guilt that followed him around like a shadow.

He tried running from it. Oh, had he tried. First there was the military. Then, after the divorce, he'd moved to West Virginia and got a job in a coal mine. Three years later, he moved back to Dark Hills to be closer to his kids. But his drinking had gotten the best of him, and when he drank, he became violent. A year ago a judge cut off his visitation rights, and his ex-wife took the kids and moved out west. Montana? No, North Dakota. Maybe Minnesota. He didn't even know.

He'd let everyone down: his ex, his kids...his old man. His dad, the popular politician on his way up the political ladder, had put it all on the line for him. What a hypocrite. Covering up for him, making sure no one knew his dirty secret. Quite a dad.

Every now and then the guilt would become especially unbearable, and that was when Glen would turn to the bottle and drown himself in a six-pack of Budweiser.

He thought about praying sometimes. He was raised in the Methodist church in town and had been a good, Sunday school–going, Bible-believing kid until he got into high school. Amazing how getting in with the wrong crowd can ruin a life.

He started drinking in the tenth grade. He and the other guys would go to the old cemetery and throw a few back, have some laughs, then go home. But in eleventh grade he started drinking heavier, and by twelfth grade he was a closet alcoholic.

Somehow, he was able to maintain passing grades and even land a spot on the first string of the varsity football team. But as soon as school was out or practice was over, he'd hit the bottle, and hit it hard.

Now he was thirty, lonely, out of shape, and depressed. His social life consisted of shooting pool at the bar almost every evening and…well, that was it. He was a loser. Plain and simple. No one could forgive him for what he did. Not even himself.

What he did.

Woody was the first to hit the kid, the retard. He swatted the back of his head, then shoved him in the chest hard, knocking the kid to the dirt. They were all drunk, coming home from the cemetery where they'd put down too many beers. When the kid stood up again, Eddie took a swing at him and knocked him back down. The kid landed solid, and Glen saw the anger flash across his face. It all happened so fast from there. Woody found the rope; Eddie held the kid. The sound of that rope beating against the kid's bony back and his muffled crying…

After a while, the kid's mother appeared at the door, screaming something about calling the cops. For being so drunk, Woody had moved fast. He pushed her inside, followed by Eddie, and, farther back, after stealing a glance at the kid, Glen. She was hollering and crying and grabbing for something to throw when Woody struck her the first time, a solid blow right to the jaw.

Things after that were always a blur.

He remembered Eddie standing up and telling him it was his turn. He refused at first, but the way they laughed at him and the anger in their eyes got him so mad. It must have been the alcohol, because he found himself blaming the whole thing on the woman; it was *her* fault. He hated her. So he did it.

As they were leaving, Eddie shoved the kid against the outside wall of the house, told him he and his mom needed to learn some manners. The kid was crying and snot was running out of his nose. His back was red and welted and bloody.

It wasn't until the next morning that the guilt hit him like a punch to the gut. And every morning after that.

Glen walked into the bathroom, set his beer can on the counter, and eyed himself in the mirror. What a disgrace! His hair was too long and shaggy, his face partially hidden behind a scruffy beard, a spare tire bulged over his belt, and dark bags hung under his eyes like week-old shiners. He wasn't even a shadow of the high school quarterback that led Southern High to the county finals.

Outside, a metal trash can tipped over and rattled over the patio, snapping Glen out of his self-loathing pity party. He went to the back door and flipped the switch for the patio light. A steady wind was blowing, and the trash can was still tumbling across the concrete slab, making quite a racket.

Glen unlocked the door, slid it open, and stepped out onto the patio. A gust of wind blasted him from the side, filling his ear with static. He shut the door and hustled across the patio, chasing down the runaway trash can.

Umph! Something hit him from behind and sent him sprawling across the concrete. He landed on his palms and struck his chin. A shock of numbing pain surged through his jaw. Lifting a hand, he gently felt his chin. It was wet. He'd busted it open. He quickly collected himself and tried to roll over, thinking the other trash can had clobbered him, but something pounced on his back and held him down. He tried to move, wriggle free, fight back, anything, but the *something* was like a car sitting on his back. Whatever it was, it was huge. He could hear its massive lungs drawing in air—long slow inhale, short quick exhale, long inhale, short exhale.

Seconds ticked by, and the *something* didn't move. Glen's mind reeled. He tried to think, form a coherent thought, but all he could think was *bear*. A black bear had found its way into his yard, rummaged through his garbage, and he'd startled it. All he could do was wait for the fatal blow, for the beast to sink its teeth into his scalp and be done with it. But the blow never came.

He had to play dead. That's what they always said on TV. If a bear attacks, play dead. He let his body go limp beneath the beast and lay motionless.

More seconds, an eternity passed, and nothing happened.

Then the bear was off of him. He could hear its claws scraping along the concrete and the sound of its breathing. He didn't know what to do. He couldn't just lie there all night. What was the bear waiting for? Maybe it would get bored and leave.

How long he lay there, he didn't know, but after some time the sound of the bear faded and Glen lifted his head and looked around. Nothing in sight.

He rolled over and felt his chin again. It was still bleeding. The patio door was only fifteen feet away. He could make a run for it.

Scrambling to his feet, he took three steps toward the door and froze. Something was behind him. The bear was back. Again, he could hear the click and scrape of claws on concrete.

Instinctively, he turned to face the beast and was immediately met head-on by two large paws, driving him backward and to the ground.

What stood over him was no bear. It was nothing he'd ever seen before.

The beast lowered its head, arched its back, and let out a deafening roar, holding it at its loudest point, then trailing it off to a low growl.

"Dear God," Glen muttered just before the mouth opened, and his face was swallowed in darkness.

CHAPTER 36

JOE WAS BESIDE himself. He'd spent the evening and then most of the night and into the early morning scouring Dark Hills for any sign of Maggie or anyone who might have seen her or knew where she was. He talked to Darlene at the diner, Hank Finnigan at the hardware store, Wanda Mitchell, the hair stylist, some guy named Rocco with a tattoo of a Shih Tzu named Pinky on his arm at the pizza shop on White Street, even the clerk at the dry cleaners. Nobody had seen her.

Andy hadn't answered the phone when he called, so he'd stopped by the station—no one was there; the building was dark and the doors locked.

Joe continued to drive the streets of Dark Hills until well after midnight, but his search had turned up nothing. Finally, with nowhere else to look, he headed over to Josiah's.

Josiah answered the door in his pajamas, sleep in his eyes, hair plastered to the right side of his head.

"Sorry to wake you," Joe said. "I needed someone to talk to. Is it OK?"

Josiah stepped aside. "Sure, sure. Come in. It's chilly tonight. You like coffee? Tea?"

"Coffee'll be great," Joe said.

"Then coffee it is."

Joe shed his jacket. "Maggie's missing." The words sounded so final, so doom-and-gloom. They fell out of Joe's mouth like a ten-pound weight. But he really didn't *know* she was missing. He was working off an assumption. It was possible Maggie just left town for the night or just wanted an uninterrupted evening without calls, questions, or intrusions. She wasn't beholden to run her schedule and plans by Joe. But then why wasn't she answering her cell phone?

Seeing the look of disbelief on Josiah's face, Joe explained himself. "Caleb had another... *writing*."

Josiah held the coffee grounds above the percolator. "And?"

"It said, *Save Gill.* Maggie left early from work, and nobody knows where she is. She isn't home, isn't answering her cell phone, and I can't get a hold of Andy or Gary." He paused, knowing his rationale rested heavily on the accuracy of a comatose boy's handwritten message. Not exactly rock-solid evidence. He might as well have been jumping out of an airplane with an untested parachute. "I'm worried. I think something's happened to her."

Josiah rubbed his chin thoughtfully. He didn't quite fit the part of a scholar in his black and red plaid pajamas and slippers, but his wisdom was deep. It wasn't the wisdom obtained from years of higher learning and book studying, but rather the kind earned from a lifetime of hard living, of experiencing life as it happened, of making mistakes and learning from them, of loving and losing. Of really *living.* It was authentic wisdom that demanded respect. "All of Caleb's messages so far have been accurate, right?"

Joe nodded. "Yes. There've only been two, but they both meant something."

"Are you sure you're interpreting it correctly? It couldn't mean something else?"

Joe shrugged. "What else could *save Gill* mean? My gut says she's in danger."

Josiah crossed his arms. "Your gut. You mean that still, small voice in your heart? God's voice?"

"You could call it that."

Josiah leaned forward. "OK. If the other messages were on, why would this one be any different?"

"You really think it's God speaking through Caleb, don't you?" Joe had seen the writing, even witnessed one taking place, and figured out what they meant. But he still wasn't convinced it was God doing it. That was a mental leap that was a little too far for him to take. It went against everything he'd been taught and believed. God didn't speak like that anymore. Maybe in the old days He did, to men with long white beards and flowing robes. Men who did miracles and fought battles. But not these days.

Josiah eyed Joe steadily. He seemed to look right past that outer wall Joe had erected and find the real Joseph Alan Saunders hidden somewhere behind it. "Joe, you gotta let God work. Yes, I really think it's God speakin'. Why not? You tell me that."

"Because God just doesn't do that anymore." Joe said it like he meant it, though as soon as the words left his mouth he questioned whether he really did.

"Who says?" Josiah paused as if waiting for an answer. Joe didn't have one. "Who says God can't use a dream, or a vision, or a comatose boy to reveal His plan? Is He limited by what we believe about Him? He used a donkey, didn't He? Is it that far of a stretch for you to believe He could use a boy?"

Again, he waited, and again, Joe had no answer. "I sure hope not," he said, leaning back and unfolding his arms like a lawyer resting his case.

Joe thought that over for a moment. Josiah did make a good point. Who was he to tell God how He could and couldn't communicate with His children? He was God, for crying out loud. He didn't have to bow to our beliefs or limit Himself because of our theology. Maybe Josiah was right. Why couldn't it be God speaking? Why not?

Joe suddenly felt very small. He had seen something most people never even dream of witnessing and dismissed it as *bad theology*. How foolish! How ignorant. How small was his faith. He had hardened his heart so much toward God that he didn't even want to listen when God was speaking.

It finally hit him with all the force of a battering ram: it wasn't God's fault that Rick was dead. Joe had wasted so many precious years—too many—blaming God and pointing an accusing finger toward heaven. He had walked out on God, not the other way around. God had always been there. The patient, loving Father waiting for His wayward son to return. Waiting to lavish him with love and welcome him back into the fellowship of His family. His heart suddenly felt very heavy in his chest, and a lump rose in his throat. His hands began to tremble. His flesh tightened with goose bumps. His mouth went dry. He knew what he needed to do. He'd always known. And tonight, right here, he'd do it. "Jo, will you pray with me?"

Josiah smiled. "It would be an honor."

Right there in the kitchen, Joe bowed his head and opened his heart. Emotions that had been bottled for ten long years, fueled by the events of the past several days, suddenly burst out, and the tears flowed freely. Great sobs shook his muscles, choking his words. For a full five minutes, Joe didn't speak, didn't say a single word. He couldn't. He just cried. He fell into the arms of his Father and cried.

Then Josiah was beside him, the older man's hand heavy on his shoulder. "Heavenly Father," Josiah prayed, "I come to You on behalf of my brother. He loves You, I know he does. Wrap Your arms around him, pull him close, and let him experience Your forgiveness and restoration. Your son has come back, Lord, and we all welcome him."

Joe sniffed and wiped his tears with his sleeve. His throat felt dry and tight as he began to pray. "Father, I owe You an apology. I know it's not enough and never will be, and I know I don't deserve Your love, but, for what it's worth, I'm sorry. Please forgive me for being so bitter and angry. My faith has been so frail. If You'll have me, I'd like to come back to You. Thank You for teaching me so many things." He sniffed again and wiped at the tears on his cheeks with the back of his hand. "I'm ready to be used of You, Lord. Amen."

By the time Joe was done praying, Josiah had a smile on his face that stretched from one ear to the other. "Welcome back, brother," he said, patting Joe's shoulder. "Welcome back. Now we've got work to do."

"Maggie," Joe said, his voice still a little shaky.

"Yes. There's not much we can do now. The whole town is asleep. Call the station first thing in the morning and see if you can get ahold of her. That's one thing. The other is Glen Sterner and Elston Gill. Owen, Hopkins, and Cummings are all gone. That leaves Sterner and Gill as the only ones left. I think we have good reason to believe one of them's next."

"What do you think is killing them?"

Josiah stroked at his chin some, then smoothed his bushy eyebrows. "Not sure about that yet. Maybe *who* is the question we should be asking."

"You don't think it's an animal? *A man-eating devil lion?* Isn't that what Yates called it?"

"Didn't say that. There's a beast involved, no question 'bout that. But my question is: Is someone controlling it? Like Yates claimed he could." He paused and nursed his eyebrows some more. "The only person all three of the victims had in common was Stevie. It'll be daybreak in a few hours. I'll pay him another visit. Alone this time."

"Why can't you go now? Wake him up and talk to him."

Shaking his head slowly, Josiah said, "Won't do no good. Stevie's not exactly a morning person. You saw how he reacted last time; it'd be worse."

"You think he's capable of doing whatever's going on around here? Of murder?"

Josiah wrinkled his brow and cupped his jaw in his hand. "Gut feeling? As much as I hate to admit it, yeah, I do. Last time I talked to him, when we were there, there was something dark in his eyes. Evil. I could feel it. Over the years, I've tried tellin' that boy about the Lord, God knows I have. But he just don't want to hear none of it. There's something dark there. Something real dark. There's other forces at work, you know. Powers and principalities. I'm sure of it."

"Fueled by revenge. Like with Yates."

"Revenge is a powerful force," Josiah said. "Why do you think God says vengeance is His? He's the only one holy and righteous enough to wield such power. In the hands of man, vengeance is evil. Wickedness."

Joe straightened up and set his mug on the counter. "This stuff is creeping me out. I just want to make sure Maggie is OK. I'll let you battle the forces of darkness. I'm gonna go see if I can get at least a couple hours of sleep. Thanks for the coffee and…everything else."

Josiah placed his hand on Joe's back. "A couple more hours of sleep sounds like a great idea. My mind's tired as a one-legged frog. Call me when you find something out about Maggie. And I think it would be a good idea to pay our friend Glen a visit. The senior Gill too. You know where he's bein' cared for?"

"Maggie said St. Magdalene's over in Quinceburg."

"You mind?"

"Not at all. I'll call you as soon as I know something. And Josiah, thanks again."

Josiah sandwiched Joe's hand in both of his. "Let's pray before we part." He then led them in prayer, asking God to protect them and give them wisdom, courage, and a humble spirit. Then he prayed for Caleb and Rosa and Maggie. When he was finished, he lifted his face and smiled at Joe, his tired eyes crinkling at the corners. "Go with God, son. He will guide us. He hasn't failed yet."

CHAPTER 37

HOURS LATER, AFTER a bout of restless sleep, Joe was up, showered, shaved, and dressed before sunrise. Maggie was on his mind. He had tried calling her house and cell before attempting sleep, but both led to her recorded voice. He'd tried praying too, but the words came sporadically, more begging for help and pleading for answers than anything else. His mind was reeling with possibilities, scenarios, horrors. Where was Maggie? Where had she gone? What if she already...

God, please no.

He picked up the phone and dialed in her number. The phone rang four times with no answer before her machine clicked on. A familiar message: "Hi, this is Maggie. I'm not home now; you know what to do."

Not home. But where? He left a message again, his fifth. "Maggie, it's me again. I'm worried about you. Call my cell when you get this message." Calling her cell again, he left the same message.

He then punched in the number for the police station. Three rings and a recording: Gary's voice, instructing the caller to dial 911 for an emergency, leave a message for a non-emergency. Joe hung up, threw on his coat, and headed out the door.

Outside, it was still dark and murky. A cold dampness had settled over the region, biting to the bone and bringing with it a thick fog. Joe shivered and climbed into his truck. He had to find Andy or Gary.

He had to find Maggie.

Michael Dinsmore had gotten up early, padded downstairs to the family room, and turned on the video player for his daily dose of cartoons. His brother, Sean, with whom he shared a room, was right behind him. Their other brothers were still fast asleep, Dad was in the shower, and Mom was rummaging around in the kitchen. It was all part of their daily routine.

Dad usually woke the boys up when he got out of the shower. Mom would have breakfast ready. They'd eat, get dressed, and be out the door by 7:15 to catch the school bus at 7:20.

But catching the school bus seemed like hours away now. *Scooby-Doo* was on, and Michael was glued to the set. Scooby and Shaggy were being chased by a monster that looked like it had just climbed out of a garbage can. Of course, it wasn't a real monster, just some dork dressed up in a dumb costume. The monster had Shaggy cornered. Scooby was hiding under a box. The monster moaned. Shaggy pulled a box over his head and hollered "Jeepers!" Scooby whimpered. The sound of cartoon music and canned laughter filled the room.

Michael only noticed the steady meowing after Scooby's moment of truth. He spun around and looked at the sliding glass door that led to the concrete patio in back of the house.

Sean jumped off the sofa. "Hey, Mike, look, the c–c–cat!"

Michael hushed him. "Quiet, dorko. You want Mom and Dad to hear you?"

They both snuck over to the door and looked at the tan cat through the glass. The cat shook the cold water from its fur and meowed again, its big eyes pleading for just a minute's worth of warmth and affection.

"It's the sa–same one from the other d–day. It looks so c–cold," Sean said, tapping the glass.

The cat lifted its paw and touched the glass where Sean's finger was. *Meow.*

Michael nudged his little brother. "Go check the steps."

Sean smiled and nodded, stood up, and tip-toed away. "All clear," he whispered.

Michael unlocked the door and slid it open just far enough for the cat to slip in. It went to him immediately and rubbed its head along his leg, purring loudly.

Sean knelt beside Michael and extended his hand to the cat. "He li–li–likes us. I wish we c–could k–keep him."

"Yeah, right. Mom and Dad would never go for that," Michael said. He stroked the cat's wet head and back.

"He's so c–c–cold. What's he guh–gonna do when winter comes?"

Michael kept on petting the cat as it purred louder. "Maybe we could hide him." He looked around the room.

"Boys!"

Uh-oh. Dad. Michael hadn't even heard him coming down the steps.

"What is that?" Dad stood over Michael and Sean, hands stuck to his hips, eyes squinched up. It was the look he gave right before dishing out a couple of good whoopin's.

"Uh, um." Michael looked at the tabby.

Sean jumped up and pleaded with his dad. "D–dad, can we k–keep him? It's so c–cold outside, and loo–look at him; he really likes us."

Fortunately, Dad wasn't in a whoopin' mood. His face softened, and he relaxed his arms. He knelt down next to Michael and ran his big hand over the cat's head. "I'm sorry, guys, we just don't have room or time for a pet." He looked at Michael, then at Sean. "You can't keep it."

"Aw, c–come on, Dad," Sean pleaded.

"We'll take care of it, and we can use our allowance money for food and stuff," Michael said, pulling the cat closer to him.

Dad sighed. "Sorry, guys." He took the cat away from Michael and cradled it in his thick arm. "He might be someone else's, or he may have some kind of disease. You just don't know what you're gettin' with stray cats." He slid the door open and let the cat fall to the concrete patio. It shook its legs, looked around, then tore off, heading back into the woods.

Michael stood next to Dad and watched as the cat bounded across the yard and disappeared into the darkness. Dad flipped the switch for the floodlight and leaned closer to the glass. His heavy hand fell on Michael's shoulder. "Mikey." His voice was hushed and serious. "You see that?"

Michael followed Dad's eyes to a spot directly behind the house, across the dirt alley. The woods. Two yellow lights hovered in the fog, just out of the floodlight's reach. He looked closer and squinted, trying to see through the murky haze. They could be eyes. Or maybe just the light playing off some water. Then they moved…and blinked. They were definitely eyes. His hands were suddenly numb. The eyes were watching him, staring right through him. Just like the monster on *Scooby-Doo.* He opened his mouth and tried to say something, tell Dad he saw it too. But nothing came out. So he just nodded.

"Son," Dad said, keeping his hand on Michael's shoulder and eyes fixed on the yellow marbles floating in the fog, "get me the phone."

Ten minutes after leaving the Dew-Drop, Joe pulled up in front of the police station. A light was on inside. He jumped out of his truck and checked the front door. It was locked. He looked inside and saw a light on in Maggie's office, then rapped on the door. A shadow moved in the office, but no one responded to his knocking. It had to be Gary or Andy. Maybe even Maggie.

Please be Maggie.

He knocked again. Still nothing. The shadow moved again.

Come on. I know you're in there.

Joe ground his teeth and ran around the rear of the building. The back door was open. He entered the darkened narrow hallway, "Hello? Maggie? Gary? Anyone?" No answer.

But he could hear movement in Maggie's office. A chair slid across the floor, file cabinet drawers rolled open and shut, papers shuffled.

Joe rounded the corner and found Andy sitting behind Maggie's desk digging through a drawer.

"Andy!"

Andy started, jumped up, knocked his knees against the desk, and drew his gun. He pointed it directly at Joe. His hands were shaking, sweat dampened his face, and his eyes were wild with terror.

Joe shot both hands into the hair. "Whoa, Andy. Hold on now." He tried to swallow the tremor in his voice. *Stay calm.* "I'm on your side. I just want to find Maggie."

Andy said nothing but kept the gun leveled.

Joe took one careful step toward Andy, hands still raised in surrender. "Andy, think about what you're doing here, man. I'm not even armed. I stopped by to see if you heard anything from Maggie, that's all. Remember I called you last night."

Andy took a step backward. The gun wavered in his hands, and sweat soaked through his shirt. "Don't come any closer. I'll shoot. I will."

Joe stopped his slow advance. "Andy, please. You don't want to shoot me. Do you? I'm just trying to find Maggie. She's in trouble. I think—"

"She's next," Andy finished. "That's what you said. Now she's missing." The tremble now took over his entire body, and for a minute Joe thought he would collapse. "Maybe it's you."

Joe nudged his hands higher into the air. "Andy, Andy. Easy, man. You know that's not true. I would never do anything to hurt Maggie." Joe's heart was climbing in his throat. *Stay calm. Stay calm. One sudden move and he'll jerk the trigger.* "Andy. Have you ever shot anyone?"

Andy didn't answer, but the shift of his eyes to the outstretched gun and back to Joe said no.

"Do you know what it's like? Feeling the trigger depress under your finger. Hearing the crack of the fire. The gun jerking in your hands. You know you can feel the impact of the bullet just as if it was your own flesh it was penetrating? You'll never forget it. Knowing you killed someone. Took a life. An innocent life." He paused. Joe had no idea what it was like to put a slug in someone either, but he was desperate and making things up on the fly.

The gun lowered a little in Andy's hand. He was thinking. That was good.

Joe took one step closer to Andy. "Andy." He looked right into the younger man's eyes. Hazel. Scared. Confused. "Andy. I love Maggie. I do. And I would never do anything to hurt her. I only want to find her. Just like you."

Finally, Andy lowered his gun and set it on the desk with a clunk. He slumped his shoulders and dropped his eyes to the floor. "Sorry, Joe."

Joe lowered his arms and blew out his cheeks. He ran the back of his hand across his forehead. "It's OK. I know you're scared, but we need to find Maggie. What happened last night? Any leads?"

Andy sat in Maggie's chair and rubbed at his eyes with both hands. His face was ashen and glistened under a thin film of sweat. "No. She's not home, not answering her cell phone, and the radio in her car is shut off. I've been up all night and got nothing." He looked at Joe, fatigue misting his eyes. "Gary's gone too. I can't locate him."

"Gary's gone too?"

Andy sucked in a deep breath and nodded. He was looking more composed with every passing second. "It's like they both just vanished. I've been tearing this place apart looking for anything that might clue me in to where they are. But so far I still have nothing. What if—"

Just then the dispatcher's voice came over the radio. "Police assistance needed at 2874 Jackson Lane. We have a report of a large animal in Yates Woods."

Joe shot a look at Andy. "You have a shotgun I can use?"

Andy ran for the radio. "Sure do." He picked up the receiver. "Andy here, Brenda. I'm on it." Then he went to the gun locker, unlocked it, grabbed a shotgun, and tossed it to Joe. "Help yourself to the ammo."

Rosa sat by Caleb's bed praying and waiting.

She had been awakened out of a sound sleep by her own screaming. Her pillow was wet with tears, and her stomach was tied in knots. She didn't remember having any dreams, but knew she had to go to Caleb. He had another message to relay.

She had arrived at Hillside at 6:30, convinced the morning nurse to let her in—visiting hours didn't start until eight—and had been praying and waiting for the past half hour. *God, speak to me.*

Ever since Caleb's message yesterday, she had done nothing but pray. Prayer was her escape, her hiding place. There was no place she felt safer than in the presence of her Lord. She called upon Him night and day, seeking Him, beseeching Him, petitioning Him, praising Him. When others, like Joe, were called to action, she was called to be still, to pray.

When Caleb's message came yesterday, she prayed. When she couldn't find Joe, she prayed. When Joe called her last night and told her the search for Maggie had been unsuccessful, she fell on her knees and prayed. When she awoke early in the morning, wet with tears, heart banging in her chest, stomach knotted, she prayed.

And now, sitting beside her son's bed, waiting for a miracle, she prayed.

"Write. Write, child. Write for Us."

I will. I'm willing.

The glow had grown, and the voice had softened to almost a whisper. There was a sense of urgency this time, not of panic or fear or distress, but of importance.

"Write for Us."
I'm ready. Use me.

Caleb's body started trembling again. His hand began shaking. Rosa jumped up, did the pencil and clipboard thing, and waited. Watching her son's hand form words sent a wave of needles along her scalp and down her neck. She was witnessing a miracle.

"Thank You, Jesus," she whispered.

It didn't take long. Caleb's hand wrote quickly, scribbling another message. When it stopped, Rosa took the clipboard and studied it. There were more scribbles this time, and the letters were harder to decipher. But once she found it, the message jumped out at her like a flashing sign: *FEar noT.*

Joe. Something was going to happen to Joe. *Dear God, protect him.*

A peace settled over her then and she knew with clarity the meaning of Caleb's message. God's message. Joe would have to decide this morning—either he would trust God completely and fully, or he wouldn't.

This would be Joe's defining moment.

She picked up her cell phone and punched in the number. *Please answer.*

CHAPTER 38

JOE BARRELED DOWN Main Street, following Andy's cruiser through the fog. It was beginning to lighten, but the fog still made visibility almost impossible. He turned onto McCormick, wheels slipping on the wet asphalt, and reached for his cell phone. He needed to call Josiah. But just as he unclipped it from his belt, it rang. It was Rosa.

"Rosa."

"Joe, I have another message."

"Another message?"

"From Caleb."

"OK. Go."

"Fear not." Pause. "Did you get that?"

Joe slowed and pulled the Ford into the Harrison's Garage parking lot. "Uh, yeah. Fear not. What does that mean?"

"Joe, listen to me. Are you listening?" Her voice was tight, and it cracked when she spoke.

Joe threw the truck into park, turned the key toward him, and shut off the engine. "Yes."

"Something is going to happen this morning, something frightening. This message is for you, for you, Joe. Whatever happens, remember that God is with you and that He is in control. *Fear not.*"

Joe grabbed the shotgun and a handful of shells from the passenger side seat. "Gotcha. Fear not."

"Joe!" Rosa's voice spiked in volume and snatched Joe's full attention. "Listen to me. Where are you?"

"Andy got a call just a couple minutes ago that Jerry Dinsmore spotted our animal in the woods behind his house. We're here now ready to go after it." He jumped out of the truck and shut the door.

"Be careful. Go with God. And fear not; He's with you. Do you hear, Joe? Fear not."

"I know, Rosa. Just pray, OK?"

"I will. Just be careful. Bye."

Joe reset his phone and punched in Josiah's number. *C'mon. C'mon.*

———————

Maggie awoke to the belligerent thump of a pounding headache. Her head felt like it would explode or implode—whichever was worse—at any moment. She was still in a half-conscious state and wasn't sure where she was. She tried to move. An aching cramp in her shoulders brought her into full consciousness and quickly reminded her of her present situation. Some muted light was filtering into the dirt-floored box she was in, and she realized she was somewhere under the trailer. That would explain the activity last night taking place above her.

Last night. The gunshot. Gary. Stevie. Was it all just a dream? Her head was still cloudy, and she wasn't sure what was reality and what were mere products of her imagination.

She tried to lift her head, but something pulled at her hair. The blood from her head wound had dried, matting her hair to a blanket under her. Her arms and legs refused to move, scolding her with cramps and spasms every time she tried to budge them. Her hands and feet were bound tight, and there must have been tape over her mouth, sealing in whatever was stuffed *in* her mouth. She tried to swallow, but her throat was too dry.

The trailer was silent. Was Stevie still in bed? Or had he already left for the day?

Slowly, memories from last night started to form. She remembered Gary and Stevie wrestling, then the gunshot, then hearing something large being dragged across the floor, and then outside. It wasn't a dream. Gary was dead; she was sure of it. She also recalled Stevie's voice reso-nating through the floorboards, saying something about Dinsmore and Sterner and Dad. No, Sterner first, then Dinsmore. Then Dad. That's what he said.

He was going to kill Glen Sterner first, then the Dinsmore boys. Panic rose in her chest. Then Dad.

Ignoring the pain in her shoulders and head, she tried to move again—she had to get herself free—but it was useless; whatever held her wrists and ankles was too tight. If she could roll onto her back, maybe she could kick at the ceiling. It was only a couple of feet above her. She took a deep breath through her nose, held it, and in one quick motion rolled herself over. Hair ripped from her scalp, her back spasmed, shoulders screamed, head throbbed. She drew in a long breath, air whistling through her nose, and let out a muted scream. It was all she could do.

Drawing her knees to her chest, she kicked her legs upward with a grunt, beating the trailer floor with her feet.

"Josiah will be here in a few minutes," Joe said, shutting his phone.

"I just called a couple of guys too," Andy said, hooking his phone to his belt. "They'll be here ASAP."

Joe looked into the woods. It was getting lighter by the minute, but the fog was still so thick the trees were only vague charcoal outlines against the gray haze, like gnarled sentinels guarding an ancient secret. The beast was in there somewhere, hidden in the fog, waiting for them. Waiting to hunt them. At the thought of being the prey, a warmth started in Joe's cheeks and spread through his face. What was it Rosa had said? *This message is for you, for you, Joe. Fear not.* Fear not. The words bounced around in his head before settling quietly. Fear not. *Lord, I know You're with me. Help me to not be afraid.*

"—Joe."

Andy was calling his name.

"Joe."

He looked at Andy and blinked.

"You OK?"

Joe peered into the fog and blinked again. "Yeah. I'm fine. Just...thinking."

Andy swung his rifle over his shoulder. "Take plenty of ammo. Once we go in there, we're not coming out until we get a kill."

"Yeah. OK."

Fifteen minutes later, Josiah pulled up in his beat-up Dodge followed by three other burly hunter types in oversized pickups. They all climbed out of their trucks, toting rifles and decked out in camo, and assembled around Andy's cruiser.

Andy made the introductions. "Thanks for coming out, guys. This is Barry Wagman." He pointed to the tallest of the three newcomers, a thick-armed giant with a rough, pock-marked face, then went from left to right: "Mike Kline," a short, round middle-aged man with squinty eyes and a full brown beard; "Dan Berwager," a husky linebacker-type with a round face, rosy cheeks, and big meaty hands; "Joe Saunders, and Josiah Walker."

They all nodded to each other, then focused their attention on Andy.

"We don't know exactly what we're looking for in there, but it's already mauled a young boy and"—he glanced at Joe—"killed three others that we know of. Whatever it is, it's a predator, a man-eater, so you can bet it'll be hunting us just the same as we're hunting it. Visibility is tight, so keep alert."

"Simba Mfu," Barry said, taking a cigarette out of his coat pocket.

Joe shot a look at Josiah, then leaned toward Barry. "Excuse me?"

"Simba Mfu, fellas, a devil lion, that's what we're hunting...or being hunted by. I've been hearing the stories going around town 'bout the lion out there. Some years ago I spent some time in Africa, traveling and hunting, running from some of my own demons. The Africans tell a tale of a lion that's possessed by the spirit of a dead man. Spends his nights prowling and hunting humans, settling old scores. He's driven by revenge. They say the lion is immune to bullets and has some kind of supernatural intelligence."

Joe swallowed hard. His throat felt like it was stuffed with cotton. Simba Mfu. That's what Old Man Yates called it too. Said it was a devil lion. His palms were suddenly wet.

Barry shoved the unlit Marlboro between his lips, making eye contact with each of the other men. He must have noticed the way they eyed the cigarette. "Don't worry, I won't light it. I'll save it for after we bag this creature. Any of you ever heard of the man-eater from Mfuwe? He terrorized a whole valley a few years back. After he killed his sixth victim he paraded through the village streets with the man's bloodied clothes in his mouth. Like he was braggin' 'bout it. And then there was the Tsavo River incident. Back in the 1800s, two lions killed over a hundred and forty men."

He pulled the cigarette from his mouth and studied it thoughtfully. The silence around the circle was almost as thick as the fog. "I've done a lot of research on man-eaters. Even hunted a few. Believe what you want, but those African tales came from somewhere; there's some truth in 'em. There's a devil lion in these woods, fellas. But that ain't gonna stop me from puttin' a hole in it when I see it."

"Just be careful, guys," Andy said. "You have my permission to shoot anything that isn't human and bigger than a dog. I only want one death today, so be careful." He lifted some handheld radios out of his car. "We'll go in twos. Joe, you and Josiah, Mike and Barry, and I'll go with Dan." He handed each pair one radio. "We'll keep in contact with these. Channel five." He turned to Joe. "Joe, you went after this thing once already. Anything you want to add?"

Joe glanced at Barry. "I think Barry might be on to something. Bob Cummings and I hunted this thing a week ago. It's stealthy, like a phantom. It snuck up on us and"—he paused to swallow—"got Cummings before he even had time to aim his rifle. I'm talking not even seconds. If you get a shot, make it count." He looked around the group, making sure he had their attention. "You may only get one."

Andy nodded. "OK. We'll start on the north side here and move south. If we can flush it out into the open field beyond the woods, we'll have a good shot at it. Joe and Josiah, you start on the west end; Mike and Barry, take the center; and Dan and I will start on the east end. The two groups on the perimeter will move toward the center. Keep in contact, guys, and partners, maintain visual contact with each other at all times. I don't want anyone getting disconnected."

The tension in the group was thick. They worked quickly in silence, loading their weapons, checking their radios, making only awkward eye contact with one another.

When they were all ready, Josiah said, "Guys, you mind if I say a word of prayer?"

No one said anything, but they all gathered in a circle around Josiah.

Joe bowed his head as Josiah prayed. "Father God, maker of heaven and Earth, we ask You to go with us today as we enter these here woods. Be our protection. Give us keen hearing, sharp eyesight, and steady hands. Let us see Your power at work today." He paused, and Joe lifted his head and looked around the group. Some of the men had their eyes open, staring at the broken and cracked asphalt; some had their eyes closed. "Amen."

Andy looked up and nodded. "Amen. OK, guys. Let's go get us a kill."

Maggie kicked at the floor above her again and again until her legs felt like lead. Letting them fall to the ground, sore and tired, she wheezed heavily through her nose. Her pulse was like a piston in her ears. Sweat trickled from her hairline. Her head throbbed. She needed to catch her breath.

As it was getting lighter outside, more and more light filtered into the compartment in which she was hidden. And now that her head was freed from the ground, she could look around. She was in a box, about six feet by six feet. In one corner was a pile of empty soda cans, potato chip bags, and candy bar wrappers. In the opposite corner was what looked like a crumpled blanket and pillow. Next to the pillow was a large black flashlight. This must be Stevie's hideout, where he came to feel safe and concealed from the outside world.

Maggie drew in a long breath. The musty smell of body odor and blood filled her nostrils. She raised her legs again and kicked at the trailer floor, letting out a muffled grunt with each blow, but it didn't budge. There was something heavy on the floor above her. It was useless. She was trapped, buried alive, and no one knew where she was. She would die here. Or worse, Stevie would return and finish the job he'd started. He obviously knew she was still alive, or he wouldn't have bound her and stuffed her in this dungeon.

She let her legs rest again and shut her eyes. An image of Joe stared at her, smiling, his large brown eyes sparkling in the sunlight. He was young, just out of high school. His face was smooth, his hair short. He was promising her the world.

Life was simple then. They were in love and that was all that mattered.

Tears mingled with salty sweat and stung Maggie's eyes. She wanted to be eighteen again. She wanted to start over and do things differently. Do them right. Never did she imagine she would wind up here—a failed cop, buried alive, left for dead. What happened? How did she wander so far off the centerline of life?

The Secret. The Gill family legacy.

Anger flared inside her. Curse the family legacy. Forget about the Secret. They'd ruined enough lives, including hers. But they would ruin no more. If—*if*—she ever got out of here, she would come clean, confess, pour her heart out, reveal the Secret, end the legacy, and take what she had coming. *Sorry, Dad.*

And Joe would help her.

No, he wouldn't. Why would he? She'd lied to him, betrayed him, deceived him, and hurt him. She'd lost him forever.

CHAPTER 39

JOE STEPPED THROUGH the thick undergrowth, holding his shotgun waist high. The fallen leaves had been softened by the moisture of the fog and didn't crunch when stepped on.

It would give his prey an added advantage.

The fog was still thick, and that, coupled with the chill in the air, made it a miserable morning for hunting. Visibility was no more than fifteen feet in any direction. It was like walking through a dark tunnel with only a candle to light the way. There was no telling what may be lurking behind the curtain of fog just feet in front of him. He had to be ready, ready to aim and pull the trigger with only a second's notice. Anything longer may be too long and...well, he'd seen what would happen.

Joe stepped over a fallen tree, making sure his feet landed softly. Josiah was a little more than ten feet to the right of him, a gray silhouette stepping bent-kneed in a half crouch through the haze. He was glad to have Josiah with him. He had grown very fond of the old farmer and admired his wisdom and insight. It was because of Josiah's courage and willingness to challenge that Joe had reconciled his differences with God—*his* differences. He now knew and accepted that the problem he had with God was *his* problem. God had never stopped being sovereign; He'd never once stepped down from His throne or turned a blind eye toward the plight of Joe's family. He was always God, always the same, and any difference Joe had with Him was *his* difference, not God's. Whether his old friend in overalls realized it or not, he had opened Joe's eyes to the truth and pointed the way. Joe guessed Josiah did realize it, knew it full well, but had enough sense to let Joe work it out himself.

Joe scanned the terrain as he walked. Trees rose from the ground like silent gray giants and disappeared into the fog above. Stands of elderberry, wild raspberry, and honeysuckle crowded the uneven terrain. He watched the wall of haze like it was a theater curtain ready to open any minute and reveal some hideous creature. He'd felt the weight of the beast, smelled its hate and anger, and kept imagining it crouching in the fog waiting patiently for him to stumble upon it and find himself once again pinned under its massive paws. He shuddered at the thought.

Andy's voice crackled over the handheld. "How's everyone doing?"

"All clear so far here," Mike Kline replied.

Joe pushed the talk button. "Nothing here yet."

"Keep pushing forward," Andy said. "And maintain visual contact with your partner. The fog seems to be getting thicker the deeper we go."

"Gotcha."

"Will do."

Joe clipped the handheld to his belt and stepped over a twisted branch.

Wait! He stopped. Josiah stopped and looked at him. Joe held a finger to his mouth and pointed into the fog in front of him. He thought he heard something. A branch break. Josiah started heading toward him, shotgun eye-level now. Joe raised his weapon as well, pushing the stock into his right shoulder, sighting down the barrel as he stepped carefully, slowly, over and around debris and leaves.

Step by step, he inched farther into the fog, listening, smelling. He heard it, he was sure of it. Not far now, just beyond the fog screen.

Mike's voice over the handheld startled him, and he almost lost his balance. "I have something. I have it." Andy answered. "What is it, Mike?"

"I don't know, it was just a shadow, but I definitely heard it. It's coming your way, Joe. We'll close in behind it."

"We're on our way too," Andy squawked.

Joe had unclipped the radio and was holding it to his mouth. He motioned for Josiah to come to him. "I heard something over here too." He spoke in a hushed tone. "Are there two of them?"

"Joe," Mike said. He was breathing heavy, and Joe could tell he was running. "It sounded like...it was running...on two legs...but I could be wrong."

"Gotcha." Two legs? Maybe the fog was distorting the sound.

Joe looked at Josiah. "It's coming our way," he whispered.

The sound came again—a branch breaking. Soft and muted from the dampness, but definitely the sound of wood snapping. Then again. It was moving closer to them. Joe and Josiah scanned the fog, eyes wide, guns ready, fingers pressed lightly against triggers, waiting, waiting for *it* to reveal itself.

Another twig snapped. This time it was behind them. Joe spun around. His stomach was in a knot, and he fought hard to still his trembling hands. He and Josiah stood back to back. Was there more than one? *God help us.*

Snap! This one was to Joe's right…and closer. He shifted his weight to his right foot and exhaled slowly. Every one of his senses was on full alert, like raw nerve endings.

Something moved in the fog. A shadow, a vague figure, darted behind a clump of honeysuckles.

Joe's heart was in his throat. His pulse beat like a kettledrum in his ears, pounding so hard he could barely hear himself think.

Think. Don't forget to think.

He inched closer to the honeysuckles, cheek against the cold metal of the gun, finger pressing into the trigger, willing himself to slow his breathing. How many pounds of pressure did it take to depress a trigger? Three, four? He had to be close. He heard Josiah behind him, moving around to his right, circling around the bush.

There was a rustling of branches and shuffling of leaves, and something took off out of the honeysuckle. Joe jumped back and jerked his gun skyward, following the dark object that exploded from the bushes. He nearly squeezed the trigger in a knee-jerk reflex.

But it was only a spooked grouse, beating its wings against the still air. Joe lowered his gun and exhaled. His fingers tingled. His heart raced.

Josiah looked at him, eyes wide, and blew out a breath.

Snap! A twig, behind him again. He and Josiah lifted their guns in unison, spun around, and watched the fog.

Andy's voice came over the handheld. "Talk to me; Joe, what's going on?"

Joe pressed the radio against his mouth and spoke in a whisper. "It's here. I'm not sure where, but I can hear it. Where are you, Mike?"

Mike's voice was still breathless. "We're coming…slow going, though…brambles really thick here…Should be there soon."

Something rustled to Joe's right, and he spun, standing his ground. Leaves shuffled under wet, muffled footsteps. *It* was pacing…stalking. Joe glanced at Josiah, caught his eye, and pointed to the fog in front of him. Josiah motioned that he would go around to the right.

Joe took a careful step forward and paused to listen. It was still pacing. His nerves felt like they would climb out of his skin. He took a deep breath and blinked, trying to calm himself. He had to keep his head. Right now, carelessness was as dangerous an enemy as the thing in the fog. And that thing was right in front of him, just on the other side of the haze. By the sound alone he could almost see it, pacing back and forth, back and forth, waiting for him.

Suddenly, something moved behind him. He spun around in time to see a brown wooly...*something* charging him.

He squeezed the trigger.

Boom!

Maggie heard the distant gunshot and flinched. Someone was hunting. Was it Andy? Joe? Being in that box, she had no sense of direction and couldn't tell where the shot had come from. The Dinsmore house was on the other side of Yates Woods. It could have come from that direction. It sounded at least a mile away. That would make sense.

But that would mean...

She was the only one who knew the truth. Panic crept over her like a cold shadow. She had to get out of there. She had to warn them. But if she was right, and the gunshot did come from Yates Woods, it may be too late for warnings. She had to *help* them. Raising her legs above her, she pulled her knees to her chest and exploded with a kick against the flooring, letting out a loud muffled grunt.

Nothing.

She cocked her knees back again and fired away. Again and again, frantically, she kicked and kicked. *Thud! Thud! Thud!*

Still nothing. The board above her rebounded after each blow.

She stopped and sucked in the dry air through her nose. Her legs burned, her back ached, her head felt like a jackrabbit had taken up residence in it. She could only think of Joe. He was out there, she was sure of it. Would he find the truth before it was too late?

Please, Joe, be safe. Please, Joe.

The creature fell to the ground, writhed for a second, then lay limp, crumpled in a heap of lifeless fur. Joe kept his gun at eye level and the barrel trained on the beast as he slowly approached it. He could feel his pulse through his trigger finger. Sweat pooled in his eyebrows. He breathed through his mouth, quick and shallow.

"Joe, you OK?" Andy's voice was strained as it vibrated through the handheld.

Joe didn't answer. He didn't want to take his full attention off the beast lying on the ground. It may be playing dead, baiting him, waiting until he was only feet away to pounce.

"Joe…" It was Mike now, still winded. "I'm right near you…say something so I can follow your voice."

Josiah came up alongside Joe and inched along with him closer to where the creature lay.

When they got within ten feet, Joe felt his heart drop out of his chest. His whole body went numb, like someone had pumped ice water into his veins. He stood still as the gray shadowy trees spun around him, and the fog closed in on him. He lowered his shotgun and let it slip to the ground.

There, sticking out from under the heap of fur, was a foot—a sneakered foot.

Josiah saw it too and ran to the beast. He nuzzled the barrel of his gun under the fur and turned the heap over.

It was Stevie. It was Stevie. It…was…STEVIE!

His back was draped with a large brown bear skin, his head covered with a monstrous lionlike Halloween mask complete with oversized canines, the eye holes cut larger to allow for better visual ability. On his hands he wore thick work gloves rigged with razor blades, shards of glass, metal, and other cutting edges, all sewn into the palms. His arms and legs were covered with what looked like gray rabbit skins that had been pieced together.

A hole the size of a baseball carved out Stevie's chest.

Josiah dropped his gun and fell to his knees beside Stevie. Stevie's wide eyes, full of shock and confusion, followed him—he was still alive. Carefully, tenderly, Josiah slid the mask the rest of the way off the young man's head.

Joe couldn't move. His feet were nailed to the ground; his arms hung limp at his sides; his legs were like rubber. Things were happening in slow motion now. Josiah was cradling Stevie's head in his arm, facing Joe and yelling something, but an eerie silence had permeated the fog. Andy's voice mumbled somewhere in the background. All Joe could hear was his own heart *thump-thumping* in his chest and his lungs drawing in short, shallow breaths.

Mike Kline and Barry Wagman finally arrived. Mike bent over and propped his hands on his knees. Barry was panting and hollering, but Joe heard none of it. He'd killed a man. Shot him in cold blood.

"—Joe." Josiah was calling to him, but his voice sounded like it was on the opposite end of a long dark tunnel.

"—Joe." Andy's voice was crackling over the radio.

"—Joe." Someone's voice was getting louder.

"Joe!"

Joe finally snapped out of his trance and met Josiah's eyes.

"Joe. He's still alive."

Joe blinked and cleared his head. Feeling rushed back into his arms and legs. He approached the limp body of Stevie.

Barry stepped out of the way. Mike radioed Andy.

Joe knelt down next to Stevie and looked into his eyes. He wanted to apologize, beg forgiveness, but the words wouldn't come. The look of fear that darkened Stevie's eyes paralyzed him. A memory, stored away somewhere in Joe's mind, suddenly bobbed to the surface. The first deer he ever shot. He was a cocky twelve-year-old and had gone on his first hunting trip with his dad. They had been out a little over an hour when they spotted a whitetail behind a patch of brambles. Joe sighted it in his scope, his heart pounding, hands shaking, breathing shallow, and pulled the trigger. The Remington 700 he'd gotten for Christmas popped, and the deer fell.

He would never forget walking up to that fallen doe and realizing she was still alive. His shot had punctured her abdomen and a steady stream of bright red blood ran out of the quarter-sized hole. But it was the look in the animal's eyes—the pain, the sheer terror—that made Joe vomit on the spot. His dad made him finish the beast off. One shot through the heart was all it took. But that look remained with Joe and haunted him for years after that first kill.

It was the same look that now shadowed Stevie's eyes.

Seconds later, or maybe it was minutes, Joe couldn't tell, Andy and Dan Berwager appeared. Dan stood over Stevie and shook his head. Andy radioed for an ambulance. His voice was hushed and grim. It was obvious to all that Stevie wouldn't last much longer.

Somewhere behind Joe, Mike said, "So *he* was the beast?"

Josiah leaned in closer to Stevie. "It's OK, son, help is comin'. Hang in there."

Stevie followed him with his eyes and moved his lips. Blood trickled out of the corner of his mouth and made a scarlet line down his cheek. He moved his lips again.

Josiah leaned closer, tilting his ear toward Stevie's mouth. "What is it, son?"

Stevie's voice was a hoarse whisper, but Joe could make out what he said. "Chief...safe..." His words then trailed off.

"Again, Stevie," Josiah whispered, laying a hand on Stevie's head. "Tell me again, son."

Stevie's lips moved but no words passed over them. He tried again. "Chief...safe...in...hide..." His words faded, and his eyes went blank, staring vacantly into the fog.

Josiah placed two fingers over Stevie's carotid, held them there a few seconds, then removed them. "He's gone."

He's gone. The words echoed in Joe's head, rattling around like bullets in a metal box, looking for a soft spot to penetrate. He'd done it. He'd killed a man.

Josiah stood up and looked at Joe, determination in the set of his jaw. "Joe, you didn't know. There's nothing more we can do for Stevie; he's gone. But Maggie isn't."

Joe snapped his head toward Josiah. "What?"

"Did you hear what Stevie said?"

Joe looked confused. "Yeah. Chief safe in hide. That's it."

"He meant Maggie was safe in his 'hideout.' A place under the trailer he used to hide when he thought someone was after him. She's alive, Joe."

Josiah walked over and picked up Joe's gun, then tossed it to him. "Let's go."

Seconds later both men were racing through the woods toward Stevie's trailer. Joe pushed on harder and harder, ignoring the burning in his lungs, ignoring the spasms in his thighs, ignoring Josiah's urging to slow down. He couldn't see where he was going, only fog, thick, smoky fog. It was crazy, he knew. He could step in a groundhog hole, trip on a fallen tree, clothesline himself on a low-hanging branch, anything. Bones would crunch before he even knew what had happened. But he didn't care. Not now. Not as long as Maggie was in that trailer. He wouldn't care about anything until she was safe in his arms.

A thought entered his mind, but he quickly brushed it aside. No, she had to be alive. Stevie said she was safe. *Please, God, let her be alive. I can't lose her again. I love her.*

CHAPTER 40

MAGGIE WAS IN the middle of another kicking outburst when she heard the trailer's storm door creak open and slam shut. She stopped midkick and listened, filtering out the sound of her own heavy breathing. Was it Stevie? Had he come back to finish her off?

Footsteps.

Her pulse thumped in her neck.

Then, "Maggie!"

It was Joe! His voice never sounded so wonderful.

She raised her legs and kicked furiously at the boards above her. "Mmmm! Mmmm!" *Here! Here!*

The footsteps thundered on the floor above, closer and closer until they were directly above her.

"Maggie?"

"Mmmm!" She kicked again. Hot tears flooded her eyes. *Joe! Joe!*

Something heavy slid across the floor. "Maggie, I'm here." The board was lifted away and light blinded her.

Andy, Mike, Dan, and Barry stood around Stevie's body as the paramedics squawked over the radio. They were having a hard time locating the hunting party in the dense fog, not to mention the arduous trek through the thick underbrush.

"It's no hurry," Andy spoke into the radio. "He's dead anyway."

"Well, why the heck are you having us come in then?" a man's voice screeched. "Ouch! I can't believe this."

Andy looked at Dan and chuckled. "It builds character, Jase. You'll thank me later."

"Yeah, right."

Barry pulled out a lighter, spun the thumbwheel, and held the flame to the cigarette dangling from his mouth. He took a long draw, held it for a second, then let a ribbon of smoke slowly escape through pursed lips. "I can't believe this crazy was the beast," he said, gesturing toward Stevie's lifeless body. "Some man-eater. What do you think got into him?"

Andy shrugged. "Beats me. Something flipped his switch. Poor guy."

"So much for your lion king. Simba Whatchamacallit," Dan said.

"Hey." It was Jason the paramedic again. "Hey, guys?"

Andy held the radio to his mouth. "Oh, c'mon, Jase. Think of it as a nice walk in the woods."

"Guys, there's something out here. Something's moving in the fog."

"It's called wildlife." Andy looked at the other guys, rolled his eyes, and smiled. "You know, squirrels, chipmunks, rabbits. Hey, watch those rabbits. I hear they can get pretty vicious."

There was a long pause. "Seriously, guys. There's something here. It's big. Circling us." Another pause. "We're getting out of here."

Beads of sweat popped out on Andy's forehead. "No. Don't move. We'll come to you. How far have you walked so far?"

"I—I don't know. It's getting closer. Can't see it. Fog's too thick."

"Stay there," Andy said. His palms were starting to sweat now too. "We're coming." He released the talk button and turned to the others. "Get your guns."

"You can't be serious," Barry said, tapping ashes from the end of his cigarette.

Andy shouldered his rifle. "Remember when Joe asked if there were two?"

Barry blew out a mouthful of smoke and picked up his gun. "Say no more."

Jason came on again. "Are—are you coming?" His voice quaked with fear. "I don't—" There was a pause and only a faint static filled the radio's speaker. "Oh my—No!" Then footsteps running, rustling, snapping. Heavy breathing. "It's—Awww!"

The radio went dead.

Joe bent over, reached into the box, and grabbed Maggie's bound wrists. Seeing her in the hole, so frail, so scared, but so alive, brought a lump to his throat. His eyes blurred with tears, chin quivered. "Watch your head, Mags."

Maggie sat up, and Joe pulled her to her feet. Her legs wobbled. Joe had to grab her under her arms to steady her. She looked up at him, and for a moment, they were alone in the world, just the two of them.

Thank You, Father. Thank You.

As soon as she was out, Joe wrapped his arms around her and squeezed. He wasn't prepared for the emotions that flooded him. He buried his face in her matted hair and let the tears come. "Maggie. Thank God. I thought I'd lost you again."

Her thin frame shook in his arms as waves of sobs escaped through her nose.

"It's OK," Joe said, stroking her hair. "You're safe now."

Joe felt a nudge on his right side. Josiah was there, holding a pocket-knife. "You gonna untie her?"

Joe wiped the tears from Maggie's eyes, then slowly peeled the duct tape off her mouth. She grimaced from the pain as the tape tore away the top layer of skin. He then pulled the rag from her mouth.

She tried to talk. Her lips moved, but all that came out was a dry wheeze. She reached for her throat with bound hands and swallowed hard.

"I'll get some water," Josiah said and disappeared into the hallway.

Joe cupped her face in his hands and wiped at her tears, smearing dirt across her cheeks. "Are you OK?"

Maggie smiled and nodded. She looked a wreck. Dried blood matted her hair and flaked on her face. Dust and dirt smeared across her gaunt cheeks. And a red rectangle outlined her mouth where the tape had been.

Joe stroked her hair and smiled. "You're beautiful, Maggie Gill."

While Joe cut away the tape from her wrists and ankles, Josiah reappeared with a tall glass of water. Maggie took it from him and drained it in four huge gulps. She swallowed again and rubbed her throat.

"We have to go," she said quietly. Her voice was raspy and raw. "Stevie's the beast. It was all a hoax. He tried to kill me, and he killed Gary."

Joe looked at Josiah, then turned back to Maggie. "Gary's dead?"

She nodded. "He came looking for me, and Stevie shot him. I think he ditched our cars in the pond along with Gary's body. I think he shot me too."

"What? Where?" Joe looked her up and down.

Maggie touched the back of her head and winced. "Here. It must not have penetrated the skull, though."

Joe carefully parted her hair and saw a golf ball-sized lump and an inch-long gash. "I don't think he shot you, Mags. It looks like he hit you with something. We better get you to the hospital; you may have a concussion."

"No." Maggie's voice was gaining strength, and she was adamant. "We have to stop him. He's going after Glen Sterner and the Dinsmore boys. Then my dad."

Josiah put a hand on Maggie's shoulder. "Stevie's dead."

Maggie looked confused. Her eyes flitted between Joe and Josiah. "What? When?"

"I shot him," Joe said. "We were hunting what we thought was the lion, and it turned out to be Stevie in an elaborate Halloween costume."

Maggie's eyes widened. "Where's Andy? Is he OK?"

"He's fine," Joe said. "He stayed behind with Stevie's body and a few other guys to wait for the paramedics. He's fine." He put a hand on Maggie's arm and stroked it gently. "Everything's gonna be OK now."

Maggie shook her head. Tears returned to her eyes. "No, it won't." She swallowed again and winced. "Joe, I did something awful."

CHAPTER 41

J ASON!" ANDY HOLLERED into the radio. "Jason! Jase! Answer me."
He released the talk button, waited a second—*C'mon, Jase, answer,
man*—then pressed it again. "Jase! You there? Jase? This isn't
funny."

Nothing. Only dead air.

Barry took another draw of his cigarette and looked at Mike; Mike
looked at Dan, then all three looked at Andy. He was still holding the
radio up to his mouth. "Jason. Jason. Come in, man. Jason?"

Barry held his gun to his chest, cigarette teetering on the edge of his
lips. "What's going on here?"

"I don't like this," Mike said, picking up his rifle and clicking off the
safety.

"Me neither," Dan added. His face had gone white, and he fingered the
trigger of his rifle as he stared into the fog.

Andy clipped the radio to his belt. He was about to lose control of his
team, and that wouldn't help them stay alive. And staying alive was the
main objective now. Something was still out there. Joe was right; there
were two. But if Stevie was the beast, what was out there? "Everybody calm
down. We'll stick together and work our way out of here. Make sure your
weapons are ready, but keep a cool head. We'll come back for him"—he
motioned toward Stevie—"when the fog lifts. He's not going anywhere."

The four men stuck close and began lightly stepping over and around
fallen trees, broken branches, and tangled undergrowth. The fog was
still oppressive, and visibility was still no more than fifteen, twenty feet,
making progress slow and tense. They pushed ahead in silence.

Andy allowed himself to fall behind the pack by a few feet. He needed
to clear his head—watch, listen, sense. He was an experienced hunter, as
were the others, but under these conditions—the fog and the unknown
that lurked in it—experience alone did little to comfort him.

When they had pushed a few hundred yards into the fog, Barry suddenly stopped and held up a hand. He pointed to his ear, then to the fog in front of them. They all stood motionless, listening, for a full minute before Mike whispered, "What are we doing?"

Barry pointed in front of them again. "I heard something."

"I didn't hear anything," Dan whispered.

"Neither did I," Mike said.

They all looked at Andy, who held up a hand. He heard it too.

They stood like statues and listened to the silence, searching it for even the slightest sound—a leaf rustling, a branch moving, a twig snapping.

Then, *snap*. They all jerked their heads forward and stared at the fog. It was faint, but definitely a twig breaking. The muted rustle of wet leaves then broke the silence.

Andy's heart pounded. With sweaty hands he gripped his rifle, eyes scanning the fog, watching, waiting. It was all he could do.

Barry raised his gun to eye level, and the others followed his lead.

The sound had come from directly in front of them, just beyond the cover of fog.

It was quiet again. Too quiet. An eerie chill blew over Andy's skin.

Then...

Snap! Crunch.

Something moved, a shadow, a phantomlike image sliced through the fog. There, then gone.

Andy saw Barry jerk his gun a few inches to the left. "No—"

BOOM!

Boom!

The sound of distant gunfire echoing off the Dark Hills startled Joe, and he jumped. "What was that?" He reached for his radio and remembered he'd turned it off. He pushed the power button, waited for the LCD screen to spring to life, then squeezed TALK. "Andy. What was that all about?"

Boom! Boom! BoomBoom! More shots fired, more echoes.

Joe yelled into the radio, "Andy! Can you hear me?"

The radio crackled and squeaked. "Joe."

BOOM! That came across the radio loud and clear.

"Joe. Something's..." Andy's voice was breaking up. "Something's...here."

The radio fell silent.

———

Something was circling them. Branches broke, twigs snapped, first in front, then to the right, then behind.

Barry spun around, following the sound. *Boom!* He fired again and quickly slammed another shell into his shotgun.

Leaves rustled in front of them again, and something moved. A ghostly shadow glided through the fog.

To Andy's right, Dan was in a panic. His eyes were wide as baseballs, sweat trickled from his hairline, and his hands massaged the gun pressed against his shoulder. "It's out there, isn't it? It's gonna kill us."

Andy stared at Dan, raised a hand, and kept his voice low. "Dan—"

Dan shifted his weight from his right leg to his left and back again. "Well, I'm not going to wait around for it to kill me. If it's a hunt it wants, I'm the hunter." His voice was shaky. His hands continued to massage his gun as he pushed forward into the fog.

"Dan," Andy said, straining to keep his voice low. "What are you doing? Get back here."

Dan ignored him and disappeared into the fog.

They all waited. A few seconds later there was a rustle of leaves, running footsteps. Dan hollered, fired his rifle—*Boom!*—then a terror-stricken scream sliced through the fog like an arrow.

"Dan!" Barry screamed, panic shaking his voice. "Dan!"

Dan shrieked again, a hideous howl that made Andy's blood run cold.

Barry looked at Andy and Mike. "Well?"

"Don't go after him," Andy said.

Barry lifted his gun and turned away. "You gonna stop me? I'm goin' in."

Andy reached for his arm, but it was too late. Barry had already disappeared into the fog.

Andy cursed, gripped his gun tighter, and followed Barry into the unknown, leaving Mike standing by himself.

—

Mike was paralyzed with fear, suffocating in the fog.

His claustrophobia was acting up, and the weight of the fog pressing in around him was almost too much to bear. He wanted to scream, run, claw at his skin, shoot himself, anything to get out of there.

—

Boom! Another shot rang through the air, bouncing off the ominous hills that overlooked the town.

"Andy. Come in, Andy."

The radio crackled. There was static, then the sound of footsteps, leaves, branches, hollering, a distant scream. Then silence again.

Maggie was beside herself, frantic. "Joe, we have to help them!"

"Joe!" Mike's voice screeched over the radio. "Joe! Help us. Please help us. It's gonna kill us all. I can't take it. I need to get out of here."

Joe could tell by the edge in Mike's voice that he was about to lose it. "Mike? Mike? Are you listening to me?"

Silence, heavy breathing, then, "Yes."

"Mike, stay where you are, OK? Is anyone else around you?"

"No. They all went after it. I think they're dead."

Electricity ran down Joe's spine, and the hair on his nape stood on end. "Stay where you are, Mike. Don't go any farther. I'm coming for you."

There was a moment of silence before Joe said, "Mike, you still there?"

"Yeah."

"Do you know where you are? How far you hiked from Stevie?"

Pause. Labored breathing. "Uh, I don't know. Maybe a couple hundred yards, maybe three. I don't know. Can't tell for sure. I think we were heading due west."

"OK. I'm coming. Hang in there. And maintain radio contact."

"Yeah."

Joe clipped the radio to his belt and turned to Maggie. Her face had gone pale. She seated herself on the sofa, held her hands to her chest, and gently rocked back and forth. "This is all my fault," she said. "Andy and Gary are dead, and it's my fault."

Joe put both hands on her shoulders and looked her right in the eyes. "Maggie, listen to me. There will be time later for talk. Right now we need to act. Are you feeling well enough to make a few phone calls?"

Maggie bit her lower lip and nodded.

"Are you sure?"

She nodded again.

"Josiah and I"—he paused and looked at Josiah, who nodded his agreement—"Josiah and I are going to go get Mike—it's Mike Kline out there. I need you to call the state police and Game Commission and tell them we need some guys down here now. Tell them there's a man-eater in Yates Woods, it's killed several men already, and it's not about to stop. Then call an ambulance and get yourself to a hospital." He looked at her, meeting her eyes with his. "Can you do that?"

There was fear in her eyes—intense fear. "Yes. State police. Game Commission. Ambulance."

He turned to leave, but she caught his arm. "Wait!" He faced her and saw the tears that had welled up in her eyes. "Be careful, Joe. I can't lose you too."

Joe knelt on one knee in front of her and put his hands on her knees. "Do you know what it is out there?"

She shook her head and lost eye contact with him. "No, not exactly. I—I think it's a lion."

Joe tightened his jaw. An image of a man-eating lion strutting through a tiny African village, the bloody and tattered clothes of his last victim hanging from his mouth, flashed into his mind. "OK. Make those phone calls as soon as we leave. We're gonna need those guys down here as soon as possible."

Joe stood up, bent at the waist, and kissed Maggie on the forehead. "Do what you have to do." Then he turned to Josiah, who had already gathered the guns and was standing by the door. "You ready?"

Josiah nodded. "Guns are loaded. Let's do this."

The two men left the trailer and entered the woods, armed with one pump-action shotgun apiece, a compass, and the handheld radio—hardly a proper outfitting for hunting a lion, if that's what it really was.

Joe unclipped his radio. "Mike. How ya doing, buddy?"

"I—I'm still here. You coming?"

"We're on our way. Keep your cool, OK? Don't do anything stupid."

"O—OK."

Joe clipped the radio back onto his belt. He tried to still the tremble in his hand and looked at Josiah.

Josiah dipped his chin and met Joe's eyes. He lifted a hand and rested it on Joe's shoulder. "Don't fear, my friend. God's here with us. He'll guide us." He then talked to the Lord, beseeching Him to guide them, to lift the fog, to protect Mike, and to give them steady hands and a sure shot if the time came. "And, Lord," he prayed, "draw Maggie to Yourself—"

"Joe?" It was Mike again. His voice was quiet, almost a whisper.

Oh, no. Joe held the radio close to his mouth. A sick feeling crept into his stomach. "Mike, what is it?"

"Something's here. I–I heard footsteps." His voice wavered with terror.

Joe looked at Josiah, who was silently moving his lips. Praying. Good. "Hold still, Mike. Is your gun loaded and ready?"

"Uh, yeah. But I only have two shells left." There was a brief pause, then, "Oh, oh, there it is again. It's in front of me."

"We're coming, Mike."

CHAPTER 42

MIKE STARED DOWN the barrel of his gun, watching the haze but seeing nothing, only hearing. A twig cracked, some leaves rustled...

Joe and Josiah ran through the woods, cutting blindly through the fog. Trees jumped out at them, fallen branches rose out of the ground, shrubs and bushes reached for them. They ran, they dodged, they jumped, all the time keeping their eyes on the ground ten feet in front of them. Joe held his rifle in his left hand and the compass in his right. Josiah gripped his shotgun with both hands, one finger on the trigger at all times.

Mike listened, his ears picking up every sound. Another rustle. Another crack. A low rhythmic hiss. Was that breathing? The sounds were moving to his right. He followed them with his eyes, with the barrel of his gun.

Suddenly, the sounds ceased. He held his breath and listened. Through the dense silence he could still pick up the low hiss. It was a little to his right. Two o'clock.

He let out his breath and rotated his shoulders. He pointed his gun at the sound, listening, separating the hiss from the rhythm of his own breathing and the thumping of his pulse.

It was hidden by the fog, but it was there. He could almost see the sound. Inhale, exhale, inhale, exhale. It was definitely the sound of breathing.

He aimed his gun into the fog, sighting down the long barrel. It was now or never.

Boom!

⏤

Joe and Josiah both flinched and pulled up when the sound of gunfire ripped through the fog like a crack of thunder.

Joe tore the radio from his belt. "Mike! Mike! Talk to me!"

The radio crackled, and he could hear ragged breathing. "I—I think I hit it." Mike's voice was almost a whisper as it cracked and hissed over the radio. "Not sure, though. I need to reload."

The radio went dead.

⏤

Mike pumped his shotgun and stood still, stock against his shoulder, metal against his cheek, watching the fog on the other end of the barrel, listening. One more shot. Make it count. His eyes studied the gray haze until it became a blur. The only sound was the wheeze of his breathing. His asthma was kicking up.

Snap.

Mike froze, paralyzed by fear. His blood went cold, skin tingled. Every hair on his body prickled. *It* was right behind him, just feet away. Its breathing was barely distinguishable from his own, but it was so close he could feel the heat of its breath. He couldn't run; it would pounce on him before he even shifted his weight forward. And he had no time to spin around and get a shot off.

He was a dead man.

He shut his eyes and said good-bye to Jody, his wife, and Pete and Chris, his two sons. He'd never see them again.

⏤

Joe and Josiah hustled through the woods, carelessly pushing ahead, making much more sound than they should.

If that thing was out here, it would hear them coming a mile away, Joe thought. But he didn't care. Let it come. He looked at Josiah and noted the determination in the set of his jaw. They were ready.

It was the scream that stopped them like they'd run into a wall. A spine-tingling, gut-wrenching, agonizing wail—Mike's wail—held at its peak, then followed by a low, mournful moan.

Another crack of the gun made them flinch again. It echoed through the woods like a gavel, announcing the final verdict—case closed.

Joe looked at Josiah. Both were panting heavily.

"It came from over there." Josiah pointed ahead of them, at a forty-five degree angle to their right. "Not far."

Both men took off. Mike couldn't have been more than two, three hundred yards away. They ran for about a hundred yards, then slowed to a walk, listening, smelling. It was there. Close. Joe could sense it. Feel it.

Slowly they pressed ahead, searching, studying, scanning the gray mist for any sign of movement, listening for the slightest sound.

Something was on the ground ahead of them, maybe a rotted log. A few steps closer and they realized what it was—a body, facedown in the leaves. The camo was blood-stained and torn, one arm twisted unnaturally around the back of the body, the ground was dark with blood. Joe tucked his boot under the hip and rolled the body over. It was Dan...barely.

Bile forced its way up Joe's throat.

Josiah held up a hand for silence. Had he heard something? He looked at Joe and gestured to their left.

The fog was finally starting to lift, and Joe now recognized where they were. They were at the top of the ridge that sloped down to the old Yates place. He ran his sleeve across his mouth and listened.

Somewhere in the distance a branch broke.

Joe stood still, listening, gripping his gun, ready to squeeze the trigger when needed. The sound was coming closer—twigs snapping, leaves rustling, steady, rhythmic, ominous. Whatever it was, was making no attempt at stealth.

Josiah inched forward. He raised his gun to his shoulder and pointed the barrel in the direction of the sound. It was closer now, louder, clearer, speeding up. Was that thing running toward them? Joe raised his gun too, and pressed his finger against the trigger.

The sound was closer still. Steady. Steady. Any second and the beast would burst from the unknown and charge them like a runaway locomotive.

But seconds ticked by and nothing happened. The sounds continued, just out of sight, concealed by the blanket of fog. Joe's heart was banging in his chest like a sledgehammer. His palms were sweaty, making his gun slippery. He tried to swallow, tried to calm himself, but it was useless. This was it. He stood on the brink of life and death. The beast, that devil lion, that *whatever* lurking in the haze, was all that stood between him and life, him and Maggie. It all came down to this moment, this place.

It would only take seconds.

He would only get one shot.

Precious Lord, rescue me.

It was a prayer of desperation. He was Peter sinking in the water, seeing his life flash through his mind like an old home movie in fast-forward, feeling death tighten its icy grip around his throat. He was Peter crying out, "Lord, save me!"

Suddenly, the sounds stopped, and an eerie silence hung in the woods again.

A shiver rippled down Joe's back.

Josiah looked around, shifting his weight from his right foot to his left, leaning into the fog, listening. There, to his right he heard it. A leaf rustled. But before he could react, a massive bulk leapt at him and bowled him over, knocking him facedown on the ground. He didn't get a chance to see what it was, but felt its weight, suffocating weight, on his back. His face was turned toward Joe, and he saw the fear in his young friend's eyes.

CHAPTER 43

J OE DIDN'T HEAR the leaves rustle, and he never saw the beast lunge at Josiah. It happened so fast. One second Josiah was standing; the next he was hitting the ground.

Spinning to his right, Joe jumped back, nearly dropped his gun, and thought for sure his heart had stopped. An icy breeze started at the top of his head, blew down to his feet, and paralyzed him. There, standing with its front paws on Josiah's upper back was a lion...

...only it wasn't a lion.

It resembled a lion, and it was easy to see how at a quick glance or even from a distance it could be mistaken for one. But it was no lion. Not a devil lion. Not a Simba Whatever. What it was, though, was another story. Its head was the shape of a lion's—large and rectangular, kind of tapering into a squarish jaw, but the skin over its face was hairless and glossy and stretched tight, like the grafted skin on a burn victim, and it was covered with large quarter-sized blisters or fatty tumors, it was hard to tell which. Fleshy pink tendrils hung like mucus from its muzzle, each one crowned at its base with wiry black hair. Its mouth hung ajar in a perfect frown revealing four razor-sharp canines and a slick blue tongue. Real blue, like a tarp, and it flitted in and out from behind curled lips like a snake's tongue tasting the air. Its eyes were also shaped like a lion's, slanted down and in, but one was yellow and one was red, the color of blood. Its ears were nothing more than wrinkled folds of pink flesh singed on the ends like they had been burned to nubs. Behind the ears and lining the neck was what might be called a mane, but the fur was matted and hung in thick cords like dreadlocks. The fur covering its thick torso and stocky legs was spotty at best, like it had the mange. Dark patches of dry skin mottled the otherwise tawny fur. The tail was also hairless and covered with the same glossy skin as the face, looking more like a rat's tail than a lion's. But it wasn't a lion. Joe noticed all this in the mere two or three seconds it took for it to register in his brain. The sight of the beast/monster/whatever revolted him, and he found his mouth tasting like bile again.

It stood motionless, like a stone effigy, its one yellow and one red eye watching Joe, piercing him like daggers, searching his soul for any weakness, any fear. Calling to him, daring, taunting, mocking. This was definitely no lion. And if it was, man oh man, if it was, it was most certainly a devil lion if there ever was one. It must have crawled right out of hell into Yates Woods.

Joe's eyes locked on Josiah's. It was the first time since he'd known the old farmer that he'd seen fear darken those gray eyes. Josiah held his gaze for a moment, then dropped his eyes to the shotgun dangling at Joe's side.

Joe got the message. In one slow, fluid motion, he raised the gun to his shoulder and peered down the barrel at the beast in front of him. His hands trembled, causing the end of the barrel to bounce around on the monster's face. He lowered the barrel until it pointed at the broad chest. Somewhere in there, between the shoulders and the base of the neck, was the heart pumping life into the creature. At least it should be. If it was a lion, that's where it would be.

The beast stared back at Joe, those eyes burning holes right through him. There was something about those eyes, one yellow, one red, something disturbing, evil…deadly. It was waiting for him to make a move, daring him to squeeze the trigger, betting he wouldn't.

Joe leaned on the trigger, depressing the fat pad on the end of his finger.

The beast let out a low growl, a deep eight-cylinder rumble originating in its chest, resonating through its throat, and finally rippling out of its snarled mouth. It splayed its paws, revealing five talonlike claws, and curled them until they dug into Josiah's back like knives.

⌒

Josiah gasped. The claws felt like hot pokers digging into his back, searing flesh, tearing sinew. Never had he felt so much pain. His eyes met Joe's again. "Pull…"

He winced and gasped again. "Pull the trigger."

—

Joe took a deep breath, shifted his weight to his left foot, shut his left eye, and sighted the monster's chest with his right.

The beast narrowed its eyes and curled its claws more, pressing them deeper into Josiah's back. It was daring him. *Go ahead. Go ahead.*

Joe shifted his gaze to Josiah.

"Do it." Pain twisted his old friend's colorless face.

—

But before Joe squeezed the trigger and buried a hundred plus lead balls in the beast's chest, it stabbed those huge canines in Josiah's left shoulder. Bones crunched; muscle ripped; nerves frayed.

"Ahhhh!" Josiah gritted his teeth and winced from the acid that flooded his shoulder and shot down his arm like a lightning bolt. The pain paralyzed him and robbed him of breath. A wave of nausea tore into his stomach.

The beast kept its head down, jaws clamped on Josiah's shoulder. He could smell the animal's putrid breath as it hissed from its throat. Then, in one sickening motion, it jerked its head back, lifting Josiah off the ground so he dangled from the huge mouth like a dead gazelle.

But he wasn't dead. The pain was all too real.

"Aaaaah!" he cried, hoping it would end soon and he could finally see his Savior face-to-face. Thoughts of first-century martyrs, mauled and eaten by lions to the cheers of thousands, rushed through his mind.

Take me, Jesus. I'm ready.

—

Joe aimed again. But he couldn't get a good shot. Josiah was in the way. That thing was dangling him like some prize it had won on the savanna...if it were only a lion. He wouldn't risk hitting his dear friend. There may still be hope.

But whatever hope Joe had imagined was quickly dashed when the monster spun to its left and dashed down the slope toward the abandoned Yates house, dragging Josiah along with it. Prey in the jaws of the hunter.

Frozen by the sudden change of events, Joe momentarily hesitated, then instinctively lifted his shotgun, pressed the stock against his shoulder, sighted the beast's hind quarter in its sight, and exhaled as he squeezed the trigger. The end of the barrel exploded in a flash, and the gun recoiled violently.

He missed. The beast had taken a hard right. He pumped the fore-end, aimed, and fired again.

Another miss. C'mon!

The beast was too far now, only a vague shadow in the fog, maybe thirty yards ahead, to the right.

Joe grunted and started after the creature. He ran pell-mell down the hill, snapping branches, stumbling, slipping on the wet leaves, trying desperately to keep up with the mutant lion and not lose it in the fog. He fell once, twice, but both times sprang to his feet and continued his pursuit. But the beast's movements were deft, precise, and quick, its soft paws finding sure footing as it wove and slipped between, under, and around the brush.

When he finally came to the clearing, he stopped and looked around, studying the gray curtain that concealed the house. There. The mutant's ratlike tail disappeared behind the stone wall of the old ruin. Joe dashed for the doorway and entered the house, gun outstretched in front of him. He scanned the first floor and noticed fresh blood—Josiah's—dotting the floorboards. He followed the trail with his eyes...the cellar, the monster's lair.

It was luring him, using Josiah as bait.

Joe stood at the top of the stairs and stared into the darkness. Little light made its way down to the dirt floor. The very thought of going down there put his back on ice. No way. He couldn't do it.

Fear not.

Caleb's message. The words rang in his mind and penetrated to his heart, momentarily banishing the chill.

Fear not.

He breathed in and slowly exhaled. *OK, Lord. You've got my attention. I trust You.* He pumped the fore-end, jamming another shell into the chamber. Ready for another shot.

Putting one foot on the top step, he began the slow descent into the darkness as if he were entering the bowels of hell itself. He stayed close to the wall, inching along, watching the hazy blackness for any sign of movement.

When he reached the dirt floor at the bottom of the stairs, he held his gun shoulder high and pressed his back against the cold stone. He saw nothing, but he could hear the beast's breathing, a ghostly whisper. It was in the far corner.

Joe stood still, battling the urge to flee. Every fiber in his body wanted to dash up those steps, back into the muted light of the morning, and holler for help. If Maggie called the police, they had to be on their way. Probably picking their way through the woods right now, looking for him.

He heard a thump in the far corner and then a muffled moan. The beast must have released Josiah. It was free to attack now, to pounce on him at will, maul him, and eat him alive. For an instant, Joe imagined what it would be like to be pinned beneath the creature, that glossy-skinned, blistered face staring down at him, saliva dripping off the blue tongue, yellow eye/red eye burning holes in him. Fear, cold and dark, spread over him like a thick shadow. His pulse spiked, a lump rose in his throat, and his hands began to tremble again.

Jesus, help me.

"Fear not." It was *His* voice. The voice of the Savior. Clear and gentle, but rich with authority, like polished brass.

Joe froze, momentarily paralyzed by the reality of the still voice that resonated through his head, no, his heart. His mind stuttered. *F–fear not? But there's so much to fear.*

"Fear not, My son."

A low growl vibrated from the corner, then another muffled groan.

Joe slid his back along the stone wall as he sidestepped to his right, gun still held against his shoulder, finger pressed against the trigger. He had to get to Josiah. There was no way he was going to leave him to be devoured by this monster.

He inched along, painfully slow, but making progress, staring into the shadows, keeping his eyes on the sound of the low hiss. His eyes were slowly adjusting to the darkness, drawing in what little light was left in the room.

Then, like an explosion, the beast burst from the shadows, a blur of mangled fur, slick skin, and fangs.

Joe had only a fraction of a second to react. He pointed and squeezed. The gun thundered with a flash. The monster rocked back onto its hind legs, stumbled, let out a yelp, and disappeared back into the darkened corner.

He hit it! Joe reached in his pocket for another shell…it was empty. He felt the other pocket. Empty too. He must have lost the shells when he was stumbling down the—

The mutant moved. Joe could hear paws shuffling along the dirt. The beast's breathing had increased and deepened. It was wounded and angry, and he was helpless—easy prey.

Suddenly, the monster appeared. It sauntered into the light at the bottom of the stairs, turned, and stared at Joe. The corners of its mouth were pulled back, making it look as if it was smiling at him, saying, *Nice try; is that all you got?*

Joe inched farther back, trying to disappear into the shadows, but those eyes—one red, one yellow—pierced the darkness like fiery darts. There would be no hiding. There would be no running. This was it. Showdown at high noon.

The beast shook its head and the pink tendrils slapped back and forth against the blisters. Its left flank was raw and red. The shot must have just grazed its shoulder. It eyed Joe steadily, puffed, growled, and curled its lips into a hideous snarl, revealing those knives in its mouth and that blue tongue darting in and out, licking teeth, tasting his scent. Then it splayed its paws and dug its claws into the dirt, bracing itself. Lowering its head, it arched its back, wrinkled its muzzle, contracted its abdominals, and let out an eardrum-ripping, thunderous roar.

Joe froze. Paralyzed. That was definitely lion. Never had he witnessed such a perfect blend of power and hate, let alone been on the receiving end of it. He was done for. This beast, this monster, was going to tear him limb from limb and devour him slowly.

Jesus. It was all he could pray, the only thing that his mind could grab on to. *Jesus.*

"Fear not."

How?

"Daniel."

Daniel?

"Remember Daniel."

Then it hit him like a revelation from heaven, like a sunbeam piercing the darkness, slicing through the fear like a double-edged sword.

Yes, Daniel!

CHAPTER 44

THE LIGHT APPEARED again. Not the orange glow but the pinhole of brilliant white light, high above Caleb, like a lonely star in the midnight sky.

He stared at it, studying its brilliance, mesmerized by its radiance.

A familiar voice was near him, muffled but almost distinguishable. It was a woman's voice, soft and kind, hushed in a whisper.

The light drew closer, growing as it floated toward him, its radiance reaching like tentacles through the darkness, wrapping around him, enveloping him in a warm embrace.

The woman's voice grew louder. She was calling to him, her voice familiar yet oddly strange.

The light grew brighter, beckoning him to follow it, but still he could not move.

Joe lowered his gun and let it slip to the floor with a clunk. Taking a deep breath and holding it, he took one step closer to the beast.

The mutant snarled, its lips pulling away from its teeth like Roman blinds, revealing canines slick with saliva. It huffed a low growl, crouched its front end, and anxiously clawed at the dirt.

Joe wanted to run, drop, surrender, beg the beast for mercy. This was insane.

"Surrender to Me. Trust Me. Let Me."

Joe slowly let the air out of his lungs and took another step. His feet were numb. His legs were numb. His whole body was numb. But he knew what he had to do.

Daniel.

With each step that Joe moved closer, the monster grew more agitated—snarling, growling, hissing, puffing, stamping its paws in the dirt, shaking its head, wagging those tendrils.

But Joe pressed on. Step by step until he was no more than five feet from the monstrosity, standing eye to eye with death itself. Time stood still as if the world had stopped spinning on its axis.

The light urged Caleb on; the woman's voice grew louder. But fear kept him pinned to the floor, hidden in his hole. The beast was out there. This was a trick, a ploy, an ambush.

"Fear not."

The deep voice was there again, intermingling with the woman's.

"My dear child, fear not."

The woman's voice called to him, his name—"Caleb."

The light grew brighter, the voices louder, filling the darkness.

"Surrender to Me. Let Me."

"Caleb. Caleb."

The beast wrinkled its nose and snarled again, batting at the air with its paw. It let out a puff of hot breath, crouched its hind end as if ready to pounce. Muscles rippled and contracted along the length of its thick torso.

Then, as if some unseen hand had closed its mouth and stroked its nappy mane, it sat on its haunches and retracted its paws. Peace fell over the beast's face. It lifted its head and yawned, its tongue curling in its mouth like a blue ribbon. It then tilted its head to the left and blinked at Joe, eyelids meeting in the middle of the red and yellow orbs.

Joe exhaled—he didn't even realize he had stopped breathing—and slumped his shoulders.

BOOM! BOOM! BOOMBOOM! A volley of gunfire exploded from the top of the stairway, filling the cellar with thunder.

Joe flinched, stumbled backward, and fell to the dirt. He saw the beast recoil, then roll onto its side.

Its left flank was open and bleeding, a gaping wound.

—

"Surrender."

"Caleb."

"Surrender to Me, child."

I will.

The light grew brighter still, blinding him until he had to squint to shield his eyes. A face appeared in the light, a familiar face, soft and caring, loving and peaceful, surrounded by light. It was the woman. Her mouth was moving, forming words that he now heard clearly: "Caleb. Caleb. Sweetie."

The face sharpened, and a sense of recognition overwhelmed him with a rush of warmth and peace and emotion.

Mom.

—

Joe sat in the dirt, propped on one hand, watching as the beast's chest rose and fell, his own chest matching its rhythm. The *thing* lifted its gnarled head and looked at Joe. The yellow eye seemed to intensify with hatred for a brief second before the light in it waned like a dying bulb. Then it blinked once, slowly, and the broad chest fell for the last time.

—

"Saunders? You OK?" A man's voice bounced down the stone steps.

Joe climbed to his feet. His legs were wobbly, and he wasn't sure if they would support his weight. "Uh, yeah. I think so."

He looked at the beast again. It was dead. Its lifeless body lay still on the dirt floor, blood pooling around it. "Josiah Walker's down here too. He's hurt bad. We need some light."

Then, as if the OK had been given, men began pouring down the steps—Game Commission officers, state troopers, paramedics, some in uniform, some in civilian clothes, but all hurrying about, flashlights in hand, filling the dank cellar with light.

Maggie had succeeded.

Joe's legs finally gave out, and he would have collapsed if not for two state troopers holding him up. He turned and saw Josiah lying in the dirt. Three paramedics hovered over him, checking his vitals, splinting his arm. One held an oxygen mask over his mouth; another injected something into his arm.

"C'mon, Joe," one of the troopers said. "Let's get you out of here." His big voice sounded familiar. Joe looked at the nameplate pinned above his right breast pocket: *Patrick*. Lieutenant Big Head.

"You believe me now, Lieutenant?"

Patrick furrowed his brow and frowned. "Yeah. I do."

"How's Maggie?"

"She was taken to Chambersburg Hospital. She'll be OK. Let's get you outside so the medics can take a look at you."

CHAPTER 45

J OE SAT BESIDE Maggie's hospital bed and prayed. He'd been finding himself doing that a lot since *the hunt*, as he called it, two days ago. God seemed to be continuously on his mind of late, and he'd catch himself praying when he didn't even realize he was. And he'd spent a lot of that prayer time petitioning God on behalf of Maggie, interceding for her, begging God to save her.

He loved her. It was that simple. After all they'd been through, after all the lies and cover-ups, he still loved her. Fact is, he'd never stopped loving her...and now realized he never would.

He put his hand on Maggie's and prayed a silent prayer, asking God to touch her heart and renew her spirit.

She stirred, let out a slight groan, and fluttered her eyelids open.

Joe smiled and gave her hand a gentle squeeze. "Hey, Mags. Good morning."

She smiled back, a tired, worn smile. Her eyes were glassy, her head wrapped in a thick white bandage, lips cracked and dried.

Joe had run into Dr. Houserman in Maggie's room and learned that she had suffered a severe concussion and skull fracture. When the paramedics brought her in, she had a blood clot on her brain from the blunt head trauma. Surgery was required to remove the clot and release the pressure on the brain. She'd be fine, though.

Maggie licked her cracked lips. "Good morning." She looked at the water bottle on the rolling table by her bed. "Would you mind handing me the water?"

Joe handed her the bottle, and she took a long sip. "Mm. I never thought lukewarm water would taste so good."

"I'll go get you some ice," Joe said, starting to stand.

"No. It's OK. Just sit with me awhile."

Joe sat back down and patted Maggie's hand. "How are you feeling?"

"My head feels like it's gonna pop, but other than that, not bad. Just really tired."

Joe stroked Maggie's cheek with the back of his fingers.

"Tell me," she said.

"Tell you what?"

"Tell me what happened. How long have I been out?"

"Two days."

Maggie sighed and blinked her eyes open wide. "Tell me what happened."

Joe continued stroking her cheek. "After the hunt, the state police were crawling all over the woods and Stevie's trailer. They found Gary's body in the trunk of his cruiser. And..." He paused.

"Tell me," Maggie prompted.

Joe hesitated, then continued. "Andy's gone. So are Mike Kline, Barry Wagman, Dan Berwager, and two paramedics. They found Glen Sterner's body too. He was killed in his backyard. Your dad's fine. So are the Dinsmore boys. Josiah was attacked, but he's OK, awake and talking, anyway. Patrick said his guess is that Stevie couldn't have been responsible for any of the attacks. Whatever he was doing in that monster getup was all part of his illness."

Tears filled Maggie's eyes. She tried to blink them away, but it was no use, so she allowed them to flow freely. "What was it?"

Joe paused. An image of the beast flashed through his mind. How could he describe it? It wasn't what they had all thought it was, that was for sure. "It wasn't a lion...and it was, sort of. It's hard to put into words, you know? It was a monster. That's the best way to describe it." He paused again, satisfied with his answer and still far from satisfied. There were some things in this world that simply couldn't be put into words...if that *thing* was even of this world. "No one can figure out where it came from. Some state troopers were going through Stevie's trailer and found a paw and Philip Yates's old journal with all kinds of African witchdoctor stuff in it. I was just over to see Josiah; he has an interesting take on the whole thing."

"Yeah? I'd like to hear it."

"Some other time, Mags. You need your rest."

Maggie grabbed Joe's hand and held it. "I'd like to hear it, Joe. Josiah may be an old coot, but I admire him. Tell me what he thinks."

Joe sighed, then smiled at Maggie. "He thinks the beast or whatever was a manifestation of Stevie's obsession with revenge. And somehow Stevie was demonically controlling it. Something to do with the witch-doctor stuff. Think about it; everyone the monster attacked at first had somehow wronged Stevie in the past. Hopkins, Owen—"

"I know," Maggie said. "Revenge. Just like Yates."

"Revenge," Joe said.

Maggie gave Joe's hand a weak squeeze. "And what about you? It attacked you and you never did anything to Stevie."

"It attacked me but didn't harm me. It had nothing on me. Josiah thinks that after Stevie died, the beast was still controlled by dark powers and went on a hunting spree. Or maybe it *was* a demon. Maybe it was a devil lion, like Barry said."

"And what do you think?"

"I don't know. It's too much to take in right now. All I care is that it's over and you're safe. For now, I'll leave the theorizing to Josiah."

"How's Caleb?"

Joe gave a little chuckle. "He's awake, doing fine, and eating like a horse. Rosa should be able to take him home soon. He'll need a lot of physical and occupational therapy, but the doctor says he should be fine. He's a strong kid."

Maggie hesitated and her face grew serious. "Joe, I need to tell you the truth—"

"Shhh. Don't, Mags. I already know everything."

"But you need—"

Joe put his finger over her mouth. "Maggie, please don't. Really, I already know everything I need to know. I know about your family's past and all the secrets. I know about the cover-ups too. Cummings and Owen and Hopkins."

"And about Gail Bauer?"

"I know about the murder."

"But there's more—"

"Mags, really, we'll talk later, OK? We'll have plenty of time later."

She sighed heavily. Her chin quivered as she fought back the sobs. "I'm sorry, Joe. I'm so sorry."

Joe squeezed her hand and smiled at her. "I know you are, Mags." He paused, and for a moment, lost himself in her clouded eyes. A wave of emotion washed over him as memories of their past crashed through his mind. "I'll be with you," he said, tears puddling in his own eyes.

Maggie bit her lower lip so hard it turned white.

"I love you, Maggie. I always have and always will. I'm not going anywhere this time."

Maggie released her lip and allowed silent sobs to shake her body. Joe put his cheek to hers.

After she had cried all her tears, Maggie lifted Joe's head and held his face in her hands. "How?"

"How what?"

"How can you still love me?"

Thank You, Joe prayed, knowing it was God who had prompted her to ask such a simple question, opening the door for him to share the wonder of His unconditional love.

He took Maggie's hands in his, bent forward, and gently pressed his lips against hers. "My dear Maggie, let me tell you about a love I experienced…"